HUM LITTLE BIRDIE

HUM LITTLE BIRDIE

A NOVEL OF CAIN CITY

Jonathan Fredrick

MYSTERIOUSPRESS.COM

OPEN ROAD
INTEGRATED MEDIA
NEW YORK

Copyright © 2021 by Jonathan Fredrick

ISBN: 978-1-5040-7558-9

This edition published in 2023 by MysteriousPress.com/Open Road Integrated Media, Inc.
180 Maiden Lane
New York, NY 10038
www.openroadmedia.com

For Calvin

HUM LITTLE
BIRDIE

CHAPTER ONE
THE PAPER CUTTER

I sat in the tenth-floor conference room of Leach, McKinney & Thurber listening to two defense attorneys ask their client the same question thirty different ways, only to —time and again—receive the same stock answer. All the while I couldn't help thinking that if Dante were to design a ring in Hell specifically for me, he'd do well to lock the double doors to this room, throw away the keys, and leave me surrounded for all eternity by a bunch of lawyers chirping at one another.

Yet here I was, of my own volition, in a meeting with three of them.

The two on my side of the table, Ed Leach and Kent McKinney, I tolerated because their names were on the front of the building and on my paychecks. The third was their client, an attorney who specialized in disability claims named Scott T. Barnhard. He sat across the black mahogany, dull-eyed and irritable from the volley of questions being put to him. Barnhard's face and body had an extra layer of blub around it that made him look swollen and unnatural, like one of those old European kings who'd had his choice of vices and chose them all. He sported a badly dyed beard and enough cologne to power a lawnmower. Barnhard was the embodiment of everything I hated about lawyers: equal parts smarm, entitlement, and bravado mixed with a load of confidence that bordered on delusion. The man seemed wholly unconcerned with the fact that he was being investigated by the U.S. Attorney's office for social security fraud.

Leach and McKinney were growing frustrated with Barnhard's indifference to their inquisition. Leach was a decent actor, could put on the right face, play whatever role the situation called for, but McKinney couldn't fake a cough. It had been fifteen minutes since he'd loosened his tie and five since he'd unbuttoned his cuffs and pushed up his sleeves. Now he placed his elbows on the table and leaned forward, hands clasped in a pleading gesture.

"I'm going to shoot you straight, Scott. I've had some dealings with this U.S. Attorney, uh . . ."

"Wilkes," Leach prompted.

"Wilkes. This woman dots her I's and crosses her T's. She does not summon you to her office unless she's ready to put the screws to you. I know you say—"

"This is a shakedown, plain and simple. That's it."

McKinney held his palm up to signal that he wasn't finished speaking. "Right, a shakedown. If you're so confident that that's all this is, a fishing expedition, then why hire us?"

"Because when people talk about the best defenders in Cain City, they talk about you two. Are they wrong?"

"No, they're not wrong," McKinney said. "That's my point. Why go to the trouble of hiring us if their whole play is a bluff?"

Barnhard twisted his head awkwardly to the left and right. The bones in his neck grinded and cracked. He settled his gaze on McKinney.

"I'm not one to sit back and let other people dictate the terms on which we deal. I refuse to be intimidated, even by the big, bad government. Fuck the government. If they want to take a run at me for whatever reason, whether to pin some bullshit charge, make me some kind of scapegoat, or just make me sweat a little, these people are going to see I'm a serious person. They're not going to roll me over like a pup who needs his belly scratched.

They want to bully somebody, they're going to see they picked a fight with the wrong person." He sat forward for the first time since the meeting began and pointed at both Leach and McKinney. "That's why I've hired the two of you. Now they know exactly how difficult it's going to be to take me down. They probably shit themselves when they heard who I got."

Neither McKinney nor Leach responded immediately. Barnhard took this to mean his little speech had had its intended effect. He glanced sideways at me, then leaned back in his chair, laced his fingers over his belly and ran his tongue over his teeth.

"So that's our main function here?" McKinney said, dismay creeping into his voice. "Public relations?"

"I'm paying you to be you," Barnhard said. "If part of that is your reputation precedes you, then so what? Is that a problem, Kent? I didn't know I had to put on my baby mittens."

Ed Leach held out an arm as if to preemptively stop an altercation between the two men.

"I think what my partner means, Mr. Barnhard, is there's a reason we are so highly regarded in our field, as you previously mentioned. That reason is because we outwork our opponents in order to outsmart them. But in this particular situation you're not giving us a chance to prepare as thoroughly as we typically would, and walking into the U.S. Attorney's office blind, well, that makes us a little uncomfortable. You understand? We go into this meeting tomorrow and they know more than we do about our own client, that's not setting us up for success. It's setting us up for trouble."

Barnhard sighed impatiently. "You guys have contacts all over town, right? You mean to tell me nobody knows why they're looking into me?"

"That's why we're so nervous," Leach said. "Everybody's mum."

"Including you," McKinney added.

Barnhard nodded toward me. "Isn't that what he's for?"

"Mr. Malick is tops at his job, there's no question about that. That's why we have him working your case. We dedicate the best resources to our clients, but he's not a miracle worker. We need to see things from the Feds' perspective. We need to know exactly how they're going to attack us, so we can take the fight to them, as you say. You're the only one in a position to help us with that." Ed Leach looked imploringly at both client and partner. "So what do you say we all put the acrimony aside, buckle down, and get through this thing?"

McKinney, for his part, appeared to have forgotten to breathe since the last time he'd spoken and was now on the verge of internal combustion. Barnhard sulked, but eventually flung up his hands as a signal of concession. McKinney released a long, wheezy breath through his nose and gestured to proceed.

Leach continued, "Just sticking to facts here, you *have* gotten a lot of people disability benefits in the last few years."

"That's my job. I'm good at it."

"Of that I'm certain." Ed Leach shuffled through some papers until he found the sheet he was looking for and pulled it out to examine. "In the last five years, you've put through approximately," he read down, "thirteen hundred disability cases."

"Sounds right."

"Are you aware that's four times the amount that any other attorney has put through in this jurisdiction in that time?"

"What, do you guys think you're the only unicorns that are smarter and work harder than everybody around here? I earned each and every one of those cases. I've dropped a fortune on advertising."

"We've all seen the commercials," McKinney said.

Leach smiled to temper McKinney's sharp tone. "They're very effective. That catchy jingle, and what's that you always say at the end? It's your life . . ."

"Take back control of your life." Barnhard gave it the same kick he did in the ads.

Leach snapped his fingers and pointed at Barnhard. "That's good. And then you say, 'Come see me, Scott T, and remember'—"

"The T stands for truth," Barnhard cut him off.

"You also make some promises in those commercials that you'll get their claims done faster than anyone else . . . and it seems like you've made good on those promises. It takes an average applicant almost two years to get approved. You've managed to cut that time by half. Likewise, only fifty-seven percent of all claims get approved. You're working at an eighty-nine percent clip."

"So the government comes after people for being good at their jobs now? You guys better watch out, you're probably next."

McKinney cut back into the conversation. "What you don't seem to comprehend, Scott T—the U.S. Attorney, she sees smoke, she's going to think there's fire. Now, I don't know if there's fire or not. Ed doesn't know if there's fire or not. We don't want to know. But we do know there's a whole hell of a lot of smoke around this case, and we have to know where all that smoke is coming from so that we can do our jobs."

"I've told you guys a hundred times already. I don't know why they're investigating me. If there's smoke, you're gonna have to tell me what it is 'cause I don't know."

My cue.

I said, "Quite a few of the people that you've gotten put on disability seem to be perfectly healthy. Smoke."

Barnhard eyed me straight on for the first time. A curious expression floated across his face. "It speaks." He turned back to Leach and McKinney. "You're going to have to do better than that. Some of the people I got benefits *seem* to be perfectly healthy? Who cares? Here's some news. Disabilities, more often than not, are mental. Not physical. You're going to have to do more than just follow these people around and see that they can buy their own groceries or mow their own lawns."

"Maybe you're right," I said. "I only spoke to twenty of your clients. Out of those twenty I'd say nine of them qualified for benefits, no problem. But the other eleven, if there's a reason they aren't fit to work, I couldn't spot it."

Barnhard made a sour face. "That doesn't mean anything. You're not a psychologist."

"Admittedly," Ed Leach said, "it's a small sample size. But Mr. Malick's only had a week to work whereas the U.S. Attorney may have been at this for months, half a year, a year, we don't know. We won't know until we get in there tomorrow. But if *we* found half your cases to be questionable . . ."

"This is insane," Barnhard murmured. He slurped his water and looked out the picture window at the far end of the room. From this high up you could see the length of downtown Cain City; a low, disparate cityscape that brought to mind a jaw-full of chipped teeth. In the distance off to the left was the golden dome of the courthouse. To the right was the shopping district. Beyond that was the floodwall, the river, and the sun dipped low in a violet sky. "And let me tell you something else," Barnhard fumed, "if this damages my practice in any way, I'll sue them. I swear I will. Drag it out for years if I have to. I'll drag them through the muck for so long they'll forget why they got so twisted up going after me in the first place."

Here, Leach feigned like he'd received a text, showed his phone to McKinney and whispered something. McKinney nodded, playing along, and both stood.

"Something's come up that we have to step out and take care of real quick," Leach said. "Stay put, if you don't mind. Won't be five minutes."

Leach told us to buzz Betty at the front desk if we needed anything. He and McKinney exited, closing the double doors behind them. This was a little gambit they ran when they wanted to get me alone with a client to see what I could get out of them.

"So you're the famous detective?" Barnhard said.

"If you say so."

"Are the stories true?"

"I dunno. Any story in particular?"

Barnhard pulled out a pack of cigarettes, shook one loose and put it between his lips. "Think they'll mind?"

"Do you care?"

He grinned and lit up, offered me one. I declined.

"I heard you were shot four times during that shootout at the old high school."

"It was just once."

"What's that feel like, to get shot?"

"Stings."

"Stings!" Barnhard exclaimed. He was enamored now. "And you killed seven of them?"

"Three. There were seven of them total, so I'm told."

"Jesus." Barnhard blew a thick stream of smoke from his nostrils. "That must have been something. Where'd they get you?"

I lifted my left arm, which was still cocked a bit sideways and would never fully extend for the rest of my life.

"It still jacked up?"

"Eh, it works. Well-placed bullet though. Severed the artery. Nearly bled me out."

Barnhard whistled and shook his head. He flicked ash onto the carpet and scuffed it into the fabric with his shoe.

"Tell me something. Did Leach really get some urgent message just now, or are they trying to play some voodoo mind trick on me?"

"You're smarter than you look."

He smacked the tabletop. "I knew it. So what, they give you a run at me, see if you can get me to talk?"

"Something like that."

"They do this kind of thing a lot?"

"Only when a client proves especially difficult."

Barnhard threw his head back and laughed as though he'd just heard the greatest joke ever told. "Well, I suppose I do fit that description, huh? Does it work?"

I shrugged. "They think I can get more out of the clients than they can for whatever reason. Because people have heard of me, because I can speak to the clients in blunter terms than they can, I don't know. Fact is, if people want to talk, they talk. If they don't, they won't. Most people feel the need to unburden themselves at some point. These two don't do themselves any favors with the way they come at you."

"You're not kidding. They'd make anybody clam up the way they hammer ad nauseum. After seeing them in action, I don't know how they've earned their reputations." He waved a hand dismissively. "But they came highly recommended . . . so."

"They are a bit eager."

Barnhard snorted. "They're like seventeen-year-old virgins on prom night."

"That's one way to put it," I said. "Me, I'm like Switzerland."

"Meaning what, neutral?"

"Not neutral exactly. More like an impartial ally. I clock in, do the work, clock out. That's it. No skin in the game. Maybe that gives people room to relax a little, breathe—"

"And spill their guts."

I grinned. "Sometimes."

Barnhard's mouth curved into a fat smile that multiplied his chins. He wiggled a stubby index finger at me. "I bet you've got your opinions though."

"Who doesn't?"

"You and I could have some real fun together. I could show you a side of this town you've never seen before. When this is all over, what do you say we let our hair down, see what kind of trouble we can get into?"

"Sounds fun. Mind if I swallow glass first?"

Barnhard howled like I was a comedy virtuoso, cigarette bouncing on his lips. When his howling petered out he sighed and said, "What do they want from me?"

"Who?"

"Scooby-Doo and Scooby-Dum."

"Oh, I don't know. They probably just want you to tell them something they can use to defend you with, that's all."

"What do they think? If I don't know why I'm being looked into, and they don't know why I'm being looked into . . . I can't just concoct a bunch of gobbledygook out of thin air to implicate myself."

"C'mon."

"What, c'mon?"

It was my turn to laugh. "It doesn't take a genius to see there's something rotten in Denmark. The U.S. Attorney's not coming after you for shits and giggles."

Barnhard bristled and glared at me. "We don't know why they've summoned me."

"If you say so."

"Quit saying that." He put the fat of his palms against his eyes and rubbed them in circles. "What do they think I did?"

"Who, these guys? They don't tell me that kind of thing. Above my pay grade."

"No, the U.S. Attorney."

"I could only speculate."

"Okay then." Barnhard stubbed his cigarette out on the bottom of the table. Flicked the butt into a potted plant in the corner. Waved away the smoke in front of his face. "Mister hot-shit detective. What do *you* think I did?"

"Doesn't matter what I think. I'm not your counsel."

"No shit. I wouldn't ask if I didn't want to know. C'mon, let's hear your theory."

"I don't care what you did. None of my concern."

"Hey," Barnhard snapped. "I'm technically paying for you, right? I say I want your take, you give me your take. You say you can only speculate? Then speculate."

I leveled my eyes on him. "Okay. Way I see it, you don't have too many options."

Barnhard frowned at me like I was dense. "How do you figure that?"

"It's all optics, like you said. Everybody's just trying to cover their own ass. That's the way of the world, right? Rubber meets the road, nobody gives a shit about anybody else. The only person that cares about you is you. Leach and McKinney, they pound away with question after question because they don't want to lose. They want to get you off, sure, but not for you. For them. They have a rep to uphold. That's why they do things like hire me. So they can tell everybody they have the very best resources at their disposal, so on and so forth. *You* don't talk because you're hoping if you never admit to anything and nothing can be proven, then maybe this whole thing will blow over. That, or you're protecting somebody else. Any way you slice it, everybody's just covering their own ass."

I leaned forward.

"But let's not kid ourselves, this isn't going to blow over. Deep down you know that. You figured out a way to rig the system. I don't know how you rigged it. Probably you had some help, I don't know. My understanding of how the whole process works is . . . rudimentary. Regardless, it's impressive. I'm impressed, and till now you haven't been caught. You get, what, about four grand for every claim you're awarded?"

"Something like that."

"That's a nice little chunk of the government's money. Bravo to you, I've got no love for the government. They've taken the same amount of money out of my paycheck for twenty years. That's not what gets me though. What gets me is where they put my money. We're all citizens, we all want roads you can drive on. I'll pay my share for that. But this government just takes my money and gives it to their buddies. Anyway, that's beside the point. Point is, the government likes their money. But like any bureaucracy, it's a big machine with a lot of moving parts. A lot can slip through the cracks of a big machine with nobody being the wiser. You took advantage of that."

"You don't know what you're talking about."

"You want to set me straight or you want me to finish my theory? You asked for it."

The muscles in Barnhard's jaws bulged. He looked as though he might leap across the table at me, but his mouth stayed silent so I continued.

"Now, I'm sure that money stole easy, spent easy, and after a while you take a little more. Then a little more. When nobody catches on, you figure you've outsmarted them this long, why not push it a bit farther? You get so used to this system you've got set up, that money starts to feel like it was yours to begin with. It becomes normal. Probably didn't even seem all that wrong anymore. And what the hell, it's Cain City, there's so much shit going on here nobody's even looking in your direction. You're liable to fleece them like this until retirement.

"But you play a game of chance long enough, the house always wins. And the government is a big damn house. Now that big ol' machine, it's onto you. Thirteen hundred cases over five years at four grand a pop, we're talking north of five million dollars, not to mention the benefits that have been doled out to all those cases. I don't know about you, but I think they're gonna want their money back. So even if it is a fishing expedition, like you say, they're fishing with dynamite. Something's going to float to the surface, probably already has. And the government, they can't let you skate on this. They're like anybody else. They gotta cover their own asses. So yeah, from where I sit, you've got about one option."

Barnhard paled. "What's that?"

I grinned, genuinely. "You gotta cover your own ass."

Barnhard took a sip of water that went down the wrong hole and sent him into a coughing fit. Once he recovered, he said, "You came up with all that from talking to twenty people?"

"And you."

His upper lip curled and he put both hands flat on the table. "To be clear, you believe that I've swindled over five million dollars from the United States government? Do you know how absurd that sounds?"

"Oh, I'm sure some of your clients were legit. You do have those jazzy commercials, after all."

"You sure do know how to spin a tale."

I leaned back casually in my seat. "You might be right—what do I know? Either way, you're in good hands with the two Scoobies, probably got nothing to worry about."

Barnhard's palms remained on the table. He stared at my forehead for a solid minute.

"Tell me. In this little narrative you've concocted, how would you suggest I cover my own ass?"

"If it were me?" I pretended to think about it. "Worst case, you walk in there tomorrow and they've got you dead to rights. Offer you a plea deal or straight to jail, nothing in between. It's a no brainer, right? You give 'em what you got."

"And if I don't have anything to give them?"

"Then I hope you have a woman you can call this evening because you're going to have a lot of cold nights in your future."

Barnhard winced and scratched at his beard. A puff of dandruff floated down onto his belly. He gazed out the window. "Let me ask you something. Who, in your mind, is the bigger crook? The man who steals a million dollars from one person, or the man who steals a dollar from a million people?"

"That's easy. The guy who stole the million. Stealing a dollar from a bunch of people is akin to a bunch of paper cuts. Doesn't really hurt anybody, you know."

Barnhard nodded. "That makes sense."

"Which one are you in that scenario?"

"Me?" Barnhard turned back to me with a placid expression. "I'm the paper cutter."

CHAPTER TWO
A TEN-STORY TOWN

I excused myself from the conference room, went ahead and grabbed my coat and flat cap from the rack in the hall, walked three doors down and slipped into Ed Leach's office, closing the door behind me. Leach and McKinney were seated across the desk from one another debating which tack to use on Barnhard next. McKinney wanted to go back in and ask Barnhard straight out if he was involved in a disability scheme. Leach advocated for a defter touch.

"Let's start with something less threatening. Maybe ask if he fudged any paperwork. Work our way north from there."

McKinney scoffed. "We already tried that. If he shuts it down, which by the way is all he's done to this point, we're left with nowhere to go. We can't jump from 'Did you forge documents?' to 'Were you involved in a criminal conspiracy?' He's going to stomp out the door and we're no better off than when we started. I want to find out what's going on with this guy."

"Me too," Leach carped, exposing the first inklings of his frustration.

"Well, at least I know I'm not the only one with a pulse around here." McKinney's eyes cut my way when he said this.

Leach took off his glasses, leaned forward on the desk and pressed his fingers into his temples. "Look, if his conversation with Nick made him squirmy—maybe he's searching for a way to get out of this mess. It's on us to make him think it's his idea. How did it go in there, Nick?"

I ran down the highlights of my conversation with Barnhard. McKinney's face turned positively fluorescent when I told them Barnhard smoked a cigarette in there. When I finished, Leach complimented me on the *cover-your-own-ass* spiel.

"Think you spooked him?"

"A little."

McKinney asked me what I thought of all the crook and paper-cutting business.

"I think that's as close as you're going to get to an admission that there's other players involved in this thing."

Both of their dispositions brightened. Leach said, "Okay, you heard what we were thinking of doing. How would you play it?"

"I don't think it much matters what you go in there and say to him or how you say it. He doesn't exactly hold you in the highest regard."

"I'm sure you didn't say anything to dissuade him of that opinion," McKinney said.

I smiled. "Nope."

Both of them sniveled for a moment. McKinney cursed under his breath. I didn't catch all of it, but it had something to do with me and the Lord. Then Leach looked up quickly.

"What about this? Assuming Barnhard has partners that he's covering for, if he's nervous enough, the night before his appointment with the U.S. Attorney would be the time to meet with them, right? If we go back in there and we're not getting anywhere, we'll end the meeting and have Nick surveille him to see if he gets up to anything."

"Listen fellas," I interrupted. "I gotta bounce. I'm already late for this thing I've gotta do."

"What thing?" McKinney protested.

I raised my hands in mock innocence. "Told you about it a week ago."

"I don't remember you telling me anything. Do you remember, Ed?"

"Yes," Leach admitted. "He told us about it right when we told him about this meeting. A celebratory dinner, right? Your girlfriend . . ."

"She's graduating from nursing school."

"Right. We said it'd be fine as long as he was here for the meeting."

"Well, that's just—shit."

To cool their jets, I said, "Look, if Barnhard wants to contact somebody, he's likely as not to just place a phone call. Not much we can do about that."

McKinney's face grew comically shrewd. "But if he's smart—big *if*, I know—but if he is, he's not going to make a call on any phone that can be traced back to him. Probably safer to meet in person."

"You guys watch too much TV," I said, but conceded the scenario wasn't outside the realm of possibility.

Leach asked how long my engagement was going to be. I told them I'd probably be free by ten. If they could scare up somebody to tail Barnhard for the next few hours, I'd coordinate with them, take over the stakeout when I was available.

"In the meantime, one of you should get back in there before this guy starts getting antsy and books a ticket to Samoa."

McKinney made a screwy face. "Samoa?"

"No extradition . . . I'm kidding."

Leach agreed that Barnhard had been left all by his lonesome for too long and headed for the conference room while McKinney got on the horn to line up a shadow. I told him to text me if the plan was a go and walked out. They mustn't have gotten far with Barnhard. Not seven minutes later, as I was steering my Tacoma down around Redding Park, I got a text from Leach saying the gig was on. Bob Lawson was in place to track the client. I sent a confirmation thumbs-up emoji.

At the edge of Redding Park I crossed over a small bridge

and drove up into the southern hills of the city. The last of the sun blinked over the western horizon and I flipped on my headlights. Woods lined the winding lane. Branches from the tall oaks, birches, and cedars stretched to form a canopy overhead. As I snaked farther up the lane, the sporadic houses that dotted the hillside grew more grand, more stately, each one looming slightly larger over the house that preceded it. There wasn't a lot of money in Cain City, but most of the money there was lived on this hill.

Near the top there were four or five offshoots of the main road. The last of these, Honeysuckle Lane, skirted the crest of the hill. I turned onto it, drove a couple hundred yards farther, and pulled into the long driveway of a palatial estate. The house was the type of monstrosity that had to have a name. A sampling of the neighboring estates found the likes of Rosebud, Bloom Hall, Darby Manor. One was called Breath Away. To my ex-wife and her husband's credit, they'd held off giving their home a moniker for a while after they'd moved in. But this last year they succumbed to the pretention of their tax bracket and christened the place Jacob's Ladder in honor of our dead son. Had a fancy plaque with gold lettering nailed to the gate.

I parked the Tacoma behind my girlfriend Karla's Nissan Sentra, got out, strolled the length of the walk and climbed the steps to the porch. A couple of 20-foot-tall pillars bracketed the top of the steps. I reached them and turned around to have a look at the whole of Cain City twinkling below me: from the factories in the west end to the hospital and housing projects in the east; from Redding Park at the bottom of the hill and the middle-class neighborhoods of the Southside, to the courthouse and the handful of eight- and ten-story buildings that defined the downtown skyline. In the tenth-floor offices of Leach, McKinney & Thurber, the lights were still on.

You could see it all from here: the river with its three bridges crossing from West Virginia into Ohio, the old high school where I lived and worked, the sprawl of Cain City College, the spires and bell towers along church row, the railroad tracks that bisected the city, the viaducts that ran beneath them.

This is what two doctors' salaries get you, I thought. *A view from the summit and so much square footage you have to name it.*

I pressed the buzzer. Musical chimes sounded inside the house. A dozen seconds later Tom Orvietto swung the big door open. Every time I saw Joanna's new husband I was struck anew by his resemblance to a circus clown, complete with the curly hair and hoola-hoop waistline.

"Thank God you made it," he said cheerfully. "I don't think I could have taken another minute of *girl* talk."

"Tom." We shook hands and he squeezed my bicep as though he were only pretending to size me up. "How much trouble am I in?"

"Plenty." Something over my shoulder caught his attention and I looked back to see what he was seeing. "Did you finally get rid of that old hoopty?"

"'Fraid so. Old girl finally gave out on me coming up under the Eighth Street viaduct. Coughed twice, started rolling backwards, and that was that. Car full of college kids felt sorry for me and helped me push it up the hill."

Tom let go of my arm and clapped me on the shoulder. "Well, maybe it was for the best. That vehicle was one of the most abominable things I've ever seen on an American road."

"Yeah, but she was mine."

"What kind of car was it?"

"Skylark."

"Skylark. Do they even make those anymore?"

I shook my head no.

Tom jiggled with laughter. "I only rode in it once, mind. But by the time I got out, I'm telling you I felt like I needed a tetanus shot. No offense."

I wondered how many times he'd regaled his friends and colleagues with that anecdote and said, "I think I will take offense to that, Tom."

He laughed again, believing me to be joking. He took my cap and coat and led me through the large foyer and living room, past the kitchen, to the dining room where Joanna and Karla sat catty-corner at the end of a long four-leafed oak table. An enormous crystal chandelier hung above it.

Neither woman stopped chatting to acknowledge our presence. Joanna wore black leather leggings with an oversized black blouse that fell off one shoulder and was tied in a knot at her hip. Her black hair was pulled into a tight bun atop her head, exposing wisps of silver that streaked back from each temple, which always brought to my mind the rather pleasing image of Madeline Kahn in *Young Frankenstein*. The all-black get-up accentuated her slender form, the sharp angles of her cheeks, jaw, and collarbone. If she was wearing any make-up at all you couldn't tell. She didn't need it.

Where Joanna was all sculpted contours and fine lines, Karla was shaped with curves that belonged in a Renaissance painting. Her typical wardrobe consisted of whatever jeans and top were close at hand, but tonight she was gussied up in a sleeveless sundress with a red floral print that I had never seen her wear before. Viewing it presently, my first thought was that she'd cause a dozen car wrecks if she walked two blocks down the street in that dress. Her pale, sea-foam-colored eyes were done up smoky, her lips matched the dress, and her honey-colored hair fell down in a muss past her shoulders.

I took in the pair of them and wondered what I'd done right in a previous life. I certainly hadn't earned them in this one. Perhaps my fortunes would get squared in the next iteration. I moved around the table, placed a hand on the nape of Karla's neck and kissed the top of her head. She reached back and squeezed the hand affectionately. I noticed Joanna taking a sudden interest in the bottom of her wine glass. I apologized for being late.

"Nonsense," Joanna said, overcompensating with a bit of forced spirit. She lifted the glass to her lips. "It's been nice to get to know Karla a little better. Hasn't it, Karla?" Joanna giggled as she drank the wine, choked on the juice going down the wrong hole and nearly coughed it back into her glass.

"You okay?" Karla asked, concerned.

Joanna held her palm aloft, then placed it over her chest and said, "I'm fine. I'm fine," though it took her a few deep breaths to regain her composure.

"It's been very nice," Karla said. She tipped her own drink back and shot me a furtive little brow raise over the rim.

"I'm sorry. We were just comparing notes on what it was like to live with you. Commiserating over our shared plight."

"I told you," Tom blurted. "You got here in the nick of time."

"Should I leave? I don't want to spoil the fun."

Joanna waved a dismissive hand. "Sit down. Sit down. We'll play nice, won't we, Karla?"

"No." Karla smirked.

"Since we're all here," Tom said, making for the kitchen, "why don't I go and get the hors d'oeuvres?"

"Mmm," Joanna said, mid-sip. She grabbed the empty bottle of wine by the neck and held it out for Tom to see. "Pick us out another rosé."

Tom's shoulders sloughed, but his voice stayed chipper when he spoke. "Maybe we should take a break. Have some water, stretch the night out a bit, eh?"

"I'll pump and dump, Tom," Joanna said sharply. "The baby will be fine. She won't starve." She softened and turned her attention back to Karla. "Besides, what's that they say? Two glasses of wine a day will help prevent giving a shit."

"What do they say about two bottles?" Tom asked.

"Even better." Joanna didn't bother to look at him. She simply slid the empty bottle his way across the table.

"Where is Ruthie?" I said. "I'd like to get a look at her."

"We just put her down for the night," Tom answered.

"She's gorgeous," Karla said. "She has two huge dimples and a little cleft chin and she can't stop smiling." Both Joanna and

Tom thanked Karla for the compliment and said something about their inability to figure out which one of them Ruthie looked like. Tom remarked that DNA was a funny thing, grabbed the wine bottle off the table and turned for the door.

"Drink, Nick?"

"None for me tonight. I've got to get back to work after this."

"No, you've got to be kidding me."

I shrugged. "Somebody's always up to something."

"Sure you can't have one? I picked up a bottle of that mid-shelf bourbon you like."

"Maker's?"

Tom nodded in the affirmative.

"Maybe one."

Dinner with the girlfriend, the ex-wife, her husband—I could have used a handful of drinks, but I stuck to my word and stretched the one through the appetizer, meatballs stuffed with cheese, and the main course, grilled scallops on a bed of pasta with white sauce. Tom had cooked the whole thing. Outside of being an amiable goof who had a lot of money and would rub Joanna's feet every night for the rest of his life without a grunt of complaint, I had never understood their match. But his culinary skills were cause enough to reevaluate the way I'd framed their entire relationship.

Despite the flow of wine and our hosts' occasional chippiness with one another, the dinner conversation stayed polite. Topics didn't stray far from the safety of our respective occupations or what television shows we watched. Karla had just put in her notice at the grocery store, so she and Joanna debated which grocer in town had the best produce, meats, and fish. They also shared an affinity for the same reality shows, as did Tom—mostly the singing and dancing stuff—so they wasted a good bit of time talking about those.

"What programs do you like, Nick?" Tom asked, slurping a chunk of pasta into his mouth.

"I don't watch TV."

"Really? That's admirable."

"Please don't tell him that. It just feeds his cultural superiority," Karla said. "Plus, it's not completely true. He watches one thing every day."

"The news!" Joanna exclaimed.

I conceded that I did like to watch the news.

Karla stated she didn't have the stomach for the news, especially the local news. Too bleak. And she didn't understand why, when they conducted street interviews, they had to pick the people that made Cain City seem like the least educated, least hygienic place in the nation. Everyone they put on camera was missing teeth or wearing dirty clothes or struggling to string together three words that could be found in the dictionary.

"I like to see what they report and what they leave out," I said.

"Now we've got to know," Tom said. "What do they leave out?"

"Plenty. Though more gets reported now than there used to be."

"Don't tell me that. Joanna is already down on this town enough as it is."

This kicked off a diatribe about the state of affairs in Cain City.

"Ever since this gang business started, the drugs have just gotten worse and worse," Joanna said. "I thought it would get better after Nick helped get rid of those thugs from Detroit, but it hasn't. Did you know that per capita we get more overdoses than anywhere else in the country? Anywhere. We're number one. The city now spends millions, literally *millions*, on Narcan annually."

"At least they've been trying to push the crime back into the east and west ends," Tom said.

"Why?" Joanna spat. "Because that's where crime belongs, with the poor and disenfranchised?"

"That's not what I said, dear. But that is where the crime

spread from, am I wrong? I will tell you one thing, though, Nick. I'm glad I'm not an EMT anymore."

"You haven't been an EMT for twenty years, Tom," Joanna groaned.

"And I'm glad of it. I wouldn't want to be out there in the thick of this mess. They never know what they're walking into. Did you see that story on the news the other day where the police found a car crashed into a ditch on the side of the interstate? Inside were a couple who still had the needles in their arms. And in the back seat, strapped into their car seats, were two toddlers."

I told them I'd seen the story.

"Drugs are the foundation for crime," Joanna professed. She was getting belligerent now, her diction sloppy. She waved her wine glass around. "And let me tell you something. It's a hell of a foundation. The amount of trauma we see in the hospital from violence is crazy. It's overwhelming. Sometimes it feels like we're in a Third World country. I never dreamed I'd become an expert at treating gunshot wounds."

"Sure glad you did," I said.

When I'd gotten shot, Joanna was the surgeon who extracted the shotgun spray from my arm, clamped my artery, and stopped me from bleeding to death.

"You were only wounded in an extremity, you big baby," she teased.

The conversation went on like that for a bit. Tom lamented the number of patients who came into his psychiatry clinic for no other reason than to be prescribed oxycodone or Percocet.

"You get through a whole session with these people who you believe want help—that's why they're there, right? They've taken the first step. And then at the end they ask, 'So what narcotics can you give me?' It's preposterous."

"That reminds me," I said. "Have you ever dealt with a lawyer named Scott Barnhard?"

At the mention of Barnhard, Tom blanched. His eyes

darted to Joanna, who was idly swirling the wine in her glass and not paying attention, then back to me. I was paying plenty of attention. He shifted uncomfortably in his seat, wiggled his eyebrows and looked to the ceiling. Tapped his lips with his fingertips as though he were racking his brain to place the name.

"I don't know. Isn't he that fellow who runs all those local ads?"

"That's the one. Him and Livingston Chrysler take turns annoying you every commercial break."

"That's right." The tension in Tom's body eased and he settled his weight back into his chair. "I've never dealt with him directly, but I'm sure some of my disability patients have gone through him. That's his whole schtick, isn't it? Why, is he a client of yours?"

"He's one of the firm's clients."

Tom poured himself a glass of wine. I sucked on an ice cube from my long-gone Maker's and watched him, trying to decipher what that initial flash of fear meant, but he had snapped back to his jovial self.

"Is he in some kind of trouble?" Tom asked.

"I don't know. We'll see."

Tom nodded solemnly.

"That's in line with what you do though, right?" I said.

"What is?"

"Affirming disability claims."

"It can be, sure." Tom shifted his focus to Karla, asked her what her plans were now that she'd graduated nursing school.

Before Karla could answer, Joanna started speaking. She squinted through glazed eyes and jabbed a serious finger into the air. "If I could go back and tell myself one thing, *one thing*, I'd tell myself to be a nurse. Pays well, you're still helping people without all the stress of, you know, their lives depending on your split-second decisions. And"—she slapped her own knee—"you're always in demand. You can travel, you can move anywhere you want. I'd love that freedom. I've told Nick for years—he has nothing holding him here. Get as far away from this town as you can."

I said, "I've told Karla the same thing."

Joanna shook her head like her brain had glitched. "Really?"

"If it were up to me, we'd be gone already."

"It feels like a lot right now," Karla said apologetically. "With me graduating and Davey just starting his freshman year. Maybe in the future."

"She says that, meanwhile she keeps showing me houses to look at online."

"Houses?" Joanna's eyes widened. "That's a big step."

Karla said, "The faster we can get out of that old high school, the better."

"Of course. I didn't know Davey was a freshman." Joanna stared absently into her wine. Her voice dropped to a hush. "I don't know if I can raise another child in this city."

"Don't say that, sweetheart," Tom said. "There's still plenty of good things about this town, and plenty of good people. Right, Nick?"

"Sure. There's good people everywhere."

Joanna nodded vaguely.

Tom clapped his hands and rubbed his palms together. "Speaking of good people. Let's get to why we're here, shall we?" He raised his wine glass. "We are very happy for you, for the two of you. Congratulations, Karla. Passing the NCLEX test is no easy feat. It's a big accomplishment and nursing is a great profession to enter into. If you need us to put a word in anywhere, obviously we'd be glad to assist in any way we can. Right, Joanna?"

"Hmm?"

"I was telling Karla that you could put in a word for her at Kyova."

"Oh, yes. Of course."

Karla thanked them for the offer, but explained that she actually had an interview in two days with Maggie's Place, a center that opened a couple of years ago for babies born addicted to opioids.

"That's important work," Tom said. "Worthy work. Can you believe there are so many of them now they need their own facility? It's appalling really."

Joanna stood abruptly. Her balance faltered and she placed a hand on the table to steady herself. "I am in need of some air," she announced. Before anybody could say anything she staggered out a set of French doors that led to a back patio.

"I'm sorry," Tom said. "I thought . . . I don't know. Joanna's been having a bit of a tough time. Ruthie still doesn't sleep through the night. She gets so worked up that only her mama can put her back to bed, no one else, so Joanna's really been stretched to her wit's end. She was up half the night last night."

"No apology necessary," Karla said. "I totally get it."

I asked if Tom and Karla minded me stepping out to talk to Joanna. Neither of them objected, so I went outside. Joanna stood in the shadows at the far end of the patio, just beyond the arc of light emanating from the windows of the house. She was gazing out at the back of their property, a vast lawn that sloped down into a dense wood. The night was clear and cool. Thick clouds drifted across the purple sky. I stepped into the shadows next to her.

"Cold out here."

"You run cold," she retorted. Immediately she regretted the words, put her fingers over her lips. "I'm sorry. I've made a complete fool of myself tonight."

"It's good to see you cutting loose, having a little fun."

"Is that what that looked like to you?"

"The first year after having a baby is always tough, you know that. Don't beat yourself up."

"Ruthie's sixteen months old."

"Year and a half then."

A wan smile crept into the corners of her mouth, lasted a few seconds, and dissipated.

"I thought it would be different after Ruthie came. I thought it would make me happier. Fill a void or something."

"Nothing will ever do that."

She turned and locked eyes with me.

"No? You seem to be doing pretty well. Better than ever in fact."

"Me? I just pretend to be a normal human. Hoping if I fake it long enough, maybe one day it'll be true. How am I doing?"

"You've got me fooled."

A tear drew a thin line down her cheek. I wiped it off with my thumb.

"Jo, that hole will always be there. This grief stuff, it works backwards. The more you try to fill the hole with other things—people, possessions, drugs, whatever—the deeper it gets. Jake's gone. Nothing is ever gonna change that. Nothing will ever fill that hole or replace him. You can't take that out on Tom and Ruthie. Jake wouldn't want you to live that way."

Joanna made a disgusted sound. "You think I don't know that?" She turned her back to me and we both gazed out at the black woods and the treetops, which cut a jagged horizon beneath the purple sky. Then, unexpectedly, she stepped backwards, bumped against me and laid her head against my shoulder. "It's ironic, you attempting to be the calm voice of reason. How come you couldn't have been like this eight years ago?"

"I had to go through it my way."

She scoffed and straightened up. "That you did."

She twisted to look back through the French doors into the dining room where Tom and Karla still sat, pleasantly chatting.

"She's beautiful."

"What can I say? I'm an overachiever."

"Very true." She crossed her arms and looked at her feet. "I'm happy for you."

"You're beautiful, too, you know. But I'm not happy for Tom."

"He's been very good to me, mostly."

"The only reason I tolerate him."

"Do you love her?"

"What kind of question is that?"

"It's just a question. You don't have to answer it."

I took a second to arrange a tactful response. "I do. As best I can."

Joanna hugged her arms against her body and nodded rapidly, as though this information confirmed something she'd already suspected.

"You're looking for a house. What's next, marriage? Kids? Did you realize that her son is the same age Jake would have been?"

"Davey's a year older. He's fourteen."

"Oh, a whole year older. He's not replacing Jake at all then, is he?"

"Are you trying to pick a fight?"

She considered the question before replying, "No."

"He's a good kid."

"I'm sure he is. When did she have him, when she was twelve?"

"Sixteen."

"Ah."

"Listen, I'm gonna go back inside now."

"I'm sorry, Nick. I—I'm not myself. Apologize to Karla for me, too, will you? And tell her congratulations. I can't imagine how hard that was, what she's done, being a single mother, getting her degree. I'd be happy to give her a rec if she needs one."

"You're not coming back in?"

"No."

CHAPTER THREE
THE HIGH-PITCHED TAIL

I left Joanna on the patio, went into the house and conveyed her message of apology and praise, omitting the patronizing bit about Karla being a single mother. Tom escorted us back through the house to the front porch. I asked him to hang there for a minute so I could bend his ear about something and saw Karla to her Sentra. She slid behind the wheel. I shut the door behind her, removed my cap, and leaned through her open window to kiss her. Her lips were cold and sweet from the rosé.

"You okay to drive?"

"I'm fine. Joanna had most of it. How was it with her?"

"I don't know. She's a little mixed up right now."

I told Karla not to wait up, I'd be working late and would sleep in my office. I spent most nights at her apartment, which was on the third floor of the old high school. My office, for the time being, was on the first floor. A new rental company had taken over the contract and they were finding ways to evict all the old tenants so they could jack up the rent. My lease expired at the end of October.

"That's too bad," she said. "I had plans for us tonight."

"Big talk."

She beckoned me to lean down once more and kissed me again, sliding the tip of her tongue beneath my upper lip. I ran my fingertips up the smooth skin of her inner thigh. Her legs parted and her skirt began to bunch. I'd nearly reached my destination when she took hold of my wrist, removed my hand from her leg, and transferred it unceremoniously to the windowsill.

"Guess you'll never know," she said, feigning remorse.

"You're a cruel, cruel woman."

Despite the numerous assets that Karla's dress showcased, it was her round, heavy-lidded eyes that still cut me to the quick. She rolled them now, told me to be safe, threw the car into reverse and backed down the driveway. The Sentra's taillights faded down Honeysuckle Lane, flickered through the trees, and disappeared. I joined Tom, who was slumped against one of the pillars on his porch. He apologized again, saying both he and Joanna had been looking for an occasion to get us all together and maybe they had rushed into it prematurely.

"I thought we were starting to get back to normal. She's been better lately, but you never know when she's going to go into one of these . . . funks."

"We had a fine time, food was great. She been struggling for a while?"

"Since the baby. Just since the baby. I keep waiting for things to go back to the way they were."

"Hate to be the bearer of bad news, Tom, but it'll never be the same. The woman you knew, whatever dynamic the two of you had, the moment that baby was born—*whoosh*—gone for good, never to return."

Tom winced, rocked back on his heels and clutched at his heart in an exaggerated gesture. "Don't tell me that. You realize you're dashing all my hopes and dreams."

"I'm good for something."

He sighed heavily, extended his big belly and rubbed it as though a genie might float out and grant him a wish. "What was it that you wanted to discuss?"

I asked him how disability claims worked from his end. He recited a bunch of professional jargon about PRTF forms and medical dispositions and nine mental health categories.

"Cut to the part where the lawyers get involved."

Tom explained that for whatever reason, be it limited means or an inherent distrust of lawyers, most people seeking disability in this area don't retain counsel until their initial application has been denied, which happens almost without fail. At that point, the only recourse a claimant has is to appeal the decision in front of an administrative law judge or re-apply. The easiest route to getting an application accepted is to win the appeal. That process shortcuts you to a judge who is able to decide your case at his discretion. And the odds of that decision falling in your favor are increased if you have a lawyer who knows the ins and outs of the system.

"Sounds like a hell of a racket. Where do you fit in?"

"If a patient or lawyer, usually it's a patient, asks me to provide an evaluation to present to the judge during the appeal, that's what I do."

"The nine categories and all that."

"Yes. And all that."

"And how many of these do you do, say, in a month?"

"It varies. I'd say the number has increased steadily over the last few years with all the people out of work, soldiers returning from the Middle East with PTSD, that kind of thing."

"And Scott Barnhard, you've never done an evaluation for any of his clients?"

I watched to see if the mention of Barnhard affected him as it had before, but Tom didn't flinch. He did, however, squish his face up into something that split the difference between a smile and a grimace.

"I can't recall off the top of my head. You know, it's a tight-knit world, I'm sure I have. My office manager keeps thorough records of all these things. You're more than welcome to come by sometime and have a look at them."

"I may do that, Tom."

That squishy grin stayed plastered on his mug. I stood there for a moment to see if he would drop it, but the expression held. Problem was, you couldn't tell if it was the topic of conversation making him nervous or if he was just awkward as hell. I decided to let him off the hook, bade him goodbye, and climbed into my Tacoma. There I texted Bob Lawson for the current location of the Barnhard stakeout.

His reply read: *across from the 21 club. in the green cherokee*

Downtown. I put the Tacoma in gear and pointed her in that direction.

21 Club was the latest attempt at an upscale drinking hole in Cain City, craft beers and whatnot. It was located on the bottom floor of the Georges Building, a ten-story relic from the thirties that operated as a hotel for its first forty years and, outside of the lobby and ground floor, had largely gone unused since. Before this current iteration, 21 Club had been a dive bar called All Saints. Before that a dance club called Rowdies, and before that a sandwich shop called Stacks.

Bob Lawson was parked beneath the marquee of the defunct movie theater, which provided a good chunk of darkness in the middle of the well-lit block and a direct sightline into the bar's plate-glass front across the street. I pulled in behind him, got out and hopped into the passenger side of his Cherokee.

"Tell me a story," I said.

Lawson looked at me as though I'd desecrated his mother's grave. He was a nondescript white guy whose flat features kind of blurred together. You'd have a hard time picking him out of a line-up even if you'd just met. This blandness was useful for tailing people, and he could be counted on for good, thorough work, but he was also a shameless try-hard and suck-ass with anyone who might hire him. His mere presence put me in a foul mood. Lawson's only remarkable characteristics were a right hand that was minus two fingers—the index and middle, due to an ice skating accident when he was a kid—

and a thin, high-pitched voice suited more to pre-pubescent boys than a thirty-two-year-old man. He always wore gloves to cover up the missing fingers. There was nothing he could do about the voice.

He said, "Hi, Bob. Good to see you. Really appreciate you helping us out on such short notice."

"Shut it. You're getting paid."

"No problem, Malick." He continued the farce. "Delighted to see you as well. How's fall treating you so far?"

"Oh, OK. Hello, Bob. You're looking healthy. Isn't this time of year so lovely? Watching the leaves change plain takes my breath away. Now tell me a fucking story, please."

"Was that so difficult? A little interpersonal communication." Lawson pointed a gloved finger toward the 21 Club. "There's your man sitting at the corner of the bar all by his lonesome."

I leaned around Lawson and peered into the bar. There were only seven people in the place, including the bartender. Barnhard was hunched over a handful of empty shots and a tumbler filled with some kind of dark liquor. Lifting the drink to his mouth seemed to take a Herculean effort—hands trembling, lips puckered as though, with a little luck, he might catch the liquid in his mouth.

Lawson said, "Oh, yeah, by the way, he's totally shitfaced."

"It's like watching a prop airplane try to land in the middle of a hurricane."

Half the drink went where it was supposed to go. The other half splashed down his chin and onto his lap. Barnhard mashed his chin against his chest and surveyed the damage, then wiped his chin with his hand and flicked the liquid off his fingers.

Lawson guffawed and shook his head. "So what, we follow our own clients now, too?"

"Guess so. The ones that drive them crazy anyway. He been on his phone?"

"Not to talk. Fooled around with it a couple times, but it looked like he was surfing the net more than texting. I don't think he could get those thumbs working now if he tried. Seems to me he's intent on a bender."

"All right. Take me through his night."

By Lawson's account, Barnhard had taken him on a walking tour of downtown Cain City. Upon exiting the offices of Leach, McKinney & Thurber, Barnhard retrieved something he couldn't see from the glove compartment of his Jaguar, left it parked on the street and set out on foot for Taco Willie's, four blocks away. Sat at the counter, ordered about twelve tacos, didn't talk to anyone or get on his phone, though he did check it quickly three or four times, likely to see what time it was.

Paid cash for the food, walked a block and a half west, north for another block to the side door of the Royal Vista apartment building. There, Barnhard halted suddenly and took a long look up and down the street, spotted Lawson and watched him as he walked past the stoop without so much of a glance Barnhard's way. Once Lawson was a good half block past the Royal Vista, he glanced back to see that Barnhard had stopped clocking him. He was punching some numbers into a keypad, which got him buzzed into the side door. After Barnhard entered, Lawson sprinted back in time to catch the door before it shut. He went in and spotted Barnhard as he stepped onto the elevator at the far end of the hallway.

Lawson hustled down the hall in time to see the elevator ascending to the fifth floor and stopping there. He took the next ride up and had a look around, but couldn't figure out which apartment Barnhard was visiting. Lawson then retreated to the shadows of some trees across the street from the Royal Vista and waited for Barnhard to come back out.

I grunted.

"What?" said Lawson.

"Eh, probably nothing. I know somebody who lives on the fifth floor of that building."

"Well, he was in there a little over an hour. Came out visibly more fucked up, stumbled the three blocks from there to here, planted himself at the bar, and here we be."

"He talk to anybody in the bar?"

"Just the bartender."

"So outside of losing eyes on him when he went into the Royal Vista, you didn't see him get on his phone or talk to anybody?"

"No. Nothing like that."

"Anybody go in or out of the Royal Vista while you were waiting for Barnhard?"

"I couldn't monitor both entrances, so I don't know about the front, but there were eleven—six in, five out—through the side door. Three people did both, entered and exited during that hour."

Lawson grabbed a long-lensed digital camera off the dashboard, tilted it to where I could view the display screen and flipped through pictures, narrating them as he went along.

"Barnhard goes in, couple minutes later these two women right here go in, arms full of groceries . . . then you've got this short little guy who hustles in a minute or two later . . . Five minutes after that, the tinier of those two women comes out . . . this fat fella flicks a ciggy into the bushes, gets buzzed in . . . The short guy comes back out carrying something. I can't tell what it is, can you?"

I leaned closer to the camera. "No idea, maybe a tablet or piece of equipment of some sort?"

Lawson kept going. "Right here a Marty's Pizza guy comes round and buzzes, this bleached-blonde woman comes down to pick it up . . . and this black girl with a pink wig comes and sits on the stoop. Nobody in or out for ten minutes before Barnhard comes out of the building. Pink girl gets up and catches the door before it shuts and locks and she goes in. That's it."

"She seem like she was waiting for him to leave or just someone to leave so she could get in?"

"Couldn't say. Him leaving was the first chance she had to get in the door if that's what she was doing. They didn't look at each other that I could tell."

I had him take me through the pictures one more time.

"Recognize anybody?" Lawson asked.

"No," I lied. I recognized a Sheriff's Deputy whose name escaped me and the girl in the pink wig, a nineteen-year-old named Renata Jones. She was the roommate of the girl on the fifth floor that I knew.

I asked Bob the same question.

"Not a one," he replied.

I asked Lawson to email me the pics with the time stamps on them and told him to bounce, I'd take up the stakeout.

"You sure? I don't mind staying, could use a couple more hours."

"Nah, this guy has somewhere to be tomorrow. I better make sure he gets tucked in nice and tight."

"C'mon, Malick. You getting yours, man, but what about everybody else? This business is a tough road to hoe, you know that. How 'bout giving somebody else a slice of the pie?"

"Let me ask you something, Bob."

"Yeah?"

"Do you consider yourself a contralto or a soprano?"

"Aw, c'mon—"

"No, seriously. Off the top I would say you're a contralto—"

"Screw you—"

"But when you whine, kicks it right up to soprano."

"Don't ask me for any more favors, all right, Malick?"

"I'm just playing, Bob. Calm down."

"No, fuck it. There ain't no motherfucking brotherhood."

"Don't be dramatic."

"How would you like it if I called you *Finding Nemo* or something?"

"The movie?"

"Yeah."

"Haven't seen it."

"He has a fucked-up—you know what, forget it. You think I would ask *you* for work if I didn't need it? You think that's easy for me?"

"All right, Bob, take it easy. Tell you what. If you went in the bar, you think Barnhard would recognize you from outside the Royal Vista?"

"I've got a change of clothes in the back."

I instructed Lawson to go into the 21 Club, sit a few stools down from Barnhard and eavesdrop on any interactions. I didn't expect anything to happen at this point, but if Barnhard did by chance contact anyone tied to his case, we were better off having an operative within earshot. At least, that's how I'd justify billing double duty to the bosses. Hell with them if they didn't like it. Lawson only made half my rate anyway.

He crawled into the back seat and swapped his beige fleece for a navy one. We got out of the car. Before he took off I cautioned him against talking to Barnhard. "Once he hears your voice, your cover's blown forever."

Lawson flipped me off, crossed the street and entered the 21 Club. I climbed into the Tacoma and watched him slide onto a stool three down from Barnhard and order a beer.

This was at 11:40 p.m. By 1:00 a.m. the three of us were in the exact same positions. With each successive drink, Barnhard's head sank closer to the bar top, but he hung in there, kept the drinks coming. I was bored out of my skull, physically peeling my eyelids apart to keep awake. It was a Tuesday, so there weren't many college kids out and there wasn't any action on the street save for the occasional car gliding by or a 21 Club patron coming out to barf in the bushes. That happened twice. Same patron.

Only real excitement of the night came shortly past twelve when a red Jetta screeched to a stop in the middle of the road maybe twenty feet in front of my truck. A young black girl in jeans and a cut-off shirt shot out of the passenger door, ran around to the front of the car and started dancing wildly in the headlights. Some song was blasting from the Jetta's speakers, throwing a sonic reverb up and down the street, the only discernable lyrics being 'work that ass,' repeated roughly three hundred times. The girl obliged the rapper and shook her shit all over the place. The light from the beams refracted off the bangles on her wrists, her necklaces, her hoop earrings, the rhinestones on her jeans and the glitter on her eyelids. She was putting on a show, a one-woman disco, but not for anybody else; not for the driver, not for me. She didn't even know I was there. The girl danced with such euphoria, such unbridled freedom—it was almost enough to make you want to relive your youth, do all the dumb shit you did all over again. When the song ended, the girl dived back into the Jetta and it vanished around the corner like an apparition.

Once again I was alone on the street.

At 1:17 a.m. Barnhard's forehead settled onto the bar and his body went slack. I got a text from Lawson: *the fuck do i do now?*

I replied: *wake him up*

Bob Lawson poked Barnhard on his shoulder a couple times and lightly shook him to no avail, so he gave up, looked out the plate-glass window toward me and threw his arms up. I cursed under my breath, got out of my car and went in. I told Lawson to go home, fill out a report, and send me the Royal Vista pictures; I'd take it from here. He didn't argue. I gave Barnhard's hairy face a few rapid slaps. The big man groused a bit, but didn't wake. A spit bubble inflated between his lips and popped. I tried flicking his ear. His arm came up and swatted at the air around his head, but his eyes didn't crack.

The bartender, a lanky guy with muttonchops and slicked-back hair, said, "Hey fella, your buddy needs to settle up."

I pulled out my wallet. "How much?"

"Sixty-eight bucks."

I wasn't that generous. I tucked my wallet into my pocket.

"Give me a glass of cold water."

The bartender sprayed some water into a cup and handed it over. I promptly lifted Barnhard's collar and poured the water down his back. That roused him. He wrenched upward, addled and bleary-eyed, blinking like he'd been knocked silly. I clapped my hands in front of his face, got his pupils focused on me and told him to pay his tab.

"Malick?" he muttered. "What the hell are you doing here?" His head started lolling. I grabbed him by the shoulders and propped him up. He whispered something I couldn't make out, so I leaned in closer and smelled the mixture of rum and funk coming off his body. "My car," he said.

"Forget your car, get it tomorrow."

"No!" he yelled, displaying a shocking burst of energy. "No! Need my car!"

"All right, all right. We'll get your car. Pay the tab."

Barnhard fumbled through his wallet and tossed a hundred-dollar bill onto the bar. The bartender asked if he wanted change and Barnhard raised his hands as if he were surrendering to authorities. I took him by the elbow and assisted him to the sidewalk. The cool night air sparked his senses and he began ranting about the great conspiracy to keep his Jaguar parked downtown overnight.

"Vandals everywhere," he said, flitting his arms about in a gesture that I presumed indicated the whole world. "You'd not believe how many there are in every bastard hole you look in. Nobody can stand to see somebody get ahead in life, have nice things, nice poss . . . possessions—" He put a fist to his chest, belched, and lurched forward as if something may have come up into his throat. If so he caught it and swallowed it back down. "Ew," he said. "Everybody wants to cut great men like me down to size. They all want to see me go down, down, down. All the way down. They even want my car."

"Nobody cares about your car. Sit down."

Barnhard looked at me like he was baffled by the sounds my mouth made, or possibly he was overcome by the toxicity of whatever he'd put into his body. Either way, he did as I said and plopped down next to the bushes where not too long ago I'd seen somebody puke their small intestine out.

For twenty bucks, this guy who called himself DD Chuck would bring a friend of his to wherever you were and the two of them would drive you and your car home. Every drunk in town had DD Chuck's number. I dialed it and asked him if he'd ever driven a Jag. Ten minutes later his Dodge Caravan pulled up out front of the 21 Club. DD Chuck was roughly my height and three times my width, with a flat-top haircut that had been abandoned by the public as a whole in 1989. He slid out of the car, pushed his glasses up on his nose and gave me a once-over.

"Ain't seen you in a good spell." DD Chuck didn't so much speak his words as chew them on the way out. You had to really listen to piece together his syllables.

"What, you miss me?" I said.

"Is a frog's ass watertight?"

"Come again?"

"Hell no, I didn't miss you."

DD Chuck lifted Barnhard to his feet, warned him not to vomit in his van, and heaved him into the back. I got into my Tacoma. They followed me to where the Jaguar was located a few blocks away. DD Chuck got behind its wheel, and his associate slid over to the driver's side of the van. I led them to Barnhard's house on the Southside, a large ranch-style home across the street from Redding Park.

They parked the Jag in Barnhard's roundabout driveway, helped him down from the van, handed over his keys, and went off to rescue some other lush. Barnhard wobbled to his front door and sifted through his keys, eventually selected one, and started jabbing it at the lock like he was trying to pin the tail on the donkey. I was considering getting out to help him when one of his stabs miraculously hit the slot and the door swung open. Barnhard tumbled through the threshold and flung the door shut. A couple lights flipped on and off in different parts of the house and then the place went dark.

I cut the engine and waited there for a bit to make sure Barnhard stayed put. I rolled down my window and breathed in the clean night air. The neighborhood was quiet, peaceful. Nary a dog barking nor a human in sight, nothing. So quiet you could hear the stream that cut through Redding Park burbling from a hundred yards away. Karla had dreamed of living in the park district since she was a little girl. She was constantly pulling up real estate websites to show me the houses that came up for sale: the number of bathrooms, bedrooms, the square footage, whether or not they had crown molding or a fireplace or an island in the kitchen, endless pictures of unfurnished rooms that she had already decorated in her mind. Maybe if I won the lottery. Course, I'd have to play the lottery.

I shot off a quick email to Ed Leach and Kent McKinney that summarized Barnhard's drunken odyssey and, when the clock struck 3, called it a night.

CHAPTER FOUR
THE PINK GIRL

The morning sun streamed in through the windows, turning the insides of my eyelids orange. I peeled them apart, rolled onto my back, and took stock of my surroundings. I'd managed to shed my coat and one of my boots before I crashed last night, but the rest of my clothes were still on. I didn't sleep in the back room of my office often, mostly on the occasions where I was up late working or drinking. Since I started working for the lawyers, the hours—save a few exceptions like last night—had more or less eased into your standard nine-to-five. The drinking, at least the heavy sort, had become rarer since Karla and I had become a real thing. This becoming a real thing happened a little over a year ago. We'd gotten into a particularly colorful shouting match in my office. Beats me about what. I'd been bombed off bourbon and had only snippets of the argument in my memory. It was mid-summer, the days were hot, windows were open, and it must have been a doozy because her son Davey, who was in their apartment two floors above at the time, still enjoyed quoting some of the more select passages.

The next day, Karla laid it out for me like this: I could drink myself into a warm, fuzzy, liver-failing stupor for all the live-long day; I could drink until my blood turned into lighter fluid if that was what I so chose. But it would be done without her. She proposed one simple term and condition. She didn't ask me to drop the booze cold, just to scale it back to a manageable level. It wasn't exactly Sophie's Choice; I needed an impetus to get off the sauce and she gave it to me, but I pretended to weigh the costs of such a decision just to get her fired up. She was stunning when she got animated.

I sat up and checked my phone for the time, but the battery was dead. I kicked the boot that I was still wearing onto the floor, got out of bed and scoured the room for the remote to the old twenty-inch analog TV that sat atop the dresser. Couldn't find it, so I hit the power button and flipped the channel until I came across *Good Morning America*. The anchor informed me that it was 8:20 on this fine Wednesday morning, the twenty-fifth of September. I plugged my phone into the charger, stripped off my clothes and ambled into the bathroom where I shit, showered, shaved, and emerged a new man.

I got dressed, took a cursory glance at the mirror to make sure I still passed for human, then looked at my phone again. Two new texts. One from Karla reminding me that her job interview was that afternoon and I needed to pick up Davey from school. The second, from Joanna, had come in three minutes ago. It read: *Sorry for all the histrionics last night*

I responded: *no sweat*

She replied immediately: *With all that's happened, all we've been through together, in my head I thought it would be really nice to be friends. But I don't think I can do it actually. I hope I'm not being even more dramatic and ridiculous. It's just all a little too much for me now.*

What the hell was I supposed to say to that? I didn't want to get involved in some lengthy text conversation—I had somewhere I had to be—so I typed: *okay. take care of yourself. take care of that baby*, hit send, and pocketed the phone. I collected my keys, coat, hat, then walked out of the back room and across my office to the door. When I opened it a small, nebbish man wearing horn-rimmed glasses and a neatly trimmed mustache nearly tumbled in on me.

I said, "Who are you?" But before the 'you' even made it off my lips I noticed the pink slip in his right hand, strips of scotch tape attached to the forefinger and thumb on his left, and knew exactly who he was and why he'd been leaning against my door.

The man attempted to gather himself, pushed his glasses high on his nose with the finger that had tape on it. The tape stuck to the bridge of his glasses and when he lowered his hand the glasses were flung to the floor.

"Oh no," he mumbled, bending to pick them up. The left lens had a jagged crack down the center. This seemed to vex the man a good deal. He put the glasses back on his face, then widened and squinted his eyes to test the best way to see around the crack.

"You okay?" I asked him.

"Are you Nick Malick?" he asked, his left eye still fluttering.

"Yeah." I nodded toward the pink slip. "What's this, then?"

"I'm—"

"—the new building manager."

"Yes. My name is Roger Holbrook. This is an—"

"—Eviction notice."

I snatched the slip from his hand and skimmed it over.

"I hate to be the bearer of bad news," Roger said.

"Do you?"

"Yes, but I'm afraid we're going to have to ask you to vacate the premises completely by the thirty-first of October."

"Ask away."

"Pardon?"

"You said you were going to have to ask. Ask."

"Oh, I'm sorry for the confusion. Tell. I meant we're telling you that you have to vacate by the last day of your lease."

"Let *me* tell *you* why that's not going to happen, Roger." I gave him a genial grin, turned my back to him and locked my door, then started walking down the hall, signaling for him to come along. With a little flurry of steps he caught up to me. "Do you know who I am?"

"Nick Malick?"

"Right. And you know what I do?"

"I'm afraid so. That is why, regretfully, we can't renew your lease. How do I put this politely . . . Your presence causes a lot of potential businesses and tenants to . . . *balk* at renting space in the building."

"So nothing to do with the fact that you want to double what you're charging for these units?"

"Oh. Well, I don't know if the markup would be double."

We turned the corner and reached the intersection of the main hallway. Next to us were two sets of double doors. One led to the old gymnasium, the other to the auditorium. I stopped walking and the little guy followed suit.

"Listen, Roger. You keep saying 'we,' so I'm gonna assume you're just a lackey working for a bunch of corporate schmucks, out here doing your job. An unpleasant job, but somebody's gotta do it, right? And you gotta collect a check somehow."

Roger neither confirmed nor denied my assumption. Unconsciously, he fingered his wedding band.

I continued, "Now, I have no doubt that what you say is true and that your bosses want me gone for more reasons than money, but let's not kid each other, when it comes down to it, it's always about the money. Just so happens I work for a bunch of lawyers that know a good deal about money. They love the stuff. And I perform a service for them that they appreciate, so if I were inclined to fight this, which I would be, my friends down at Leach, McKinney & Thurber would do me the solid of taking my case on pro bono, and they'd drag it on and on, as long as was necessary to make your company feel the hurt. Because the one thing they like almost as much as money is winning." I handed Roger the pink slip. "So you go ahead and return this piece of paper to your boss and tell him what I said. Then he can tell his boss and he can tell his and so on. They can have a conference about it and if, after that, they decide that it's worth it for them to come after me, well then, Roger, you just bring this notice on back and we'll get the party started."

Roger stared at the pink slip. He raised his finger and opened his mouth to speak, but not much came out, just a little squeak from the back of his throat. His hand lowered slowly back to his side, but his mouth stayed hanging there as though the hinges had sprung loose. I started down the main hallway toward the exit.

Without looking back, I said, "And if your bosses want people to feel more at ease, maybe do more to mend the bullet holes than spackle over them." I pointed to exhibits A, B, and C on the walls of the hallway where there were large white splotches in the otherwise smooth umber-colored brick. There were about twenty more of those white blots visible from where Roger stood, remnants from the night seven men had come to kill me.

Outside, the sky was clear and cloudless, the air pleasantly cool. I stood on the portico and admired the progress made in the neighborhood over the last six months. The strip mall across the street had been down to two businesses, a shoe store called Sole Brothers and Plenty's, a yogurt shop. The other four spaces had been vacant for a couple years but, one by one, new businesses had moved in: a Container Store, a UPS mailing center, and a deli, leaving only one empty property. Catty-corner from the old high school they built a new Sessions Bank that had been up and running for a few weeks. Even the gas station on the north side of the street had gotten a facelift: new pumps, new neon logo, remodeled interior. Cain City was willing away its own decline, trying to improve, trying to grow. It was possible that I'd never given the town the credit it deserved. In spite of its many shortcomings, Cain City was a scrapper.

I trudged down the stone steps and around the side of the building to the parking lot. This new management company had assigned parking spaces. Mine was beneath a light pole in the middle of the lot, number 42. I climbed behind the wheel of the Tacoma and pointed her north, crossed under the viaduct and emerged downtown.

The Royal Vista was a non-descript six-story building in a town full of them. I parked in front and climbed the four stairs to the entrance, punched in the four-digit security code and went in.

The building had a sterile feel: florescent lights, grey-tiled flooring, walls and ceiling painted the same off-white color. A couple generic paintings of landscapes hung loosely from nails. I walked down to the elevator and rode it up to the fifth floor. The apartment I was going to was at the far end of the hall, number 512. I knocked on the door. The TV was blaring inside, but nobody answered. I banged.

There were some shuffling footsteps and the door swung open. Renata Jones, the girl with the pink wig whom Lawson had photographed sitting outside of the back entrance the night before, stood there, slumped and shapeless. She'd ditched the wig. Half her hair was pulled into a short ponytail, the other half sprouted off perpendicular to her head. An oversized t-shirt with the sleeves cut out was the only visible article of clothing on her body. Her boobs were half-flopped out of the sleeve holes. She held a bowl and cereal in one hand, spoon in the other, and was chomping away on a mouthful.

"You," she said flatly, scanning me up and down. Dark circles ringed her eyes and her moving them seemed like a massive chore.

"Me. Where's Birdie?"

Renata didn't say anything, just scratched her scalp with the handle of the spoon and stood aside to let me enter. I stepped in. She kicked the door shut behind me and moped over to the couch, pointed a remote at the TV and unpaused an episode of *South Park*. I knew the show because Davey watched it all the time.

The apartment was dingy with a low ceiling and random pieces of furniture that had been cobbled together from thrift shops and street corners. It had a faux parquet floor and an island that separated the kitchen from the living room. The smell of rotten poultry filled my nostrils. Dirty dishes and empty fast food containers were everywhere.

"Got a dollar says someone's about to kill Kenny," I said to Renata.

"Huh?"

I pointed to the TV. "Someone always kills Kenny."

"Riiiight."

I walked down the short hall and rapped a knuckle on Birdie's bedroom door. No response. I called her name but still got nothing, so I twisted the knob and peered in the room.

Birdie Bryant was sprawled face down on the four-poster bed, motionless save for her nostrils flaring with each breath. Her cheek was smushed against the bare mattress and her body was tangled up in a comforter. I couldn't tell if she had any clothes on beneath the blanket.

I raised my voice and called Birdie's name again, to no avail. Dead to the world. I stepped in and inspected the room. It was an atypical bedroom for a nineteen-year-old: neat, clean, minimalist, scents of vanilla and citrus. A total contrast from the squalor of the living room. An old-fashioned vanity sat against the wall opposite the bed and there was a matching chest of drawers in the corner. The closet was two floor-to-ceiling mirrored sliding doors. Beside that was a door that led to a bathroom. On the far wall was a sliding glass door that opened onto a small balcony. Nothing was strewn about—no clothes on the floor, no make-up on the vanity, no hair ties, no headphones. The only blights in the place were the lump of human on the bed, a lava lamp that cast a sleazy red glow over the otherwise-austere aesthetic, and the remnants of some crushed pills next to a library card on the bedside table. There were also some colorful silk scarves tied to each bedpost.

I leaned over and jostled Birdie by the shoulder. When that didn't work I lifted her mattress until she slowly started to roll down. That did the trick. Her eyes popped wide and she jolted upright, sucked in a panicked breath and looked around as though she didn't know where she was. Then she saw me and her world snapped into focus.

"Shit," she moaned. "What you doing here?"

"It's Wednesday," I said. "Get up, get dressed. You're going to be late."

Birdie cursed again and flopped back onto the bed. She stared at the ceiling for a moment, then sniffed, rubbed her nose, and sat up with a resigned expression. "All right, give me a minute."

I went back out into the living room and sat on the opposite end of the couch from Renata. Her only acknowledgement of my presence was to grunt and pull her legs farther up under her, so we sat silently watching the cartoon. The characters in the show were sitting at a long table eating pizza in a tableau that looked like *The Last Supper*, and one of them was going to have to sacrifice themselves to save everybody. I wondered if Renata understood the references the show made or if she just liked the crass humor. I wondered the same thing about Davey.

The bastards killed Kenny. The episode ended.

Renata finished her cereal and slurped the remainder of the milk from the bowl. When she finished she set the bowl on the floor and wiped her chin on her shirt.

Another episode began. Renata started scratching at her upper arms, which were dotted with acne scars and cigarette pocks, like she wanted to tear her skin off.

"You all right?" I asked her.

She stopped her scratching and glared at me. "I'm fine. *You* all right?"

"Peachy. How was your night last night?"

"What do you care?"

Just then, Birdie hurried into the room. She was wearing a beanie, jeans, a modest sweater, some fuzzy-topped suede boots. All in all, she looked remarkably fresh compared to just ten minutes before. She was holding a small stuffed unicorn with a rainbow-colored mane.

"You ready?" she said, a touch frenetic. I got up from the couch. Birdie scoured the room, found her purse under one of the beanbags, and stuffed the unicorn into it. She took a quick look in a mirror to fix the beanie on her head just so and apply some ChapStick. She smacked her lips together and flounced over to the door where I was waiting for her. "Later, Renata."

"Yeah, laters."

CHAPTER FIVE
HUM LITTLE BIRDIE

"You look great, Birdie, don't worry."

She was examining her reflection in the Tacoma's visor mirror. She flipped it shut and sat back. On the whole, Birdie was a smooth customer with a seen-it-all attitude, largely unshakeable, but these weekly visits to her daughter's foster home stripped her of her composure. Sitting next to me, she picked at her cuticles and tapped her foot incessantly in an effort to not crack into a thousand pieces.

The foster home was in a little 'burb called Becksville, fifteen minutes east of Cain City. I merged onto Interstate 64 and told Birdie to buckle up. She stopped fidgeting long enough to roll her eyes, pull the belt across her torso and strap in.

"How's your week been?" I asked.

"You know, same old. Shit don't change. How my brothers and sisters doin'?"

"Good. The families they've been placed with are still getting them together every other Saturday. You haven't been going?"

"Nah," Birdie said, shaping her mouth into a pout that seemed disingenuous. "Haven't had the time."

"Have you made the time to study?"

"Man, why you forever pressing me with that garbage?"

"I'm not pressing shit, Birdie. I'm trying to help you. The test is in three weeks."

"Yeah, well, did I ask for your help? I seem to remember being just fine before some crusty ol' white dude shows up with your savior complex and all that. Just because you had some weird thing for my mom and I look like her or some shit."

Birdie laid her head back on the headrest and looked out the window at the trees, the greens, reds, and yellows of the leaves blurring together as we sped past.

"Do you want to get your daughter back?" I asked.

She made a smacking sound with her mouth. "What you think?"

"Then you gotta pass the GED. You gotta get a real job. You gotta get your driver's license. You gotta show that you've got your shit together and are capable of taking care of her."

"Tell me something I don't know. If it was easy as all that, it'd have already been done."

"Nothing's easy. Is what you're doing now easy?" She didn't say anything. "And you gotta stop with the drugs."

"What are you doing snoopin'?"

"I wasn't snooping. It was right on the table for anybody to see."

"Anybody that barges into my room—"

"You're never gonna get her back if you're doing drugs—"

"—is snooping. Nobody told you you could come in there. How am I supposed to. . . ?" Her sentence trailed off. She clenched her teeth, let loose a muffled scream and banged her head against the window.

"Easy, okay? Easy."

We both stayed mute for the next few miles.

"I didn't have a thing for your mom," I said, breaking the silence. "I told you, we—"

"You worked together. Yeah, I know, 'cept she was a stripper and a hooker. So 'worked together'"—she air-quoted—"could mean a lot of things."

"It wasn't like that."

"Hmm."

"And I'm not crusty."

"Hmm."

"I'm a little old, but I'm not crusty." Birdie side-eyed me skeptically. "You're gonna be forty one day too, you know."

"Yeah, but I ain't gonna be no crusty."

"You better stock up on some lotion then."

"Was that a racist joke?"

"No, it was a black joke. I can't tell a black joke now?"

"Naw. Don't you know what year we live in? You can't say nothing like that no more. It's against the rules."

"Yeah, well, don't you know what city you live in? The rules of polite society don't apply."

"I heard that shit."

I glanced over at Birdie. With her high, round cheeks, deep brown skin, doe eyes, pert little nose, and thick lips, she was a striking replica of her mother.

"DNA is crazy," I said. "You even got the sass."

"You don't have to tell me. I know my mom was all that. Every night when I was little I'd sit there Indian-style on the floor, watching her put her face on in the mirror before she left, hoping one day I'd be just as beautiful as she was. She'd say I looked like a little birdie waiting to get fed, sitting there like that. That's how I got my name. I ever tell you that?"

"No."

"When I get Aisha back, I'm gonna call her Little Bird. And she can call me Big Bird. That's cute, right?"

"Yeah, it's cute."

Birdie smiled, picturing this future in her mind's eye. The expression faded. "How am I gonna learn to drive?"

"I'll teach you."

"When?"

"Whenever you want."

Birdie looked at me seriously. "Why you doing all this for me? For real."

I shrugged and searched for some sufficient words. "I don't know, your mom, I just—"

"Shoo, she must of had you whipped on that snatch."

"I told you—"

"I know, I know," she yawned, "you just *worked* together. Can we listen to some music or something?"

I said sure. Birdie scrolled through the dial and landed on a retro station playing a block of Prince songs.

"Hold on," I said, before she turned it loud. "Before we get there, I've got something else to talk to you about."

"Ugh. What now?"

"I know we agreed that I'd never ask you about the people that come to see you."

"Nope, I ain't answering no questions about no clients."

"Birdie, this isn't me asking you about your life, your work, or whatever. This is about someone I'm investigating. I need to know if he came to see you last night."

Birdie folded her arms beneath her chest. "You can ask, but I ain't answering."

"White guy, about six foot, a little beefy, beard that looks like he colored it in with a magic marker, hair a little thin on top, slicked back." I gauged her to see if anything I was saying resonated or struck a chord, but she was stone-faced. "Deep voice, kind of an asshole. Nothing?"

"I told you a long time ago and I told you just now. I don't talk about that and I ain't never gonna talk about it."

"Last night he was wearing navy slacks, cream-colored shirt, and a striped tie, different shades of blue. I just need to know if you were with him, or if you saw him talking to anybody, heard him talking to anybody on the phone, anything like that."

Her lips were sealed. But she would have said no if Barnhard had not come to see her, just to shut down my inquiry if nothing else, so I at least had that answer.

"All right," I said. "Crank it up."

Birdie twisted the knob and Prince's "Purple Rain" filled the truck with that smooth, synthetic timbre of his. Birdie sang along; her voice wasn't half bad. She kept right up with the Purple One, even when his range shifted north or south or he let rip one of those screaming runs he was famous for. She knew all the lyrics by heart. I asked her if she had ever seen the movie of the same title or its sequel, *Graffiti Bridge*. Birdie said she hadn't.

"What they about?"

"You know, love, loss, fear, obsession, jealousy, all the good stuff."

"Sounds dope."

"Gett Off" came on the radio next. With her in the car, the lyrics made me uncomfortable, so I tried to switch the station, but Birdie slapped my hand away and kept the performance going. She had that song down pat, too, even throwing some gravel into her voice for the man's part.

"You can really sing," I told her.

"Shut up."

Midway through the song we arrived at the foster home. I shut off the engine. Birdie took one more peek into the visor mirror and shut it.

"You look great," I assured her. "It's going to be fine. Aisha lives for these visits." Birdie forced a nervous smile and took a deep breath.

"See you in an hour," she said, and stepped out of the truck. I always stayed in the car when I brought Birdie to these appointments with her daughter. I didn't want to impose on their time together—the woman who ran the foster home was legally bound to perform that duty enough as it was—but on days like today when the weather was nice they would come out to the front yard where there was a slide and swing set.

I enjoyed watching them play. Aisha was a gorgeous little girl, a few months shy of two, with big blue eyes and butter-colored skin that paired well with her mother's features. Her hair, various shades of gold with streaks of blonde running through, fell in thick curlicues down to her shoulders. Aisha's father was most likely white, though nobody knew for certain. I figured Birdie must have her reasons for not divulging his identity, but it's just as possible that she wasn't sure who the man was herself.

I rolled down the windows to let the fresh air blow through and listen to their playing. Birdie doted on Aisha during these visits. In turn, Aisha beamed at the sight of her mother. She clutched her new unicorn to her chest as Birdie pushed her gently on the swing. The foster mother, a benevolent older woman named Dottie who had a pronounced hunch in her shoulders, stood to the side. She always gave Birdie an update on Aisha's week and then let them be for the rest of the hour.

"I took in a new child on Monday," Dottie told her. "A little boy only a few months older than Aisha. His name is Zachary. Sweet little thing, but he and Aisha have butted heads a couple of times. Nothing serious. I think they're just feeling each other out."

"So you got three now?"

"That's right. Aisha, Zachary, and Cassie, who's three. They're both inside with my sister, who helps me out, as you know. Three is my limit. I won't be taking any more unless one of the children is adopted permanently."

Birdie's posture went rigid. She stuffed her hands into her pockets and started chewing her lip.

"But you're not looking to get Aisha adopted right now, like you said."

"No, no, I meant Zachary and Cassie. Sorry, I didn't mean to worry you. I will take care of Aisha as long as I can, dear. They don't start to make a big push to get them adopted permanently until they hit school age, so you have some time."

Birdie must have started to get teary because she sniffed and dabbed at the corners of her eyes. Dottie apologized again and proposed they restrict any further topics of conversation to Aisha.

"She's really getting fast. She's faster than Cassie who's a full year older."

"She hasn't said no words yet?" Birdie asked.

"No," Dottie said apologetically. She forced a sunny expression into her face. "Wait until you see what she started doing this week though. Let me show you and I'll leave the two of you alone." Dottie slowed the swing to a stop and bent down to Aisha's eye level. "Let's show Mommy what we learned. Can you sing Mommy a song? Can you sing 'Twinkle, Twinkle'?"

Aisha turned bashful, tucked her chin into her chest and smooshed the unicorn into her face. Dottie tickled her belly, which elicited a giggle, and whispered something in Aisha's ear that coaxed the unicorn down. Then, to prompt her, Dottie started singing.

"Twinkle, twinkle little star, how I wonder what you are—"

Aisha hummed the next notes in the tune, timidly at first, but when she saw her mother beaming down at her she relaxed into the melody and hummed as clearly and as on-rhythm as her mother had sung Prince, all the way through to the end. The two women clapped and made a lot of fanfare over Aisha, who soaked up the adulation with delight. Dottie explained that they played nursery rhymes for the kids all the time, but Aisha had never even danced or clapped or anything until a couple days ago, when she started humming along to the entirety of every song they played.

"Who needs talking when you can sing?" Dottie said. Birdie concurred. She leaned over, cupped Aisha's cheeks in her hands and kissed her forehead. Dottie listed some other songs Birdie could try with Aisha and excused herself. Birdie knelt down to eye level with Aisha, took hold of her hands, and began a new rhyme.

It was remarkable, watching them. Birdie gently sang the words of song after song as Aisha cooed the music in unison. *DNA is crazy,* I thought again. They began an "Itsy Bitsy Spider" duet. Thoughts of my own son at Aisha's age slipped into my brain. Decade-old images of a two-year-old Jake: the way he'd run into my arms full bore; splash in the bath until the whole room was soaked; fit perfectly on my chest to watch TV, a cartoon for him or a ballgame for me. The way he'd repeat every word we said and work through the syllables in his mouth afterward, how he'd giggle until he was breathless when I tickled him, then squeal *again, again!* Joanna had refused to cut Jake's hair for the first three years of his life and he would whip his head from side to side to feel it flip in and out of his face.

My phone buzzed. I checked the display—Ed Leach—and answered.

"We have a problem," he spat. "Scott Barnhard hasn't shown up to the meeting at the U.S. Attorney's office."

I checked the time. 10:10 a.m.

"Shit."

"Yeah, shit. He's not picking up his phone either. I think I've filled up his voicemail in the last twenty minutes. How blotto did he get last night?"

"The guy thinks he's going to jail. He got wrecked."

"Jesus. Get over there and get him up, douse him in mouthwash, do whatever you have to do. Just get him here. They extended us twenty minutes. If he doesn't show, they're going to have him picked up."

"I'm in Becksville."

"Then step on it."

I got out of the truck and jogged over to where Birdie and Aisha were sitting on the grass out front of the house.

"Something's come up at work. I have to go, but here." I handed her a piece of paper. "If I'm not back, call this cab driver. He'll come get you and take you home. He might look a little sketchy, but I know him. He's harmless. I've got a running tab going so I'll take care of it, okay?"

"Everything all right?" Birdie asked, shielding her eyes from the sun to look up at me.

"Yeah, just have to deal with some idiot. You know how it is."

"Say bye-bye to Mr. Nick," she said to Aisha. Aisha grinned and opened and closed both her hands.

"Bye-bye, sweet girl," I said.

I flipped a U-turn in the middle of the lane and kept to the speed limit through the neighborhood, then opened her up when I got on the interstate and made it to Barnhard's by 10:23.

His Jaguar was still parked in the roundabout where DD Chuck left it. I pulled in behind, got out, walked over and banged on the front door. Nothing stirred inside the house. I pressed the doorbell a couple dozen times and listened to the ring bounce hollow off the interior walls. Tried the knob to see if I'd get lucky. No dice. I cupped my hands and peered in through the small rectangular windows that bordered the doorframe on each side, but the foyer was dark and the glass was too thick to make out anything through the distortion. I scoured all the nooks and crannies where there might be a spare key tucked away and came up empty.

Waist-high hedges surrounded the outer walls of the house, so it was difficult to get a good look in any of the windows. I walked along the perimeter in search of a way into the residence or, at the very least, a break in the hedges. Out back of the lot was a wide lawn with a large patio, a guest house, jacuzzi, and an in-ground pool. Most people closed their pools up around Labor Day, but there was no tarp on Barnhard's. The morning sun flicked a thousand glints of bright light across the surface of the water. Either Barnhard was lazy or kept his pool heated year-round. I guessed the latter.

There were two entries at the back of the house—a sliding glass door off the patio, and an auxiliary door at the far corner that opened to a laundry room. Both were locked. I had a look in all the windows back there as well, but still caught no sign of Barnhard. I stood on the patio and vaguely considered breaking into the place.

The time on my phone was 10:27. The meeting at the U.S. Attorney's was fucked.

The firm made it a policy to give me the cell phone numbers and email addresses of all the clients I worked with. I scrolled to Barnhard's contact info and hit the call button. The ringer sounded in my ear and a half beat later I heard a soft chime coming from the other side of the sliding glass door. I peered into the dark living room again, straining my eyes to locate the source of the chime. My gaze landed on a pile of clothes at the edge of the room: the same slacks, cream-colored shirt, and striped tie Barnhard had been wearing the night before.

And before I could think, *Why would his clothes be piled up in the back of his house?* Before the question could fully articulate itself in my brain, I wheeled around and ran to the edge of the pool. There, below the shimmery surface at the bottom of the deep end, was the body of Scott T. Barnhard.

In I went.

CHAPTER SIX
FAT MAN'S FLOAT

"All right, Malick. Take me through it one more time," Detective Willis Hively said. We were sitting on foldout portable stools under a police tent at the far edge of the lawn, a safe enough distance away from the scene by the pool where the techs were working. Hively cut a handsome figure with his shiny blue tie and grey suit, tailored to show off the fact that he had more fast-twitch muscles than everybody else. My clothes were sopping wet. I'd jumped into the water and attempted to haul Barnhard to the surface, but he had been too waterlogged and too dead to move.

Someone had put a dry towel around my shoulders. I used it to wipe my face and said, "Don't perp-talk me. I just told you what happened. None of the details are going to change."

"Humor me."

Hively readied his pen and notebook for the second go-round.

"We got a problem, Willis?" I asked.

"You mean besides the dead body in the pool?"

"Yeah, besides that."

"Why don't you tell me your version of events again, like I asked you to, and I'll let you know if we have a problem."

Hively was a good cop, still young, a tick over thirty, idealistic to a fault. Not a speck of jade on him. He was raised in the Malcolm Terrace housing projects and could have easily settled on the criminal side of the law, came up with plenty of guys who flipped that way, but Hively made a different choice. That street education is what honed his instincts, made him a natural detective. He had the ability to think like a criminal. But those hood associations also necessitated he keep his rep clean, unimpeachable.

Back in the day we had a kind of mentor-mentee thing going, but Hively operated beyond the greys. His world was morally absolute; there was always a high road to be taken. That's where he and I fell out. Hively didn't agree with the way I'd handled the last case we worked together, the Cash City business. A gangbanger named Cupcake had taken a swan dive out of a fourth-floor window and Hively was sure I'd had something to do with it. Wouldn't be persuaded otherwise and I didn't have the energy or inclination to change his mind. Since then he'd looked down upon me from his proverbial high horse with a mixture of pity and disdain. As he was now.

I rehashed my story front to back: Bob Lawson tailing Barnhard to 21 Club—me joining the stakeout—Barnhard passing out at the bar—DD Chuck chauffeuring him home—Barnhard no-showing for the U.S. Attorney's meeting—my coming here to fetch him—finding him in the pool—jumping in to get him—soaking my phone—kicking in the laundry room door—calling the police.

"And here we are," I finished.

Two med-techs wearing wetsuits lugged a metal gurney into the backyard and set it by the side of the pool. They pulled on some flippers, fitted goggles over their eyes and mini air-tanks onto their mouths, and lowered themselves into the water.

"Why was the law firm having their own client tailed?"

"You'll have to ask them that," I said, distractedly. Something about the scene didn't make sense and was gnawing at me. I was trying to figure out what, exactly, as I watched the action by the pool. The two divers waded into the deep end and disappeared underwater.

Hively said, "I will. Why don't you give it an educated guess?"

"They didn't trust him. Did you see the pile of clothes in the house?"

"Yeah. Why didn't they trust him?"

"Did you see that they were wet?"

"Yeah, Malick. Answer my question, please."

I sighed and gave in. "Barnhard wasn't cooperative, even with his own counsel."

"What was the meeting with the U.S. Attorney about?"

"You'll have to ask the U.S. Attorney."

"Did anything you saw last night lead you to believe that Barnhard was in some kind of trouble, either from outside parties or from himself?"

"No."

One of the divers surfaced at the edge of the pool, grabbed the gurney, and dived back down with it.

"He meet up with anybody while he was out?"

"No."

"Talk to anybody?"

"No."

"What about when Bob Lawson was watching him?"

"You'd have to ask him, but to my knowledge, no."

"Except when he visited someone at the Royal Vista apartments. You don't know who he went to see there?"

"Right."

"No idea?"

"None," I lied. I wasn't getting Birdie caught up in this if I didn't have to.

The divers brought the body up. Two additional techs helped slide the gurney onto the pavement and tried to lift it, but it was too heavy from saturation. They called a couple of uni's over for reinforcements and the four of them, with a concerted effort, were able to hoist the gurney onto a roller.

Barnhard's meaty body was bloated and obscene. Water poured off it in strings. His skin had purpled and in the sunlight it possessed a slick, serpentine sheen. When I'd dived in and tried to grab hold of him, his skin had warped like putty in my hands. Now it seemed to be slipping off his flanks and upper arms like melted wax.

Barnhard had on red swimming trunks with a Hawaiian floral print. For some reason, the red of the trunks and the purple of his body brought an image of Papa Smurf to mind. His head flopped sideways on the gurney toward us. The tip of his tongue poked through his teeth.

We could tell from the expressions on the techs' faces that the corpse had started releasing its death gases, which happens when you move a body that's been dead for a while. The only smell worse than the gases from one dead body was the gases from two of them. The team went to work on him, scraping beneath the nails of his fingers and toes, and taking samples of hair from his head, eyebrows, eyelashes, and body.

Hively got back to the questioning.

"What time did you drop Barnhard off here last night?"

"2:15 . . . 2:30."

"And this DD Chuck will confirm that?"

"If you can find him." I was distracted, still watching Barnhard get processed and working over the scene in my head.

"DD Chuck got a last name?"

"I'm sure he does. I don't know it."

Hively closed his notebook and leaned forward. "Aren't you just a convenient source of fuck-all information?"

I turned to him, snickering. "What do you want from me? I don't know what I don't know."

"You think I believe a word you say?"

"Here we go. Now we're getting to it."

"You want to know what I see?"

"I got a fucking choice?"

Hively's mouth drew tight. A spasm started bouncing in the cheek below his right eye. He wiggled his features around to regain control over his face.

"Look here," I said. "You got a problem with me, fine. But it's your problem, not mine. And I'll tell you something else. One day you're gonna arrive at an impasse where there are no right or wrong choices, only a bad one and a really fucking bad one. You stay in this line long enough, that day will come. And it's not gonna announce itself. It's not gonna give you time to prepare. It's just gonna show up, right then and there, and you're going to have to make one of those choices. We'll see where you stand after that. Maybe then you won't be such a finger-tight asshole."

"Give me straight answers, Malick. That's all I fucking want or care about right now. The rest of that shit you're spouting means nothing."

"Ask away."

"What made you think to look in the pool?"

"I didn't at first, but it struck me that the pool was still open when most people's are closed by this time of year. When I called his phone, heard it ringing in the house, I looked in, saw his clothes from the night before on the floor, and something told me he was in the pool."

"So you saw him and jumped in?"

"Correct."

"But you couldn't raise him up."

"No." I nodded in the direction of Barnhard's corpse. "Look at the fat fucker."

"So you kicked in his side door to call us?"

"Right."

"With Barnhard's cell phone that you found in his house 'cause yours took a bath when you jumped in the pool?"

"Look at us," I said. "One talks, one listens. I think they call that communicating."

"Let me see your phone."

I dug my cell, heavy from being soaked, out of my pocket and handed it over. Hively hit some buttons, nothing happened, and he tossed it back, satisfied.

"How drunk was he?" he asked.

"Scale of one to ten? A twelve."

"Excuse me, detective," a voice from behind me said. It was a technician who had been examining Barnhard. Her badge read *Gloria Andrade*. I looked past her and saw that a plastic sheet had been placed over the top of Barnhard. Andrade stepped into the shade of the tent. "We're finished with our on-site procedures. Would you like to have a look at the body before we transport?"

"What's your take?" Hively said.

"No visual signs of undue trauma. Nothing visible under the nails. No defensive wounds. The capillaries in his eyes have burst, but that doesn't necessarily mean anything. There was a lot of vomit found in the first-floor bathroom sink with a wide spatter radius, which indicates a fairly forceful evacuation. The capillaries could have just as easily burst during something like that as they could have in a drowning, if that is indeed the cause."

"That's what it looks like, drowning?"

"Yes, sir. All initial appearances point to an accidental drowning. We won't know more until we get him into the lab."

"Okay. Give me a minute and I'll be over there." She went away. Hively looked at me, started to say something, but stopped short of speaking, shook his head and stood up. I stood with him. The water in my boots made a loud *squish*.

"We're done," he said.

"Can I look at the body?"

"No, you can't look at the body. What do you think this is, a viewing party?"

"This wasn't an accident," I insisted.

"I'll be the judge of that, thank you. You can go."

Hively started toward Barnhard's gurney.

"I'm telling you, something's funny here," I called after him.

"Fuck's sake." Hively wheeled back round. "You won't give me a straight answer to anything I ask, but you'll tell me that 'something's funny here'? I look around, the only thing I see out of place is you. Now if you know something that I should know, now's the time to tell me, because the way it looks is: your rich-boy client was hammered, made a stupid decision to go for a swim at 3 a.m., and got himself drowned. Is there something else I need to know?"

"No, not from me."

"Then listen to the words coming out of my mouth, Malick. Get gone."

"I need to see that body."

Hively took three aggressive steps toward me and stopped.

"Do you even know what your dumb ass is saying? If it's not an accident, then you're the last person to see the man alive and the first one to see him dead. Which makes *you* the main suspect. You think of that? To top it off, you've already admitted to breaking into the house, so no, you can't see the fucking body."

"You really think I'd implicate myself in a murder that I committed? Of my own client?"

"I don't put anything past anybody. Especially you. Now get out of my crime scene."

"So you do think it's a crime scene and not an accident?"

Hively tossed his hands in the air and did a couple full turns as though he were appealing to the heavens. For what, I don't know. Guidance? Serenity now? I pondered my talent for getting people worked up and waited for him to finish his rain dance. Eventually, when he did stop twirling, Hively put his hands on his hips, rolled his shoulders back, jutted his neck forward and turned to face me.

"You okay?" I said. "You dizzy or anything?"

Hively raised a finger to caution me. "Okay, one chance. What makes this look funny to you?"

"Why are all the doors locked?"

Hively frowned. "He's drunk, locks himself out. Not a stretch."

"Why were his clothes on the inside of the house wet?"

"Could have happened twenty different ways. You sifted through them yourself when you were looking for a phone. Maybe you got them wet."

"Give me a break. Those clothes were completely saturated. What'd I do, dry off with his pants?"

"This isn't your job anymore. It's mine, got it?"

"Wait, do me one favor."

Hively's eyes bulged with disbelief. "Do you a favor? Are you . . . Man, you . . . you're something."

"Yeah, I get that a lot. Listen, if somebody drowned him—"

"You gotta be kidding me, man—"

"They had to hold his head down—"

"Carson!" Hively hollered. A stout young officer standing near the patio came hustling over.

I spoke faster. "Just have the examiner shave the back of his head to check for bruises, okay?"

"Escort Mr. Malick to his car and see that he leaves the property please."

"Is that necessary?" I said.

Young Officer Carson dutifully took hold of my arm. I wrenched it from his grasp.

"All right, all right, I'm leaving."

Carson gave me a solid push to get me moving and then kept nudging me toward the gate. I said, "Quit pushing me, asshole," then called over my shoulder, "Back of the head. They won't do it if they think it's an accident."

I don't know if Hively heard that last bit or not. He had already pulled back the plastic sheet on Barnhard, and Gloria Andrade was pointing something out to him.

CHAPTER SEVEN
BLOOD FOOLS

Out front of the house, some members of the press and a few idly curious bystanders had congregated behind the yellow DO NOT CROSS tape. A field reporter from WSAC was powdering her face and checking her teeth in the mirror of her compact as her cameraman set up a tripod on the curb. I was making a beeline for my truck and had the door open when I heard a familiar, nasally voice squawking my name.

"Malick! Hey, Malick!" Ernie Ciccone, the crime reporter from the *Cain City Dispatch*, a paper renowned for its practice of truthiness, beckoned me over. I shut the door and signaled for him to meet me at the corner of the tape, out of earshot from the rest of the spectators. Ciccone bumped his way through the crowd and scurried over to where I was, gave me the once-over, and said, "You fall in the toilet or what?"

"The *Cain City Disgrace* hasn't fired you yet?"

He winked. "No one can wallow through this muck like I can, Malick."

"I suppose you need to have a knack for which stories to report and which ones to bury."

"It's been two years, Malick. How long you gonna hold that over my head?"

"I'm thinking maybe"—I squinted and feigned like I had to mull it over—"yeah, maybe forever. You gonna ask me a question or not?"

"Straight to business, I like it. Word is, they found Scott Barnhard dead in there. That true?"

"True."

Ciccone grinned, showing off his prominent overbite. He raised up on his tiptoes like a little boy unable to contain his excitement. "No shit. Who found him?"

"I did. But you can't report that. My name stays out, understand?"

"Sure, yeah, whatever. Where'd you find him?"

I gestured to my whole, wet self. "Look at me, take a wild guess."

"In the bathtub? He drowned?"

"Pool. And maybe. But that's the wrong question."

"What's the right question?"

"Whether he was murdered or not."

Ciccone's smile turned greedy. He glanced furtively down the line of reporters, all of them oblivious to the fact that he was getting the scoop.

"You for real? He was murdered?"

"I'm not sure. But the police are going to come out here and tell the microphones that this has all the markers of an accidental drowning. That it's not suspicious. But it is. It's very suspicious."

Barnhard scribbled my words down on his steno pad. I started for my car.

"Wait, Malick, how are you involved in this one? Why were you here at Barnhard's house in the first place?"

"Write what I told you. Leave me out of it, and you'll get more story from me later, got it?"

"Yes, sir, oh captain my captain," Ciccone said sarcastically, saluting me as I walked away.

I climbed into my truck. A policeman made a hole in the tape and parted the tiny crowd so that I could pull out of there. I drove to my office at the old high school. There, I opened a window and put my phone on the sill to soak up some sun, got out of my wet clothes, and took a hot shower to wash the chlorine from my pores. Chlorine from a pool that had interred a dead man.

I got dressed and checked my phone for any sign of life. Nothing. The buttons didn't even click when I pressed them. I looked at the clock on my microwave, 1:27 p.m. Davey's school let out in just over an hour and a half at 3:05. I figured Leach and McKinney would want an explanation as to why their client went from being delivered home by me to a death by drowning shortly thereafter, so I found a pair of old boots in the closet, tugged them on and grabbed the essentials: keys, wallet, coat, cap, dead phone. I was about to leave when it dawned on me that a little precaution might be necessary. I got under my desk and unlocked the safe to retrieve my shoulder holster and sub-compact Beretta. Checked the clip, strapped it on, hit the door.

All the lunchtime traffic had cleared out of downtown and the streets were nearly vacant of cars and people. I parked my Tacoma in the same spot Barnhard's Jaguar had occupied the previous night, went into the building and rode the elevator to the tenth floor. When the doors split, Willis Hively and his nifty suit were standing on the other side. We stared at each other blankly for a moment, then I made to step out and he stood aside to let me pass.

"Willis."

"Nick."

"You move fast."

"Everybody moves fast when you only go one speed." Hively boarded the elevator. "Better get in there. I think your bosses might be a little peeved they had to get their report from me." He punched the button for the lobby and the doors began their slide together.

"Speaking of, any news on our murder?"

"Not unless you want to confess. And it's not your case."

"Oh, I might poke around a little anyhow," I said, just as the doors closed.

I walked down the hall to where Betty, the firm's lifetime receptionist, was sitting behind her desk with the phone to her ear, nodding along and making dull noises to confirm whatever the person on the other end of the line was saying. Seeing me, she perked up and wagged an arthritic finger in a manner that suggested I'd been naughty.

She put her hand over the phone and mouthed, "Where you been?"

"Swimming," I said, and gestured toward the partner's offices. "They in?"

In a few swift strokes, Betty put her caller on hold, patched a line through to Kent McKinney, said, "He's here," shooed me away, and was back on the original call before that person even knew she'd been gone.

I went into McKinney's office. The both of them were in there, Leach standing pensively with his arms crossed and a fist tucked under his chin, and McKinney sitting wide-legged in a chair facing the door, hands gripping his knees, as though he were waiting for his teenager to come home after breaking curfew.

"Joy to the world, look who decides to show their face," McKinney said.

"Cool it, Kent," Leach said. "Give him a chance to explain."

"Did you forget how to answer a phone, Malick? Do you know who we just had in here grilling us?"

"Kent," Leach pled again.

"Fine," McKinney said sharply. To stifle his temper, he clawed down on his knees, which only served to make the red in his face rise like a thermometer. "Explain."

I strolled over to McKinney's desk, hooked a hip over the corner and leveled my gaze on him. As pleasant as I could muster, I said, "A client just died. I understand how that could cause your cholesterol to rise a little. I understand how that's not the best advertisement for your business. But there are other lawyers in town and if you speak to me like that again I'm gonna be working for them, not you."

"None of them will pay you the retainer we pay you," McKinney spat.

"I'll manage."

"Please," Leach interjected, "guys. Nick's right, this is a situation unlike any we've ever been in and we're more than a little on edge, admittedly. Let's all calm down and sort through this mess, okay? Together."

"I'm calm," I said.

"Okay, we've got a few questions."

"Me too. You ask yours and I'll ask mine."

"Where've you been?" McKinney asked evenly. "We've been trying to call you for hours."

"Hively didn't tell you?"

Leach said, "He told us they found Scott Barnhard at the bottom of his pool. That the early read is an accidental drowning, but they'd wait until all the forensics were back before making the final determination."

"What's that have to do with you going AWOL?" McKinney squawked.

"I'm the one who found him. Hively didn't say that?"

"No, he did not."

"I dove in and tried to fish him out." I pulled my phone from my jacket pocket and tossed it to McKinney. "That was in my pocket when I jumped in."

He examined the phone, saw that it was kaput, and held it up to show Leach.

"Hively questioned me at the scene. When he was done I went home for some fresh clothes, then came straight here. I didn't pass Go or collect two hundred dollars."

"Why didn't Hively tell us any of that?" Leach asked.

"He probably saw how nervous you were and thought it'd be fun to jam me up. He and I go back. He has some hard feelings."

"What'd you do to him?" McKinney said.

"Couple years back a suspect took a nosedive out of an upper-floor window at the Greenleaf building. He thinks I had something to do with it. I didn't, but he'll believe what he wants to believe."

Leach said, "You're talking about the leader of that Cash City gang."

"Yeah."

"That was you?"

"I just told you it wasn't. Now, what'd Hively ask you?"

"Well," McKinney said, his eyes flicking up and to the left, "he wanted to know what the U.S. Attorney's meeting was about. If Barnhard's behavior was strange during our meeting yesterday evening. And why we felt it necessary to have him surveilled."

"If we knew of anybody that might have wanted to harm him," Leach added. "And if we knew what your movements were last night."

"Hmm. What'd you tell him?"

"What could we?" Leach replied. "His behavior was normal—"

"For him," McKinney clarified.

"And we were largely in the dark as to what the meeting with the U.S. Attorney was going to be about, and that's why we had you and Bob Lawson follow him. To see if he was hiding anything."

"We showed him the email you sent us last night," McKinney said. "He was very curious about that."

"Did he ask you to *speculate* what the meeting with the U.S. Attorney might have been about?" I said.

"Yes," McKinney answered. "We told him that Barnhard might have been scamming the government for money, but that he denied it."

"You didn't tell him about the paper cutter thing?"

"No, that was secondhand information."

"What about if somebody wanted to hurt Barnhard?"

McKinney looked confused. "What about it?"

"You said he asked if you were aware of anybody who might have wanted to hurt him."

"He did, but how could we know that?" Leach said. "It's not like someone sent in a threat."

"Well, somebody did," I replied.

"Did what? Sent in a threat?"

"No, hurt him. More than that. Somebody killed him."

"That's the direct opposite of what the police just told us," McKinney said. "How can you be so sure?"

I explained to them about the large quantity of vomit in the bathroom, the locked doors and the wet clothes, and how the whole thing felt off-key.

I said, "Who pukes their guts out, thinks to themselves, 'You know what would be a good idea? Going for a swim with all my clothes on.' Then jumps into a pool, thinks better of it, gets out, and goes and puts on some trunks. And then jumps back in."

Leach shrugged. "People in a crazed state of mind do crazy things. All of us here have seen that. Plus, that's all circumstantial, isn't it? There's no proof."

"Everything's circumstantial," I retorted. "That's why so many murders go unsolved. The burden of proof is for a court of law. That's your department. Mine is, I'm telling you somebody put Barnhard into that water. And unless you want to be known as the law firm where clients go to die, I think we need to find out who did it and why."

"Whoa, whoa." McKinney extended his raised palms out in front of him. "This is a police matter now, it has nothing more to do with us."

"Kent is right," Leach said. "There's no benefit for us to get involved."

I stood up off the desk. "You are involved. He's still your client."

"No, Nick. You're thinking like a police officer. We don't represent the dead." The look on my face must have been one of bewilderment because Ed Leach came over and patted me on the shoulder. "We know you might feel responsible for this since you were the one watching him when he passed."

"And apparently the first to see him dead," McKinney pitched in.

"I wasn't the first to see him dead. Whoever killed him was."

The two partners glanced at each other and pursed their lips as though they were wondering how much longer they'd have to put up with my conjecture.

"And even if I was," I went on, "I wasn't the last person to talk to him. That was you two. What'd Barnhard say after I left?"

"What do you mean?" McKinney barked.

"Was he spooked? Did he give you any indication that he might sing?"

McKinney opened his mouth to speak, but Leach cut him off with a curt "No." McKinney flinched at the verbal slap, but he shut his mouth and the two partners shared some kind of non-verbal communication I couldn't decipher.

"He was your client. Don't *you* want to find out what happened to him?"

"Sure, we want to find out," McKinney said, cracking a jovial, shit-eating grin that set my blood to boil. "We'll keep tabs on the police investigation."

"They're not gonna figure it out," I snapped. "They'll turn over a rock or two just to say they did it, the forensics will come back inconclusive, and they'll chalk it up to a fluky accident and move on."

McKinney frowned. "You don't have much faith in the justice system."

"No shit, wonder why."

"If the evidence comes back inconclusive, then maybe it is just that, a fluke," Leach said.

"Or the person or persons who killed him knew how to make it look that way," I countered.

"Either way," McKinney said, straining to get up from his chair, "it's no longer our concern."

"And to be frank, he was one of the worst clients we've had in thirty years of practice," Leach admitted.

"Well, I'd like to look into it."

"Not on our dime," said McKinney.

"I need to see the file you've got on Barnhard."

McKinney grunted involuntarily, veiled it by clearing the phlegm from his throat. He said, "Detective Hively warned us not to show the file to anyone. He may need to obtain a subpoena for it."

"He doesn't have one yet, does he?"

"No."

"So let me see it."

"We don't think that's a good idea, Nick," Leach said apologetically. "We think it's best to toe the line on this one, professionally speaking."

"What fucking line?"

McKinney walked to the door of his office as though I should follow him, opened it, and said, "I don't think we have anything else going right now, do we, Ed? Maybe take a few days off. Check in, oh, beginning of next week and we'll see if there's something we can scrounge up for you to do."

I looked back and forth at the two of them, with their soft bellies and patrician faces, and marveled at how smoothly they could wash their hands of the whole affair, at their latent amorality couched in decorum. I couldn't help but shake my head and laugh. Fucking lawyers. I kept on laughing as I walked out of there.

"See you next week," Ed Leach called after me.

CHAPTER EIGHT
THE HIGH ART OF BULLSHIT

I drove down past Cain City College and under the Twentieth Street Viaduct onto Clifford Avenue. This took me past some run-down East End neighborhoods, the Malcolm Terrace housing projects, Kyova Memorial Hospital, and on out to the edge of town where the consolidated high school, Piedmont, was situated atop a hill near the interstate.

School hadn't let out yet. I maneuvered around the queue of cars and buses and pulled the truck into the loading zone at the far end of the parking lot, near a side door. A bell rang and fifteen seconds later a mass of kids poured out of the school. Davey emerged from the side door with his backpack on, Reds ball cap cocked to the side, skateboard in hand. His brown hair had grown long, down past his chin. He was still gangly, but after a big spurt this summer he was just a couple inches shy of my height now and would probably surpass me in no time. Suddenly, you could see hints of what he'd look like as a man. It shocked me sometimes, the swift metamorphosis of youth.

Davey put the board down and coasted the sidewalk to where I was parked, then popped it up and climbed into the passenger side.

"'Sup, Malick?"

"Kid. How was your day?"

"Boring as hell."

"Tell me one thing you learned."

The kid looked at me like I was ridiculous, but then something clever came to him.

"Oh, I learned how to fall asleep with my elbows on the desk and my thumbs kinda propping up my head. Like this." He demonstrated the technique with an unwarranted amount of pride. "That made the day go faster."

"Innovative."

"I thought so. Got me through Western Civ and Biology."

I swung around the building and made it into the first wave of cars heading onto the two-lane road that snaked down the hill and merged back onto Clifford.

"Where we going?" Davey asked.

"I'm dropping you off at home."

"You got work?"

"Yup."

"That why you strapped?"

I looked down to see if the Beretta was making a bulge or if there were any other signs that I was carrying. There weren't.

"How can you tell?"

Davey looked pleased with himself.

"Your posture changes a little bit when you got it on."

"No shit?"

"Yeah, you kinda hold your arm out with your shoulder forward. Just a lil'. Not much."

"Huh."

"So like, I haven't seen you packing weight in a long time. Something going down?"

"No, nothing like that. But I might be sticking my nose around some blind corners so, you know."

"Gotta be prepped for the shit *to go down*. I got you." Davey nodded and I could tell he was working his way toward something. "So like, maybe I could help."

"Not a chance."

"C'mon, man. What am I gonna do at home all by myself? I'll tell you what I'm gonna do, one of three things. One, I'm gonna play video games all night, probably lose my eyesight a little, develop carpal tunnel. Two, I'm gonna go out and see what kind of trouble I can get into, which I know you don't want. We've all seen where that leads. Or three, I'm gonna jack off a bunch and get a shit-ton of viruses on the computer. Then Mom will get mad as hell, you know how she gets, and I'll tell her, if Malickay McDoogan would have let me come with him, all of this could have been avoided. I wouldn't be sitting here in juvey, far-sighted, unable to use my hands, with no sperm left to make you grandbabies."

"Your mom has anti-virus software. Knock yourself out."

"Damn, you ice cold, man. You the coldest in the world."

I shook my head. You had to hand it to the kid. He committed. "You really are a marvel of modern bullshit," I said.

"Yeah, well, you're a marvel of some stubborn, geriatric, delusional shit."

"Geriatric?"

"Yeah, you can look it up in the dictionary. It means old as hell, like pre-historic old."

"I know what it means. You got any homework?"

"A little," he pouted. "Nothing big."

"All right, quit your whining. My phone died. I have to go get a new one. You're more than welcome to go with me if you want."

"What about after that?"

"You're going home."

"Whack. Forget it."

I dropped Davey off out front of the old high school, fished a couple twenties out of my wallet and handed them to him.

"Your mom should be home in a little while. She had that interview this afternoon, so I'm cooking."

"So what, you want me to order some pizzas or something?"

"Pizza, breadsticks, whatever. Tell your mom I'll be back by seven."

I watched Davey take the stone steps two at a time up to the portico, throw open the double doors, drop his board down and skate into the building.

My next stop was the phone store. The closest Verizon outlet was twenty minutes away at the shopping mall in Becksville. I hopped on the interstate and made it there in fifteen.

The service rep, a young girl who was chomping on a wad of gum, took one look at my phone, blew a giant bubble until it popped, and said, "Yeah, no, all your data is loooong gone. You're gonna have to start from scratch. Let me see if you're due for an upgrade." I wasn't due. She half-heartedly pitched the newer models, but my phone was still under warranty so she activated a new version of the same one I'd had. My contact list was on the cloud, so she pulled that out of the ether and reinstalled it as well. I sat in the store and got busy setting up the securities and email.

When my email linked with the World Wide Web, five new messages cropped up. Three were spam. One, from Kent McKinney, had been delivered at 10:45 a.m., him wondering where the hell I was. The last had come at 12:03 p.m. from Bob Lawson, an attachment with all the pictures of people he'd seen outside Birdie's building while Barnhard was in there. They'd slipped my mind until just then. I scrolled through the pics to reacquaint myself with them.

Lawson had sent two or three snapshots of each person: the two women with armfuls of groceries; the husky guy with the cigarette; the slight little man who, even in the still frames, looked to be in a hurry. Then the pizza guy from Marty's delivering to the skinny bleached-blonde woman, and Renata in her pink wig.

I opened a browser and typed in the URL for the *Cain City Dispatch*. Ciccone had already published a brief article about Scott T. Barnhard's death. It didn't give any details beyond the who and the where. A headshot of Barnhard accompanied the story. He was dressed in a bulky suit and red tie, posed in front of an American flag and grinning fatly at the camera. I saved the picture to my phone and set out for downtown Cain City.

As I cruised west on the interstate tufts of gray clouds spread over the horizon, and by the time I reached the exit for Clifford Avenue the downpour had commenced. Thunder boomed overhead. Jagged cracks of lightning slashed the sky and took stabs at the earth. I flipped my wipers on high and squinted through the onslaught of rain. The base of the Twentieth Street viaduct had already amassed a few inches of standing water. I rolled through that and made it to the Royal Vista, where I parked out front of the building and hustled up to the entrance. I shook the water off my coat, punched in the door code to let myself in and hopped on the elevator to the fifth floor.

Nobody answered the door. Birdie or Renata, one or the other, was always home so I kept knocking. Some fat old man from three doors down stepped into the hall wearing nothing but boxers and shouted for me to knock it off. I told him that I was the police and he needed to get back in his apartment and stay in.

"'Bout time," the old man grumbled as he shut, bolted, and chained his door.

I don't know how long it was, couple more minutes, but my fist was plenty sore when the door was finally flung open. Birdie didn't look particularly happy to see me. She'd tossed a silk robe haphazardly over her body. Her face was heavily made up with purple blush and silver, Egyptian-style eye shadow that smeared out past the corners of her lids.

"What you doing, man? Don't you know how to use a phone?"

I stepped past her and scanned the kitchen and living room. Both were empty.

"Um, did I say 'come in'? Why you all wet?"

"Lose the guy."

"What guy?"

"The guy in the back. Get rid of him."

"*Psshh*, are you crazy?"

I cocked my eyebrows and gave her a look to let her know I wasn't playing. She thrust her neck toward me and, in an exaggerated manner, mirrored my expression.

"All right, then." I went down the hallway to Birdie's bedroom and pushed the door open. A thin, loose-skinned white dude with moles all over his back was hurriedly yanking on his pants. I didn't recognize him.

"Yoo-hoo," I called out.

The man, who was half bent over trying to get his second leg in, whipped around, caught sight of me and froze. The red glow from the lava lamp deepened the ghoulish shadows of his face. He still had his condom on.

"Who are you?" he said, voice so weak I could barely hear him.

"Pussy police. Time's up, pal. Take a hike."

The guy must have gotten the impression that I was another of Birdie's customers. He ripped the condom off and threw it on the floor, then thrust the second leg into his pants and stood upright with his fists on his hips.

"The hell I will," he bristled. "I don't know who you think you are, but this is not how this works. I've paid for a service until the end of the hour and I intend to get what I paid for. So you can march right back out of here and wait your turn."

I felt like fucking with this guy a little bit, so I pulled out my gun and held it loosely at my side. "I'm not asking."

The man's eye sockets doubled in size. "Are you shitting me?"

"Keep talking and find out."

The man frantically collected his possessions—socks, shoes, belt, shirt—that had been strewn about the floor. While he did that I went over to the vanity, opened up his wallet and extracted the ID. Phillip Wilmer Woolwine was a forty-seven-year-old Gemini who stood five-foot-eight, weighed a hundred and forty-five pounds, and was an organ donor.

I tapped a button on the side of his phone and the screen lit up with a picture of two smiling boys in a pile of leaves.

"Cute kids, Phil."

"Hey!" he screamed. "Give me that." Phil dropped the articles of clothing in his arms and rushed toward me. He snatched his ID, wallet, and phone out of my hands and jammed them into the pockets of his khakis.

"Time to get," I said.

He picked his stuff back up and led the way out of the room. Birdie was slumped against the wall in the hallway, holding her robe closed.

"Sorry 'bout this, Phil."

"Who is this, Birdie?"

"Somebody who likes to fuck with my livelihood."

"I can't go home smelling like this," Phil pleaded. "I need a shower. She's going to know."

"Guess it's just one of those little shits of life, pal," I said, prodding him forward.

Phil stumbled into the hallway, arms chock-full of clothes, and spun around to look at me. "You should pray I never find out who you are."

"You should pray I never show up outside of 817 Twelfth Street," I said, and shut the door in his face. I tucked my gun away.

"You happy?" Birdie said.

"I've got some questions for you."

"So?"

"So you're gonna answer them. Go get dressed."

Birdie looked at me like a second head had just that moment sprouted from my neck.

"You think I'ma do anything you say right now after you barge in here all macho and shit, kicking my clients out and shit? You know what you just cost me? You have any idea? Phil's a good tipper. Shoo, I ain't doing nothing for you."

"You remember this morning when I asked you about a guy who came to see you last night?"

"Kinda."

"The beefy white guy with a dark beard?"

"Yeah, I didn't stutter. I said I remember."

"That guy is dead now. Probably he was murdered. So unless you want the next people banging on your door to be the police, you need to answer my questions and you need to answer them now. Understand?"

Shock seeped into Birdie's face. She pressed her fingers against her temples in an effort to compute the words I'd just spoken.

"Wait a minute, he's dead?"

"Yeah."

"Since when?"

"Last night."

"Say what? But I just . . ." Her thought trailed off and the resistance drained from her. All at once she looked exhausted. "Give me a minute."

Birdie wandered into her room and three or four minutes later emerged wearing jeans and a white t-shirt, her face scrubbed clean of make-up.

"Let's sit outside and watch the storm," she said.

I followed her into her bedroom, she grabbed the comforter off her bed, and we went out onto the small balcony. There were a couple of wrought iron deck chairs out there, a little table between them. Birdie wrapped herself in the comforter and sat with her legs folded beneath her. I settled into the other chair. The overhang from the balcony above shielded us from the downpour. Silently, we watched the world go by for a bit. Sheets of rain gusted one way with the wind, then the other. Lightning zigzagged across the gloomy firmament. The air felt electric, clean. Night came on. Below us on the avenue, cars flipped on their beams. A pickup going too fast hit a puddle and nearly skidded into the middle of a four-way intersection. Everyone leaned on their horns.

"Ready for your first driving lesson?" I asked.

The question snuck up on Birdie. She snorted and hiccupped simultaneously, producing some abhorrent noise that, in forty years on earth, I'd never heard the likes of. Even Birdie was taken aback by the anomaly that came out of her mouth. Seeing the mixed expressions of disgust and concern for her intestines on my face, she burst into laughter.

"What was that?" I said.

Birdie was laughing too hard to answer, so hard that she clutched at her stomach and tears squished out of her eyes; it was a free, pure laugh, endowed with a spirit that I had rarely seen from her. In that moment, she looked like the nineteen-year-old she would have been if she'd been born into different circumstances, to a different mother, in a different town.

Birdie must have seen sadness in my eyes, or sensed it in my demeanor. Her laughter tapered away. She sighed, wiped the joyful tears from her cheeks, and in a blink was somber again.

"What do you want from me?" she said, her voice soft, tired.

I pulled out my phone, brought up the picture of Scott Barnhard that I'd screen-grabbed from the website, and held it out for her to see. She glanced at the image and turned her attention back to the drenched city.

"Was he here last night?"

Birdie nodded. "Yeah. Scott T. He really dead?"

"Yeah."

"How?"

"I think someone drowned him in his pool last night. Do you have any idea who could have done that?"

Birdie flung a cold glare my way. "Drowned? How would I know about anything like that?"

"I gotta ask these things, Birdie. If you don't want to talk to me, that's your prerogative, but I want to protect you. To do that I need to find out what happened. The next people that question you about this aren't going to give two shits about you."

"Yeah, I got police coming my way. I ain't trippin' over that." Birdie took a deep breath that she gently expelled. "But see, I tell you certain things and certain people find out I'm the one told you those things, I'ma be in big trouble, you heard."

I knew all too well, maybe even more than she did, how right she was.

"Birdie, if you're linked to someone who got murdered, the night they got murdered, you might be in trouble anyway. You gotta think about it from that way. But I promise you, whatever information you give me, I will never let anybody know where I got it from, you understand me? I'll keep you out, make sure nobody can make that connection."

Birdie shuddered. "You really think I could be in danger?"

"I don't know. But I'm going to look into this thing. I'm gonna make sure you're safe, okay? Whatever I gotta do, I'll do it. I don't want you getting caught up in this thing if you don't have to be."

She tugged the comforter tighter around her body and worked out whatever she needed to work out in her head. "Why are you doing this for me? My mom long dead. What's she got over you?"

"It's complicated," I said, but that was a lie. The truth wasn't the least bit complex. I simply couldn't bring myself to confess to her that I was the reason her mother was shot in an alley. Her body discarded in a dumpster, like garbage, for doing exactly what I was asking of Birdie—to give information, to inform, to be an informant, to speak a few words aloud that separately held no meaning, but said together, in a particular order, could cost her her life. That's all I was asking.

"Did you love her?" Birdie asked.

"No."

"You one of her baby daddies?"

"No."

"Did you kill her?"

"No," I answered again, though that was its own special brand of lie.

"You didn't love her, fuck her, or kill her, then what's so complicated?"

I didn't have an answer. "Maybe someday, Birdie."

"Someday," she mused. "What an empty word. That and 'forever' are the two emptiest words in the dictionary. Two words that don't mean nothing. You were there the night my mother died, weren't you? Down in The 4 ½. Showed up right when they was hauling her up out of there." She was speaking wistfully now. If you weren't listening to the words you would have thought she was recalling some fond memory.

"I didn't know if you remembered," I said.

"I remember everything. You know, I didn't even hear the shots. I was up in our apartment asleep with my brothers and sisters. Didn't hear a thing. Later I heard the commotion though, went down there to see what there was to see, just being nosy and stupid. If there was a show to see, then I wanted to see it. Popped out the backdoor of the building, right away saw her leg hanging up outta that dumpster. Knew it was her. Recognized them red thigh-highs."

"I'm sorry, Birdie."

"Probably wouldn't have changed nothing." A sorrowful resolve came into her face. "Okay, Slick Nick. For you, one time. One time, you can ask me whatever you need to ask me about my business—"

"Birdie—"

"—and that's it. You understand? Once and never again."

I said, "Deal." Then, "How many times has Scott Barnhard been a client?"

"Shoo . . ." Birdie gazed upward to calculate the number of times Barnhard had paid to use her body. Saying the question out loud conjured a revolting image in my mind—him crawling his fat, suffocating body atop hers, wheezing with every thrust, his rancid flop sweat soiling everything within a ten-foot radius: sheets, pillows, the carpet, Birdie, all of it; the wad of bills he probably left on the nightstand. However, if Birdie felt any animosity toward Barnhard, she didn't show it. Instead she spoke of him with an air of affection. "Scott T . . ."

She squinted as though the memory of an ogre penetrating her weren't visceral, but rather a vague, hazy mirage that felt as though it may not have even happened. Or maybe Birdie liked him. Maybe Scott Barnhard was sweet to her.

Finally, she said, "Once a week, maybe every other week, going back this whole last year at least. Could be longer."

"He take any drugs when he was here last night?"

"He always takes something. Last night it was coke, molly, the usual shit. Smoked a fat J out here when we was through."

"How do you get these guys? How did you get set up like this? The guy I kicked out, Phil, Barnhard—how'd you build your clientele?"

"I didn't. I was recruited."

"Recruited?"

"Yeah. Couple months after I had Aisha I had to get back to work, you know. And my body bounce back pretty quick-like. So I'm out there and this dude approaches me on the street. White dude I ain't never seen before, starts talking all this mad smack 'bout how I'm too fine to be working the alleys and he could set me up real nice, have me an apartment, pay no rent, hook me up with high-class johns, that kind of thing. I said, yeah yeah, you know, whatever, I ain't believe it. But then he brings me up here, shows me the place. That's that. Here I am."

"What about Renata, she do the same thing?"

"Naw, Renata didn't have that spark they was looking for. She still working them alleys. They say she can live here long as she don't mess with my hustle none. Ghosts whenever I got a client."

"What's their cut?"

"I don't know. They pay me seventy-five for every guy I see. And the guys usually leave some kind of tip."

"So the clients don't pay you, they pay, who? This guy that set you up?"

Birdie gave a minimal shrug. "I guess. All I know is, I do what they say, I don't see anybody else 'cept the johns they send me and in return I get to live here. Them's the rules."

"How do they pay you?"

"I got a P.O. box at the UPS Store down around the corner. They drop my money there."

"When?"

"Saturday, Sunday. Sometime over the weekend. I don't know. I check it on Mondays usually and it's always there."

"This guy that set you up here, you seen him since?"

"Yeah, he shows up every once in a while for what he calls a spot check, make sure everything's up to snuff, you know. He random as hell. Makes me and Renata step out when he does it. Mostly though he just calls or texts, tells me when to be ready for an appointment."

"He got a name?"

"I'm sure he does, but he ain't never told me what it was. He a real redneck sounding mug though, so I always call him Billy Bob."

Sitting there listening to Birdie relate these truths of her life so matter-of-factly, the thoughts in her mind having long ago been divorced from the actions of her body, wrecked me clean through. My lips drew tight. I gritted my teeth and shook my head in frustration. How had I thought this whole time that I'd been helping her? What good had I actually done? I shuttled her to see her kid once or twice a week. Repeatedly lectured her to work her shit out. My voice had probably become white noise. I'd done nothing. Worse, I'd done just enough to enable her to remain right where she was, not going forward, only staying on her back. I was useless.

Off my expression, she said, "Don't feel sorry for me."

"You gotta get out of this, Birdie."

She stared, pensive, into the black night. The rain had slowed. Fat droplets dripped down from the ledge above and plinked against the balcony's railing.

"Where can I go?"

"I have a spare room in my office. You can stay there for as long as you need."

"I'ma stay with you? Yeah, right. Careful what you promise."

"I'm serious. We can go tonight if you want. Pack your shit and go."

"You're gonna house me?"

"Yeah."

"You don't know what you're sayin'. They ain't gonna just let me out from under this. They ain't gonna just let me walk. I'm like an investment. That's what Billy Bob calls me. An investment."

"I'm gonna help you, Birdie. Protect you. I promise."

"Yeah." She smiled wanly. "Let me think about it, okay? I can't just up and go like lickety split."

"Why not?"

Birdie searched for an answer that would be sufficient for both me and her. She came up with, "I can't leave Renata hanging like that. I gotta give her a chance to find another place."

"Sure, okay."

"Maybe *someday* you'll tell me why my mother has such a hold over you."

"Someday," I said, the word coming out hollow.

"I got some money saved up. Maybe I can get me an apartment of my own soon. With a bedroom for Aisha, too. Might even have enough left over for a car. If you gonna give me driving lessons that'd be good, right? I always wanted one of those cute little bug cars."

"Yeah, yeah, that'd be good." A knot rose into my throat. I swallowed it down. "Couple more questions, Birdie. Okay?"

She sighed. "I'll give you two more."

"Did Barnhard talk to anybody on the phone last night, or was there anybody else here that he might have come in contact with?" Birdie's mouth opened to speak, then shut. "This is important, Birdie."

"He didn't talk to anybody on the phone."

"But he saw someone?"

"Yeah." She hesitated. "Billy Bob was here. I didn't see

him, but I heard them talking in the hallway before Scott T knocked on the door to come in."

I leaned forward. "Did you hear what they said?"

"Naw, not really. It was all muffled-like. Only thing I heard was Billy Bob saying something like, 'Keep cool and this ain't gonna be no thang,' or something like that."

"You're sure it was him?"

"There ain't no mistakin' that voice, trust me."

"What's this Billy Bob look like?"

"Ugly."

"What makes him ugly?"

"I dunno. He's short, wiry. Kind of jittery, like he's always moving. Head shaved. Not bald, short all around. He's got these weird eyes where it don't look like he has eyelids, know what I'm saying? Like you can see the white all the way around his irises."

I brought my phone back out and flicked through the pictures Bob Lawson had sent me, stopped on the one of the shrimpy guy who looked like he was carrying something and walking fast down onto the sidewalk.

"This him?"

Birdie checked the photo. Right off, she said, "Mm-hmm, that's Billy Bob. That snap from last night?"

"Yeah, we were following Barnhard. See if you recognize any of these other ones."

I scrolled through the other photos. Birdie knew the bleached blonde who had picked up the pizza, said she lived on the second floor. And one of the old women with the groceries lived upstairs. Then Renata in the pink wig. She didn't recognize anybody else.

"Can we be through, please?" Birdie asked. "I'm done."

"One more question."

"C'mon, you taking advantage now."

I raised my hand as though I were swearing in. "Last one."

"Make it count."

"You hungry?"

CHAPTER NINE
CUSTOMER SERVICE

On the way home, I stopped at a gas station to pick up some French vanilla ice cream. When I slotted the Tacoma into its assigned parking spot at the old high school it was nearly eight o'clock. Birdie got out, followed me up the portico stairs and through the double doors into the building. She was curious about the place. In the entrance hall she stopped to examine the glass display cases, full of team photographs and trophies from generations past. The cases were relatively new—the previous ones were shot to pieces in the gunfight I'd gotten myself into a couple years previous. Birdie wandered down to the end of the corridor and peered into the old gymnasium and auditorium.

"My mom went to school here," she said, opening and closing one of the original built-in wall lockers that still lined the halls. "She ran track."

"My office is an old classroom. I'll show it to you after we eat."

We hiked up the two flights to the third floor. I fished out my key and started to open the door to Karla's apartment.

"Wait," said Birdie.

I looked at her. "It'll be fine, Birdie. They're gonna love you."

"It's not that. Listen, that money I talked about, the money I got saved."

"Yeah?"

"It ain't in a bank or nothing. It's in a box in the ceiling panel above my bed."

"Okay."

"You got me thinking. If something were to ever happen to me, somebody should know where it is."

"Nothing's gonna happen to you, Birdie. We're gonna figure it all out, all right?"

"Yeah, okay. But just in case, now you know."

"Now I know. Ready?"

"Yeah."

I turned the key. We went in. The TV was on, some reality show where people were attempting some absurd obstacle course, but nobody was in the living room or the adjoining kitchen. With one sweep of the eyes, Birdie assessed the apartment.

"You live here?"

"Kinda." I called out, "Hey?"

From the back bedroom, Karla hollered, "Hay is for horses. And the people who eat it."

I could tell Birdie didn't know what to make of the hay bit. I asked if she'd ever heard it before.

"No. That some weird cracker shit?"

"Pretty much."

Davey popped out of his room, mouth already moving. "You don't write, you don't call. We thought we were gonna have to contact a bail bondsman or something, get a search party . . ." He spotted Birdie and froze stiff, the rest of his sentence paralyzed in his mouth. If there were a record playing it would have skipped.

"Cat got your tongue?" I asked. "Birdie, this sudden mute is called Davey. Davey, Birdie."

"'Sup?" Birdie said coyly. Davey shoved his hands in his pockets and mimicked her greeting and tone. I asked Davey if there was enough pizza left for us or if he'd hogged it all.

"We got two pies like you said." Davey pried his gaze away from Birdie to address me. "It's hella cold now, though."

"We'll heat it up. You like Marty's, Birdie?"

"It's all right."

"How many slices you want?"

"One's fine."

"Have a seat." I indicated the circular table and chairs that divided the living room and kitchen. She went over and plopped down. Davey stayed standing as though his feet were shackled in cement. I asked him if he wanted to join us.

He stuttered, "I mean . . . I've already eaten, so like—"

I showed him the tub of ice cream. "Got some French Vanilla."

"Yeah, yeah. I'll have some of that." He shook his feet loose and bounded over to the table, sat across from Birdie. "So how do you know my main man Nick here?"

"He's my youth pastor and spiritual advisor," Birdie deadpanned.

"Word. I shoulda known. That's how I met him, too. He was on a corner with a bullhorn warning us about the next apocalypse with one of those big 'Jesus Saves' signs around his neck and we just hit it off. Minds just totally melded together. I'm a total Jesus freak, really. I used to wear like eight of those 'What Would Jesus Do?' bracelets and everything. Two on each limb."

"You don't wear 'em no more?"

"No, I decided I was showboating too much. You know, flauntin' how much more faith I had than everybody else and all that. So from now on I just wear 'em in my heart, you know, where people can really see them."

The kid was quick, I had to give him that. He could talk nonsense with the best of them. And Birdie, you could tell, was entertained by his particular brand of bullshit.

"How full of baloney are you exactly?" she said.

"Oh, hundred percent," Davey answered.

I left them to their banter and went into the kitchen to heat up the pizza and dole the ice cream into bowls. Karla emerged from the bedroom, barefoot in cut-up jeans and an old, threadbare Aerosmith concert t-shirt. She sidled up next to me at the counter and dipped her finger into the tub of ice cream. I smacked her hand, but she'd already scooped a good chunk out. She shoveled it into her mouth.

"So this is the fabled Birdie," she said, hushed so that only I could hear.

"That's her. I think the kid's in love."

"*Really*?"

"You should've seen it, he was struck dumb. She had him tongue-tied, if you can believe that."

Karla boosted herself onto the counter and observed her son's interaction with Birdie. "Looks like he bounced back fast. She's very pretty."

"Not as pretty as you."

"Do you think it's smart to bring her around here?"

I twisted around to regard the two teenagers. Davey was regurgitating some conspiracy theory he'd heard on TV about how the pyramids in Egypt were created by aliens and how there were ancient carvings found in an Osirian temple that depicted spaceships and helicopters. I was sorry that I missed the connective thread he'd made to leap from Jesus to aliens.

"Look at him go. I'm more worried for her."

"You know what I mean."

"He's fine. She'll toy around with him like a kitten with a ball for a little while. Then she'll get bored. She's not a bad person."

Karla looked at me dubiously.

"Trust me." I got the pizza and breadsticks out of the microwave and put them on plates. "Come meet her."

Karla's disposition eased. She dipped her finger into the French Vanilla again, licked it off, wiped her hand on her jeans and slid down from the counter. I handed her a couple bowls of ice cream to carry and we stepped over to the table. I made introductions.

My experience of Birdie in a social environment was limited, but what I had seen, whether it be with Dottie—Aisha's foster parent—or a doctor, a county magistrate, or a server in a restaurant, was that she could very quickly evaluate the personalities in front of her and adjust her character accordingly. With Karla it was no different. The two women took measure of one another, traded a few flattering comments, and were both instantly smitten.

"How does a beautiful woman like you end up with all *this*?" Birdie gestured in my general direction.

"Hey now," I said.

"No offense, but usually I see a woman that looks like Karla here with a dude that looks like you, that kinda discrepancy, you gotta be rolling in stacks of money, know what I'm saying?"

"I wish," Karla said. "What can I say, Birdie? Slim pickin's in Cain City. You gotta take what you can get."

"Have your fun," I said.

"I'm just playing, Slick Nick. You ain't *that* busted."

Davey, anxious to insert himself into the conversation again, said, "So what do you do, go to Cain College or work or what?"

"I work."

"Oh yeah? See, I keep trying to tell these jokers that you don't have to go to college to be successful. What kind of job you got?"

Karla shot me an enigmatic look. I continued to wolf down pizza and pretended not to see it.

"I'm in customer service," Birdie said.

"Cool. That ever get on your nerves though, having to deal with people all the time?"

"Yeah it can wear on you a bit. What do you do, Karla?"

"I'm a nurse."

"Mom just got a new job."

"At the hospital?" Birdie asked.

"No, I'm going to be working at Maggie's Place. It's a facility that takes in babies who are born with drug dependencies because the parents are addicts—"

"I know what it is," Birdie said quickly. "My baby went there when she was born."

Karla's face flushed. "Oh, I'm sorry. I didn't know that."

"Naw, it's no thing. I don't do none of that stuff no more, so."

The table fell quiet except for my chewing. I swallowed the bite and said to Karla, "You got the job? When were you going to tell me?"

"When you asked," she replied coolly. "I was hired on the spot. I don't know if it was anything I did. I think they just need people."

"Well, congratulations."

"Maybe I could do something like that someday," Birdie mused.

"Is that something you would like to do?" Karla asked.

"I dunno. It sounds good anyway."

"Well, if you decide that it's something you'd like to pursue, I'd be glad to help you."

"Y'all sure are some good people. Always trying to help us poor black folk out."

"Birdie, you okay?" I said.

"I'm sorry. I don't know why I said that."

"We understand," Karla said. "It's no thing."

Birdie brightened. She played the rest of the night nonchalant, but now I could see the effort she was having to put into the interaction. Mentioning Aisha seemed to dislocate something inside her that wouldn't easily shift back. When it was almost ten she thanked us for feeding her and announced that she had to get home and go to work.

"Night shift," she explained to Davey.

I told Karla not to wait up, I had to stop back by the firm for a bit and didn't know how late I'd be working. She knew that meant I'd likely be sleeping in my office.

"Okay," she said, disappointed.

"Some things happened today," I explained. Davey was eavesdropping so I didn't want to elaborate further. "I'll tell you about it later. Let's go out to dinner tomorrow night. Get some reservations at Savannah's or wherever, anywhere you want. We'll celebrate your new job."

"Oh, we going fancy?"

"You earned it, fancy girl."

Birdie said her thank yous and goodbyes and we left. As we stepped into the hall and Karla shut the door behind us, Birdie's whole body sagged as though every last ounce of energy had been sapped from her body.

I said, "C'mon, let me show you my office."

"Do we have to?"

"Just real quick."

We descended the stairs to the first floor and I led her through the maze of hallways to my office, an old converted classroom that still had the tile flooring. I showed her through to the back room, which used to be a teacher's office. Karla had some storage boxes and other junk piled in there, and some of my clothes were scattered about on the floor.

"We'll clear all this out," I said, waving at the boxes, "and clean up, obviously. There's a shower in back there and we can get you a little fridge or something if you want. Or you can use mine in the office."

Birdie's eyes wandered lackadaisically around the space.

"Cool," she yawned. "Can you take me home now?"

We drove back downtown in silence, Birdie with her head leaned against the window, watching the street slide by. I pulled to the curb by the side entrance of the Royal Vista. She sat up and unbuckled her seatbelt.

"See you," she said.

"Wait, do me a favor, will you?"

She groaned, perturbed. "Depends on the favor."

"Next time Billy Bob shows up, call me, text me, whatever you gotta do, just let me know that he's here, okay?"

"Nuh-uh, you crazy. That's asking too much. I'ma get myself buried if I do some stupid shit like that."

"He'll never know. I'll track him and won't approach until he's far away from here. I just need to talk to him about Barnhard. He'll have no idea, okay?"

Birdie looked at me, too weary to protest further. "I'll think about it."

"You really gotta work tonight?"

"Yup."

She slipped out of the truck, trudged up the stoop, and disappeared into the building.

CHAPTER TEN
PLAY THE FADE

I stepped off the elevator and into the darkened offices of Leach, McKinney & Thurber. All the personal offices were locked. Keeping the lights off, I scoped out the rest of the floor, the conference rooms, break room, bathrooms, and kitchen, to make sure I was all by my lonesome, no partners or associates skulking around, billing absurd hours. There was not a soul to be found. I sat down at Betty's desk and booted up her computer.

I didn't have access to the firm's data system, but at various times I'd witnessed Leach task Betty with locating a document or looking up past case files on the PACER database. Betty, in her age and wisdom, kept all her passwords on note cards taped to the back wall of the top drawer in her desk. I slid the drawer open, shined the flashlight from my snazzy new phone, and copied down her passwords to log into the system and sign in to the firm's PACER account. The database charged thirty cents a page and three bucks flat for a full document. I planned on downloading every disability case Scott Barnhard had ever appeared on, but found that Betty had already done that leg work for me. All of Barnhard's old records had been downloaded and sorted into a nice little folder on the desktop labeled *Barnhard, S.T.*

I began poring over the documents and earmarking the individual pages that specified the court's ruling on the case, the judge who'd presided over the ruling, and the doctors who'd either testified or filled out the qualifying paperwork on behalf of the claimants. I created a separate folder and copied all the selected docs over. All told, there were 1,314 cases. It took me the entire night to work through them all. By the time I finished it was nearly six a.m. Traces of blue dark were creeping over the black horizon outside. I saved the new folder to a thumb drive, deleted it from Betty's computer, shut the PC down, and got out of there.

The circuitry in my brain felt like it was about to short out, with my motor skills following suit, but there were a couple more things I wanted do before I crashed. One was to see if the police were going to open an investigation into Barnhard's killing or if they'd be content to play the fade, accept the findings that pointed to an accidental drowning and move on. Two, I needed to know the identity of the man in the photograph. The man Birdie called Billy Bob.

I had some time to kill before my next stop, so I got in the Tacoma and steered it three blocks down the avenue to the IHOP, where I was the morning's first customer. I ordered a Denver omelet and poured seven cups of coffee down my throat. The meal and caffeine provided enough of a boon to keep me from going narcoleptic right there on the countertop. I paid, hopped back in the truck and drove the half mile to the police station.

The elevator was out of order, so I hoofed it up the stairs to the third floor where the Special Investigations Bureau was housed. The overnighters were still manning the shop. I gave the officer clerking the front desk my name and told her I was there to see the head honcho of violence.

"I know who you are," she said brusquely, directing me to a row of empty benches against the wall. "We got our first-class and our business-class seats available. Have your pick. Hale should be in at nine or thereabouts."

The clock on the wall read 7:36 a.m. Hour and a half to wait. Maybe he'd get in early. What else was I gonna do? I took a seat, leaned my head back against the wall and shaded my eyes with my flat cap, thinking I'd just power down for a cat nap. Next thing I was aware of was a smattering of voices and noises blending together in my ears. Also, someone was solidly, repeatedly, kicking my feet. My neck was crooked from where I'd fallen asleep funny. I slowly rolled my head back to perpendicular and creaked my eyes open to let the light in. Above me were the familiar contours of a bulky figure with a thick torso, no neck to speak of, and limbs that had gone scrawny with middle age. His gray and black hair was short on the sides and combed straight back from a widow's peak on top. Those traits, in combination with a nose that had been flattened its fair share, once by me, made for more than a passing likeness to a gorilla.

He kicked me again even though he saw that I was awake.

I said, "All right, all right, you've had your fun."

Bruce Hale grinned down at me. "You gonna sleep all day, you old crank, or you gonna get up and cause some trouble like always?" He was sucking on a lozenge or something and his words came out a little garbled.

I sat up, rubbed my eyes loose and took a gander around the station. While I'd been zonked, the shift had changed. Roughly thirty people had filed into the place and all of them were off and running on their day.

"What time is it?"

"10:40. We had a pool going to see how long you'd stay comatose with your mouth hanging down like a dead grandpa's. Leave it to you to exceed expectations, you outlasted everybody's bets. Carol had 10:30. Only Red Lewis put in for anything past that. His was 1:45. We all thought he was being silly, but . . ." Hale extended his arms toward me to indicate my current, in his estimation pathetic, state. "I reckoned leaving you there for that long would constitute cruel and unusual punishment, so here I am, kicking you."

"Gee, thanks."

"To what do I owe the pleasure? Or should I say to whom?"

"Scott T. Barnhard."

"T-for-Truth himself. Now how'd I know you were gonna say that? C'mon."

He signaled for me to follow and strode off through the rows of desks where the detectives worked. Knees bowed, arms dangling, he even walked like a primate. I got to my feet, stretched my legs a bit, and followed him through the bullpen. There were some snickers, some *Sleeping Beauty* references, and one jab about how someone thought beauty rest was supposed to make you less ugly, not more. I saw some familiar faces: Jerome Kipling, Clyde Sturges. Red Lewis fanned out a half-dozen ten-dollar bills like a hand of playing cards and thanked me for his steak dinner. Willis Hively glowered at me from behind his computer monitor like I'd murdered his puppy or something. I gave him a pageant wave and went into Bruce Hale's office.

Hale was already seated behind his desk, cracking his knuckles. I took one of the visitor's chairs. On the edge of the desktop was a large gold placard for all who entered to admire. It read:

Bruce J. Hale
Captain
Violent Crimes Division

The office was cluttered with file boxes in the corners and papers and notebooks strewn around a computer monitor on the desk. A senior portrait of Hale's late daughter, murdered nearly two and a half years ago, was perched in a silver eight-by-eleven frame next to that mess.

"How you been, Bruce?"

"Good, good. Things are good. We had a hell of a time, helluva time, fending off those gangs who tried to come in here and pick up where Cash City left off. Factions came in from all over the place—Columbus, Atlanta, hell, all the way up from Tallahassee—but things are finally swinging in our favor. We've pushed the pushers back to the neighborhoods they came from, Walnut Hills, Spring Road, the Terrace. Back to dealing more with local riff-raff now, which is much . . . uh . . . simpler."

"I read all about it in the paper. That's not what I was talking about."

"Ah." Hale's lips cinched tight. He assumed a regretful tone. "You know Cindy and I are divorcing."

"No, I'm sorry to hear that."

"Yeah, well, after all that happened with Charity . . ." His voice faltered and he put a hand over his mouth, glancing quickly at the portrait on his desk.

"We don't have to talk about it."

"It's okay, who else can I talk to about this shit, you know? A pastor? Please. That's what Cindy does." He fluttered his hand in front of his face like he was trying to clear the air of odor, or smoke, or the past. "I'm living in an apartment down by Redding Park, not too far from the house. Nice place, all I need. Cindy's keeping the house. I had to get out of there, too many memories."

"Memories are a double-edged sword."

"Yeah." Hale looked again at the framed pic of Charity. His face went slack and he went somewhere in his head for a moment. Then his eyes popped wide like something bright had come to him, and he was brought back to the present. "Speaking of papers." He sifted through the chaos on his desk, came up with the front section of today's *Cain City Dispatch*, and tossed it in my lap. "Guess what I woke up to this morning?"

The bold headline was plain to see: *Prominent Lawyer Found Dead In Pool: Foul Play Suspected.* I unfolded the paper and skimmed the article. It didn't expand on the headline much. Ciccone made good on his promise to keep my name out of it, citing a "source close to the investigation" for the inside scoop on the possible homicide.

"Ciccone's at it again, huh?" I said, folding the paper and tossing it back on his desk.

"Now, who do you think that *source* of his is?" Hale asked.

"Beats me. Ciccone's your boy. Why don't you give him a call and ask him?"

"Oh, I did. He's not answering for some reason. Pretty ballsy, don't you think, after all I've let that little bastard get away with. Anyhow, I thought *you* might be able to enlighten me."

I shook my head. "Haven't seen him."

"No? Didn't cross paths at the scene yesterday?"

"Nope."

"Okay, Nick, if that's how you want to play it."

"I'll show you how I'm playing it." I pulled the flash drive from my jacket pocket, leaned forward and placed it on top of the paper mess in front of him.

"What's this?"

"Evidence that Scott Barnhard was involved in something that probably got him killed."

Hale's interest was piqued, though he eyeballed the flash drive as though it might be booby-trapped. "Why are you so sure that Scott Barnhard was killed?"

"You have the initial forensics on the body back yet?"

"Maybe."

"Care to share?"

"What do you want from me, Nick? What's your angle?"

"Do I need one?"

"No, but usually you have a few to spare."

"You show me yours, I'll show you mine."

Hale narrowed his gaze on me and drummed his fingers on his potbelly. "Willis Hively's the lead on this and he hates your stinking guts. Won't have a thing to do with you."

"I'm sorry, I thought you were the boss. Is there someone else I should talk to if I want to get something done around here?"

"Fuck off. He hates my stinking guts, too, and you know why. If he wasn't the best I had I'd bounce him to Property Crimes."

"It'll be extra fun to make him cooperate with me then. Twist the knife a little."

"You're killing me." Hale sat back in his chair, thoughtful-like, and worked his tongue in the cracks of his teeth as if he had half his breakfast stashed in there. He tapped the desk beside the flash drive. "You gonna cut to the chase, tell me what's on this thing? Or do I have to plug it in and see for myself?"

"Scott Barnhard was scheduled to be interviewed by the U.S. Attorney's Office yesterday morning, presumably to discuss a conspiracy to defraud the government out of millions in disability benefits."

"Millions?"

"Presumably."

"What the fuck does that mean?"

"It means he wasn't very cooperative, not even with his own lawyers, so nobody was gonna know exactly what was what until we got into that meeting. Which he never made it to."

"And you have evidence of that conspiracy on this thumb drive."

"On the drive is a record of every ruling on every disability case Barnhard handled in the last five years. Over thirteen hundred."

"That proves what?"

"To get a scam like this going, Barnhard would need two things: doctors to testify to a claimant's disability, and a judge to rule in his favor. Now, there's lot of doctors named on those records, some a lot more often than others. More interesting, there are two administrative law judges for this region, Judge Vicky Dunlap and Judge Rutherford Blevins. Now they split cases from what I understand, down the middle fair and square, so you'd think it'd be a pretty even draw of Barnhard's, right? Flip of a coin, maybe one gets a little more than the other. Wanna know what the split was between Dunlap and Blevins?"

"Not particularly."

"Blevins presided over 947 cases out of 1,314."

"This is what you're standing on? Some crackpot theory based on, what? Some shoddy math? That in no way points to Barnhard being murdered? Which, by the way unless you forgot, is my bag, mur-der." Hale flicked a finger toward the gold placard. "You see what that says?"

"You certainly have climbed the ladder. It's very shiny."

"It is fucking shiny, and it says *violent* crimes, not white-collar who-gives-a- bullshit crimes. You're losing a step, Nick. You gotta come with more than smoke and mirrors if you want to give me a stiffy."

"All right, all right, don't have a heart attack. I've got more."

"You'd better. For your sake I hope it's not a fucking mathematical proof. And for your information, I've got a resting heart rate of like forty beats a minute, fuck you very much."

"You use a stopwatch or just count Mississippis?"

Irritation was starting to peek through the cracks of Hale's congenial manner. His cheeks were getting rosy and a good amount of saliva had pooled on his lower lip. A couple more well-placed barbs and I'd get a face-full of spittle. I grinned with the intent of defusing the situation, but whatever Hale read off it must have put a fright into him. His shoulders sagged and his face turned dopey.

"Aw, shit, what are you gonna pull out of your sleeve now?"

"I repeat. You show me yours, I'll show you mine."

CHAPTER ELEVEN
THE MAN IN THE PICTURE

Hale swung his door open, hollered, "Hively!" left the door ajar, and moved back around the desk. As he passed by me he clapped me on the shoulder, harder than necessary. "This should be fun."

Hively appeared in the doorway, his glower now tinged with paranoia, took one step in and moved no further.

"Come on in," Hale told him, indicating the empty wooden chair next to me.

"Why?"

"Malick here has a theory on your case."

"I don't bite, Willis," I said. "Not too hard and not unless you ask me to."

Hively stayed put. "I don't think it behooves us to consider anything from a person who, if my guy was offed, was sitting on a silver platter right in the middle of the crime scene—means and opportunity already accounted for."

"What, no motive?" I said.

"You're a sociopathic asshole with masochistic leanings and a homicidal streak. How's that for motive?"

"Seems a little thin. Big words though."

"Pretty spot-on profile if you ask me," Hale quipped.

"Tell me, Willis, did you come up with that diagnosis just now, or have you been waiting to drop it on me for a long time?"

"Willis," Hale said, interceding before things leapt too far off the rails. "Sit down, listen to what Nick has to say, and if it's bullshit, then we can both tell him to go fuck himself and get on with our day. That'd be a pleasant experience, right? And while we both know that he's a select breed of asshole, along with all those other attributes you so concisely stated, we also can be pretty certain he didn't kill Scott Barnhard."

"I don't know that," Hively said. "I don't put anything past him. Or the two of you together, for that matter."

Hale's laconic demeanor dissolved instantly. "What did you just say to me?" he said through gnashed teeth, his words choked with fury. "I do know it. And if you know what's good for you, you'll shut the goddamned door and sit your ass down right now. You understand me?"

Hively dragged his feet a little to show us he didn't like it one bit, but he obeyed the order, closed the door, then crouched on the edge of the chair next to mine like he was ready to make a quick getaway if needed.

Hale said, "Tell Nick about the autopsy."

"What about it?"

"What you told me earlier."

"Are you serious?" Hively protested.

"Dick cancer serious. Tell him."

"How 'bout I take a stab at it first," I interrupted. "Initial tox report showed signs of multiple drugs in his system. Cocaine, molly, marijuana, alcohol of course, and Viagra or whatever dick pill he uses. There was a lot of shit brewing in the crockpot, so to speak, so despite whatever indicators there are for an intentional drowning—say blood vessels burst in the eyes, or an enlarged heart, water in the lungs, the weirdness of the wet clothes inside a locked house—nothing can be automatically deemed suspicious because the water's too murky with all this other garbage. So for now, I'm assuming the cause of death was classified 'undetermined.' How close am I?"

"That's about the sum of it," Hively mumbled.

Hale chortled and shook his head, half perturbed, half astonished. "How can you know all that? The autopsy wasn't finished until an hour and a half ago. You were asleep on the damned bench out front."

"I've still got some moves," I said, winking at Hively.

"Where did you get your information?" he said. "Or did you feed him the drugs yourself?"

I ignored that. "Did you have the back of his head shaved like I asked you to?"

"The shaved head was your idea?" Hale asked.

"There was bruising on the skin at the back of Barnhard's skull," Hively conceded. "Doesn't mean he was murdered. Could mean somebody was grabbing a fistful of his hair during sex. We found half a strip of condoms in the pocket of those wet pants you're so fond of mentioning."

I ignored his jab. "Doesn't mean he wasn't killed. Whole lot of coincidences."

"Didn't you tell me once upon a time that there was no such thing as a coincidence in an investigation?" Hively retorted.

"No, I said you can't investigate a coincidence."

"You're making my point for me." Hively shifted his ire to Hale. "What am I even doing in here?"

"Let's get to it, Malick," Hale agreed. "We showed you ours. Your turn."

"You want a motive?" I said to Hively. I regurgitated the same stats that I'd given Hale about Barnhard's disability cases, as well as the rulings, the judges, the doctors, et cetera. To his credit, Hively didn't immediately dismiss the information. But he still needed some convincing.

"So what? You got some far-flung hunch, so now I'm supposed to go out and interview every person the guy ever crossed paths with professionally?"

"I don't think it's far-flung, and we could narrow the list down a bit."

"Hold up," Hively said. "There ain't no 'we' here, and there ain't never gonna be a 'we.'"

Hale stifled a yawn and said, "I still don't hear anything that falls very far from the speculation tree, Malick."

"It's solid enough to check out, don't you think? Or are you gonna play it to fade because your solve rate is lousy and this one's easily chalked up as an accident?"

"First off," Hale said, "nobody gives two fucks about our solve rate. Nobody has a good solve rate, here or anywhere else. If they do they're cooking the books. We're here to do the job to the best of our abilities. That's that."

"Swell. Prove me wrong."

Hively leaned forward with his elbows on his knees and contemplated the carpet between his legs.

Hale held up the front page of the paper again, continuing, "Secondly, you made damn sure we're not going to be playing the fade. But we got too much going on and not enough bodies for me to dedicate resources to something that *might* be a murder."

This time, I didn't bother to deny that I'd been the source in Ciccone's story. Instead, I said, "Try this on for size. I have a witness says they overheard a man having a conversation with Barnhard the night before he died, pressing him to keep his cool or else." The "or else" bit was a fabrication, but what the hell, these guys needed a cattle prod to get them to budge.

"Give me the witness," Hively said.

"I can do you one better. I've got a picture of the guy." I brought out my phone and scrolled to the picture of the small man with the keen eyes that Birdie identified as Billy Bob. I held it out for Hively to see.

"Shit," he said.

"Who is it?" Hale asked.

"It's Maurice Morrison."

Hale's cheeks puffed up with air that he expelled noisily. "That's not nothing."

"No, it's not nothing," Willis Hively agreed.

I said, "Who the fuck is Maurice Morrison?"

Hale lurched forward, smacked his hands together and exulted, "So that's your angle. You needed to know who was in that picture."

"Nobody ever said you weren't quick."

Willis Hively looked at us both like we should be banished to a corner and made to wear dunce caps and muzzles. "You took this the night Barnhard died? While you were surveilling him?"

I nodded in the affirmative. "Can you tell what he's carrying there?" I offered the phone again.

"Naw, something square. Laptop maybe. You're positive Maurice Morrison was the guy Barnhard spoke with?"

"Hundred percent."

Hively swiped his hand from his forehead down over his face, looking vexed.

"Anybody want to tell me what's so special about Maurice Morrison?"

As it turned out, Maurice Morrison, aka Momo, was a rising lieutenant in the Stenders, a gang of white separatists that lorded over all illegal activity on the west end of town. Rumor had it the Stenders held sway over many of the local unions in the southern part of West Virginia, thus having a hand in many legitimate business dealings as well. The gang's general M.O. was to keep their dealings on their turf and let the blacks war with the police and each other in Cain City proper.

The Stenders were unique in that they didn't flaunt their money or influence, of which they had plenty. They weren't in this game for the moment; they were in it for life, and acted accordingly—no risky dealings that would draw excessive heat, no business with people they didn't know, no selling out in the open, no selling to kids. Their enterprise was so tight that no one ratted, no one testified, and no one outside their ranks, not even law enforcement, had the first clue as to how they conducted their business, how they got their product, how they distributed it. *Nada.*

Even the exact location of the gang's headquarters was unknown. All people said was that it was somewhere deep in the forest, which was acres upon acres of dense, nearly unnavigable woods; a no-man's land referred to collectively as The Trees. If the street jabber was to be believed, there were more than a hundred bodies buried six feet under the earth in that forest. Bodies that would never be recovered. Maybe this was myth, but over the years enough people had run afoul of the gang and gone missing shortly thereafter, so what once was legend had more or less become accepted truth.

Per Hale, Momo had pushed up through the ranks quickly. He also had a stellar criminal pedigree to boot. Father was in Moundsville for life on a double homicide rap. Mother was some kind of relation, half-sister or something, to the gang's leader, Fenton Teague. Momo was twenty-six years old, had a lengthy juvenile rap sheet that ranged from shoplifting, to breaking-and-entering, to assault, to armed robbery. But nothing major on his adult record. Any felonies he'd committed had been expunged through community service or some bullshit, his record redacted. He hadn't caught any charges for the past few years, but nobody with half a brain believed that his criminal streak had fizzled.

"He's a live wire, that one," Hale said. "Total miscreant, but smart, smarter than he lets on, has this whole good ol' boy act he puppets. When he was a kid in school, he was in the talented and gifted program while simultaneously failing all his classes. Nobody'd seen anything like him. Methodical like his uncle, too, but more impulsive and short fused. More apt to get reckless if he's pissed off."

"So let's light the fuse," I said. "What's the best way to rattle his cage?"

Hale stared at me, dead-eyed, and shook his head as though I were an exasperating child. He shifted his gaze to Hively. "What's going through your head, Willis?"

Hively tossed his hands up in a gesture of futility. "I don't know what to think."

"You set the meet with the U.S. Attorney?"

"Yeah." Hively consulted the digital clock on his phone. "Forty-five minutes."

"So you *are* investigating it further," I said. "I want in."

"I've got a detective on it. Don't get wet yet," Hale chided. But then, out of the other side of his mouth, he added, "I want you to take Nick with you, Willis."

Hively's posture stiffened with alarm. "Hell nah, I've got a big problem with that."

Hale kept his cool, though I could see the spittle gathering on his lip. One more false move and his DNA was gonna go flying all over the place. He flung his hand about to indicate the world at large. "You see a whole bunch of kittens around waiting for you to have the pick of the litter?"

"I don't even know what that means," Hively replied.

"It means we'll take what we can get, help-wise."

"Give me anybody else," Hively said, voice low and deliberately calm. "Give me Sturges."

"Sturges?" That first *s* did it. Saliva took flight. Some of it misted onto my hand. Hale wiped his mouth. "Jesus Christ, why not just pick a receptionist at random and take them? You can have Sturges if you want, for all the good it'll do you, but you're still taking Nick."

"This is so fucked," Hively said.

"Nick, give us a second, will ya?"

I said, "Gladly," and stepped out. An empty swivel chair was vacant at a nearby desk, so I sat there and swiveled for a few minutes. I also tried to log in to the desktop PC with a generic catchall password from back in my days on the force, but it didn't take. Willis Hively emerged from Bruce Hale's office, said, "C'mon then," and bee-lined straight past me, back through the maze of detectives' desks and down the steps. I got up and followed, catching up to him as he flung open the station doors and stepped out onto the street. The sky was a pale, stark mat of gray that gave no hint as to where the sun might be hiding.

"I'm driving," Hively said.

"What a gentleman. You gonna open the door for me, too?"

Hively unlocked the doors to his Celica and grabbed the driver's side handle, but stopped short of opening it. His nose wrinkled up. He grazed it with his thumb and sniffed as though he were repressing some obscure, masculine emotion.

"Not another word, Malick," he warned.

"Fair enough."

We both got into the car. The engine failed to turn over and after a handful of tries it flooded. Hively let loose a streak of curses that weren't particularly original, but I admired the fervor of the tantrum. When he was through I asked him if he wasn't sure he wanted me to drive. He warned me to shut up and tried the starter again. The engine sputtered to life. Hively peeled away from the curb, flipped a U-turn in the middle of the avenue and headed east.

"The U.S. Attorney's office is back thataway," I said.

"I've got a stop to make first."

CHAPTER TWELVE
THE WASTELAND

Hively turned south, crossed under the Twentieth Street viaduct and hooked a left to continue east. We pulled parallel with the train of coal cars chugging along the tracks in the same direction and kept pace with it for a half mile until a red light halted us. The train slid around a bend and disappeared behind a row of run-down houses with rust-stained facades and weeds sprouting up through caved-in porches.

"Why are you even sticking your nose in this shit?" Hively grumbled.

"We talking now?"

The light turned green and Hively accelerated through the intersection, drove two more blocks and turned right onto Clifford Avenue.

"Seriously, I don't get it. You bored or something? Your pride hurt because Barnhard died on your watch?"

"What do you care?"

"You're stepping all over my toes on this one, that's what I care."

"I'm not trying to step on your toes. Am I bored? Yeah. Is my pride hurt? Maybe a smidge. But not enough to get me out of bed. Something's rotten about this one, I can smell it. And I want to find out what it is."

"All right, I'll bite. What smells rotten?"

"Nobody wants me to look into it, for one. And if Barnhard was murdered and somebody went to the trouble of making it look like a freak mishap, then yeah, call it professional curiosity. My turn to ask a question. After Hale asked me to leave his office, what'd he say to you?"

"He said enough."

"Enough of what?"

"Enough to get me here in this car with you. Bickering. Enough for that."

We passed the Malcolm Terrace housing projects, block after block of identical two-story rectangles, red-bricked with concrete stoops, flimsy screens, and cheap plywood doors. Hively turned left from Clifford Avenue onto Spring Street. Rows of houses were stacked tight on either side of the road. Half were boarded up and the other half bowed and slouched like they were gradually being consumed by the earth. Hively pulled over abruptly, threw the car in park and faced me. "My turn. Did you know when you left Hale and the suspect alone in that apartment in the Greenleaf that he was going to kill him?"

"Honestly?"

"No, feed me a bunch of bullshit."

"I thought he might beat him to death. I didn't know he was going to send him skydiving out the window."

Hively took my measure for a few seconds, then grimaced and settled back into his seat. He stared through the windshield. A few years back there was a city referendum to deter narcotic trafficking on Spring Street by cutting down all the maple trees, which would serve to provide less cover for the dealers and the dopers. So now there was a tree stump for every dwelling, an unobstructed view for half a mile, and the dope crews had plenty of warning when the cops made their token weekly patrols. There were three crews within view of the Celica now, spaced out strategically a block or two apart. And all those eyes were on us.

"Look at this place," Hively muttered. "It's like the ancient ruins of the goddamned American dream."

"Tell me, what was going through your head when you left the Greenleaf that day?"

Hively shook his head absently. "I never even saw the suspect. Far as I made it was the hallway, remember? Hale ordered me to leave the premises. He was my superior, what was I supposed to do? I didn't have a choice."

"Whatever you gotta tell yourself. That suspect is the one who killed Charity. You know that, right?"

"That for sure?"

"Yeah, it was for sure."

We stayed parked for a minute, sitting in silence while Hively wrestled with the shit in his head. "Y'all shouldn't have put me in the middle of that mess without letting me know what was what."

"Fair enough. You gonna tell me what we're doing here, or are you just gonna drop me off in the middle of your old neighborhood and see if I can make it out alive?"

"Shit, you wouldn't last two minutes in these here streets." Hively kicked the car into gear and started driving. "It'd be like throwing an alpaca in the middle of a lion pride."

"The fuck's an alpaca?"

Hively ignored me. Instead he studied two of the drug crews as we rolled past them. "Plus, if you died out here I'd get to feeling guilty about it, and you ain't worth feeling guilty over."

"That's comforting."

"You don't make it easy to like you, you know that?"

"I've been told. Where the hell we going?"

"Right here."

Hively stopped the car, threw it into reverse, and backed up to the curb in front of the dope crew we'd just passed. There were three of them, two sitting on the stoop of the shuttered corner house and one leaning against the wall. The two who were sitting stood up lazily. The one against the wall pushed off it and his hands went into the pockets of his parka. He stepped forward next to his pals.

Hively told me to wait there. He hopped out of the car and walked around the front of the Celica with his arms extended at his sides and his hands open-palmed. He said a few words that I couldn't make out. The two men who were listening to him relaxed. I say men, but neither of them could have been older than twenty. The short one had the type of peach fuzz on his upper lip that looked like the first growth after puberty hit. The one with his hands in his parka stayed focused on me, didn't even glance at Hively.

Willis reached cautiously into the inner pocket of his suit jacket and produced a business card. He handed it to the taller of the boys, who examined the card, nodded his head, and said, "Bet."

Willis came back around and got into the car while the crew assumed their same positions on the stoop and wall.

"Friends of yours?" I asked.

"Yeah, they babysit my daughters. Have them over to the house time to time for barbeque." Hively flipped a U in the intersection and got back onto Clifford Avenue. "Stupid little motherfuckers. Barely making enough money to feed themselves, feeling like there ain't no choice but to sling out here on the corner. Highest they hope for is to live to twenty-five."

"You don't think you're gonna live past twenty-five, there's not a thing in this world worth caring about. Their life, other's lives, hold no value. Nothing matters."

"Right."

"But you never know," I went on, "maybe one of their rap albums will break out and the rest of them can be hangers-on, contribute a verse now and again to the definitive chronicle of Appalachian street hustle."

Hively's jaw flexed. His eyes shot me some sidelong venom. "That's some racist garbage. You even realize how prejudiced that is?"

"Is it racist because I said it, or racist because everybody who's ever stepped foot on a Spring Street corner thinks they can flow?"

"Both. There was a time I was about *this* close to working one of those corners." He pinched his thumb and forefinger together to demonstrate how close *this* close was.

"You got flow?"

Hively cocked his head in my direction and regarded me for a moment before cracking a lopsided grin. "Mad flow. Bet."

We drove back under the viaduct, past the college campus, then Church Row, and on into the main stretch of downtown. There, between the original 1920s storefronts and the floodwall that guarded the city from the river, lay a wide swath of wasteland, twenty square acres' worth, that had been earmarked by civic officials as the centerpiece of their efforts to revitalize downtown Cain City. Locals dubbed the empty lot "Cruise Avenue" because it used to be a hot spot for teens and college kids to park their cars, carouse, and smoke weed. This was back when the city was safer, when weed was the hardest drug anybody could cop. You couldn't even score coke back then. The scariest thing you'd have to worry about was some knucklehead bringing a knife. Now coke was quaint and knives were a joke.

One of the many mistakes local politicians had made was rejecting a plan to build a shopping mall on the Cruise Avenue site twenty years ago, when the strip was in its heyday. Citizens thought a massive shopping complex would spoil the city's character. Instead the mall was built out in Becksville, which thrived from the boost in commerce while Cain City's economy, along with its population, dwindled.

Now the decision makers were trying to remedy that blunder, two decades too late. Real estate development companies had been making proposals and bidding on the site for months. The winning bid, as well as the plans for the property, were set to be announced that afternoon. Presently the street was closed as vendors and event staff prepped for the occasion, which, according to the huge banner strung across the road, was being dubbed "The Cain City Century Celebration."

"Say that five times fast," I quipped.

"I forgot about this jazz," Hively said, maneuvering the Celica into the logjam of vehicles jockeying for a route around the blockade.

I nodded back toward the direction we came from. "Back there, that pertain to us or something else?"

"I came up with the dude who runs the east side of town now."

"Nico Blakes?"

"Look at you, Malick, keeping up with the power structure in the 'hood."

Hively swerved the car into an alley between Fourth and Fifth Avenues. 4 ½ Alley, as it was known, was an established junkie and prostitute hang out. As soon as we started rolling down The 4 ½, figures on either side of the lane retreated into the nooks and shadows of the buildings.

"You and Nico tight?" I asked.

"Twenty years ago. Look here, from where we sit, the Stenders and the East End bangers have had this understanding, uneasy as it may be, for what, three decades now? More? The wicked in the west stay in the west, wicked in the east stay east. Everybody thinks it's a cold war, like there's no connect between the two, but that doesn't make any sense. You trying to tell me you keep a truce like that, for that long, with no back channel or nothing? There has to be times when it becomes necessary to contact the other side. Has to be a way set up to do it."

"You think Nico can get us a line on Momo Morrison?"

"Worth a shot, don't you think?"

CHAPTER THIRTEEN
FACE OF A THOUSAND CREASES

The U.S. Attorney's office was on the ground floor of a drab concrete building with banks of mirrored windows. The interior lobby had three large paintings on the wall that looked like someone had shit mauve over the canvases and done some finger painting, but it provided some color anyway. Hively and I had been twiddling our thumbs for half an hour. I was starting to wonder if the paintings weren't some kind of pastel Rorschach test, when Debra Wilkes came out glad-handing three men in suits. She was a short, sturdy woman with close-cropped gray hair dispersed evenly over her small head, and a collection of outsized features that looked as if they were in a battle for supremacy over her face.

Whatever she was saying to the men had them in stitches, though nothing about the interaction seemed genuine. She made a crack about one of their golf games, they laughed dutifully, and she bade them goodbye. When the door clicked shut behind them, Wilkes ditched the collegial act and cast a withering glare our way.

"Who's who here?" she said, waggling a finger between the two of us.

Hively and I stood. He said, "I'm Detective Hively. I spoke with your assistant this morning."

"And your mystery date?"

"This is Nick Malick. He's consulting on the case."

"Malick?" Debra Wilkes's face went tart and cinched into a thousand creases. "You the investigator who was supposed to be babysitting Scott Barnhard?"

"I am."

"Really gobbed that one up, didn't you?"

"Yes, ma'am, I did." I motioned toward the paintings. "I like the art you've got here."

"Oh yeah?" She turned her nose at the paintings as though they were giving off a pungent odor. "What do you see when you look at them?"

I regarded the three mauves once more and said, "Not a damn thing."

"Me neither. I think you're supposed to project life's meaning onto them or some such nonsense. My receptionist says one of them looks like the rays of the sun filtered through a cloud-covered sky. She's an optimist. I don't know what I can do for you fellows, but we can do it in my office or we can do it here." She twisted a large-faced wristwatch around and checked the time. "I've got seven minutes until my next appointment."

We opted for the office. The three of us took our assigned seats and Hively apprized the U.S. Attorney of our investigation.

"Murder?" Debra Wilkes said. "I was told Barnhard got stoned and drowned in his pool."

"That was the initial take," Hively said. "Evidence has come to light to indicate otherwise."

"Well, that changes things, doesn't it? However, I'm still at a loss as to what it is I can do for you."

"Easy. Give us what you had on Barnhard."

Debra Wilkes's lips parted as though she had a sharp retort on the tip of her tongue, but she raised her fingertips to her mouth, suppressing the impulse. Her censored response came forth slow and measured. "As you know, Detective, I have no legal obligation to share that information with you."

"I can get a warrant," Hively mused.

"You can try."

"If you want to make me work for it, I'll work for it, but is that really necessary? We're on the same side here, ma'am."

"Our inquiry included, but was not limited to, an investigation into Scott Barnhard's possible misconduct. This inquiry is very much ongoing, though I'll admit his death puts the scope of our inquiries in jeopardy. My bosses want heads to roll on this one. And if I was to give you what we have, which is highly confidential, the whole thing could go poof." She closed her fists and opened them quickly to illustrate what "poof" meant.

"Who's the whistleblower?" I asked.

"Excuse me?"

"The whistleblower," I repeated. "Look, there's got to be some common ground we can stand on to help each other out. I have an inkling about where you were aiming your investigation." I laid out the racket that I believed Barnhard was running, down to the dollar amount he'd scammed from the government. In the time it took me to do that, Debra Wilkes's demeanor morphed from one of mild curiosity to acute vigilance. Where previously we had been a benign irritant, gnats in her periphery, now we were genuine in-her-face nuisances who could wreck her whole stratagem.

"How close am I?" I said.

"Close enough."

"You want to find out who all's involved. We want to find out if this is why Barnhard was killed. If I'm right, he was the cog that made the whole thing turn."

Hively leaned forward. "You give us a name, give us something we can work with, and anything we find along the way that can help your end of things, it's yours."

"Tempting." Debra Wilkes removed her glasses and scrubbed the lenses with a tissue, held them against the light to look for smudges, then placed them back on their perch. "Why should I trust the two of you?"

"You said yourself your whole operation is in jeopardy," I answered. "What do you have to lose? Ask around if you feel the need. Hively here is the best detective this city has to offer, and I—well, I have something to make up for, don't I?"

"I can't give you any names, even if I wanted to," Wilkes retorted. "Deals have been struck, confidentiality agreements signed, etcetera, etcetera. What I can tell you"—she drew a breath—"is that ten months ago a disability caseworker grew suspicious of Barnhard's, shall we say, productivity. She was of the opinion that not all of Barnhard's clients fit the requirements necessary to receive benefits. So that was run up the chain, and eventually it was looked into. This being the government, progress was slow as molasses. I swear, you have to have thirteen people sign off on a request for a new printer cartridge around here. But recently we gained some traction with three different doctors implicated in the scheme. We squeezed them, deals were proffered. In exchange for immunity, each of the doctors agreed to testify that Barnhard paid them a lump sum, in around five hundred bucks, for every medical record or PRTF or whatever they falsified. It got to be so frequent, two of the doctors started getting kickbacks for legitimate claims. Barnhard had so many cases going, he never took the time to vet whether they were real or fudged. Lazy ass just forked over the cash and pushed 'em through the system. Anyhow, with the doctors' sworn statements locked in, we had the ammo to go after Barnhard, which we were going to do yesterday. And once we cracked that nut, we'd be able to see if the trail kept leading up the chain, or if it were only him and the doctors, how many doctors—you get the idea. If we'd have been able to snag Barnhard on the hook, we could've exposed the whole shebang."

"So with Barnhard's death, what happens to the deals you struck with the three doctors?" I asked.

"Void, for all intents and purposes. He was the fulcrum of the investigation. If we get lucky and are able to unearth anyone else who's involved, then maybe we can still use their testimony."

"And if not?"

"I hope it doesn't come to that, but"—Debra Wilkes flipped her palms up—"it's like I said, somebody's head's got to roll."

"One of those doctors Tom Orvietto?"

Debra Wilkes blanched and a noise akin to a stuck fur ball escaped her throat. She swallowed the lump down. "Now how the hell could you know that?"

CHAPTER FOURTEEN
THE LEFT-HAND MAN

As soon as Hively and I got out of the building he stopped cold and turned on me. "It's time you quit fucking about and clue me in to what's what, Malick."

"Jesus, Willis. You look serious."

"I am serious. I'm tired of this bullshit, you keeping knowledge close to the vest until you decide if and when it's beneficial to *enlighten* me."

"That's not what I was doing."

"You're gonna answer these two questions or I'm done with you, you understand me? You're out, I don't care what Hale says. He won't do jack about it either. You know it, and I know it."

"Okay, shoot."

"How'd you know which one of the doctors had turned informant? And don't give me that bunk you gave Wilkes about combing through all the case files and it being an educated guess."

"I'll give you two answers for the price of one. How 'bout that?" Over Hively's shoulder, I clocked three men lounging against a shiny black 4Runner parked directly behind Hively's Celica. They looked to be waiting for us.

"I'll settle for the straightest answer you got," Hively groused.

"I got it from combing through the case files."

Hively bared his teeth. "That's it. We're done."

"Wait now, here me out. Did you hear when Wilkes said that one of the fabricated documents was called a PRTF?"

"Yeah, so?"

"In a disability claim, that form is only used by a psychologist or psychiatrist. The doctor I mentioned, Orvietto, was the psychologist Barnhard used the most."

"There's your educated guess. What's the second answer?"

I explained that Tom Orvietto was Joanna's new husband, and about his reaction when I mentioned Barnhard's name at the dinner party two nights previous.

"Damn," Hively exclaimed. "Joanna's husband read dirty to you?"

"No, never would have guessed it. Reads as clean as they come. Guy doesn't even jaywalk."

"One more before you're off the hook. Who's the witness that puts Momo together with Barnhard the night he died?"

"I've got a more pertinent question for you," I said, side-stepping the inquiry. "How tight exactly were you and Nico Blakes when you were pups?"

"What's that got to do with anything?"

I tilted my chin to the street beyond Hively. "'Cause I think we're about to find out how he feels about you now."

Hively twisted around and saw where I was looking. Positioned between the two other men, decked in all black, baggy jeans, oversized hoodie, hair cornrowed, puffing on a cloved cigarette, stood Nico Blakes. He raised up off the car, stepped forward, and exhaled two long columns of smoke from his nose.

Hively faced me again. His eyes pinballed around like a million thoughts were sprinting through his brain at once. He bowed his head to collect himself, then raised back up and focused on me. "All right," he said. "You strapped?"

"You telling me we're about to throw down right now? I'm not really in the mood."

"Lose your edge working for them cushy lawyers?"

"Yeah. I probably did."

"We should be fine. Just making sure the playing field is even."

I reached inside my jacket and flipped the safety off on my Beretta. "I'm set."

"All right. Let's go see what's what."

We descended the five steps down to the walk and started toward the trio. The two men on either side of Blakes came up out of their leans and took their places beside him.

"Who are the flunkies?" I whispered out of the corner of my mouth.

"One on the right is the muscle, Junior Brown. Oversees the downtown trade."

"I remember Junior. Gained some weight. Who's the left-hand man?"

"Arkell Prince."

"You come up with them, too?"

"Junior, yeah. Prince is Nico's protégé. He's young. Don't know much about him."

The three gangsters standing in a row looked like a progression chart of mankind. Junior Brown was short and squat, slightly hunched at the shoulders. Then came Nico Blakes, who was of average height and build. Lastly was Arkell Prince, who was tall and stringy with a long, alien-like neck. Everybody had their hands at their sides and not in their pockets, which I took to be a promising sign that we weren't going to shoot it out right there on the lawn. Regardless, I advised Hively, "Shit goes down, you take Junior, I'll take Prince, and we'll meet in the middle with Blakes."

"Bet."

As we drew close, Nico Blakes' mouth spread into a wide grin that read equal parts convivial and menacing. "Little Willie," he boomed.

"Nico. Junior."

"Willis." Junior smirked as if Hively's name alone were funny.

Nico waved the clove cigarette at us like it was incense and he was blessing us with the holy trinity. "Seems like y'all was getting heated. You need more time to settle y'all's lover's quarrel or whatnot, we can step away. Let you settle."

"Nah, we're good," replied Hively.

Nico took a long drag off the clove. His eyes roved over Hively from top to bottom and back up again. "Look at them duds, boy. *Fancy.* Styled out better than a pastor on Sunday. Damn near makes me feel inadequate. What you think, June?"

"He ain't shopping at Penny's," Junior put in.

"No, he ain't. Fresh to death. Who's your tailor, Willis? I'm going to have to get up with him, see if he cain't take my measure for my burial suit and shit."

Junior Brown chuckled. This made his whole body jiggle. Prince, for his part, didn't twitch. Didn't even blink. He was inert as a statue save for his gold eyes that slid lazily between me and Hively as if he were observing a meandering tennis rally. Something about his placid manner got the hairs on the back of my neck tingling.

"Plan on dying soon?" Hively asked.

"Never know when your last day has dawned. Gotta be prepared for that shit." Nico narrowed his eyes on Hively. "You know, I squint hard enough, I can still see back through the decades to when we was young bucks. You still in there, Little Willie, underneath all that polish."

"How'd you track me so fast?" Hively said.

"Shit, you ain't *that* hard to find." Nico wet the tips of his thumb and forefinger, used them to extinguish the clove, and stashed the dead cigarette in the front pocket of his hoodie. "Been a long spell since we heard two peeps from you, Willis."

"It's been a minute."

"That it has. That it has. So you can imagine my surprise when one of my pigeons delivers me this." Nico raised his hand, twiddled his fingers around, and like a magician produced the business card Willis had given the kid on Spring Street not two hours ago. "Said you needed a favor. That right, Willis? You need a favor? From me? 'Cause, see now, *that* piques my interest. I like favors. I like the idea of you owing me a favor."

"We need to find a guy."

"You goin' have to be more specific."

"Momo Morrison."

The name perked Nico's ears. Junior rolled his shoulders back and straightened his posture. Arkell Prince yawned as if we were boring him into a coma. Nico glanced back at Junior, who made googly eyes and shook his head like he had never heard anything so dense. When Nico turned back to us, he had a bemused expression on his face, as though he were waiting for a punch line.

"Y'all for real trying to find Momo?"

Hively nodded that we were.

"'Cause see, I don't see that as me doing y'all no favor. Quite the opposite. I don't know what Momo's done, but if it's anything short of killing somebody, I might, uh, go on and let that shit slide if I was you."

Neither Hively nor I responded.

"Oh," Nico exclaimed, "so he *did* kill somebody?"

"We just need to talk to him," Hively said.

To this point in our interaction, Nico's gaze hadn't strayed from Hively. Now he turned and scoped me out.

"This your partner, Willis? You know, way back when, me and Willis used to be partners. Thick as thieves." Nico clucked his tongue. "Thick as blood brothers."

"This is Nick Malick," Hively said.

"Malick?" Nico put a finger to his temple as though he were activating a memory. Then his eyes went large, he pointed the finger at me and feigned pulling a trigger. "You the man started that war with them Detroit boys."

"It was more like a skirmish."

"Shit, I ought to be thanking you. We was in a pickle there, boy. You did our dirty work for us. Heard you was mixed up in that fuss too, Willis."

"I played a bit part."

"Bit, huh? Bet you did. So y'all looking to get in some more trouble?"

"Like I said, we just have a few questions for Momo."

"That's trouble enough." Nico contemplated the blank sky for a moment, tocking his head back and forth as he mulled things over. "All right," he said, bringing the wide, false grin back for another go-round. "Y'all want it, I'll see what I can do. Thing is, I put the word out you trying to find Momo, more likely than not it's gonna be Momo finding you. Y'all sure you ready for that?"

"Fine by me," Hively said. "Saves me the legwork."

Nico Blakes held up Hively's business card again and twined it through his fingers. "I know where to find you." He made for the passenger door of the 4Runner and signaled for the others to follow. Junior walked around to the driver's side, hoisted himself in and started the car. Arkell Prince, who hadn't spoken a word the whole time, stared us down for an extra couple beats before moseying over to the back door and sliding in. His lanky, flat-footed gait reminded me of the way Goofy walked in all the old Mickey Mouse cartoons.

As they pulled away from the curb, Nico Blakes rolled down his window. "Good seeing ya again, Little Willie."

Hively didn't return the sentiment. He just watched them go. When the 4Runner was half a block away I reached under my jacket and switched the Beretta's safety back on lock. The 4Runner rolled through the stop sign at the next intersection, swung a left, and vanished behind the Hearing Aid Center on the corner. Hively gazed into the void where the 4Runner had just been as though, at any second, it might reappear spraying bullets.

"Guess he liked you well enough," I said, in a clumsy attempt at levity.

Hively expelled a deep breath of air. "That's the ghost of Christmas past, present, and future all rolled into one for me right there. That could have been me." Hively had never reflected much on his coming up in the Malcolm Terrace housing projects. At least not to me. He checked the time on his phone. "Shit, it's two-thirty already. You hungry?"

"Famished."

CHAPTER FIFTEEN
MAN ALIVE

We sat at the counter of The Spaghetti House, a Cain City institution that opened on Third Avenue, the main downtown thoroughfare, in 1938. Employees still donned the same style uniforms they'd worn back then, clean white smocks with green aprons. The old lady tending to us looked as if she might have been working there since the day they cut the ribbon on the place. Her name tag read *Geraldine*.

It was between the lunch and dinner rushes and there were only a couple other diners in there besides us. Geraldine delivered us our food and we plotted our next moves over plates of pasta. Because of my personal relationship with Tom Orvietto, I would approach him solo to see what I could glean. Hively was scheduled to interview Barnhard's law firm colleagues that afternoon. We called the office of the honorable Judge Rutherford Blevins to set up an interview, but his court docket had been cleared for the day and he was out of the office until tomorrow. His clerk was reluctant to schedule a meeting without the judge's strict approval, so unless we wanted to show up on his doorstep, we'd have to wait a day.

"What about the other administrative judge, Vicky Dunlap?" I asked between bites. "If her counterpart was large-scale robbing their employer, aka the United States of America, she'd have to have an inkling."

"You'd think. Should we question Dunlap before or after we take a run at Blevins?"

"Doesn't matter so long as we get to them one right after the other. Thataway they don't have time to compare notes. If one of them crosses the other up, we walk across the hall and put it to them simultaneously."

Geraldine brought over the pie of the day, peanut butter with a graham cracker crust, for us to salivate over.

"You won't regret it," she said, flashing her big false teeth at us.

"My waistline will," Hively said.

"What waistline?" Geraldine retorted, inching the pie closer to our noses.

A block north, the celebration at Cruise Avenue had commenced. A young couple came in and the sounds of cornets, tubas, oboes, and snare drums came wafting in with them.

"You hear the big news?" Geraldine asked. "They're finally going to put in a bunch of stuff down round the corner on Cruise. Restaurants, bookstore, some shopping, ice cream place . . . oh, and a big ol' movie theater, fourteen screens they said. Be nice to see some foot traffic downtown again."

Geraldine carried on for a bit about what a vibrant town Cain City used to be back before all the jobs went to China and all the morals went the way of the devil. When she shifted gears and started speculating which department stores we would get and what ice cream flavors the new parlor might offer, I interrupted her mid-sentence.

"Mercy sakes, woman. Give me a slice of that pie."

Hively caved and ordered a piece, too. We scarfed the pie down, paid the bill, and he drove me back to where my Tacoma was parked outside the police station.

I turned to him before I stepped out. "Hale said he'd assign you Clyde Sturges, yeah?"

"I asked for Sturges to prove a point. People do whatever they have to do to avoid working with him. Man doesn't know his ass from his elbow."

"He can read, can't he? Take Hale up on it. Get Sturges to comb through all the records, police notes, and case files he can find on Judge Blevins, Momo, hell, all the Stenders. Have him go through the Barnhard files again. Who knows, maybe he'll find a needle. Can't hurt."

Hively conceded that he couldn't see the harm and agreed to get Sturges paper-hunting, then made me promise to tell him if I got anything out of the shrink.

"What, like a super pinky promise?"

"You know what I mean."

"Not really."

"You gonna make me spell it out?" Hively huffed. "You tend to be selective with the truth you tell."

"Me?" I said, feigning naivety. Hively didn't trust me to play it above board with Tom. You had to hand it to him, he saw me coming. I crossed my heart and hoped to die and got out of the car.

I got into my truck and steered toward Cain City College. Tom Orvietto's psychiatry practice was in a shit-brown one-story building with a matching gabled roof off the east edge of campus, sandwiched between a diabetes center and some student housing. I'd called ahead and knew Tom's last appointment would be finished at 4:30.

I arrived just before then, checked in with his receptionist, and sank into the leather sofa in the waiting room. Chakra music was playing lightly over some speakers mounted in the corner. I picked up a copy of *Time* magazine and tried to read a story about the latest government shenanigans, but my vision schizzed sideways and I gave up a few paragraphs in. My eyelids felt like weights were anchored to them. I struggled to remain conscious, but was losing the battle. The music didn't help. Just as I started to drift, the receptionist slammed her partition shut, startling me awake. The clock above the frosted partition read 4:29 p.m. Less than a minute passed before a tall, rough-looking man outfitted in head-to-toe denim and a black Stetson came out and hustled past me without making eye contact. Tom appeared in the doorframe behind him, a nervy grin plastered tight on his face. I stood up.

"This is a pleasant surprise," Tom said.

I gestured to the cowboy, who was already out the front door and halfway down the walk. "What'd you do to him?"

"Oh," Tom hemmed, "you know. They come in with a problem and leave with a catastrophe."

"Psychiatry humor?"

"Yes, but it's also true. Facing yourself usually makes things worse before it makes things better."

"Remind me never to do that."

"Dr. Orvietto?" the receptionist called out from somewhere beyond the partition.

Tom held up a finger to place-hold our conversation and stepped back into the interior office. He and the receptionist held a quick muffled exchange that I couldn't make out and I heard a door to the outside open and shut. The chakra music stopped and Tom rejoined me in the lobby.

"Sorry about that. Is this about Joanna? I feel like it's my fault. I shouldn't have been so adamant about having you and Karla over. She seemed so keen on the idea; I should have known better."

"Not here about Joanna."

"Oh," he said, flustered. "Then to what do I owe the pleasure?"

"You've gotten yourself in quite the fix, Tommy."

Tom's eyelids fluttered and he blinked thickly to make them stop. His tight smile looked like it wanted to run for the hills, but he forced it to stay put.

"I'm not quite following." He exaggerated his features to look confused, swallowed hard, and, with one last vestige of hope that I'd come to see him for any other reason than the one I was there for, said, "What fix?"

"Scott Barnhard," I stated bluntly. I was tired and in no mood to coddle. Tom's smile fell to pieces and his rosy cheeks turned ashen.

"I was afraid you might say that."

"Go ahead and assume I know everything, but want to hear it straight from the horse's mouth."

"I'm going to sit down."

"Do that."

Tom placed his hand on the armrest of the couch and delicately dropped down onto the cushion. He took a moment to compose himself. I took the seat adjacent to him.

"I'm afraid I'm not at liberty to discuss it with you, Nick."

"You referring to your deal with the U.S. Attorney? About that, it's pretty well fucked now that Barnhard took a formaldehyde bath."

"What?"

"Now that he's dead."

"But I phoned the U.S. Attorney's office yesterday. They told me to hold steady and not to worry."

"What else are they going to tell you? Make sure your passport's ready because if you want to remain a free man for the next five to fifteen years, you might want to scram for the border? I just came from there. Here's what they told me."

I put Tom's situation in context for him. When I was finished he sat there for a while breathing heavily through his nostrils. I asked him if he needed a paper bag or something, but he shook me off.

"So I'm going to be their scapegoat?"

"They'll look for bigger fish, but if they can't find anybody with links to Barnhard and your testimony is moot, then yeah, you and the two other doctors they got to confess will foot the bill. It's a lot of government money we're talking about here. Somebody's head's gotta roll. Wilkes's words. Know who the other two doctors are?"

"No idea."

"All right. I'm going to need you to walk me through it. How it all started with Barnhard. How the Feds approached you. What you told them. Everything."

Tom opened his mouth wide and worked his jaw around. "I need a drink."

"Got anything here?"

"No, not in the office."

"I know a place." I didn't want to prolong the meeting any more than I had to, but a splash of liquor could soothe his nerves, jog his tongue loose. On the flipside, it could also turn him into a sobbing mess. I put the odds at 50/50 with Tom. Less maybe, in his current state of panic.

"I have to pick up Ruthie from day care in ten minutes."

"Can you call somebody else to get her?"

"I always have dinner ready when Joanna gets home at seven."

"She can handle take-out for one night."

"But," Tom hesitated, trying to sift the muck in his brain to form a coherent thought. A protest, a reason to get away from me and pretend none of it, not Barnhard, not his forging medical reports, not the U.S. Attorney's investigation, ever existed.

"There's no getting clear of this, Tom. The U.S. Attorney's case is at a dead end. I'm your only shot."

He summoned up some vitriol. "Why would you help me? You hate me. It's obvious." It occurred to me that he was moving, rather rapidly, through the stages of grief.

"I don't hate you. I just don't like you very much. And I wouldn't be doing it for you anyway. I'd do it for Joanna and that baby."

"You still love her, don't you?"

"Not in the way you're referring."

"Love is love is love, isn't it?"

"Hardly."

Tom scrutinized my face, as though if he looked hard enough he might be able to determine whether or not I was a threat to steal his wife out from under him. He pivoted back to the topic at hand. "But what can you do that the U.S. Attorney can't?"

"Try," I stated plainly. "If they can't come up with an easy solution after a while, they've already got you and the other two docs, whoever they are. They'll dance with the partners they can."

Tom closed his eyes and whimpered. "Let me try my sister."

He got on the phone and arranged for his sister to pick up Ruthie and take her to her house, then texted Joanna to tell her where Ruthie was and that something had come up, he'd be home late.

I got back into my Tacoma and led Tom in his Escalade west along the edge of downtown. We turned left, drove under the Eighth Street viaduct and came up into the Southside. Just beyond the viaduct was The Red Head, my dive of choice back when bourbon was my favorite pastime. It was a dank, musty establishment, the clientele could be a little rough, your shoes might stick to the floor, the flusher on the men's room toilet only worked about half the time, but it had a shuffleboard table, a good jukebox, an old phone booth that still worked, drinks that were stiff and cheap, and it was one of the last places in town that hadn't sold its old, crusted soul for the sleek, generic millennial dollar. Additionally, it was a block and a half from the old high school. So, convenience. We pulled into a small gravel lot between the bar and the building next door, which was a bakery once upon a time but now sat vacant. I parked the Tacoma against the old bakery, Tom followed suit, and we went in.

The place was dim. It took a moment for the eyes to acclimate and see past the dust particles that swirled in the beams of light shining in through the front windows. The jukebox was silent. The only noise was the murmuring from a hockey game playing on the thirty-inch screen mounted above the bar. Two sallow-faced old-timers I recognized from my days as a regular were nursing beers at the counter, chomping on peanuts. One of them had a Boston Terrier snuggled on his lap. Other than them the place was empty.

The bartender, Tadpole, wore his stringy gray hair in a ponytail and had two squirrelly eyebrows and a bristly mustache that hung down far enough to tickle his lower lip. When he saw me the 'stache wriggled at the corners. He slapped his rag on the bar top. "Man alive, if it ain't Slick Nick Malick. I was starting to think you were never gonna darken these doors again. That, or somebody'd finally put you out of your misery."

"Tadpole, if I didn't know any better I'd say you almost missed me."

"Not gonna lie to you, it was nice not having to worry about your shenanigans for a bit, but this place has been so quiet and peaceful, like to bore me to death. What can I tell ya, my mama always said I had a sentimental streak for the irredeemable soul. Who you got here?"

I introduced Tadpole to Tom, Tom to Tadpole, and told them they were both in the same profession, listening to blowhards and bullshitters all day.

"What'll it be, fellas?" Tadpole said. "Tell ya what, I'm feeling generous today. Make ya a deal. Fourth one's on the house."

"That might be the best marketing plan I've ever heard, Tadpole," I said.

He jabbed a finger into his forehead. "Came to me just now. Spurt of inspiration."

"Give me a Maker's on the rocks."

I looked to Tom, who fretted between a gin and tonic or a single malt scotch for a lengthy duration before going with the latter. Tadpole got to pouring.

"Hey, Doc," Tadpole said. "You ever heard the one about the blonde who saved up and bought her dream car?"

I rolled my eyes. "Here we go. Tadpole's got one of those joke-of-the-day books under the bar. Every day he tells a new blonde joke to any sucker willing to listen."

"That's not true," Tadpole said, feigning offense. "I do not get my material out of a book. I get it from the internet like a respectable person."

"Let's hear it," Tom said.

"So this blonde woman finds her dream car, this vintage Jaguar convertible, listed on Craigslist for cheap. Too cheap almost. She's stoked as hell, right, but worries the deal is too good to be true. She's thinking there's gotta be something wrong with it, but she calls the owner up, zips right over there to take a look at it, and sure enough, this thing is pristine, shimmery gold body, not a nick on it. She still don't trust it, but this is her dream car. She can't pass an opportunity like this up." Tadpole slid our drinks across the bar and clapped his hands together. "Buys it right there on the spot, straight cash homey, *bam*, plops them funds down. Gets behind the wheel and off she goes. At first this puppy is running smooth. I mean it's really purring, but then sure enough, she gets the thing revving 'round about forty miles an hour and the engine starts to sputter, tailpipe starts coughing out black bile, so she swings it into the nearest service station. Now at this point, she's just hoping for the best, you know, this being her only chance at her dream car and knowing full well the transaction has already been made—that cash she plunked down ain't coming back to her. So the mechanic flips the ignition and listens to the car very intently, then pops the hood and starts tinkering around, again very intently, grunting the whole time. Meanwhile, by this time the blonde is upset, you know. Real consternated, biting her nails, just praying that she didn't just throw away all that dough. 'Mm-hmm,' the mechanic grunts. 'That's what I thought.' 'What is it?' the blonde says. 'I'll do anything to restore this car, just tell me what I gotta do.'" With Tadpole, you always knew when the punchline was coming because he'd get tickled two or three lines before he hit it. Presently he stifled a little giggle. "So the mechanic grunts again. 'Crap in the carburetor.' The blonde, she nods along real serious and says, 'Okay, how many times do I have to do that?!'"

As soon as the last words from the joke were uttered, Tadpole, always his own best audience, cackled so hard his face turned beet red and he started choking on his own spit. He inhaled deeply a couple of times to get some oxygen into his lungs and his breathing under control, then repeated the punchline for good measure: "How many times do I have to do that?!" The old-timers down at the end of the bar must have already heard the joke a time or two. They just shook their heads and hunkered over their beers. Tom and I laughed enough to make Tadpole feel good about himself, Tom paid for the drinks, and we moved over to a booth on the other side of the shuffleboard table.

I slid into my side, Tom squeezed into his. The edge of the table pressed against his belly but he didn't seem to mind. I let him get a couple swallows of the scotch in him before we got down to business.

"I've driven past this place a thousand times," Tom said, looking around. "Never been in."

"Not your kind of haunt?"

"No, I suppose it's not." He swirled the scotch around in the glass and took a long drink. "What do you need to know?"

"Start with what you told the U.S. Attorney. Then, if there's anything you left out, tell me that, too."

"What do you mean, left out?"

"Anything you may have omitted. Kind of like when you go to the doctor and they ask you how many drinks you have in a week, how much you exercise, sexual history—people answer those questions, but they skirt around the worst of themselves, knock the edges off. Same thing happens with police. Anything you left out of your statement, however innocuous you may think it is, I need to know about it."

"All right, I get it." Tom took a moment to sort the story in his head, made some glum faces, unconsciously twisting the wedding band around his stubby ring finger. "It started innocently enough."

"Always does."

"Scott Barnhard was the lawyer for a couple of my patients who were applying for disability. This was a few years back, before I'd even met Joanna. I filled out their paperwork, the standard forms and whatnot, and sent them on their way. Didn't think twice about it. A few days later I get a call from Scott thanking me for doing such top-notch work for his clients. That's what he called it, I remember, 'top notch.' I tell him I was simply doing my job, it was nothing special, which it wasn't, but he says no, no, you'd be surprised how many doctors don't really care about their clients, don't fill out the paperwork properly, et cetera, and how that creates a real clusterfuck for him and his clients. Anyway, his gratitude was really profuse and he said he wanted to thank me in person and asked if I could meet him for dinner or a drink. What can I say, I'm a sucker for positive affirmation. I met him. Worst mistake of my life."

Here, Tom swilled the remainder of his scotch, loosened his tie and undid the top two buttons on his shirt. A greasy thatch of chest hair sprang free. I signaled Tadpole for another round.

"The fuck I look like to you, a waiter?" Tadpole grumbled, but he fixed the drinks and brought them over. Tom proceeded. Barnhard treated him to dinner that next night, and it was there that he mentioned a few of his other clients who he thought deserved benefits, but had been denied for one reason or another. All they really needed, he impressed upon Tom, was a solid, unbiased psych evaluation. Barnhard was charming, he paid for everything, and Tom agreed to assess the patients.

There were four of them. Two were unable to work for certain, there was no question about it, and the other two were borderline. Tom leaned toward declaring them fit for work, but over another dinner Barnhard detailed their failed work histories, their inability to obtain subsequent employment. These people had families, Barnhard claimed, families who would be on the street soon if something didn't give. Tom acquiesced, graded them eligible for benefits, and in that moment Barnhard had Tom under his thumb.

There were more clients, more dinners. In Tom's mind, the relationship became a true friendship. After a while Barnhard started expressing his gratitude with more than free meals.

He insisted Tom accept a cash gift, and slipped him an envelope with five hundred dollars in it. Tom declined the money initially, but Barnhard was persuasive, said it was the least he could do in return for all the "top notch" work Tom had done and continued to do for the good folks who needed him.

It all escalated very smoothly. The payoffs became standard operating procedure: five hundred dollars for every client who was awarded benefits. Those five-hundred-dollar bills multiplied rapidly. Tom knew what he was doing was wrong, unethical. He protested a little, but those protests held no teeth. He knew it, Barnhard knew it. Soon the dinners stopped altogether and Tom was being sent patients with less and less qualifications for disability, but he was caught up now, culpable.

"And just like that." Tom snapped his fingers. "No way out."

"But then it stopped, right? Cold turkey, year and a half ago. Why?"

"I had met Joanna at that point, obviously. We were about to have a baby. I was as happy as I've ever been in my entire life, yet here was this one thing hanging over me. I wanted to be done. I had wanted to be done for a long time. I took her out to dinner one night, down to Charlton's over in Ceredo."

"I know the place."

"It was one of the restaurants where I'd meet with Scott. I saw him there that night. Here I am with my pregnant wife, belly out to here, and I see him at the same table he had always sat at with me. And he's with this other man, yucking it up, cigars, wine, the whole nine yards. I walk over and say hi. Scott introduces me to the man. He's a medical doctor. Right then and there I knew. I knew that he had this thing going with more than me. He had it going all over the place. I quit. I refused to see any more of the clients he sent over."

"And that was that? No blowback from Barnhard?"

"No." Tom closed his eyes, gave a little shake of the head and opened them again. "That's all I told the U.S. Attorney, but that was not that. This is where we get to that part you mentioned. The omitted bits."

CHAPTER SIXTEEN
NEW DADDY

The clock-out hour was upon us. Cain City's working class started filing into the bar. Outside, the gray sky went grayer with dusk. Someone with a flame for Woodstock got the juke going: Joplin; Hendrix; Blood, Sweat & Tears; Jefferson Airplane. We were forced to speak up in order to hear each other.

Tom held his empty glass aloft. "Can we get another?"

"Why not?"

He rolled awkwardly to the side so that he could retrieve the wallet from his back pocket and passed me some cash. I accepted the money and bellied up to the bar, caught the tail end of Tadpole's blonde joke again, and collected two more drinks. Willis Hively texted to check up on me. I told him I was in the middle of getting the goods.

Where? he wrote.

Me: *red head*

Hively: *I'm gonna swing by*

Me: *no need*

Hively: *Yes need. See you in 5*

I handed Tom his scotch and scooted back into the booth.

"You're not driving home," I told him.

"No, I suppose I'm not," he smiled wanly.

"I'll call you a cab."

Tom slurped the top off the scotch and began his account of the night two men paid him a visit outside his office. He had unlocked his car when they appeared, seemingly out of thin air,

148

flashed pistols, and instructed him to get into the driver's seat. One of the men got in on the passenger side, the other in the back.

I scrolled through to the picture of Momo Morrison on my phone and tilted the display for Tom to view. "Was this one of the guys?"

Though the picture was grainy and from a distance, Tom shook his head definitively. "No." I zoomed the picture in on Momo's face, but Tom was certain. "No, these guys were both big. The one in the back seat was very tall. I remember he had long curly hair on the sides and was bald on top, maybe a little comb-over. The one in the front, the one who did the talking, was beefy. Not like me, more in a muscular way. And he was quite intimidating. The skin on his scalp where hair should have been instead looked warped, like it had been graphed on or burnt. The oddity of it was the edges of the scars formed a perfect hairline across his forehead."

"Both of them were white?"

"Right."

"And they threatened you?"

"Certainly."

"How?"

Tom cupped a hand over his mouth. He expelled a short, hard gasp through his fingers. His fat body deflated and he looked about to cry.

"I'm quite ashamed of what I'm about to tell you," he murmured.

"Oh," I said, unmoved.

Tom talked around the matter for a while as a means of working his way toward whatever disclosure he had to make. He spoke of his dating life, or lack thereof, prior to Joanna. His failures on all the matchmaking websites, his inability to move past the first date. The way women's eyes glazed over whenever he attempted conversation.

"I needed someone to see beyond the surface, to see all the positives I had to offer, but that's not how the modern dating world is set up, I'm afraid."

"You have money. That usually gets you somewhere."

"Right? That's what I thought. That money was supposed to be the great equalizer. That's what I had always been led to believe. You see these men walking around with these women and you think, what has that guy got that pulled her, you know? The answer was almost always money. I mean, I never knew if I was ever going to have a partner in this life." Tom was getting downright blubbery now. Snot bubbled from one of his nostrils.

"So you went to prostitutes."

This startled Tom, rendered him dumb. He stammered, "How did you. . . ?"

"I'm a rocket scientist."

Tom wiped his nose off on the sleeve of his dress shirt. "You're a snarky son of a bitch, aren't you?"

"C'mon, my mother could take two looks at you and tell you've been to hookers."

"I can only imagine what type of woman your mother must be," he snapped.

"Careful."

Tom held up a hand by way of apology. "Yes, I paid for companionship. But it wasn't hookers, plural. It was one."

"Name?"

"I don't want to get her in trouble."

"We're past chivalry at this point, Tom."

"Barnhard set me up with her. I'd told him my sexual woes and thought he was just being a solid pal, you know? He said she was totally clean, I had nothing to worry about. She got checked out every month, would show me her medical records if I so desired."

"Tell me you wore a condom, Tom."

"Yes, well, I had to if I wanted to get my money's worth. She was a professional, you know, and she was very good at her job."

Just then, out of the corner of my eye, I caught sight of Willis Hively coming in. His eyes roved over the place, locked onto me, and he started our way. Subtly, with my hand below the tabletop, I signaled for him to stay put. He read the sign and veered toward the bar.

"I'll bet she was. Was this a young black girl we're talking about?"

"What? No, she was young, sure. But she was white. Very white, in fact. Very pale. Thick red hair, curly. Very Irish." He gesticulated to different parts of his body. "Lots of, you know . . . freckles."

Internally, I breathed a huge sigh of relief that Birdie wasn't the hooker Tom had been mixed up with. That there was no chance of his being Aisha's father.

"This was all before Joanna?" I wanted to know.

"Yes, yes. As soon as I met Joanna, I stopped it all, I swear it." Tom took a healthy slug from the scotch. "You think I'm a weakling, don't you? A weakling and a fool?"

"I wouldn't consider you a bastion of strength or wits."

"Fuck you."

"That's the spirit."

"You've always held it against me, my relationship with Joanna, haven't you? That she dropped you and picked me. You've never thought I was deserving of her."

"You've got me there, pal."

"You just can't stand the thought that I might be the love of her life, not you."

"Listen, let's not get crazy. I'm not here to assuage your insecurities. You don't want to know what I really think of your marriage."

"Insecurities?" He scoffed, took a drink. "Let's hear it, jackass. Do your worst."

"All right, but this might hurt a little."

"Will you skip the disclaimer and get on with it?"

"Sure thing. Joanna went through a trauma greater than any human should have to bear. Coming off that she needed something safe and secure. A dull, reliable partner she could set her watch to. You check off all those boxes with flying colors. There's nothing so safe and predictable as a fat, rich man whose self-esteem is zilch and who's just happy to be in the game. She took it for granted you came as advertised. A durable doormat, built to be walked all over and last for decades. But you're not the man she thought you were, are you? She was wrong. Now she's paying for it. And you're paying for it. But if you want to flop 'em out and measure, I'd be happy to do that, too."

Tom glowered at me. "You're probably right. She was always too good for me, too much for me."

"Let's get to it, Tom. How's this circle back to the goons that pushed you around at your office?"

"Well, it was clear why they were there. They didn't have to spell it out. But I thought they were going to threaten me with bodily harm, that kind of thing. So right off, I told them I had no reason to ever talk, you know. I would be in just as much trouble as anybody. And they said, that's good, because if, for whatever reason, I did talk or strike a deal, or even mumble the wrong thing in my sleep, they had video of my escapades with Destiny and it would be sent to the police and the media and to my new wife. And wouldn't that be such a shame for her to have to see, having just had a baby and all. That's exactly the way they put it. Escapades."

"Destiny. That's her name?"

Tom nodded. "The name she went by. I never knew her real name."

"You never saw this video?"

"No."

"And Joanna knows all this? That's why she was so upset the other night at dinner?"

"Yes, she knows. When the U.S. Attorney cornered me with what they had, I knew I couldn't keep my indiscretions from her anymore. I had to come clean. It was eating me alive. Don't get me wrong, the post-partum depression is real, too. But I think this is what upset her the most. It's like you said, I'm not the man she thought I was."

"But why confess to Joanna more than you did to the U.S. Attorney?"

"If I told the authorities about the tapes, they'd go looking for them, wouldn't they? God forbid they found them. Then what? I hoped—I'm hoping, those things never see the light of day. I can live with losing my practice, my license, but the shame those tapes would bring . . . Cain City is a small town. Joanna's a doctor. Everyone would know. She'd walk down the corridors of the hospital and everyone would whisper behind her back, 'There's the doctor who married the fat guy that got caught up in that hooker scandal.' The gossip it would engender, I couldn't bring that upon her. Ruthie'd hear about it someday, too, eventually. I had to tell Joanna. Get out in front of it. She deserves to be prepared if those tapes ever do come out. She'd never have forgiven me if the whole situation was sprung on her. It'd be one of those moments, you know, one day you wake up, you think your life is settled, sound. Then something happens and it's never the same again."

"I think that day's come and gone, Tom."

"Maybe. But this way, she may be mortified, but at least she's prepared. And maybe she can forgive me someday. Someday."

Tom's eyes went glassy again. His head sank into his hands. Quietly, he sobbed. His crying sounded like a bird with the hiccups; little tweets and in-sucks of air, but his big body trembling shook the whole booth. The people in the box behind ours turned around to see what was jostling their seat, realized what was happening, and averted their eyes.

Willis Hively had been monitoring us from the bar. During the crying jag we caught eyes and he mouthed the words, *what the fuck?* I responded with a flummoxed gesture and waited for Tom to buck up. When his emotions were finally spent, Tom removed his hands from his face and stared at them, flipping them over and back to examine them from all sides, as if his beefy palms or stubby fingers held the secrets to why he'd made the choices he'd made.

"I really am an imbecile."

I didn't argue. "Tell me more about Destiny."

Tom didn't have many additional details to provide, save for the address where he visited Destiny: apartment 619 at the Royal Vista. One floor above Birdie. I summoned the cabbie

I knew, a guy named Dennis Maynard, put Tom in the back seat, and told Maynard where to take him.

Before I could shut the door, Tom seized my wrist. The neon lights from the exterior of The Red Head cast his mottled features into a deeply shadowed, demonic red glow.

"Do you think she'll forgive me?" he said urgently. "Will it ever get better?"

"How do I know, Tom? It'll take a lot of work I'd imagine."

He slumped back into the pleather seat of the cab, dejected. "Okay," he muttered. "You'll do your best to see me through this, won't you, Nick?"

"I'll do my best," I agreed. I shut the door, slapped the roof, and sent the cab on its way. I watched it coast down the avenue until its taillights receded from view and I thought to myself, *There you go again, making promises.* I went back into The Red Head and joined Willis Hively at the bar. He was peeling the Bud label off his empty bottle.

"Want another?" I asked. I took my hat off and tossed it onto the bar top and hopped onto the stool next to his.

"Nah, I'm good. Why'd you go and make the good doctor cry like that?"

"Didn't take much. Just told him he was probably going to prison for the next five to fifteen years."

Willis rolled his eyes and shook his head, but couldn't suppress a grin. "That's cold, Malick."

"Whaa?" I said, feigning innocence. "With good behavior he'll only serve a third."

We compared notes from our respective inquiries, him with Barnhard's colleagues at the law firm, me with a weepy shrink. To a person, everyone that worked with Barnhard admitted knowing that he bent the rules, though not one of them confessed to being aware of any flat-out illegal transgressions. Nor were any of them privy to the federal government's investigation into his activities. For my part, I relayed Barnhard's methodical courting of Tom Orvietto into the scheme: the dinners, prostitutes, cash, up through the heavies that threatened Tom outside his office, though I neglected to mention the particulars of their threat, i.e. the alleged videotapes. I also skipped a few other key details that might pull Birdie into Hively's orbit, specifically the name of the prostitute Tom frequented, Destiny, and her address at the Royal Vista.

"Makes sense," Willis said. "None of those lawyers are going to implicate themselves in any way. Our best shot with them is to find a paper trail with one of their signatures on it. Something they can't deny. I'll add it to Sturges's bucket."

"Speaking of, he find anything worth mentioning?"

"Naw, he's been reading through all that legal mumbo jumbo all day, probably can't even see straight at this point. Oh, I almost forgot. I got Judge Blevins on the books for tomorrow morning. His clerk called, said he'd push court for a half hour to accommodate us."

"That's interesting."

"Yeah. You coming?"

I told Hively I'd be there. Afterwards, I'd see if there was anything worth pursuing in the prostitute angle.

"Careful with that," he warned. "If I remember correctly, last time you got intel from a working girl she ended up full of bullets in a dumpster not too far from here."

"You know what, I'd forgotten all about that incident. Thanks for reminding me."

"What was her name again?" He snapped his fingers a few times. "That's right, Gum Drop. What happened to all those kids of hers?"

"Don't know," I lied. "Last I heard they were headed into the system. Probably spread all over the place by now."

"Poor kids." Fury swept across Hively's features. "This fucking city, man."

"This fucking world," I replied.

"Yeah. That too."

"It's been a day. Sure you don't want to cap it off with one more?"

"I gotta get home," Hively demurred. "Tabby's pregnant again. If she knows I could have been home at a decent hour and chose to drink instead, she'll have my sack."

"Another kid? Jesus, man, at this point you should let her clip your shit."

"Heh. Another girl, too. That's all I make are girls."

"Oh, you're fucked. We gotta have another drink then. Tadpole," I hollered. He slid down the bar, eyeing the two of us.

"You're friends with this here rabble-rouser?" he said to Hively, indicating me. "If I'da known that, I wouldn't have let you through them doors."

"*Friends* is a strong word," Hively said.

"Willis here is having a baby," I put in. "Give him another Bud Heavy and fill me up, will ya?"

Tadpole congratulated Hively, popped the cap off another Bud and poured my bourbon. It was my fourth, I pointed out. On the house. "So there's this blonde," he said to Hively.

"Oh, no," I interrupted. "I've already heard it twice, Tadpole."

"Well, daggum. Don't spoil it. New daddy here hasn't heard it once." And so it came to pass that I suffered through the blonde joke with the crap in the carburetor again. At least I had a fresh Maker's to console myself with.

"'How many times do I have to do that?!'" Tadpole howled.

Hively laughed politely. From behind us came a loud chortle. A tinny voice piped up, "Y'all like jokes? I got one for ya."

I peeked back to see who was doing the chirping. Standing not a foot from me was a little waif of a man with the imitation of a smile plastered across his face. He had shorn blond hair, an upjutting nose, and shifty, wide-spread eyes that bulged like a toad's. His tiny gray teeth looked as though they'd been sanded down to resemble a chainsaw blade. He was wearing the same Carhartt jacket that he'd had on in the picture Bob Lawson had taken of him.

I knew at once that this was none other than Momo Morrison.

CHAPTER SEVENTEEN
THE GARGOYLE

Birdie had called Momo Morrison ugly. She was being polite. He had the face of a gargoyle. You couldn't look at him all at once, you had to take him in in spurts. Standing behind Momo was a colossal human being that nearly doubled him in height. The giant's oblong head was so large it was a wonder he didn't tip over. He had a few strings of hair on top and black curls that hung down around his ears like Orthodox ringlets. The ears stuck out from his head like coat racks. His long face lacked structure, as though his skull were missing its cheekbones. Skin seemed to slide straight down from his eye sockets to his slack jaw, which gave him the look of someone who'd suffered a botched lobotomy. I took this to be one of the two flunkies who'd threatened Tom Orvietto in his car.

"Y'all are gonna love this one," Momo said. "Here it go. What do you call a row of trees in a black neighborhood?" He thrust his neck forward, inviting anybody to guess at the punchline. When nobody did, a smug look came into his face and he focused his attention on Hively. "Transportation."

Momo's grin, real now, took on a nasty quality. I glanced at Hively. He sipped his beer, face as placid as if he were gazing upon one of the Seven Wonders of the World. I burst into a fit of laughter; a loud, hysterical laugh full of condescension.

"Wait a second." I stopped. "Was that indecent? Should I be offended?"

"I don't think the offense was meant for you," Hively said, even-keeled.

"Oh, good. Because if somebody said something that ignorant to me, shoo, I might have to get mad." I kept the friendly act up, but fixed hard eyes on the jokester. "You must be Momo Morrison."

He tapped his nose. "Bingo. I ain't trying to get nobody riled, I'm just joshin'. Funny you should use that word though, mad. 'Cause that's the precise response I felt this morning when I heard two cop boys were looking for me simply because somebody somewhere turned up dead. And apparently, when somebody somewhere turns up dead, cop boys don't have much more imagination than to think to themselves, must have something to do with Momo Morrison."

"I don't remember that being the way of it," I said. "Was that the way of it, Hive?"

"Naw," Hively said distractedly. He had taken out his phone and was texting away, as though a conversation with Momo Morrison was about the dullest thing going.

"No, I don't think that was our line of thinking," I said. "Tell me something. People been finding us fast all day. We have a tracking device on us or what?"

"It don't take much asking around to find out all kinds of interesting little tidbits about the one-armed cop boy. I might have been the only person in Cain City didn't know where you quench your thirst on the regular."

"Should have probably learned then that I still have two arms and I'm not a cop."

"I'm not gonna bother getting semantical with you. Word is one of them arms don't work all too well. And you're working with the cops, ain't ya? Potato, po-tah-to, it's all the same to me."

I eyed the big man behind Momo. "You're a tall drink of water, aren't you? You speak words or are you mute?"

"Lil' Mike Mike speaks plenty of words," Momo said. "Don't ya, Mike Mike?"

"I speak plenty of words," the goon confirmed.

"Well, that settles that mystery. If you're Lil' Mike I'd hate to see what Big Mike looks like."

"Mike Mike's pappy wudn't too big, was he, Mike Mike?" Momo said. "He just came first. Name's more metaphorical. Got his proportions from his mama. Didn't ya?"

"I got it from my mama," said Mike Mike.

"I'm sure she's quite a woman."

"All right." Momo pushed his fists into his palms and cracked his knuckles. "Enough of this fluff talk. What do you say we dispense with the pleasantries?"

"This is pleasant?" I asked.

Tadpole, who had been listening to the whole thing behind the bar, had heard enough to get worried. "Listen, fellas," he said, a little quaver in his voice. "I don't know what's going on here and I don't want to know, but I don't need no kind of trouble in my bar, so you're gonna have to take it somewhere's else."

"Don't get your hackles up, Groucho." Momo held his empty hands out to his sides to demonstrate his pure intentions. "We ain't causing no fuss."

"Don't make me call the police," Tadpole warned.

"C'mon now, Groucho. Ain't no need for that kind of foolishness. We're just talking. Besides, this black fella right here is the police. He'd probably pick up the call." Momo made a sweeping gesture with one of his hands. "This a nice place. This your bar? We ain't gonna shoot your bar up or nothing, swear on my grandmommy."

"This will just take a minute, Tadpole. Then they'll be gone," I assured him. "Right?"

"That's right," Momo said. Tadpole didn't say anything else. From down at the other end of the bar someone beckoned him for a drink. He skulked thataway, but kept a watch on our party. Momo stuffed his hands in his pockets, focused back on Hively and me. "Now, ain't much that rankles more than being around a bunch of smart-aleck cops, but I had to see what kind of hooey the keepers of the peace were trying to put on Momo now. So this is your one chance, coppers. You ain't gonna get another."

"We better make it count then," I said. "Where to start? What do you think, Hive?"

Hively hit the button for the display on his phone to go dark, tucked it away, and got straight to the point. "What were you doing fucking about downtown on Tuesday night? I thought you Stender boys stayed to your side of the tracks."

"I didn't know we was segregated," Momo chirped. "Thought this was a free country."

Hively bobbed his head up and down. "You're right, you're right. You are totally free. You can walk out of this bar right now if you want to. Or you can tell us why you were inside the Royal Vista apartments talking to Scott Barnhard a few hours before he was murdered."

Momo scratched at a patch of fuzz on his chin. "I was downtown Tuesday night, sure 'nough, but I don't know nothing about no Skip fucking Blowhard, and by the sounds of it, I ain't never gonna know."

I said, "Before you go any further down this route where you pretend not to know what we know you know, I feel obliged to make you aware that we were surveilling Barnhard Tuesday night. We saw you talking to him. Have the pictures to prove it. You can see them if you want to."

Momo's lips peeled back, revealing red, swollen gums above the chainsaw teeth. He cocked his chin up, looked down the slope of his nose at us. "Y'all ever been out to The Trees?"

"Can't say that I've had the pleasure," I replied. Hively shook his head no.

"No, you wouldn't have been." Momo ran his tongue over the fronts of his tiny teeth. "Because a funny thing happens to a lot of people who come out there, trying to sniff around, thinking they bloodhounds. See, thicket's so dense out there, huge cedars, pines and such, well, you can't hardly see the sun. It's easy to get turned around. You'd be more likely than not to lose your bearings. Not know which direction is which. Some people go in and they don't never make it out. *Poof*, they gone forever. Shame really. You'd think folks would have learned by now, just ain't no reason to go into a place that dangerous when you don't have to. Ain't no benefit to it. Why risk it? Because you're curious or think you're smarter than all those many folks who went in before you? Wasteful, I say."

I delayed responding to make sure he was done with the monologue. Just long enough to make the air between us awkward. Then I said, "I can't tell. That sounded almost like a threat. Was that a threat?"

"Believe so," Hively agreed.

"Oh, that was good." I clapped my hands facetiously. "Was that improv'd or do you rehearse this stuff in the mirror?"

Momo took a step forward, leaned in close to where I could smell the gingivitis, and whispered, "You best be careful now. 'Cause you keep pressing me, you're gonna look back on this moment right here as the fondest memory of your ever-lovin' life. You'll pine for the day threats was all you and this darkie got from me. 'Cause next time there ain't gonna be no words. Next time it'll just be those trees you see, blotting out the sunlight."

I stood my ground. "You asked around about me, right? Then you'll know that careful's not really in my nature, Momo. But I'll tell you what. You give us the details of what you and Barnhard were talking about on Tuesday night. Give us an alibi for your whereabouts from two o'clock to six o'clock that next Wednesday morning. If it checks out, I'm sure Willis here will leave you alone. And you'll be free of me now and forever, God as my witness, till death do us part."

"I'm not obliged to tell you shit," Momo sneered.

"True. And we're not inclined to leave you alone. So that leaves us in a bit of a pickle, doesn't it?"

"You sure you want to dance with me, friend?"

"Ah, why not? My card's pretty empty."

"Oh, I'll fill it up for you. To the brim." Momo's mouth split again into that false smile that looked carved from wax. He stepped back away from me. "Till next time, fellas."

"Looking forward to it," I said.

Momo turned his back to us and strode out of the bar. Lil' Mike Mike followed him like a trained hound. As soon as they were gone, Hively hopped off his stool and hustled to the window. He peeled the curtain back an inch and peered outside. After a minute he replaced the curtain and came back to the bar.

"I didn't like him very much," Hively said.

"Can't imagine why. What was it that did it for you, the racism? Stupidity? Or just his general disposition?"

"All of the above."

"They gone?" I asked.

Hively nodded in the affirmative. "Get this, they were driving a white minivan. A Kia."

"Kia, huh? Interesting choice of transportation. That a solid minivan?"

"Oh yeah, the works, automatic sliding doors and everything."

"Sounds luxurious."

"I texted Sturges to haul his ass down here to tail them when they left," Hively said.

"He make it?"

"Pulled out right behind them. If they don't make him in the first thirty seconds, maybe we'll catch them going somewhere interesting or doing something nice and illegal."

I took a drink of bourbon. It tasted better than usual.

"Think I pissed him off enough?"

"Oh, I'd say so. Some may call that particular skill your forte."

"Some may."

"Though, toward the end there, it was looking a little flirty. If I didn't know any better I'd say it was getting downright intimate the way you two were whispering sweet nothings to each other."

"I have that effect on men, what can I say?"

Hively pulled out his wallet and sifted through some bills. I told him his money was worthless, the drinks were my treat as long as he named the baby after me.

"Nikki Hively?" he said, annunciating the syllables, testing the name out loud.

"Has a ring to it." I sipped the Maker's. "My namesake."

Hively pretended to mull it over. "Yeah, not a chance in hell."

"Fine, I'll pay anyway, you mooch."

Hively left the bar. Tadpole made his way back down to where I was posted. I apologized for being a walking nuisance. This prompted him to twist the ends of his mustache thoughtfully.

"You know all that stuff I said earlier about being bored, missing your shenanigans? Yeah, now that I got a little taste of it again, I'm fairly certain that was just nostalgia talking. You catch my meaning."

"Fair enough."

I reached into my jacket to get my wallet and settle the tab when I felt two buzzes in quick succession. I pulled both my wallet and my phone out. There were seven missed texts, all from Karla.

"Aw, shit."

The first had been sent almost three hours ago: *reservation at Savannah's for 7:00!!!* Three exclamation points at the end. The time was now 7:35 so I was pretty certain that I was in for a thorough chewing-out. The middle texts escalated from questions of logistics to declarations of anger to concerns for my well-being. The one that had just come through combined the latter two: *if you're okay you better fucking let me know right now*

I replied, *home in 5*, tossed some money onto the countertop, snatched my flat cap, and went out. The night had turned cool and damp. Quiet. The traffic on the avenue was scant and there were no customers at the hot dog stand across the street. The strings of lights that dangled from the stand's roof swayed in the breeze, the tiki torches that bracketed the seating flickered, and the faint drone of The Beach Boys' "I Get Around" carried to where I stood. The old man who ran the place was perched in the window with his head in his hands, dozing off.

I put my hat on, tugged my coat tighter around me and walked around the corner into the gravel parking lot. I fished my keys from my jacket and hit the button for the Tacoma to unlock. The truck beeped, taillights flashed. A black Explorer had parked at an odd angle too closely to my car, forcing me to turn sideways in order to squeeze between the back bumpers. I pictured the dumb redneck or oblivious college kid who would park in such a manner when there were plenty of other spots available, and I cursed the state of West Virginia for issuing a license to such a blatant moron in the first place. As I tugged on the door handle, a faint crunch of gravel came from the front of the vehicles. I looked over.

The old bakery was cast in shadow by The Red Head, and the two cars parked so close together cut a deeper shadow along the bottom half of its wall. There, in the layers of darkness between the Tacoma and Explorer, was the black silhouette of a huddled figure. My eyes narrowed to acclimate to the dark. The figure raised up from his crouch. He was a hulking man who matched me in height and doubled me in width. In his hand was an extended baton, cocked at the ready. The light of the moon reflected off the man's bald dome, making clear the scars and craters that disfigured its entire surface.

The second goon.

"Aw, shit."

CHAPTER EIGHTEEN
OCULUS RIPPED

He rushed me. I went for my gun, got my hand around the grip, finger on the trigger, but before I could take aim the baton came crashing down on my wrist. My fingers went rigid and the Beretta went skidding across the gravel. The scarred man stepped forward and raised the baton to strike again. I grabbed the driver's side door and slung it at him. The baton smashed through the window. Glass sprayed across my face, puncturing my skin. The man kicked the door shut and swung the club wildly, whacking dents into both cars. I sidestepped one blow, ducked another and blocked a third with my bum arm. The hit sent a bolt of pain through the limb and into my chest. I ratcheted backwards to avoid his next swing, but the club glanced off my cheekbone and spun me around. Fireworks screamed through my brain and skewered my vision. I bounced off the side of the truck and crashed onto my knees.

I scooped up a handful of gravel and flung it behind me at the looming brute. The rocks caught him flush in the face and he yelped in surprise, then squealed like a castrated boar and brought the baton down hard across my back. My limbs went limp, splayed in all directions, and I crumpled onto my stomach. My mouth busted on the gravel. The air in my lungs exploded out of me. I attempted to crawl under my truck, but the man stomped hard on my back to keep me still. My hand brushed against something serrated and metal amongst the rocks. I realized it was my keys and snagged them just as the man yanked me to my feet.

He twisted me around to face him, lifted me by the collar, and slung me back and forth against both cars a couple times. My head smacked against the roof of the Explorer. Then he slammed me against the cab of my truck, clamped his thick fingers around my throat and lifted me off the ground. A rush of blood screamed through my ears. I thrashed and chopped at the crooks of his arms. They didn't budge. The man squeezed until it felt as though my head might pop clean off my body like the cork from a champagne bottle. Then, just as my brain was about out of oxygen and my vision began to flicker, he dropped me onto my feet. I bent over, clutched my knees and coughed for air.

The keys, I realized, were still in my hand. They'd sliced my palm from the vise grip I had on them. I maneuvered the longest one, the key to the Tacoma, between the middle fingers on my fist and secured the fob against the heel of my hand. The man gave me a few seconds to catch my breath, then took me by the shoulders and straightened me out against the truck. He spoke for the first time. Voice raspy and guttural.

"You had your fill or you wanna keep going?"

"Not particularly," I wheezed.

"Keep your nose out of places it don't belong or next time I won't be so gentle. Got it?"

"You call this gentle?"

The man jabbed the end of the baton into my xiphoid process. I pitched forward and vomited. He took my face in his mitts and put me back against the car. I hocked out a chunk of puke that hit him in the forehead. Didn't faze him. He cuffed me on the ear and pressed the baton across my neck.

"Walk away while you can still walk. That clear enough for you?"

"Eh, could you be more specific?"

The thug's face contorted with rage. "They said you might need some persuading." He removed the club from my larynx and raised it to clout me again. Before he had the chance I summoned what little might I had left, reared back and punched him in the face. The blow didn't land clean, it rattled my fist, but the man staggered back against the Explorer. Maybe I'd surprised him. I braced for another flurry from the baton, but nothing came. The man stood there stock still, his hands fixed like claws in mid-air, as if he'd been frozen in carbonite. My eyes were fully oriented to the dark now, and I saw why he wasn't moving. The key to my Tacoma was jutting out from his left eyeball. The rest of my keys jangled on the keyring below it.

The man's functioning eye flashed around its socket before finding purchase on the foreign object dangling from his skull. He dropped the blackjack to the gravel. Taking great caution, he lifted his hands to his face and touched around the contours of the key ring.

"Holy mackerel," he mumbled. He took firm hold of the Tacoma's key fob and, without preamble, yanked the key out. The eyeball came with it, along with the muscles and nerves that attached the eye to the inside of his head. They stretched like a rubber band, then ripped clean apart. The scarred man winced but didn't make any noise. He just stood there gaping at the bloody sphere impaled on the blade of the long key.

"Holy mackerel," he repeated.

I scanned the ground for my Beretta, spotted it behind the back tire of the Ford Explorer, scurried over and retrieved it. I leveled the gun at the man's head.

He wasn't much concerned with my weapon, nor me for that matter. The eye that remained in his head fixated on the one which had been plucked. Carefully, the man pinched the eyeball between two fingers and slid it smoothly over the teeth of the key. When it came off, he cupped the ruined eye in his hand and examined it closely, as a jeweler might examine a precious stone.

The man still had a hold of my keys. I ordered him to give them over. He opened his palm and let my keys fall to the ground, then stumbled around to the other side of the Explorer—all the while muttering, "Holy mackerel," as though all other words had been excised from his vocabulary. I kept my Beretta trained on him. He clambered into the SUV, got it started and backed out slow and steady.

I noticed now that there were no license plates on the vehicle. Traveling at about two miles an hour, the cyclops preceded to sideswipe three cars on his way out of the lot. Metal bending and crunching into metal. As he pulled onto the avenue, he nearly collided with a bus that laid on its horn for the next half block. From there the Explorer coasted through a red light and dropped out of sight under the viaduct.

I holstered my Beretta and took a look around. No one else was lurking between cars or in the shadows. Across the street, the old guy was full-on asleep in the window of the hot dog stand. The song wafting over from the speakers now was "Earth Angel." I couldn't remember the group that sang that one. I considered calling 911 or possibly Willis Hively or Bruce Hale, but weighed it all out; the hassle such a call would bring, having to give a statement, getting checked out by EMTs, as well as the likelihood nothing would be gained from reporting the assault. I decided against it. I'd see Willis in the morning, tell him then.

I took inventory of my body, rolled my jaw around to make sure my mandible was still attached to my skull. It was. Although my mangled arm had taken a hard blow from the baton, the feeling was coming back with a burning, tingling sensation. I could wiggle my fingers and make a weak fist. My back was throbbing, but I could bend and twist okay. My lip was split. My cheek was gashed and swollen. Knees were banged up from falling on the gravel. A few slivers of glass were embedded in my face, and I had half a dozen lumps on my head, a large welt across my wrist. My palms were skinned up and my knuckles were sore from punching the guy.

Apart from that I was intact.

I picked my keys and flat cap off the ground, dusted the hat off, and tucked it into my coat pocket. Then I retrieved the weapon my assailant had left behind: a twenty-six-inch-long retractable steel baton, heftier than the ones the police were issued or the ones available for purchase online. This puppy was designed to crush skulls and turn brains to mush. It had nearly fulfilled its purpose. I tossed the blackjack into the passenger seat of the Tacoma, swept some glass off the driver's seat, and slunk in behind the wheel. Remnants from the scarred man's eyeball were still on my key. I wiped it off on my pants, slotted it into the ignition, and drove the two blocks home.

CHAPTER NINETEEN
BODY LANGUAGE

I dragged myself up to the portico landing of the old high school and then the three flights of stairs to Karla's apartment. I let myself in. Nobody was in the living room, though the TV was on, screen paused in the middle of some video game about war. I set the baton down, eased my jacket off, then my shoulder holster, and stood there for a moment, too tired to move or call out. Davey came bounding around the corner, headphones round his neck, skateboard in hand. He got a look at me and stopped abruptly.

"Whoa, shit. What happened to you?"

"Got into a fight with Godzilla. Where's your mom?"

Before Davey could answer, Karla emerged from the kitchen. She was wearing a black slip dress that looked as though it had been vacuum-sealed onto her body. Her make-up was done to show off her round cheekbones and the big, bluesy eyes that held sway over the other features of her face. Her blonde hair was pulled tight into some fancy configuration atop her head. The dress didn't hurt, but dress or no dress, make-up or no make-up, hers was a beauty that would make you forget your name, date of birth, and country of origin. For a moment I even forgot the pain. She was everything a man could ever want or need, and more than any man would ever be equipped to handle. She was also ready to give me an earful.

"Do you have any idea," she began. Then, "Oh my God." She covered her mouth with her hand.

"I'm okay."

Karla rushed over to me and reached for my face, but hesitated to touch it for fear of hurting me.

"Have you been drinking?" she asked.

"A little."

I took hold of her left hand, kissed it, and guided it to the spot on my face that didn't ache.

"What happened?"

"Says he got into a fight with Godzilla," Davey offered.

"That's just about true," I said. "He even had scales."

Scrutinizing my wounds, Karla make a *tsk* noise. "You have shards of glass in your face."

"Yeah. Sorry I whiffed on our date. I didn't get your texts until it was too late. You look stunning."

"Shut up and tell me what happened."

I gave Karla and Davey the CliffsNotes version of events, showed them the blackjack. Davey snatched it up and played around with extending and retracting it.

"Did you report this?" Karla asked.

"Yes," I lied.

"Why were you at the bar?"

"I needed to get somebody's tongue loose."

Karla frowned. "This was for a case?"

"Yeah."

"You could have been killed."

"Nah, they just wanted to send a message."

She traced the gash in my cheek with her fingertip. "Some message."

"Know any good nurses who might be able to patch me up?"

Davey pretended to barf and made a beeline for the door. "I'ma go check out the truck."

I extended my arm to bar him from passing. "Not with the stick you're not." Davey handed over the blackjack. "Where you off to?"

"I dunno. Down to the park for a skate or something. How 'bout you tell me where you been and I'll go the opposite direction."

"West side of the park's fine. Stay away from the east end, okay?" He agreed and I lowered my arm. "Don't touch the truck. There's probably still glass all over it."

"Yes, sir, captain sir." Davey saluted me and loped out the door. As soon as he got into the hall he dropped his skateboard. We listened to him roll away. Karla took me into the bathroom and sat me down on the toilet. I caught a glimpse of myself in the mirror. The side of my face the blackjack struck was swollen and caked with blood.

Karla shined the light from her phone into my eyes to make sure my pupils were dilating properly. They were. She wetted a rag in the sink and set to cleaning my wounds.

"You might need a stitch or two," she said, dabbing around the gash in my cheek.

"You know what they call two stitches?"

"What?"

"A band-aid."

"Suit yourself. It's your face."

"It could stand a little character."

Karla retrieved a pair of tweezers from the medicine cabinet and got to working on the glass in my face.

"The last thing your face needs is more character."

"I'll take that as a compliment."

With each piece of glass that Karla extracted, little rivulets of blood slid down my cheeks. She said it looked like I was crying a bunch of O negative, or like I had stigmata or something.

"Jesus didn't cry tears of blood," I told her, and explained to her what stigmata was, in the Catholic sense, with the crown of thorns and the spikes through the hands and feet and all that.

"You know an awful lot about religion for someone who doesn't believe in God."

"That's just it. The more you know about religion—our God, their God, *the* Gods—the harder it is to believe in any of it."

"So what? Me and everybody else who believes in a higher power are stupid?"

"I didn't say that."

"You've said it before."

"No. I said that religion is a coping mechanism."

"That's right. And what are we coping with, exactly?"

"Existence," I replied. "Are we talking about this now?"

"No."

"Is this your ploy to try to get me to church with you on Sundays?"

"No. Forget I said anything. Now's not the time."

"You think?"

Neither of us spoke for a while. Karla dug a sliver out from deep in the skin under my eye, and dropped it in the mini trashcan beside the toilet. She finished with the tweezers, dabbed some peroxide on the cuts, and ran me a bath, then helped me out of my clothes and put me in it. The water was damn near boiling, and it felt amazing. Felt cleansing. Karla brought in a couple of frozen bags of vegetables for me to hold against the swell in my face and wrist. I asked her if she'd be so kind as to fix me a bourbon. She advised me to fuck off; if I wanted a drink so badly I could get out and get it myself. The hot bath and frozen peas were feeling exceptionally pleasant just then, so I stayed put.

I sank down into the water, lapped some into my mouth and spit it out. Blood was mixed in with the spit. I watched the bright red swirl and dilute, then leaned my head back against the tub and closed my eyes. Karla removed the knot from atop her head and shook her hair loose, then sat on the edge of the tub next to me. She dipped the rag and commenced to washing my body.

"He really worked you over, didn't he?"

"That he did."

"You're lucky you're not hurt worse."

"You know, that's the same thing I thought when he cracked my arm with that baton. I thought, 'Man, I sure am lucky. That could have been my face.' Then when he belted my face with it, I thought, 'Man, I sure am lucky. That could have been my back.' Then, when he—"

"Don't be mean. You know I'm right."

I opened my eyes so that I could roll them at her, then shut them back.

"You told me that you were through with dangerous cases," she said softly. "You told me that working for those lawyers, you'd never get yourself into any kind of situation like that again."

"Some things can't be helped."

"What was the message?"

"What?"

"You said he didn't kill you because he was there to send you a message. What was it?"

"Nothing. He just wants me to stop working the case, that's all."

"So do it."

"Do what?"

"Stop working the case. Why not?"

"You can't just quit a case because some asshole tells you to. Besides, I've made some promises that I have to keep."

"So what?"

"What do you mean, so what?"

"I mean, who cares what you promised? Why can't you walk away from something that is obviously very dangerous? Something that puts your personal safety in jeopardy."

I opened my eyes and sat up in the tub.

"Because that's the name of the game. Safety's an illusion. And in case you haven't figured it out, this matters to me. It matters to me that I do what I say I'm going to do. If I don't, then what good am I to anybody?"

We fell back into silence. Karla ran the rag over my busted arm and I flinched.

"Maybe you should go to the hospital."

"I'm fine."

"At least call Joanna and let her have a look at you."

"I'm fine."

Karla stopped scrubbing my arm. She ran the rag over my chest and stomach.

"What about the promises you've made me?" she said, her voice barely audible now. I didn't answer. I knew where she was headed with this line and didn't want any part of it. "You promised me things too, Nick. You said the cases you'd get working for lawyers would be puff cases. You said they'd be simple and you'd never be in harm's way. You promised you'd stop drinking."

"What do you want from me? I barely drink anything anymore. I work in a profession where sometimes shit happens that I can't control."

"I don't want to fight with you."

"Could have fooled me. I've done everything in my power to be the person you want me to be. I love you, I love your boy. I stayed in this godforsaken town for you. What more do you want?"

Karla rang out the washcloth and laid it across the corner of the tub. "Don't put that pressure on me," she said coolly. "That I'm the only reason you're here. That isn't fair."

"Okay, I'll lie. I stayed for the swampy summers and the icy winters. I stayed for the outdated, backwards culture and the quality of life."

"You want to know what I want?"

"I asked the question."

"I want to know that this is real. That we have a real future together. That this thing between us is enough for you. You're not just play-acting the part, emulating who you think you need to be for me to keep up the status quo, and then one day you're gonna get tired of it and be done."

Her voice wavered and she twisted away from me. I reached around and nudged her chin to make her look at me. Tears had pooled in her eyes.

"What's this all about?"

"Nothing. It's just—you say you love me and I hear it, but I don't always feel it. Sometimes it just feels like a facsimile of real emotion."

"A facsimile? You've been reading too many of those self-help books. What does that even mean, facsimile?"

"You say you're here, but you're only half here. At best. The rest of you is always somewhere else. Mired in the past or occupied with whatever business you've got going on. You're never all here. Never all in."

"What are you talking about, the past? Maybe I'm just bored with this bullshit conversation you keep coming back to, you ever think of that? This is who I am. This is what I do. If you're having buyer's remorse, sweetheart, there's still time to get a partial refund. We never signed a contract."

"Don't be cruel."

"I'm being cruel? I just got my ass handed to me. I look like I ran face first into a flock of cactuses, and now I have to deal with this fucking garbage."

"I shouldn't have said anything. It wasn't the right time."

"No, you shouldn't have, but it's said now, isn't it?"

"I'm sorry."

"I love you the best I can. I give you all I can give."

"Okay. You're right."

"Is that not enough?"

"No, it is."

Karla dipped the rag into the water again and began running it idly over my chest. I grabbed her hand to make her stop. She couldn't bring herself to look me in the eye.

"I need to know you're not going to leave," she whispered.

"I'm not going anywhere. I never will. I stayed in this town for you."

"Maybe you shouldn't have."

"What is that supposed to mean?"

"Nothing," Karla said.

"Nothing meaning everything."

"What if it's like you said? What if it's something you can't control?"

"Look at me," I said. "Look at me. Am I that hideous?"

She did a quick, rapid shake of her head to clear her senses, sniffled, and then set her fierce eyes on me.

"Nothing is going to happen to me, Karla. I'm not going anywhere."

She wasn't convinced. I couldn't blame her. I didn't believe a word of it myself. For whatever reason, whatever words you wanted to assign to it—love, fear, weakness, strength, preservation of the status quo—she decided to play along.

"Is that a promise?"

"I swear it."

"You're full of shit, Nick Malick."

"Possible," I conceded. "Come here."

She leaned in, slightly. She needed me to make up the rest of the distance. I reached out, caressed her face and pulled her toward me. She didn't object. We kissed softly and for a long time. When we parted and she sat back up she had fresh tears in her eyes and my blood on her lips. The desperation, however, had gone from her face, replaced with something else, resignation maybe. She wiped the blood off her mouth and got up from the tub. I reached out and gripped her wrist.

"I love you," I said.

"I know. I love you, too."

"It'd be a shame to let that dress go to waste."

Karla looked down between my legs. What she saw there made her cough up a laugh.

"You've got to be joking."

"Despite all outward appearances, my penis has absolutely no sense of humor."

"You're incorrigible," she said, twisting her wrist to extract it from my grip. She dabbed at the tears in her eyes and stepped backwards from the tub. I half expected her to tell me to fuck off again. Instead she faced me. Slowly, deliberately, she slipped the spaghetti straps off her shoulders. Watching her undress was my favorite pastime. Karla knew it and milked it for all that it was worth. She peeled the dress down, setting free her immense breasts, and shimmied it on down over the curves of her ribs, her smooth belly, her hips and thighs. She let the dress drop to the floor and stepped out. Beneath was a red thong, nothing else. She stood there on display, dauntless, her bare skin an unblemished canvas of pale cream. Hers was a body at the forefront of evolution. As if her ancestors had been selectively bred over generations to finally arrive here, now, in the perfect form. It was enough to make me believe in God and all the Revelations.

"Is this what you want?" she asked.

I tossed aside the sack of vegetables.

She allowed me to drink in the whole visage for another moment before turning on her heels and slinking into the adjoining bedroom. With every step her lush ass quaked. The red thong disappearing and reappearing in the slit. She slid onto the bed and stretched her limbs like a lazy cat about to sharpen its claws, angled her ass in the air.

I got out of the tub.

The sex was vigorous and greedy, as if we were trying to ruin one another; no words, only sounds, the weight of our bodies colliding, smothering, melting into one. Nothing existed outside of Karla's hands, her mouth, her neck, her skin, her sweat, her thighs clamped onto my neck. The tastes, tart and bitter, sweet, blood on our lips, salt in the crease of her leg. When it was over I lay there numb and panting, devoid of all senses, an empty husk of myself. Karla seemed restored. Her body glistened with the work we'd done. She propped herself up on an elbow, ran a finger over my chest and stomach, and gazed down to watch me wilt.

"Did I hurt you?"

"Head to toe."

Karla made an exasperated groan like I was clowning or being melodramatic. I wasn't. Her destruction of me was absolute. I couldn't move. I couldn't catch my breath. She rolled off the bed and slipped into a robe, went to the kitchen and came back with a couple tall glasses of water and peanut butter sandwiches. Neither of us had had anything to eat. I was too tired to chew.

"Davey's back," she said, between bites.

"Good."

"He's barricaded in his room."

"You think he heard us?"

"I assume that's the reason for the barricade."

I chugged the water and a little life came back into me. Karla nestled in next to me under the sheet and broached the prospect of house hunting over the weekend. In two years she had never pushed for marriage, but she never let up about getting a house. You had to give her credit, she knew the best time to bring the shit up. Karla was specific about what she wanted—a mid-century redbrick, three stories, tiled shingles—and where she wanted it, the Southside. She brought out her phone and showed me some pictures of the homes available that fit her specifications, went through the numbers of what we'd have to put down, what our mortgage would be, taxes, what she would do with each space, and so on. I bobbed my head, made all the appropriate noises and comments.

Getting a house was about the last thing in the world I wanted to do. I'd put Karla off, saying we needed more money, more time together, that we needed to wait until she graduated from nursing school and got a job. Truth was, I could think of nothing more torturous than having to mow the lawn every week, spread bags of mulch every spring, rake leaves every fall, string Christmas lights every winter, host barbeques and play nice with neighbors. Remodel room after room.

I'd go for the marriage in a heartbeat. A marriage was cheaper and easier to get out of, for one thing. Dividing a house in half, metaphorically speaking, was a monstrous pain in the ass. I'd done it once and wasn't eager for even the possibility of having to do it again. But now I was making decent money, Karla had gotten her nursing job, and I was fresh out of procrastinations. She wanted that house. She wanted her own appliances. More than that, she needed them: she needed the roots, the stability, something she could call her own. These were things she'd never had. And I wanted her. From the moment I laid eyes on her I was bewitched. In two years those chemicals hadn't worn off. If anything, they'd gotten more potent.

When we met I never thought I'd love, or be loved, ever again. I thought that part of me was broken and gone, never to return. Now here I was, lying in this bed, knowing unequivocally that I was about to buy a goddamn red-bricked money-sucking house on the Southside of Cain City. Mulch, grass, the works. How long before we'd have a dog that I'd have to walk every night and pick up shit after?

At ten o'clock we watched the news. The lead story was on the Cruise Avenue land sale to a development company called River Path Group. The anchor gave some background on the company, the large quantity of real estate they'd already purchased in town, and the proposed plans for the site.

They showed a three-dimensional simulation of what the property would look like when the project was completed, ran footage of that afternoon's celebration, and followed that with some spirited sound bites from three of the attendees. Ethel Rae Morris, an eighty-one-year-old lifetime Cain resident declared this was the best thing to happen to the city in decades. Leland Guthrie, a forty-seven-year-old dockworker, thought this was the first step toward making downtown a place where people would actually look forward to visiting and socializing as opposed to the ghost town it had been for years. And lastly, a thirty-two-year-old mother of three named Bethanie Stark said it'd be neat for her kids to throw pennies in the fountain and make wishes.

After the interviews they ran a short clip from a speech given by a representative of the River Path Group. A dapper middle-aged man wearing a suit stood on a platform with a small group of spectators in front of him. He raised a fist and shouted into a microphone, "It's been a long time coming, but the wait for Cain City to be brought into the 21st century is finally over." This elicited some whistles and hoots from the gathered crowd and seemed to spur the speaker on. "This company, with the help of you fine people, is wholly committed to restoring Cain City to its former glory!"

I wondered how far back this River Path guy was expecting to turn the clock. I'd been a resident of Cain City for seventeen years and had yet to see one glorious thing about the place.

"Ten days from now," said the news anchor, "construction crews are scheduled to break ground on the new compound. An exciting new era for downtown, for the city and for the state, really." From there they segued into a piece about a fortune cookie hoax perpetrated on Sing's, the only Chinese restaurant in town. Someone had switched out the positive, life-affirming fortunes with duplicate slips of paper that read, *One Day You Are Going To Die.* I laughed at that. Karla didn't see the humor in it.

"That's horrible," she said, admonishing me. "Think of who reads fortune cookies. Little kids. Think of them cracking open their cookie all excited to see what the future holds and that's what they get. Something morbid about dying."

"They're not lying, though," I retorted.

Karla gave me a cutting look.

"I'm just saying."

"Do you have to be so cynical all the time?"

"You're right, no, you're right. Ignorance is bliss."

Karla got out of the bed, threw off her robe and pulled a T-shirt and some drawstring pants out of a drawer.

"C'mon. I said you were right. When you're right, you're right. I shouldn't have laughed. What are you doing?"

"Nothing. I'm getting ready for bed."

"You're mad at me about fortune cookies now? C'mon, what's going on?"

"Nothing. I'm not mad. I'm tired and I'm going to bed, that's all."

She pulled the pants on and went into the bathroom. I heard the faucet come on, followed by the electric hum of her toothbrush. The news cut to commercial. And there he was: T-for-Truth himself, Scott T. Barnhard, alive and well and in high definition on the television screen. No one had thought to pull his ads from the air. He had a bunch of different ones running. Most had little to do with disability insurance. This particular ad featured a line of chorus girls doing kicks in a parking lot, as well as a local celebrity who had come in fourth place on one of those reality singing competitions. The college's football coach was also tossed in there for good measure. It was all a little confusing and I was too tired to make sense of the narrative. All the ads ended the same though. They cut to Barnhard, cocksure as ever, standing next to the chorus girls this time, imploring the viewer to take back control of their life. Then a pleasant little jingle followed by Barnhard in front of a green screen, saying, "Come see me, Scott T. And remember . . ."

"The T stands for truth," I muttered in harmony with him. At this point, my eyelids felt the gravitational pull of sleep. Before I succumbed to it, a couple final thoughts skipped through my head. Karla's been in the bathroom a while—when was the last time I slept—ah, that morning—the bench at the police station—seems like a month ago—what do I need to do when I wake up?—meet Hively, the judge . . . oh yeah, the judge . . .

Whatever was left slipped through the margins of my mind. I closed my eyes and fell off the face of the earth.

I don't know how long I was down, couldn't have been more than five minutes. Karla was shaking me awake. I'd gone so deep so fast it took me a second to figure out where I was and what the hell was going on.

"What's wrong?" I said.

"Look." She gestured to the television.

It was Birdie. She was on the news, standing at the mouth of an alley, which I recognized instantly to be The 4 ½. Hooker Row. One of the station's roving news reporters asked a question I didn't hear—the volume was low—and she thrust a microphone into Birdie's face. Renata was on there too, sulking in the corner of the frame behind Birdie.

"What is this?" I said to Karla.

"It's part of that series they're doing on people's lives in Cain City."

I grabbed the remote and cranked the volume. Birdie was in the middle of a diatribe. I scooted to the bottom edge of the bed and listened.

"People like to judge and think we're the problem. But we ain't the problem, we the by-product of the problem. You think we want to be out here in these streets? What we supposed to do? The people that are out here don't have no advantages. Nobody cares about us. We have to fend for ourselves. We aren't born with many choices in this world, and those choices get boiled down to nothing before we're old enough to know any different."

In the background, Renata nodded her head vigorously in support of everything Birdie was saying.

"And what nobody seems to realize is we wouldn't be out here if there wasn't a bunch of motherfuckers willing to pay for it." The curse was bleeped, but Birdie's lips were easy to read. She glared directly into the camera now, a portrait of defiance. "We. Are. Not. The. Problem," she declared. Then she turned back to the reporter. "We the solution."

"That's right," Renata hollered from the back.

"What kind of people come to see you out here?" the reporter prodded.

"Oh, you'd be surprised who we get down here."

"Mm-hmm, shocked," Renata added, though you could barely hear her since she was back from the mic.

The reporter didn't pay any attention to Renata. "What do you mean by that?" she asked Birdie.

"Just what I said. People think it's just riffraff, you know, low-class people that be coming down here, but we get all kinds. We get doctors, policemen, lawyers, government people, mailmen, everybody. You married?"

"I am."

"And right now you think, no way it could be my husband. She ain't talking about my man, but let me tell you something. It could be all y'alls."

Birdie stepped toward the camera and jabbed a finger that actually knocked the lens.

"What is she doing?" asked Karla.

"Trying to get herself killed."

Before the segment ended, I started ringing Birdie on the phone. My calls went straight to voicemail. I got my clothes on.

"What are you doing?" Karla asked.

"I have to go down there."

"Why?"

I made sure I had everything—wallet, keys, phone, gun—and made for the door. Karla followed me to the front of the apartment, helped me into my jacket.

"Does Birdie have something to do with that murdered lawyer?"

"Yeah, she does."

"And with the man who beat you up?"

"Yeah."

Karla drew a sharp breath and touched the tips of her fingers to her lips. Her eyes got wet.

"Okay. Be careful."

CHAPTER TWENTY
LITTLE PIG, LITTLE PIG

I parked on the sloping street next to the side entrance of the Royal Vista. Before I got out of my car, I scoped the area to make sure there were no Momos or Mike Mikes or thugs with scarred heads milling about.

Everything looked quiet, serene. A few cars on the avenue, no foot traffic. I got out and scaled the three steps to the side door, punched in the code and entered. The elevator wasn't working, so I hoofed it to the fifth floor, careful to tread silently and check all the blind corners in the stairwell. Some drunk stinking of booze was passed out on the third-floor landing, snoring loudly, but that was it. Nobody else was around.

I pounded on the door of apartment 512. No answer. The old man a few doors down threw open his door and stepped into the hall ready to give somebody the business. He saw it was me, turned his fat ass around and went back in. I kept beating the door. Something inside the apartment stirred.

"I hear you in there. Open the door or I'll kick it in. Your choice. One way or another I'm coming through."

Some shuffling. The door creaked open. Renata, in an oversized white T that extended down past her knees, yawned and rubbed her glazed eyes.

"Damn, man. What you doing? Trying to huff and puff and blow our door down or some shit?" Then, as I came into focus. "Whoa, what happened to you?"

"I ran into a wall."

"How many times?"

"Quite a few. Where's Birdie?"

"How I know?" Renata shouted over her shoulder, "Bir-diiiieeee? Birdie!?" She turned back around. "See. She ain't here."

"You don't know where she is?"

"Nuh-uh."

"Know when she'll be back?"

Renata sniffed and wiped her nose on the back of her hand, then looked to see if anything had come off on it. I repeated my question.

"Lemme go fetch my crystal ball and I'll tell you."

I pushed past Renata and made for Birdie's room in the back.

"What you doing? I didn't invite your ass in."

"Good thing I'm not a vampire."

"Huh?"

Renata trailed me down the hall, fussing all the way. "Who does this mug think he is? Man, you got some gumption. Anybody ever told you that? Barging in here like you own the motherfucker."

Birdie's door wasn't fully shut. A strip of light shined from inside. I pushed it all the way open. The lamp was on. There was a suitcase on the bed, half-filled with clothes, couple pairs of shoes. The colorful scarves that had been tied to her bedposts were stuffed in a side pocket. The closet was open. In there were some storage bins and empty hangers. I glanced at the ceiling panels above the bed where Birdie said she kept her money stashed. None of them looked like they'd been disturbed.

"What's that all about?" I asked, indicating the suitcase.

Renata peered past me, made a puzzled expression and shrugged. "I dunno. Maybe she fitting to go on vacation."

I'd hoped Renata would say something snarky about how Birdie was packing to move in with me, but if that was indeed

Birdie's plan, Renata seemed to know nothing of it. The goons who had threatened Tom Orvietto implied that they had him and the girl he saw, Destiny, on video. If that were true, there was a fair chance Birdie was being filmed as well. I frisked the room.

"I'm gonna tell her you doing this," Renata said as I looked behind the vanity. "Invading her privacy. She ain't gonna like it."

"You do that. Tell her to answer her damn phone while you're at it, will ya?"

The room was so sparse and clean there weren't many places to search. I checked the dresser, the curtains, the closet, and came up empty. No hidden cameras.

"What you looking for?" Renata asked.

"Nothing. Saw you on the news tonight."

"Oh yeah? We don't have cable. How'd we look?"

"Like two idiots who want to get arrested. Birdie didn't say when she was gonna be back?"

"Nuh-uh."

"You think it'll be tonight?"

"Dunno, just depend."

"On what?"

"What she doing, I guess. Man, you thick."

I scanned the room one last time and walked out. "Tell Birdie to call me," I said. "It's important."

"Yeah, okay."

CHAPTER TWENTY-ONE
THOSE SNEAKY DEMONS

I drove back to the high school with my windows rolled down to keep me awake. I parked in the lot, trudged up the portico steps and the three flights to Karla's apartment. Everything was still, quiet. I stripped my clothes off and collapsed on the bed.

Karla stirred, murmured, "What time is it?"

"After one."

"Birdie okay?"

"Yeah," I lied. "She's fine. Go back to sleep."

I closed my eyes, felt myself diving toward unconsciousness. On the dresser next to my face, my phone lit up, buzzed two quick vibrations that indicated a text. I fumbled around, got hold of the phone and squinted against the glow of the screen to read the name.

Birdie.

I sat up and read the text.

I'm ready. come scoop me tomorrow

I texted back. *I came to your place*

Birdie: *I heard*

Me: *Bad idea to go on news*

Birdie: *I don't care. fuck em all*

Me: *You home now?*

Birdie: *Yeah.*

Me: *I'll come get you now then*

Birdie: *no got work*

Me: *get out of it. I'm coming*

Birdie: *no u not. he already here. one last one. then its over*

Me: *Who's there?*

Birdie: *not ur bizness. Tomorrow*

Me: *What time?*

Birdie: *Whenevs*

Me: *I'll be by in the morning*

The little thought bubble popped up momentarily, went away, and didn't return. I set the phone aside and lay back next to Karla.

"You need to go?" she asked.

"No." I gently ran my fingers over her eyelids to shut them. "Sleep."

And that's what I tried to do. Sleep. But it wouldn't come. My whole body felt stiff and swollen. Everything hurt. Breathing hurt. The text exchange with Birdie had gotten my mind to racing. I thought about Barnhard's murder, the Stenders, the blackmailing of Tom Orvietto, Birdie servicing the more nefarious of Cain City's upper crust, appointment by appointment, how all these things were linked, how they had to be, but why, and to what end?

It was a puzzle. A puzzle missing half its pieces. Nothing was going to be accomplished by turning it over and over in my cerebral cortex at three o'clock in the morning, but that didn't stop my brain from trying. It wanted to magically solve the damn thing before sunrise. I tried to force quit all conscious thoughts. This only served to keep me awake. After a while, the circuitry in my brain went haywire, synapses zinging all over the place. A thousand thoughts competing with each other, jockeying for position. *This must be what schizophrenia feels like,* I thought.

Minutes crawled by. I watched the light outside change from shades of black to shades of gray until five-thirty a.m., when I finally cursed myself, got up and splashed some water in my face, got dressed and out of the apartment before anybody else was awake. I stopped by my office downstairs and straightened up the back bedroom a bit—stuffed all my crap in the closet, cleared out a few drawers for Birdie's things, made sure the cable box was working, put some fresh sheets on the bed. One last look around the place. It was cramped and dusty, but good enough for the time being.

The Cain County courthouse was the oldest and most expansive building, square-footage-wise, in the city. The grounds took up an entire block in the middle of downtown. The Beaux-Arts styled architecture was stately and imposing, which, depending on who you talked to and what side of the law they fell on, gave the impression of either a prison or a palace. Rising from the top was a three-tiered clock tower that was capped by a gold dome. I was admiring the dome when Willis Hively pulled his Celica to the curb out front of the courthouse ten minutes before nine. He stepped out looking fresh in one of his cut suits, dark brown with a crisp dress shirt and green tie. Next to him I looked like the neighborhood pauper. I greeted Hively with a coffee. He thanked me, got one look at my barked face and blanched.

"Jesus Christ, man, what happened to you?"

I recapped the altercation with the scarred thug in the Red Head's parking lot: the ambush, the lopsided beatdown, the plucked eye, and the five-mile-an-hour getaway. When I was done, Hively gestured to the lower third of my face.

"Your mouth is bleeding."

I dabbed at my lip, came away with red on my fingers.

"Shit, too much talking," I said, jutting my head forward so the blood didn't drip all down my front. I went to my truck, got a napkin out of the console and pressed it against the lip.

"Why didn't you call me? Or the police?"

I shrugged. "No plates. Reckon it didn't make much difference whether I told you last night or right now."

Hively thought about that, figured I was probably right, and moved on. "I know who that is. Real name is Buddy Cleamons. Folks call him Buddy The Face because he used to fancy himself a ladies' man before he caught his own hair on fire. He's a Stender."

"Yeah, I put that together. How'd he catch his own hair on fire?"

"Who knows? Lot of product, I guess. We'll put out an APB on him, check with the hospitals, see if anybody's seen him. You took one of his eyes?"

"Yeah."

"Jesus. You've got a knack for taking out eyes, huh? First Teddy Horseman, now Buddy Cleamons."

Two years ago I'd been goaded into a bar fight with a drunken imbecile, smacked him across the face with a bottle and blinded him in one eye. An eyewitness told police that Teddy had started the fight and that I had acted in self-defense. If you squinted hard enough, it looked close to the truth, so I was never charged with anything. Hively had been the one to spring me from jail.

"Guess I do," I said. "What happened with Sturges last night? Momo lead him anywhere?"

"Yeah, he led him down Four Pole Road into the west end to where it runs parallel with the tracks down there. Momo bolted across in front of an oncoming train. Sturges lost him."

"So Momo picked up the tail right away."

Hively lifted the coffee to his lips. "I think that's safe to assume." He took a swallow and his Adam's apple leapt in his throat. He made a gagging sound and spat the coffee out onto the grass.

"Careful," I said. "You almost ruined your snazzy shoes."

"This coffee is cold as shit."

"I put a lid on it."

"When, last night?"

"Couple hours ago."

"How long you been here?"

"Couple hours."

"Why?"

"Couldn't sleep."

Hively tossed the rest of the coffee out and puckered his mouth trying to scrape the taste off his tongue.

"So you've just been waiting here for the last two hours?" he said.

"I fiddled around on the internet, looked for anything interesting about the Stenders." I nodded in the direction of the courthouse. "Or the judge."

"Find anything?"

"The Stenders don't have much of a digital footprint. But did you know our honorable Judge Blevins presided over a criminal court for four years before switching to the appellate court?"

"I did not. That mean something to you?"

"Dunno, but I'd be interested to see what his record was, what cases were tried in front of him, ask him why he switched."

"All right." Hively nodded. "Let me handle the talking, okay? I'll work it in."

"It's your show. How you gonna play it?"

"Just two friendly and dedicated officers of the law trying to get to the bottom of a suspicious death. Crossing our I's, dotting our T's, nothing more. See if we can get him to let his guard down."

I nodded. "Couple problems. One, I'm not an officer of the law. Two, I'm not in a very friendly mood."

"That's why I'm doing the talking," said Hively. "You just stand there and try not to bleed all over the place."

We walked into the building, passed through security, and ascended the circular stairs of the rotunda to the second floor, Hively's fancy shoes clacking all the way, echoing to the top of the dome. Judge Blevins's chambers were down the corridor past the assessor and probate offices. When we walked in, his clerk had the phone pinned in the crook of her neck and was riffling through stacks of files on her desk. She was young and attractive, save for the head of frizzy blonde hair that, coupled with her beleaguered expression, made her look like the before side on one of those hair commercials. She blew some frizz out of her eyes and, getting her first clear look at my mucked-up face, recoiled as though whatever was going on with me might be communicable. She waved in the general direction of a couch. We sat there. The clerk put whoever she was on the phone with on hold and patched a line through to the judge.

"Your nine o'clock is here. Yes . . . Mm-hmm . . . okay . . . almost." She pressed a couple more buttons, cupped her hand over the receiver and leaned toward us. "He'll be right—"

Before the clerk could finish her sentence, Rutherford Blevins came barging out of the adjoining door, giving her a start. She squealed and bounced in her seat a little. The files on top of the stacks began to slip. The clerk lurched to catch them before they fell off the desk and ended up knocking a good number of them onto the floor. Dead trees went flying. She immediately got down on her knees and began gathering the pages.

The judge marveled at the paper carnage scattered across the floor, then turned his attention to us. "Gentlemen," he boomed. Blevins was a tall, lanky man with a distinguished air about him. He had a full head of coarse white hair and neatly trimmed gray eyebrows and sideburns to go along with it. His face had a blunt, sturdy quality that harkened back to a different era, like it should be carved into a mountainside, or put on money. He was already decked out in his judge's robe, ready for court.

We stood from the couch. The judge strode our way, smiling wide enough to make his eyes disappear. He extended his arms and gave Hively, then me, a vigorous two-handed handshake. I took Blevins to be around sixty, though with all the verve he put on display, he could easily be mistaken for a much younger man. Hively made introductions.

"The police are farming out cases to private investigators now?" the judge inquired. "I didn't know things had gotten that desperate."

"Only when the circumstances call for it," Hively said.

"And these circumstances call for it?"

"They do."

"I see." The judge turned sullen. "Scott T. Barnhard," he said, a wisp of regret in his voice. His accent had too much music in it to be local, sounded like it belonged a state or two south of here. "What a promising life cut short, am I right?" he continued. "That kid had it all, the smarts, the drive. He was a force to be reckoned with in the courtroom too, let me tell you. A real bull. Lawyers around here didn't want to go toe to toe with him, no sir. No, Scott had the world by the short hairs, so to speak." The judge looked off in the middle distance and grimaced. "Shame," he sighed. "It's a real shame."

"He was hardly a kid," I said.

Judge Blevins fixed me with his best wizened-old-man expression. "Well, no, you're right. You get to be my age, thirty-eight years in this profession under my belt, the definition of what a kid is changes, I suppose."

"We're sorry to bother you about this," Hively cut in. "We just have a few questions regarding your professional relationship with Mr. Barnhard."

"My relationship with Scott extended much further than the professional arena."

"Oh?"

"Most certainly. I thought that was why you wished to speak with me. When I was in the private sector Scott was something of a protégé. I'd go so far as to say I was the reason he entered law in the first place. Did you know, when Scott was in high school he interned with my law firm?"

"We did not know that."

"I still remember what I said to him that got him interested in the field. I took them—there were always three, so him and the two other interns—I took them into one of the courtrooms here in this building, I sat them down in the jury box, and I told them the most awesome thing about being a part of the law is that we are upholding the Constitution, a document that has shaped the history of this country and of the world, and by doing that we become a part of that history. We influence that history. However large or small that may be, we are a part of it now and forever, and that contribution can never be erased. Our actions will echo until the last man stands." Here, Judge Blevins glanced back at his clerk. "Now, that's what I tell all my pets. Isn't it, Judy?"

Judy, still combing through the drawers, gave a perfunctory smile.

"It's become something of a running joke now. Maybe I am a little romantic about it, but that doesn't make it any less true. I still remember the way Scott lit up when I said that." The judge cocked his head and stared at a spot in the wall behind us for a spell. "I hadn't thought of that moment for years and years, but it came back to me when I got word of his passing. Clear as day." Blevins's eyes snapped back to the present. "Scott always had demons that'd poke their heads up from time to time. I'd hoped they would never catch up with him. But that's not the way life works, is it? The demons always come to collect their bounty, eventually."

Hively nodded sympathetically, then said, "Did you know that Mr. Barnhard was being investigated by the U.S. Attorney's office?"

Judge Blevins again glanced back at Judy, who either hadn't heard Hively's question or was purposefully ignoring it.

"Would you like to do this somewhere else?"

"Scott did mention something along those lines, but I didn't know there was a full-on investigation taking place. He assured me that nothing was amiss with his practice, that he followed the letter of the law and everything would be cleared up in no time. I take it this wasn't necessarily true."

"No. He was apparently defrauding the government for rather large sums of money."

This piece of news didn't seem to shock the good judge.

"Define *large*?"

"Millions."

"Millions? Plural?" Judge Blevins sucked some air in through his teeth. "Scott always did think he was smarter than everyone else. He was, to be honest. But this led to him quite often taking shortcuts. He was so talented, usually he got away with it."

"Not this time," said Hively.

"Those sneaky demons," I said.

Blevins clamped his teeth together and winced. "Indeed."

"No one from the U.S. Attorney's office has come to talk to you about Barnhard?" Hively asked.

"No. This is the first I've heard of it."

The judge looked at the clock on the wall and suggested we move our discussion to his courtroom, explaining that he liked to be in the empty space for a few minutes before it filled with lawyers and claimants and their families. Proceedings could get a little raucous, especially the families, he told us, and this was a ritual that helped to center him before the chaos of the day. A meditation of sorts.

We exited his chambers and walked down the main corridor to Courtroom Three. Along the way Judge Blevins greeted every person we passed with some personal anecdote, asking after their children or their golf games, what have you. He asked one lady about the perennials in her garden. I wondered whether he was stumping for mayor or if he was just the most gregarious man I'd met in my forty years of life.

He produced a ring of keys from beneath his robe and let us into the courtroom. Behind the judge's bench was a bank of high windows, the American flag, the West Virginia state flag, and tall shelves stocked with volumes of very distinguished-looking books. High on the walls were painted portraits of judges past. I looked around for the painting of Blevins. There wasn't one.

"I find an empty courtroom has the same feel to it that an empty sanctuary does," the judge mused, lowering himself into the front row of the gallery. He took a long sniff, as if to inhale the purity of the room. Hively leaned against the railing. I stayed standing. Hively made some small talk before transitioning back into the inquiry, asking the judge where he was from, if he preferred being a judge to being a litigator, that kind of thing. Turns out Blevins *was* from a few states down on the map. Alabama.

"How'd you end up in Cain City?" Hively asked.

"I was accepted into WVU's law school, met a girl. She was from Cain City, blah blah blah, you know the story."

"I do. Sounds like Nick here."

"Oh, really?" the judge said, his eyes twinkling with interest. "Where are you from, Mr. Malick?"

"Chicago."

"Chicago, my kind of town. That must have been quite a culture shock, from there to here."

"I think Cain City comes as a shock no matter where you come from."

"That's true, that's true. There are good people here though. Hardworking people. Like the two of you. People who care. That want to make this city as it once was. Make it great again."

"It was great once? Must have missed that day."

"Certainly. Certainly it was. The best river city north of Memphis, I dare say. This was before your time, I imagine. Do you miss Chicago?"

"Only when I'm there."

"Isn't that funny how that works? I feel the same about Birmingham. And the lady, how'd that pan out?"

"Divorced."

"Ah, same for me. Happens to the best of us."

"Yeah, it happened to me, too."

The judge looked at me, perplexed for a moment, then picked up on the jape, tapped a finger to his nose and pointed at me. "Clever. Kids?"

"No."

"At least you were spared that ignominy. I have four.

Grown now, supporting themselves, thank God. More than I could say for their mother. Milked me for every penny, never had to work a day in her life."

I gestured to the portraits. "Where's yours?"

"They paint you when you retire or die. Apparently, they want all the years of service to show on your face."

"Which will it be for you? Retirement or death?"

"I don't enjoy fishing or golfing enough. This is what I do. So I'm going to stay in the game until I die or go mad, whichever comes first."

Hively jumped back in. "Thirty-eight years you've been at it, you said. That's pretty amazing. Where'd you work when you first started?"

"Out of law school I was hired by a little firm called Thurber and Grayson."

"Is that the same Thurber that now belongs to Leach, McKinney & Thurber?"

"No, not Buck Thurber. His father, Alan, was who hired me. That's who first showed me the ropes here in Cain."

"But the firm is the same one that later became Leach, McKinney & Thurber," Hively clarified.

"It did. This was long before it had reached the lofty heights on the tenth floor of the Carpenter Building." He said this with just enough of a hint of derision that made me wonder whether his split with Thurber and Grayson wasn't the least bit acrimonious. I saw Hively pull out his Steno pad and scribble something down, and I filed it in the back of my mind for later.

Blevins continued, "It was just a mom and pop shop back then. Little three-room place over on the east end of downtown."

"Huh. And you worked there all those years until you became an appellate judge six years ago?"

"No, no. I switched firms in around 1989, went in with Winston Engles for a long time before becoming a criminal judge for four years, which led me to my current position."

"You were a criminal judge? We didn't know that."

Blevins smiled benevolently. "I've had quite the vagabond career, I suppose. Good fodder for my autobiography."

"What prompted the switch? From criminal to this?"

Judge Blevins sat upright and placed his hands on his thighs, again taking time to arrange his words.

"It was burnout, if I'm being honest. All I saw, day to day, was the absolute dreck of humanity. I started to lose faith in my fellow man. I lost my empathy. I couldn't be impartial anymore. This position opened up. I thought, at least here, maybe I could do some good, so I went for it."

A door off to the side of the judge's bench opened. A sheriff's deputy, bailiff, and a person I assumed to be a stenographer came in. They were yucking it up about their weekend plans, something to do with a cooler full of beer and a pontoon boat, when they spotted us and hushed their mouths.

"Everything alright, sir?" the deputy asked.

Blevins told them everything was fine and informed them as to who we were.

"There's a big group already out there, sir, waiting to get in."

"Is it 9:30 already?" Blevins shook the sleeve of his robe up his forearm and looked at his wristwatch. "So it is. Gentlemen, I'm sorry to have to cut this short, but I've got a courtroom to run."

Hively apologized for occupying his time and said, "We just have a couple more questions, Judge, if you don't mind."

Judge Blevins's eyes turned steely. "I don't know what more I could possibly help you gentlemen with. Scott's death is a great loss for me personally. There's not much else to say."

"I'm sorry. Just real quick," Hively demurred. "We can finish now and not have to come back later."

Blevins looked behind him to the double doors. There was a murmur of noise from the gathering crowd beyond them. He tapped on his thigh impatiently before raising two fingers toward the civil servants. "Give us two minutes, will you please?"

"Sure, sure," the deputy said. They didn't leave the room, but they stayed a polite distance away, back by the flags. Hively set his jaw in such a way that I knew he was about to go to work on the judge.

"It's our understanding that most of your cases are split evenly between yourself and Judge Dunlap across the hall, is that correct?"

"That's right."

"But three-quarters of Scott Barnhard's disability cases were heard in your court. How do you explain that discrepancy?"

The judge contemplated his next words and leaned forward as if they could only be spoken with the utmost discretion. "Scott was brash, uncompromising. He rubbed some people the wrong way. A lot of people. Vicky was one of them, unfortunately. They were natural enemies. Vicky is an old-school bra-burning feminist, and Scott would feign this machismo, say misogynistic things just to piss her off I think. If that was his plan, it went swimmingly. She loathed him in the same way that I loathe, say, a fat-fingered proctologist with long nails." Blevins chuckled to himself. "Anyway, she knew that I had a bit more of a rapport with him, so she and I came to a kind of quid pro quo. I'd take on more of Scott's cases. In turn, anyone who got under my skin, she would take those cases in her courtroom. Now, I know that's probably not the most ethical way to go about it, but it's perfectly legal, I must point out. You see a lot of things in this profession. Things that can grind you down if you're not careful. In my opinion, whatever can be done to alleviate that is better for all involved in the end. I'm sure your profession is very similar in that respect."

"Judge Dunlap can verify this agreement that you had?" Hively asked.

"Yes, of course."

"So maybe he learned it from you," I put in.

"Excuse me?" Judge Blevins scowled. His neat gray eyebrows bunched toward each other. "Learned what exactly?"

"How to cut corners. You said yourself, Barnhard was your protégé. He sees you do things like palm off cases to others, maybe he thinks it's okay to work the system a little for one's own gain or convenience."

"I hardly think there's a correlation between my placating a workplace conflict between colleagues and extorting the government," the judge huffed.

"Maybe," I conceded. "But I was told once that if it's in the cat, it's in the kitten."

"That so? Well, someone once told the honey bee to be careful where it puts its stinger."

"Did that sound like a veiled threat to you?" I said to Hively, feigning as though I were puzzled. Hively didn't answer. His countenance didn't change. He scrutinized Blevins.

"It's a figure of speech," the judge spat impatiently.

"Really? I've never heard that one before."

"There was nothing veiled about it. This has always been the problem with the police. You're like a bad wife. You take everything someone says and you twist it around however you can, however you have to, to fit your own purposes."

"That's funny coming from a lawyer."

Blevins was getting mad now. He glared at me as though he wanted to take out the good cutlery and slice me from my trachea to taint, or vice versa. Hively intervened before the judge or I said something inflammatory that neither of us could walk back.

"Did Barnhard have any enemies that you were aware of, sir?"

"Enemies?" Blevins peeled his eyes off me and put them on Hively. "How should I know? I just got through telling you he rubbed people the wrong way."

"Yeah, but we're not talking about the kind of enemies that snub you in the hallway or unfriend you on Instaface," I said. "We're talking about the kind that hold you down by the scruff of the neck and drown you in your own pool. Those kind of enemies."

"Instaface? What are you talking about? Are you telling me that Scott was murdered? Is that what you're alluding to?"

"Now you're putting it together," I said sardonically. "Barnhard intimated that there were other people involved in this little con of his. People in much more influential positions than he was. You know anything about that?"

"I—but—that's not—why would I know anything about that? What are you trying to say?"

I gave him an affable grin. "I think I'm saying it." My lip split with the grin. Blood ran down my chin. I kept the smile going.

Blevins gaped at me. "Are you here because you think I'm a part of this ridiculous scheme? Not because Scott and I were close? That's—that's ludicrous. Jesus Christ, you're bleeding all over yourself."

"Oh, you noticed."

"What happened to your face?"

"Rabid squirrel."

A quizzical expression crossed the judge's face. Then his whole countenance puckered like an asshole. He was about to give me a piece of his mind, but was preempted by the deputy hollering, "Judge," from back by the bench. The deputy gestured to the courtroom doors. The cacophony out there had grown louder. "The enemies are at the gates. We gotta get started soon."

"You heard the man," Blevins said, shrugging his shoulders and flipping his palms up, as if he didn't select the decorum for the courtroom. "Duty calls." He stood from his seat, knees creaking like a couple of rickety floorboards, clutched his low back and arched backwards to stretch it out. "Never get old, gentlemen. Age is a pitiless bitch. Frank here will let you out. Frank?"

Hively shook Judge Blevins's hand again and thanked him for his time.

"Hope it's been helpful," Blevins said earnestly. Then to me, "You ought to get those injuries looked at."

"Looked at them in the mirror this morning."

The judged tutted at me as though I were a mischievous child. He swatted the air like he was trying to get rid of a gnat and ambled off toward the bench. Deputy Frank led us to the back of the courtroom.

"So you guys are city gumshoes, huh?" Frank said. "It's enough to come in contact with these degenerates in a courtroom every day, but facing them down on the street? Forget it. Brutal."

"Yeah, you've got it real cush in here," Hively said. "Don't ever leave."

"I don't plan on it."

I stopped and swiveled around. The judge was climbing the three steps to his perch on the bench. "One more question, Judge," I said.

The judge waved his hand dismissively. "Go ahead."

"Back when you were a criminal judge, you ever have any cases involving the Stenders?"

Blevins put his knuckles on the bench at the top of the rise and leaned forward over them.

"In this line, son," he said, "you are bound to come across the Stenders at one time or another."

CHAPTER TWENTY-TWO
MALICK'S PROVERB

We parted the crowd that had gathered outside the courtroom doors and made our way to a quiet corner of the hallway, next to the bathrooms and water fountain.

Hively said, "So much for getting him to let his guard down. You can't help yourself, can you?" He held his tie and bent over to drink from the fountain.

"Guess not. Sorry if I stepped on your toes."

Hively came back up, wiped his mouth on the back of his hand. "No, it was good. We might not get another clean run at him. Might as well have a go. What's your take? You think he's on the level or is he hiding something?"

"He's smooth. Says all the right things."

"Didn't deny his relationship with Barnhard."

"No, he did the opposite, didn't he? He leaned into it."

"It's possible he just had a soft spot for the guy," Hively suggested.

"Possible."

"You don't buy it? You think he's too smooth?"

"I think he's way too smooth. Barnhard as much as said there were people involved that were higher on the totem pole. Who else could he have been referring to?"

He frowned at this. "I don't know."

"Who benefits from Barnhard dying?"

Hively thought about that. "Sounds like maybe a lot of people."

"Maybe. Did you see how the judge reacted to my face?"

"He didn't."

"Not at all. Everybody else says something or at least flinches, like his clerk, Judy, did. But it doesn't register with him. No double take, nothing. Like he already knew about it. He didn't like it when I started in on him a little harder either."

"Who would?"

"Fair enough."

"How could he have known you took a beating last night?"

"I don't know, but I'd like to find out. Here's what else I'd like to know—" A man in a suit stepped out of the bathroom and slid in between us for a long slurp from the fountain before moving on. I waited for him to get out of earshot before resuming my thought. "I'd like to know how many of the cases Blevins presided over involved the Stenders. What the results were."

"I'll get Sturges on it," said Hively. "You know what I'd like to find out? If that little *quid pro quo* with Judge Dunlap worked the way he says it worked."

"Did you pick up on the 'lofty heights of the tenth floor' bit?" I asked.

"Yeah, wrote it down."

"I'd be interested to know if something happened at his old firm that caused the split."

"You mean his old firm that eventually became the firm you're currently employed by?"

"One and the same."

We agreed that before we left, Hively would check to see if we could get an audience with Judge Dunlap, and I'd pay another visit to Rutherford Blevins's frizzy-haired clerk, Judy, see what information I could glean from her.

"You know, it's too bad I can't trust you as far as I can piss," Hively said. "We do all right together."

"Yeah, well, I only play well with others in short spurts."

"You ever think about joining back up? Way I hear it, Hale gave you a standing offer to come back into the fold, same rank."

"He's mentioned it."

Hively waited for further elucidation, which I felt no need to give.

"You considering it?" he asked.

"Oh, I dunno. How would you feel if I came back on?"

Hively flinched like there was a glitch in his wiring. He measured me before answering honestly. "Conflicted."

"Relax. I'm not one for institutions."

"Yet, funny thing. Here you are"—he waved his hand to indicate the grand building in which we stood—"always buzzing around the largest one in all the land."

I shrugged. "Gotta make a living."

"Uh-huh. Keep telling yourself that."

"There's a big difference between being on the outside looking in or on the inside looking out," I said.

"Yeah," Hively agreed. "You can effect a lot more change, a lot more good from the inside."

"Aren't you cute, still thinking your effort in all this mess amounts to a hill of beans. Listen, you want to be a man of the people, fight the good fight, that's your prerogative."

"So you're just out for yourself now, that's it?"

"Why would you want me back, anyway? You don't trust me, remember? Just yesterday you were trying to pin it on me and toss me in the clink."

Hively looked at me with an incredulous expression. He opened his mouth as though he were about to refute this assertion when, all of a sudden, his face lit up with what I assumed was the heretofore forgotten revelation that he'd tried to jam me up with Barnhard's murder just two day previous.

"That's right." He nodded mirthfully. "I'd forgotten. Never mind."

"Fuck off. Go do your job, honey bee."

We split up. Hively into Courtroom Two, me back down the corridor and into Blevins's chambers. Judy was gone. The file stacks were gone. I snooped around Judy's desk a bit, didn't find anything interesting—PC was password protected, no calendar, drawers were locked—so I planted myself on the couch and waited.

Twenty minutes later she came in through the hallway door with a scone in one hand and a cup of tea in the other. She nibbled on the scone, chased it with the tea, and didn't notice me on the couch until she sat at her desk and reached to boot up her computer.

"Lordy mercy!" she shrieked, nearly tumbling from her seat. Half the tea splashed onto her lap and desktop. She lifted her arms and assessed the spill. "Shit."

"You're a jumpy thing, aren't you?"

Judy set the teacup down, flicked some of the liquid off her fingertips, and pulled a wad of tissues from the box beside her computer. She layered the tissues over the puddle on her desk and dabbed at her skirt. "I'm sorry," she fretted. "The judge is in session. He usually takes a break at eleven or so. If you'd like to question him further, you can come back to see if he's available then."

"That's okay. I'm here for you."

"Me?" Her nervous eyes flashed to both exits, calculating distances, assessing which direction provided the best chance of escape if she needed to flee. I don't know what I did to strike the fear of God into the girl, but she looked as though she were on the verge of panic.

"Nothing big," I said, standing. "Couple questions."

She scooted forward to the edge of her seat. "I'm not sure how I can be of any help to your investigation."

"Tell you what, I'll ask the questions, you give the answers, and I'll be the *judge* of whether or not it adds up to anything."

"I see what you did there," Judy said, taking a breath and relaxing her posture. Her eyelids did a little involuntary flutter. "I don't think Judge Blevins would like me talking to you without his permission."

"That's fine," I said, smiling as much as I could without re-opening the gash in my lower lip. "I'll fetch my colleague and we'll take you down to the station if you'd prefer."

"No, I can't—I've got work to do. I don't have time for that."

"Won't take a minute," I assured her.

"Fine," Judy replied dubiously. She patted her frizzy hair to make sure all of it was accounted for. "But you're wasting your time. I don't know anything about Scott T. Barnhard."

"The judge you work for saw him in court every week. Rendered verdicts on dozens of his cases every month. I'm betting you know something, even if you don't know what that something is."

"That should be a proverb."

"Oh, I'm full of them, just wait."

"What do you need to ask me?" she said, a tad too snippy for my liking. "I've got too much work to do and too little time to do it."

"You're the one making jokes. How often was Scott T. Barnhard in this office?"

"This office? Quite a bit. As the judge told you, the two of them were close. They'd lunch once or twice a week."

"You ever hear them talk about anything other than work?"

"Like what?"

"Life. Women, men, hobbies, fleecing the government for a few million dollars, anything."

"What? No. What are you talking about? Judge Blevins doesn't have any hobbies that I know of."

"What about Barnhard?"

"What about him?"

"What was he like? Nice guy? Funny? Cocky?"

Judy began to respond but hesitated.

"He ever hit on you?"

"No, nothing like that. I mean, he was flirty, but they're all flirty."

"What then?"

Words were on the tip of Judy's tongue, I could tell. But whatever is was, some piece of confidence, a revelation, an insight, she stifled it. Instead, she answered my question with a query of her own.

"Why are the police dredging up information about Scott Barnhard anyway? He's dead. He's gone. Let the man rest in peace."

"Well, the man was murdered. It's our job to find out who did it. So the resting in peace part is gonna have to be put on hold for the time being."

The murder slant was news to Judy, but it didn't compel her to divulge anything of note. I prodded her a bit more on Barnhard, on Judge Blevins. In response I got a bunch of stock answers that'd make her boss's chest swell with pride. She'd decided to keep her lips sealed. Nothing I said was going to loosen them. For shits and giggles, I asked her if the judge had ever done anything that might be considered unethical. This, of all things, got her seething. Apparently her devotion for her boss overwhelmed her fear of my jacked-up face. She dropped the wet kitten act and gave me a thorough scolding for attempting, in the privacy of his own office, to *impugn* the honorable Rutherford Blevins's character.

"Can you use smaller words?" I said. "I don't speak the King's English."

"Surely even someone as dense as you can infer context."

I stared at her blankly, as though she were speaking Greek. She continued her lecture on Judge Blevins, the great man, a beacon of morality, the most upstanding civil servant she had ever personally encountered, a man who had devoted his whole life to the betterment of this festering ass-boil of a town. Her words, not mine. She prattled on another minute or two. If Judy was to be believed, Judge Blevins was no mere man, but a deity here on Earth. When she was done with the soliloquy I looked at her with newfound admiration. She'd morphed, in front of my very eyes, from a mousy soft touch into a veritable firebrand.

I made a show of examining her like a strange artifact, then stood to leave. "All right, Judy, I get it. You want to be him when you grow up."

"I'd be honored to have a career half as varied and rewarding as Judge Blevins's has been."

"Jesus, if you laid it on any thicker we'd both have to pull our feet out."

"*Excuse* me?"

"Varied is an understatement," I said and walked out.

I made my way over to Courtroom Two, which had the exact same layout as Blevins's courtroom. Only differences were the faces on the portraits that lined the walls. Judge Vicky Dunlap was in the middle of declining a claim.

"There is nothing here to indicate to the court," Dunlap said in a droll, uninflected tone, "that you are not capable of walking out those doors back there and going to work. The only factor stopping you from obtaining gainful employment, far as I can see, is your own abject laziness."

"Ma'am, I been all the way to Charleston at one end and Pikeville at the other," the claimant pleaded. He was a thin-limbed man in a short-sleeved dress shirt tucked into some jeans. "There just ain't no jobs left anywhere in a hundred-mile radius. None that I'm fit for."

Judge Dunlap leaned forward and pointed a bony finger straight down to the ground. "On the first floor of this building there is a job placement service, Mr. Brewer. I suggest you utilize that resource." She bent the finger in the opposite direction and extended her arm toward him to emphasize her point. "First floor." She sat back, adjusted the reading glasses perched on the end of her nose and peered down through them at some papers. "I see here this is the third time you've filed for disability in the last five years. That's nonsense. Barring some physical or mental catastrophe that leaves you incapacitated, I don't want to see you in this courtroom again. Ever. Do you understand?"

The man called Brewer threw his head back, hands in the air, a silent plea for clemency from the heavens. Nobody answered. He dropped the arms, started to stutter out some objection. Judge Dunlap cut him short, telling him there was only one right answer to her question.

"Yes, ma'am." He pouted, then shuffled up the aisle, past me and out of the courtroom. The judge called for the next claimant to step to the lectern. Hively was sitting in the fourth row back. I slipped in next to him.

"She seems fun," I whispered.

"This lady's badass, man. Doesn't take guff from anybody. How'd you fare?"

"I learned that Judge Blevins is the most noble human being to ever don the black robe in these hallowed halls. Anything on your end?"

"I called Sturges. Told him to go through all Blevins's case records, working backwards from the most recent through to when he was a litigator. See if that kicks up any dust. Spoke to the deputy. Next recess he's gonna pass the word to Dunlap that we'd like to speak with her, so we'll see."

The next recess came half an hour later. The bailiff cleared the courtroom, but signaled for us to stay put. He disappeared through the small doorway next to the judge's bench and, after a few minutes, came back out and told us the Judge could see us now and to follow him.

He led us back through a cramped, dimly lit hallway to Judge Dunlap's chambers. Dunlap was sitting behind her desk, sipping iced tea through a straw. She'd already removed her robe and exchanged the reading glasses for a large octagonal pair. Dunlap's face was hard and craggy, like an old piece of earth. Her white blouse was frilly around the neck and at the cuffs, and hung from her diminutive shoulders as if from a hanger. A perceptive person could see that, before the decades had stacked up and wilted her into her current incarnation, she was once a handsome, elegant woman.

When Hively and I attempted to introduce ourselves, Judge Dunlap raised a palm to stop us talking and informed us that she knew exactly who we were and why we were there. Apparently Rutherford Blevins had texted to warn her of our possible arrival. Without our prompting she owned up to the arrangement between the two of them, explaining that it had been she, not Blevins, who had suggested swapping cases in the first place. Such practices weren't uncommon among appellate judges—and not illegal, she added, though maybe frowned upon in certain circles.

"What circles?" I asked.

"The right-wing Bible-thumping hypocrites with assholes tighter than a Cheerio that populate this wretched town," Dunlap said. "Walk out the door and throw a rock and you'll hit one. Pardon my crassness."

Badass indeed. You couldn't help but like the woman. We doled out some more questions, but by readily admitting the handshake deal that she and Blevins had struck, she didn't give us much of a place to go. Much like Judy the clerk, Vicky Dunlap spoke of Rutherford Blevins with reverence. She had been an appellate judge for twenty-three years. In that time she'd seen four other judges take up residence in the courtroom across the hall. Blevins, far and away, was her most admired and trusted colleague. They worked as a team—the exchanging of cases stood as one example—and enjoyed each other's company socially on occasion as well. Blevins and her husband had become good friends; they golfed and fished together.

Scott T. Barnhard was another matter. Dunlap couldn't get his name out of her mouth without her nostrils flaring into an insipid sneer.

"What was it about Mr. Barnhard that made you find him disagreeable?" Hively inquired.

"Disagreeable? That's a polite way to put it. Is *everything* an acceptable answer? You laugh, but I'm serious. The man thought he was God's gift to jurisprudence. Our profession attracts a particular sort of individual. Much as yours does. There are those, like Rutherford Blevins, and I'd like to think myself, that genuinely want to be of service to their constituency. To leave things better than we found them, that old axiom. Then there are those who get into this line simply because they like the power, the money, the influence, the status that this job can bestow. Unfortunately, the latter is what you see more of. Because those types don't just want it. They need it.

So they fight for it harder. The former, those who want to do the good work, half of them are quickly disillusioned within their first year out of law school. The other half, well, those are rare birds. Rarer still in this day and age.

"All those stereotypes about lawyers are there for a reason. All those jokes, there's always some truth to them. Scott T. Barnhard"—there was that sneer—"was the worst. We're not all born with a silver spoon in our mouths. I was," she admitted, placing a hand over her chest. "My father worked his way up from nothing to become an entrepreneur. Owned a series of businesses that all did well. Dry cleaners, car washes, that kind of thing. Anyhow, the two of you, maybe you were, maybe you weren't. But when you are fortunate enough to be born in the one percent, you have to at least acknowledge the wonderful hand that you've been dealt. The privilege granted to you at birth. If you don't recognize it, don't recognize that you came into the world holding a full house, then that's one strike in my book. When you look down your nose at those who were born on the other end of the spectrum, born with nothing, into a society that gives them little chance, the very people you're supposed to represent, that's two strikes. When you're a pompous, entitled, insolent little prick, that's three strikes. Scott Barnhard had about twenty strikes. Was he good? Sure, he was okay. Who cares?" Her hand flitted in front of her. "It's not that hard to be a decent lawyer," she continued. "We're not flying to Mars here. We're not curing disease. I never understood why Rutherford was so enamored with him, other than the fact that he took him under his wing when he was just a pup. Scott Barnhard would change in front of Rutherford, too. Act different. He was condescending as hell with everyone else, but with Rutherford he was always sucking up. Rutherford was blind to it. Maybe he didn't want to see it. You know, this might sound crass, being that his body has yet to be put in the ground, but I wasn't sad to hear of his passing. If you want to know the truth, it'll be a relief not to have to deal with him anymore."

CHAPTER TWENTY-THREE
THE HONEY BEE STINGER

We descended the circular stairs, went back out past security, and walked out into the crisp blue day.

"Everybody seems to love your boy Blevins," said Hively.

"Funny, I didn't like him one bit."

"Me neither. But either everybody's in cahoots covering for this guy, or we're wasting our time trying to make something out of nothing."

"Somebody killed Barnhard. Somebody had to benefit from it."

"I'm with you, but who? If everyone is to be believed, the good judge might be just that: good. If Sturges comes up empty on him, we're gonna have to start kicking up some different rocks."

We reached our cars, made some vague plans to touch base later in the day. Hively promised to keep me in the loop and let me know if they tracked down Momo Morrison or his scar-headed stooge, Buddy Cleamons. Just as I was stepping up into the Tacoma, his phone jangled in his pocket. Hively checked the number, took the call, and listened for a second before hollering for me not to leave.

"Yeah . . . yeah . . ." Hively said into the receiver. "Who's the lead?"

I stood on the Tacoma's running board and spoke down to him over the roof of my cab. "What's poppin'?"

Hively listened to the person on the other end of the call for another moment, then hung up the phone and looked up at me, a curious mix of suspicion and puzzlement in his face.

"Got a 187."

Every atom in my body pricked up. Fear immediately wrapped around my intestines, my lungs.

"Where?" I said, my voice coming out in a low growl. "Who?"

I know what I was hoping, that the next words out of his mouth would be 'down at the Terrace,' 'Spring Street', or 'West End', followed by the descriptors 'adult male,' 'young male', or even just 'Caucasian'. Any combination therein would suffice. I willed these phrases from his lips. Willed anything other than what, deep down in my gut, in that place that separates instinct from reason, from knowledge, what I knew the answer was going to be.

Hively's mouth moved. The words came. "Royal Vista Apartments."

And so it was. I didn't wait for the who. I swung down into the cab of my truck, started the engine, kicked it into gear, and peeled away from the curb.

"Wait a minute!" Hively screamed after me. "Is this about Barnhard?"

I sped down Fifth Avenue. City Hall, The Spaghetti House, the *Cain City Dispatch* building, Church Row, all of it blowing past me in a blur. I don't know how many red lights I ran. Three, at least. At a certain point I heard a siren behind me, saw the blue lights flashing in my rearview. I didn't stop. I punched the gas.

Three squad cars and a forensics van were blocking the front of the Royal Vista Apartments. I swerved left onto Thirteenth Street and screeched to a halt at the down-sloped curb in front of the side entrance. A small queue had formed where two police officers, a man and woman, were checking IDs up on the platform, taking note of everyone going in or out of the building. I hopped down from the truck and weaved through a group of people who were bunched at the back of the line.

Some of them had their phones raised above their heads, videoing the scene in case something broke out.

The officers were scrutinizing the ID of the old geezer wearing track pants, a tuxedo jackets with tails, and a bucket hat.

"Do you live here?" asked the female officer.

"Says right there I do, don't it?" replied the geezer, sticking a gnarled finger toward the ID in her hands. She double-checked to make sure the old man's face matched the image on the card and began copying his information onto a steno pad. I scaled the three steps and tried slipping past the officers. The male officer, a pink-faced, meaty sort, crowed, "Whoa, whoa, whoa," and threw out his fat arm to bar me from entering.

"Live here," I said quickly. "Six-nineteen."

"The hell you do," the male officer said. "You don't remember me, do you?"

I took a cursory glance at his beefy face, placed him instantly, replied, "No," and tried again to push forward. He shoved me back, hard, and I knocked against the old geezer with the bucket hat. Felt his body give with the blow. I flipped around and took hold of the lapels of the man's tuxedo to keep him from tumbling off the stoop.

After I got him steady on his feet, the geezer spat, "Watch it," and slapped my hands away as if the whole thing were my fault. I wheeled on the policemen.

"You oughta thank me," I told them. "I just saved you from a lawsuit."

"Save the drama for the papers, Malick. You may not remember me, but guess what" —the piggy officer jabbed his stubby, swollen finger into my chest—"I remember you. Holy cow, somebody take a weed eater to your face or what?"

"Your wife forgets my safe word sometimes."

"Ha, nice try. I ain't married." He spoke out of the corner of his mouth to address his colleague. "This guy fooled me not once, but twice, to gain illegal access to a couple of crime scenes. One time he pretended he was a doctor to get past me. Had this whole get-up, lab coat, clipboard. You should've seen it." He laughed and shook his head as if reminiscing on some prized memory, then abruptly stopped and contorted his broad features into the best mean-mug he could muster. "Not this time, Jacko."

"When was that, two years ago?" I said impatiently. "And they still got you working perimeter? Maybe it's time to find a new trade."

"So you do remember me."

"How could I forget someone as stupid and ugly as you are? Christ, it looks like someone's fattening you up to slaughter. Squad'll take anybody these days."

The officer took a threatening step toward me and flicked the bill of my flat cap, hard. It fell off the back of my head.

"Wes," the female officer advised, "dial it back."

I casually bent over and retrieved my cap, slapped it against my leg to knock the dust off, and fitted it back into place.

"I'm going into that building," I stated calmly. "Try and stop me and by dinnertime tonight you'll be shitting your own teeth."

Wes wrapped his sausage fingers around the handle of the police baton. "You wanna test me?"

I looked down at the baton, then back up to him. "I'm not averse to it."

"Wes," the female officer said, her voice low and controlled. "Be smart. There are literally three iPhones filming you right now."

"Yeah, Wes," I prodded him. "Be smart."

"Let him through," someone commanded from behind me. Hively. He stepped up onto the stoop. "He's working in conjunction with the department on this one. He has clearance. Let him through."

The fat officer's eyes bore into mine. He had more stones than I gave him credit for. "You're a lucky son of a bitch, Malick," he said through gritted teeth.

"You're the leprechaun," I replied, and brushed past him. Hively followed me into the building. We walked down the dimly lit corridor to the elevator, which was being held on the bottom floor by another officer. We got on.

"Who haven't you pissed off in this city?" Hively asked.

Not a bad question. Had to think about it for a moment. "Well, I haven't met everyone yet," I said, pressing the button for the fifth floor.

"How do you know which floor the victim is on? You want to clue me in so I'm not walking into this room blind?"

"Who is it?" I said.

"Young black female. Didn't get the name. Roommate called it in. That's all I know. You took off and I had to chase your ass."

The doors split open and we stepped off. Hively walked out ahead of me to explain my presence and secure my passage through the security outside apartment 512. They handed me a pair of plastic gloves and some overshoes. I put them on.

"Ready?" Hively asked. I nodded. Before we went in, two things occurred to me almost simultaneously. First, that Renata may be the deceased person in question, not Birdie. I didn't know why that very logical thought hadn't crossed my mind previously. But then, on its heels, a realization. If Birdie were the one to find Renata dead, she'd never have called the police first. She'd have called me.

A calmness washed over me, a state of numbness. Most likely that was my body's defense mechanism prepping itself for what I was about to encounter. Through the threshold we went. The apartment was quiet, hushed with the reverence for the dead. Junk was all over the place. Worse than the night before when I'd been there. Dirty dishes piled high in the kitchenette, starting to mold and stink. Garbage can overflowing. Take-out food cartons, a half-empty bag of chips on the floor, along with some plasticware and a few wadded-up napkins. Clothes strewn about, ripped-out pages from magazines scattered all over the place.

Whatever optimism I'd had—if you call wishing for one person's death over another's optimism—was dashed when I saw two detectives, Red Lewis and Jerome Kipling, squatted on their haunches at the edge of the couch, trying to softly coax something out of Renata. She looked very tiny, Renata did, sitting there like that, arms crossed tightly over her chest as if she wanted to wrap herself in a cocoon. She was wearing only a sports bra and jeans. Her face was swollen with tears. Snot ran down from her nose into her mouth and she was taking in short sucks of air, trying to summon the correct answers to the detectives' queries, having a hard time at it. When she noticed someone new had come into the room, she glanced over, saw that it was me. Her lips began to tremble. Her whimper turned into a sob that turned into a scream. A sharp, piercing scream to set your teeth on edge, got your ears to ringing.

Hively made a beeline for Red Lewis, pulled him aside, said something I couldn't hear over Renata's moaning. After listening to Red's response, Hively looked over to me, realization dawning on his face. He got it now. Who the victim was. Who she was to me.

I kept moving. My feet pulling me, as if by magnetic force, back through the narrow passage to the door at the end of the hall.

Birdie's bedroom.

A forensics team, goggles, gloves, full-bodied protective coveralls, the whole kit, processing the scene. Scouring the carpet in and around the doorway for any trace evidence: blood, hairs, fibers. The click of a shutter where someone was snapping photographs.

I slid around a forensics analyst who was busy dusting the lower half of the doorframe for prints and stepped into the room. Daylight streaming in from the windows cancelled the glow from the lava lamp and gave the space a starched, sterile feel. The techs paid me no mind.

And there was Birdie. Sprawled facedown across the four-poster bed, fully clothed except that her pants had been yanked down below her knees, exposing her ass and thighs. Her arms and legs were tethered to the posts with the scarves I had seen in my previous visits. The same scarves that had been poking out of her suitcase the night before. She had a large gash across her left temple. The hair around the wound was matted, glistening with blood. Not a profuse amount of blood, but enough to snake down past her ear, under her chin and across her neck, forming a soaked spot on the sheet beneath her head, which was turned toward the door where I stood. Her eyes were open, the whites turned red, so red from busted capillaries they were nearly phosphorescent.

And, like that, the number of visions that would haunt me for the remainder of my days increased by one.

When I was a rookie cop in Chicago's 11th Precinct, I'd been the first to arrive at the scene of a murder-suicide involving an entire family. The dad had put a shotgun to the heads of four children under the age of five, three of them while they slept. The fourth, the only girl, the oldest, he found cowering in the bathtub and ended her there. Then he tied the mother to a chair in the living room, stabbed her and cut her over three hundred times before eating the shotgun himself.

Then there was my son, Jacob, a gentle, curious boy, aged six. His slight, disfigured body found floating in the brown murk of the Ohio River. His memory now relegated to a modest gravestone in Spring Hill Cemetery and a plaque on the gate of an opulent house named after him.

And now this sight, now Birdie. Another dead body in a bed, just like the kids in Chicago. Birdie who deserved better, deserved a more decent world than the one she'd been born into. Birdie, aged nineteen, with a pair of blasted-out red eyes that would burn a fiery hole in my psyche, that would never stop watching, judging, condemning. Her death was on me. A hundred percent on me. Just like her mother's before her.

I must have shuffled backward because I banged against the wall, hard. Hard enough to draw the attention of the investigators in the room. All at once a kind of delirium came over me. My mouth turned to chalk, my body became clammy, and my vision fogged at the edges. My heart started beating faster and faster, faster than an insect's wings, and my legs felt as though someone had taken the bones out of them. I slid down to the floor. The walls of the room stretched like rubber into a faraway ceiling that receded farther and farther into the space above me, almost out of sight.

"Who are you?" a disembodied voice echoed. A figure with a plastic hood cinched tight over their head floated into my hazy periphery, their nose and mouth the only things visible beneath the hood and goggles. The person's mouth opened and shut, made a few noises. As if on a delay, a second or two later, those noises reached my brain. A woman's voice. "You can't be here . . . Are you okay? . . . Breathe . . ."

"Suitcase?" I murmured.

"What?"

"Where . . . suitcase?" I tried again, but now my words came out slurred, indecipherable.

My eyes started playing tricks on me. The woman in the plastic coveralls stretched long and tall, as though she were made of elastic. Her head disappeared, too high into the sky, too far into the clouds for me to see. Then there were plastic arms, gloved hands, more cinched faces. Lifting me, dragging me out of the room, away from the scene, away from Birdie. I felt weightless in their arms, floating, like gravity had cut me loose.

CHAPTER TWENTY-FOUR
SITTING, DRINKING

Next thing I knew, I was sitting against the wall in the hallway outside of the apartment. Hively hovering over me. He snapped his fingers in front of my face.

"Nick? You okay? Nick?"

Gradually, the delirium subsided and the world around me racked slowly back into focus. A cold, wet rag had been placed on the back of my neck. A paramedic, some baby-faced kid, was squatted down beside me inflating a blood pressure cuff that had been wrapped snugly around my bicep. I yanked the cuff off and told him to go away.

"I need to check your vitals, sir."

"Fuck off. That vital enough?"

The kid frowned, gathered his kit, and stalked off.

"Well," said Hively. "You've met *him* now."

"She's dead," I rasped.

"Yeah, Nick. She's gone. It's Aisha Bryant's daughter. You knew who it was though, didn't you? Knew as soon as I told you the location."

I bobbed my head up and down, dropped my face into my hands.

"Was she your source that placed Momo here the night Scott Barnhard was murdered?"

Another bob of the head.

"C'mon, let's go somewhere. Can you get up?"

"Maybe."

I lifted my arm. Hively took hold of it and hoisted me to my feet. After a momentary wobble, the ground evened out beneath me. We walked back down the corridor, hopped the elevator to the ground floor. Outside, a slew of lookie-loos and reporters crowded the yellow tape that had been strung up in the short time since we'd arrived. News Channel 3's field reporter and cameraman were setting up. Ernie Ciccone from the *Cain City Dispatch* was there, having jockeyed his way to the front of the horde. He spotted me and whistled sharply to get my attention.

"Malick! Hey, Malick!"

I ignored his calls and drafted behind Hively as he sliced through the throng of onlookers to get to his vehicle parked at the curb. Hively unlocked the doors, I collapsed into the passenger seat and leaned my head forward against the dashboard. Ciccone rapped on the window by my head. I waved him off.

"Not now, Ernie."

"If not now, when?" he yelled through the glass. "These bodies are stacking up quick. One have anything to do with the other? Who's the vic? Can you tell me that at least?"

"Later," I told him.

Hively started up the car, pulled away from the chaos of the sidewalk and began driving through downtown. After circling the shopping district a couple times, he asked where we were going.

I raised my head from the dash, mumbled, "Red Head," and laid it back down. There weren't many customers in the bar, a few perched on the stools eating catfish sandwiches, a specialty item Tadpole served only on weekends. Tadpole had seven kids. A couple of the sons fished the Ohio River and supplied a fresh catch at the end of every week.

"Whole bottle?" Tadpole asked after I'd placed my order.

"Whole bottle," I confirmed. "Two glasses."

Tadpole looked to Hively, who gave an affirmative nod.

"That'll be forty bucks flat, gents. Throw in some of that catfish if you'd like, on the house." Neither Hively nor I had an appetite. Tadpole bent down, rummaged through some bottles and came up with the Maker's. "Say, I tell you fellas the one about the two guys who come home from golfing?"

"Just the drinks today, Tadpole," I said.

"Oh, you gotta hear this one," he insisted, unable, apparently, to gauge our dispositions. "You know Old Dan Tucker?"

"The song?"

"No, the man. Comes in here all the time. Short fella, big old potbelly, mustache like mine."

"Don't know him."

Tadpole peeled the wax seal off the top of the Maker's bottle, popped the cap and poured the bourbon into our glasses. "Anyway, Old Dan told it to me. It's an all-timer."

Like every bad comedian in the annals of history, Tadpole believed his jokes could cut through any sour mood or melancholy.

"Get it over with," I said wearily.

Tadpole slid the bottle and the two highball glasses over. "So this guy brings his friend home after a round of golf, right, and his wife comes down the stairs—"

"Fuck this," I said. I grabbed the bottle and my glass and walked away.

"Who pissed in his cereal?" Tadpole griped. Hively apologized on my behalf and explained that we'd been just been at the scene of a homicide. He said something else that I couldn't hear, to which Tadpole responded, "Aw, shit. Not again."

Yes, I thought. *Again*. I sat in the back corner booth, took my hat and jacket off and settled in for the duration.

Hively dropped two twenties and a fiver on the bar, made his way to the booth and slid in across from me. The first drink passed in silence. I moved to replenish Hively's cup, but he placed a hand over it and told me he was good with one.

I shrugged, filled my glass to the brim and kept them coming.

"Birdie Bryant?" he said, more as an open-ended question than anything else.

I answered him with a question of my own. "What's Renata's story?"

"Said Birdie had a client so she left the apartment—she wasn't allowed to be there when Birdie had somebody up. She went to work in the alley, came back around 2 a.m., didn't hear anything. Went to bed. Woke up, didn't think anything was amiss. Said Birdie often slept in. Was going to go grab some late breakfast, went to check if Birdie wanted anything. Found her like she was. Called us."

Hively asked me what I knew about Renata.

"Not much. She was Birdie's roommate. Friends from the time they were kids, I think. That's it. She a suspect?"

"We'll check out her story, see if we can track down anybody she came in contact with last night, but Red said she's been hysterical since they got there. Seems unlikely."

The pair of us sat quietly for a few minutes, drinking. Hively asked about Birdie again. There was nothing left to protect, nothing worth concealing, so I disclosed everything. How I'd been ferrying her to see her daughter a couple times a week for the last year and a half. How we'd recently decided that she'd stay at my office while she tried to get her life together, maybe gain custody of Aisha. Birdie's connection to Barnhard, to Momo Morrison.

Hively puzzled over the information for a bit. "She was coming to stay with you today?"

I showed him my text exchange with Birdie from the previous night.

"That's where I was headed from the courthouse. To go get her."

"Damn." Hively grimaced. "We found her phone, but it was wiped clean, presumably by whoever killed her. Only had a few numbers saved in it. Mostly food places within walking distance of the Royal Vista. And yours. We'll track the numbers, see if our tech guys can retrieve any of the data. That's why you were asking about the suitcase?"

I explained how I'd stopped by the previous evening to check on her, how I'd seen the packed suitcase on the bed, and how it wasn't there, at least not visible, when I'd been in the bedroom just now.

"It was in the closet. Looked like it'd been tossed in there haphazardly. Clothes spilling out. Why do you think she'd do that? Client coming over?"

"I should have gotten her out of there a long time ago," I muttered, more to myself than to Hively. "I should have forced her to come with me." He said nothing.

I shut my eyes. A series of images unspooled like a soundless, slow-motion replay against the colorless backdrop of my mind's eye: me walking down the hall, past the techs, round the corner into Birdie's bedroom. The sooty smell of graphite. Comforter on the floor. Lamp turned over, the shade off it, naked bulb glowing hot. Birdie, tied to the bedposts as though she were being quartered. Pants yanked down, her head bludgeoned. Something picking at the periphery of the image. Something I was missing. I opened my eyes.

"She had some money stashed in one of the ceiling panels above her bed. It was for . . . it was for her daughter. See if it's still there, will ya?"

"Yeah, I will. So if Barnhard was a client, then Momo was what, her pimp?"

"I don't think it was that straightforward. From my understanding, Momo set the appointments for some guys initially. After that, sometimes they scheduled through him, sometimes through Birdie. But the johns never paid her. It was more like a . . . mutual arrangement. That's how I understood it, anyway."

"If the clients she saw didn't pay her, who did they pay? The Stenders?"

"Beats me. She told me some of the men might tip her, but there was no set rate for whatever service. She got an allowance of sorts delivered to a P.O. box down the street from the Royal Vista, and the apartment was taken care of. That's all I know."

"So that's why you got tangled up in this? To protect Birdie?"

"Not to start. I was curious to find out who killed Barnhard on my watch, sure. A little miffed that somebody thought doing that was a good idea, you know? What a joke. Then you were hounding me about my involvement so I wanted to solve it before you did, if I could, or at least get you off me and pointed in the right direction. But when I found out Birdie was mixed up with it, yeah, I wanted to make sure she stayed clear of trouble. I was trying to help her to go straight, get her daughter back."

Speaking that last sentence aloud gutted me anew. Whatever future was to be for Birdie was now gone. Never to return. Without warning or prelude, I began to cry. Big, fat tears that stung the cuts on my face as they rolled down. I let them roll. Hively waited patiently. He didn't judge, didn't feel embarrassed for me. I cried through two more slugs of bourbon. Then I pressed my palms against my eyes, rubbed them dry, and pulled my shit together.

"You think that's what got her killed?" Hively said.

"Probably. Could be anybody. She also gave an interview to the news yesterday, you know that?"

"No. What about?"

"The type of men they get down there in The 4 ½."

"Why would she do that?"

"I dunno. Because she thought she was out of that life. Because I filled her head with hopes and possibilities and lies. I swear to God, everything I touch—" I closed my fist and then rapidly opened it, pantomiming an explosion. "You should go back and watch the interview. News Channel 3, I think. Seems like she just wanted to give all those people that used her, all those men, a big 'go fuck yourself' before she dropped out. But she's the one who got screwed. Not them. Her. Like usual." I swilled the bourbon, wiped my chin with the back of my hand. "Either way it was me, my fault. I'm the one who got her killed. Like her mother before her."

"Shit, Nick. You can't hang yourself with this. That's too much to carry."

"She'd have been better off if she'd never met me," I said viciously. "Her and her mother both. They'd be alive, anyway. Probably. Anyhow, that interview expands your suspect pool to every red-blooded American male in the city. Good luck with that."

"I'll look at the interview. She keep any record of her clients that you know about?"

"No. I don't know."

"Okay. I'm sorry, Nick. I didn't—" He struggled for the right words. "I didn't know you had that in you."

"Had what? Some decency? Hell—" I downed another shot, the bite sliding smoothly now, down my throat and into my chest. "I'm not decent. I'm a curse. Everybody I care about gets killed. That's not the whole of it though, is it? They don't just get killed, I get them killed, don't I?"

"That's not being fair to yourself. You were trying to help the girl get her life together."

"Is that what I was doing? Or was I trying to atone for getting her mother shot in the first place? Assuage my own guilt. Settle my own account? That's more like it. I was doing that shit for me. Trying to get back to even in my own mind." I forewent the glass and poured the bourbon straight from the bottle into my mouth. "Fuck it. Doesn't matter. I'm too far gone now. My debt's too great."

"Listen," Hively said curtly. "Red Lewis is the lead on Birdie, but I'm going to be investigating the connection to the Barnhard murder. I'll keep you up with it. As soon as I get the coroner's report, or as soon as I get a bead on Momo Morrison or one of his lackeys surfaces, I'll let you know, okay?"

"Don't bother," I said. "I'm done. *Finito*. Never to return. All I do is make things worse."

"Making things worse never stopped you before."

I lifted my gaze from the bottle to him. "I'm fucking done."

The way I said it must have sounded convincing. A look of astonishment came and went from his face.

"You gonna fold up shop 'cause things went sideways? That's not the Malick I know."

"Who *is* the Malick you know? Can I meet him? What do you know about me, Hive? Really?"

Hively began to formulate a response. I saved him the trouble.

"That was rhetorical. You know jack shit. Here's what I'm gonna do. I'm gonna sit here and drink this bottle until all of my senses are fucking obliterated, or I go into a coma, whichever one comes first. And if that doesn't work, I'll go get another bottle and drink that one. So on and so on until the job is done."

"Don't do anything stupid, Malick," he said. "Rash."

"Yes, daddy."

"I'm serious, Malick. Give me your car keys."

"Give you what?"

"Hand them over. You'll get them back tomorrow."

"What are you, the new DD Chuck? Whatever. You want them, take them."

I fished the keys to the Tacoma from my pocket and tossed them over the table. "Have her back by midnight, will ya?"

"Now your gun," he said.

"Don't push it."

Hively started to snap back, but something stopped him. His mouth drew tight.

He rose from the table and smoothed out the front of his suit jacket. "I'm going to have to speak with Tom Orvietto. Maybe your ex, too. I know you were trying to protect them."

"Do your worst."

Hively grimaced. "Okay. I'll see you tomorrow."

"Don't hold your breath," I said, not looking up at him.

He left. I drank.

More Simon and Garfunkel. A Mamas & the Papas set. Then Joe Cocker. The Doors. Somebody was always hankering for the Sixties in this place. I lost track of the music. I lost track of time. I watched the 750-milliliter bottle of bourbon diminish, incrementally, like a time lapse effect from a shitty movie. Down, down, down it went as I poured one glass after another into my throat. The liquor coursed smoothly into my bloodstream. Smoothly into the chemicals of my brain.

At some point in the day, around midway through the bottle, I got a call from my employers at Leach, McKinney & Thurber. I answered it.

"Yeah."

"Malick, is that you?" McKinney's brusque voice.

"Wrong number. This is your mother's house. She's got a mouthful, asked me to take a message."

"Excuse me?"

"What do you want, Kent?"

"Did you go down to the courthouse this morning and harass Rutherford Blevins about the Scott Barnhard case?"

"You two still friends, are you? Harassment is a bit of an exaggeration."

"That's how it was described to me. To a word, in fact. As I recall, you were told very specifically, Malick, to not have any further involvement in this matter. To leave it to the authorities, were you not?"

"Yeah. Funny thing, those same authorities asked for a little assistance in the matter. Being that you told me to take the rest of the week off, I figured I'd go ahead and . . . do whatever the fuck I want."

From his voice I could tell that his grip on the receiver had just gotten tighter.

"Well, this is the straw that broke the camel's back. We've just had a long conversation here—"

"Are you all right?"

"What?"

"I know it's hard for you to string ten words together before you start wheezing."

"What are you talking about?"

"Your lung capacity."

A pause on the other end.

"Are you drunk?"

"Very."

"You're a piece of work, Malick. I'm afraid our generosity with you has been extended beyond the level with which we are comfortable. Leach, McKinney & Thurber will no longer be using your services."

"Fine by me. Hey, you know what you should be afraid of?"

"What?"

"You said you're afraid, your generosity, blah, blah, blah. But you know what you should really be afraid of, you limp-dicked, heart-diseased fuck?"

"I should have known you'd take this with no class."

"Me. Coming round some corner someday and seeing my face. That's what."

"I'm going to see to it that no lawyer—"

"Fuck yourself."

I hung up the phone, turned off the ringer.

I don't know how long it took me to finish that first bottle of Maker's. Time was irrelevant. When the last drink was drunk, the evening sun was streaming in through the bank of windows at the entrance, creating columns of light so thick with dust they looked solid, tangible. Tadpole, against his better judgement, furnished me with another bottle. By The Red Head's lofty standards of compliance, my behavior had been tame to this point, and he was probably scared that I'd wreck his bar if he denied me service. He wasn't wrong. I was in the mood to destroy something. Or be punched in the face a few dozen times. I wanted for some asshole to come in and give me the slightest provocation, look at me funny or make some snide comment that I could use as an excuse to fight. No assholes came. No one commented.

Day gave way to night. Natural light morphing into a neon haze. The place grew younger, livelier, more fragrant. The decibel level rose. The jukebox skewed toward hip-hop, some shit I didn't know, though most of the people on those songs announced their name at some point early on in their verse.

In intervals, people started coming in looking for me. First through the door was my old buddy, Captain Bruce J. Hale of the Violent Crimes Unit, there to offer condolences, vow diligence in the investigation, ask if there was anything he could do, that kind of bullshit thing.

By this point I was basically monosyllabic. "Sit," I said. "Drink."

Willis Hively's used tumbler was still on the table. I poured some bourbon into it and shoved it Hale's way. He demurred at first, but eventually went to the bar, got a fresh glass, some soda to cut the bourbon with, and squeezed back into the booth. We toasted to our dead children, tossed the liquor down the hatch, and bumbled around some conversation.

Hale lamented his impending divorce and waxed nostalgic about the lives we used to lead back when we were young, naive, newly married, newly minted detectives; before we were both ruined by grief and vengeance and a hundred too many run-ins with the dregs of humanity.

"How good did we have it? We didn't even realize," Hale said.

"You never do till it's gone."

"Till it's gone," he echoed. "Mmm, before I forget, thought you might be interested to know. Your girl's cause of death was not the trauma to the head."

"No?"

"Nuh-uh. She was strangled. Asphyxiation. Crushed larynx."

"Ligature marks?"

"None. Bruising on her neck consistent with fingers." Hale raised his hands to his throat to demonstrate, as though I might be too inebriated to fully understand his meaning.

So someone had bopped her on the head, wrapped their hands around her neck and strangled the life out of her. They'd killed her with their hands. Just like whoever had offed Scott Barnhard. Up close and personal. Hale lifted his glass, looked into it as though he were reading the tea leaves, and set it back down without taking a drink.

"Fucking Cain City, huh?"

"City of a thousand nightmares."

Hale reaffirmed his pledge to devote as many resources as needed to solve Birdie's murder. Swore he'd keep the case alive and active until the perp was brought to justice. I wasn't particularly confident in his ability, or that of the Cain City police force, to follow through on that promise, so I afforded him a facetious thumbs-up and sent him down the yellow brick road.

As Hale shuffled out of the place, I couldn't help but think of how he, in the two years since his daughter had been killed, had become a feeble, sallow-skinned, bloated and bent old ruin. His bulk, which had always been solid, had gone spongy and weak. I wondered if people thought the same when they saw me. That I, too, was a casualty of time, of tragedy; that the best of me, of what I had to offer to this world, was a long way gone. So what if they did? I concluded. Who gave a flying fuck? I'm a speck on a speck floating on a speck. No more, no less. I don't matter. The human species doesn't matter. This world is nothing more than a bit player in a billion-years-long cosmic pinball game. A blip in time.

These bleak thoughts sloshing through my brain were spoiling my buzz, making me nauseous. I squeezed my eyes shut and pressed my forehead against the tabletop for a few seconds, no more than that. When I lifted my head, the kid, Davey, was there, all moppy-haired and long-boned and Adam's apple. He was a stealthy one, that kid. Always had been. Probably been privy to a thousand things he wasn't supposed to have seen or heard, simply by virtue of being light-footed. Once, middle of the night during that gang war that went on in Cain City, he'd crept up on me in the parking lot outside of the old high school. I'd nearly shot him.

"Kid." I stifled a belch. "You're as sneaky as a blood clot to the heart."

"Huh?"

"You shouldn't creep up on people. It's dangerous."

"Ain't nobody creeping on your old ass. I strolled up in here like a normal person and sat down. How else was I supposed to come over here? Announce myself when I walk in the door? Have somebody blow a trumpet or some shit?"

"You say so."

"Yo, you all right?"

"What?" I twiddled my fingers in front of my wrecked face. "Not an improvement?"

"Nuh-uh. Shit looks worse than it did yesterday."

"What are you gonna do?" I shrugged. "Want a drink?"

"Naw." Davey laughed uneasily. "I know better than to mess with that venom you be chugging."

"What are you, a wine cooler kinda guy now? Oh wait, I remember, I remember—Co-ro-na." I poured another portion of said venom into my cup. For good measure, I splashed some of it onto the table as well. "For the homies," I said. "Did I get you?"

"Naw, you straight. I'll get some napkins." The kid went the bar, grabbed a handful of cocktail napkins, came back and spread them over the spill. "You sure you're okay though? You don't seem so fresh."

I tapped my nose, winked and clucked at him. "You've seen through my ruse, kid. What gave it away?"

"That detective came by, told my mom a little bit about what's going on. He seemed, like, worried about you."

"What detective?"

"The black one. Hively."

"Oh, yeah? He came by? That's sweet of him. He pass her my keys?"

"I dunno. I'm sorry, Nick."

"Sorry for what, kid?"

"You know, about Birdie and all that."

"Why? You kill her?"

"What? No. She was—she just seemed pretty cool, that's all."

"She was pretty cool, kid. Pret-T cool." I collected the sopping napkins and piled them over to the side of the table, rubbed my hands on my pants leg to get the stickiness of bourbon off them. "She didn't get a fair shake, our Birdie. Never had a chance."

Davey didn't know what to say to that. He let the awkwardness sit a moment. "Mom wants to know if you're coming home tonight."

"Sent you down here to sweat me, did she?"

"Yeah. Well, no, actually. I asked if it was all right if I came down to see how you were doing. She's been calling you, but said it kept going to voicemail. She said if you were set on getting blind drunk then there's nothing we can do to stop you. We'd just have to wait it out."

I felt my equilibrium going a little wobbly, so I opened my eyes wide and shut them tight a few times before taking another drink.

"Smart woman. Tell her not to wait up."

"M'kay. I'll tell her. I guess I'm gonna dip, less you want me to keep you company."

"Nah. Your mom has the right idea. Best to leave me be."

"Okay." Davey scooted out from the booth. "You sure you don't want to come home with me? We can walk back together."

"Appreciate the offer, buddy. I'll see you soon, all right?"

"Yeah, all right. See you soon. Like, be careful and all that."

"You know me, kid. Safety first."

"Yeah."

Davey weaved through a crowd of college kids that were congregated around the shuffleboard table. At the door he hesitated, took a disappointed look back at me, and evaporated into the night.

CHAPTER TWENTY-FIVE
NIGHT DIVIDES THE DAY

The last person to seek my company at The Red Head was Ernie Ciccone, the reporter from the *Dispatch*. He stopped by the bar and picked up a Rolling Rock before wandering over to my booth.

"Jesus," he said, surveying the two bottles of liquor in front of me, one empty, one well on its way. "How do you take yours? In quarts?" He tossed his satchel into the opposite bench. "Need a drinking buddy?"

"Not you."

Ignoring that, Ciccone plopped his ass down.

"Take a load off, Fanny. Don't mind me. I'm only sitting here." My words came out sloppier than I would have preferred.

"Don't be a cock drip, Malick. There's nothing more pathetic than a solitary bender."

"I can think of a few things," I said, taking care to annunciate. "Hale tell you I was here? You two still giving each other the reach around?"

"There, there. Come now," he cooed, as if he were speaking to a toddler, "all that's water under the bridge. Everybody learned their lesson there, didn't we? Besides, all the hoopla and malfeasance going on in this town, been a long time since I was hurting for stories or sources or recognition."

"Good for you. Go scrape the gutters somewhere else then."

Ciccone rolled out his best shit-eating grin. It made him look like a deranged rodent with a toothache. "Now, is that any way to talk to someone who wants to help in what is obviously a time of great agony for you?"

"You looking out for somebody besides yourself," I clucked. "That'll be the day. Quit leering at me, will you? I'm afraid you're gonna start gnawing on my fingers with those teeth."

Instead of going away, Ciccone's expression only grew more dubious and feral.

"You're a legend in this town, Malick. Damn near mythical in stature. Bullets, gangs, bounties on your head, homicidal stalkers, you've survived it all."

"Serving it up a little thick, aren't you?"

"It does neither one of us any good to be at odds with one another," he went on. "Who does that serve? Not my readers. Not your clients."

"What'd you learn?" I said abruptly.

"Come again?"

"You said you learned a lesson from that"—I waved my hand around—"Detroit nonsense. What'd you learn?"

"Well." Ciccone took a couple gulps of beer, put his fist against his chest, and made a satisfied sound. He gazed over my shoulder with a ponderous expression. "Let's see. I learned that good men sometimes make bad decisions that can put them on the wrong end of the ledger. When it comes to compromising one's ethics, I learned the juice is never worth the squeeze. Just how slippery that slope is. And I learned to never, ever, under any circumstances, get on your bad side."

Ciccone nodded to himself, pleased with the answer he'd come up with, and took another long swig of beer.

"Jesus Christ, if you wrote with as many platitudes as you talk with, you wouldn't be allowed to report for the school paper. What are you trying to do, stay out of detention? Listen here, Ernie." I wagged my finger for him to come closer. He leaned in. "You want to stay off my bad side? Let me give you a tip. Get out of my sight. Pretend you're wearing a shock collar that'll zap you if you get to within a hundred yards. Better yet, go buy a shock collar. I think I'll name you Rocco."

Ciccone sat back. "I'm going to chalk this up to you being wasted and very upset about this young woman, Aveena Mae Bryant's, death. Rumor is you were close with her."

"Chalk it up to whatever you want, you little rat turd."

Ciccone chuckled. "I haven't heard anyone use the word 'turd' since I was twelve."

"You're welcome to quote me on that. You're a buck-toothed. Little. Rat. Turd."

"You know it's my job to write a story about this, right? This is what I do for a living."

"Heard you got a prize for the last one I served up."

"That's right. The West Virginia Society of Journalism honored me for distinguished service in the pursuit of justice. Just a state-level award," Ciccone said, feigning modesty.

"The pursuit of justice?" I laughed long and hard until I was out of breath and hiccuping. "What a crock."

Ciccone stood up hastily, yanked his satchel from the booth and grabbed his beer off the table.

"You know what, Malick? I came here out of courtesy to you. Out of decency. I thought you'd like to have a chance to speak about this girl. Have a say in how she is going to be portrayed publicly."

"Who gives a shit. She's dead."

Ciccone slugged down the wash of his beer, slammed the bottle on the table, and turned to go. "Don't say I didn't try, Malick."

"She didn't go by Aveena," I said, acquiescing. Ciccone whirled back round like he'd never intended to leave in the first place. "Nobody ever called her that," I continued. "She went by Birdie. Her mother gave her the moniker when she was just a little girl. Stuck."

Ciccone lunged back into the booth, whipped out a pen and notepad from his satchel and started scribbling.

"Her mother, who was killed—"

"Yeah."

"Never solved, right?"

"No, not officially."

"Tragically similar fates."

"Yep."

"Anything to link the two that you know about?"

"Just me."

Ciccone stopped writing and fixed his beady eyes on me. "Care to elaborate?"

"They were both involved in investigations I was conducting."

"With the mother it was the Detroit gangs?"

"That's right."

"And with Birdie?"

"Scott Barnhard. He was one of her johns."

"Holy shit, Malick," Ciccone exclaimed, writing frantically. "Just when I thought you weren't even gonna be good for a blurb. Can I print this?"

"What do I care?"

"But it's true? You're not jacking me over?"

I swallowed some bourbon. "It's true."

I proceeded to tell Ciccone some select details from the case. Some I knew to be facts, some were educated guesses designed to stir the hornet's nest. Namely, that Birdie catered to many in the upper echelons of Cain City society, not just Scott Barnhard. I directed him to the interview she gave yesterday on the local news. I also clued him in on the money scam Scott Barnhard was running—possibly with Judge Rutherford Blevins—and the U.S. Attorney's investigation into his actions. I left out the stuff about the Stenders. I didn't want to get Ciccone killed, however tempting that may have been.

"This is explosive stuff, Malick. How do I corroborate it?"

"Beats me, that's your job."

Ciccone smiled through his worry and attempted to sound casual. "This isn't your way of getting back after all these years, is it? Because look, I know in the past I may have written some unflattering things. Things I never totally made amends for, but your reputation has been largely restored—"

"I don't care about past grievances," I said impatiently. "I'm not that conniving or petty. Besides, I don't have the energy it takes to hold a torch for some bullshit like that. No, what I want is for you to blow the roof off this goddamned city. I want to shine a light into the cracks and see what kinda roaches come scurrying out."

"Sounds good to me. So Scott Barnhard hoodwinked the government—?"

"Allegedly."

"Allegedly," Ciccone repeated. "Possibly in league with one of Cain City's most decorated judges. Feds get wind of it and start digging into the allegations. Barnhard decides he's gonna cooperate with the investigation, possibly turn government witness against whoever else is involved, but before he gets the chance, he's murdered. Two days later, the prostitute he frequents, who happens to also service some of his associates, she's also murdered. Possibly because of what she knows about Barnhard's demise. That about the sum of it?"

"More or less."

"And police have already questioned Judge Blevins?"

"Yep."

"What'd they get out of him?"

I made a zero with my hand, closed one eye and peered through the opening as though it were a periscope. "*Nada.*"

Ciccone whistled. "I'll do the same thing I did last time, cite you as a source close to the investigation, if that's okay by you."

"Nah." I shook him off. "Go ahead and name me. Everybody'll know who it is anyway."

Ciccone, feverish with excitement now, ran a hand over the few hairs he had left on his head like he was making sure they hadn't moved. "Won't that get you in some hot water?"

"I've been in hot water before. I can handle it. Wait and see who comes after me for it. Then you'll be scratching the surface of the real story."

"You think the two murders are really connected? Could just be wonky timing."

I shrugged. "Could be. Weirder things have happened. But both murders were done up close and personal. Birdie strangled. Barnhard drowned. But who can prove it?"

"Strangled? That detail hasn't been made public yet."

"My gift to you," I said, opening up my hands in an exaggerated sacrificial gesture.

Ciccone put forth some more questions about Birdie, what she was like, the effect her mother's murder had on her, if she had any hopes, dreams, ambitions. Little detail questions to round out his characterization of her. I did my best to paint Birdie in a good light, to do her justice, and requested that Ciccone do the same.

"Yeah, sure," he said, reviewing his notes. "Lawyers. Prostitutes. Murders. This could be a monumental story, Malick."

"Maybe this time you'll get a regional award. You'll be known from Cain City to every podunk hamlet in Kentucky and southern Ohio. The champion of truth. The scribe of Appalachia. Hey, then you can thank me in your speech to whatever distinguished panel of ass-hats would honor you in the first place."

"One last question," he said, ignoring my belligerence. "You know how long Birdie was living there in the Royal Vista?"

"Year. Little over a year, I think."

"Huh."

Ciccone's face scrunched tight as though he were trying to ward off a sneeze. When the sneeze didn't come, I said, "What's 'huh' mean?"

"Wanna know something interesting I found out today?"

"You're sixty-three percent Mongol."

"What?"

"Turkish?"

"What are you blubbering about? No, after I found out who Aveena . . . who Birdie was, what she did for a living, I had a hunch, went down to the Assessor's Office to have a look through the residential records."

"Uh-huh."

"Her name wasn't on the lease to that apartment in the Royal Vista."

"I'm not shocked. Whose was?"

"That's just it. Nobody was on the lease. Not only that, but that apartment has been registered vacant for four years. No one, officially, has lived there for that long."

"So she was squatting. So what?"

"Maybe. If it were another building, maybe I'd assume so. But who gets away with squatting for over a year without anybody knowing? Tell me that. She wasn't skulking around the place, right? Sneaking in and out or anything?"

"No."

"Here's the interesting part. You know who owns that building?"

"No."

"River Path Group, the outfit that's been gobbling up property all over town for the past decade."

"The ones who are gonna build the outdoor mall or whatever on the Cruise Avenue site downtown?"

Ciccone leaned forward and wiggled his eyebrows as if her were about to disclose something salacious. Despite the fact that the juke was blasting and the crowd was humming too loudly for anybody to hear anything beyond a foot away, he whispered, "Those very ones."

He sat back and waited for a reaction from me that didn't come.

"From what I understand, they have very big plans for Cain City," he continued, jabbing his finger into the middle of the table as if that were the exact center-point of the town. "Word is they run a pretty tight ship, do everything above board. I couldn't find so much as a fine or a code violation on them. Nothing. Ambitious company like that, you wouldn't think they'd let a bunch of prostitutes run amuck in one of their properties."

"No, you wouldn't," I agreed. "Who runs River Path?"

"Don't know, I've gotta find out. Put a call in today that went unanswered. They're privately owned and operated. Got a modest little suite down on Centre Plaza that's listed as their business address. From what I've heard it's a bunch of local bigwigs that all function as silent partners."

"Well," I tipped my glass in his general direction. "Good luck to you."

Ciccone stuffed his pen and pad into his satchel and stood to leave.

"Thanks, Malick. Next one's on me." He tossed some bills onto the table. "*Quid pro quo* going forward? Keep the lines of communication open, backscratchers handy?"

"Sure, Ciccone. Anything for you."

"In that case, think you can get me a sit-down with Willis Hively?"

"Not in this lifetime."

"Worth a shot. Take it easy on the hard stuff, Malick. You're gonna be hurtin' for certain tomorrow."

"One can hope," I muttered.

After Ciccone left I sat there for a while staring into nothing. The surroundings of The Red Head blurred into a solid, meaningless backdrop of bodies and noise. No matter how much I drank, I couldn't rid my mind of the thoughts that plagued it like an ambient scream. How did these elements—Birdie's murder, Barnhard's murder, the Stenders, the real estate outfit—how did it all fit together? The connective tissue, the answer, elusive as it may be, seemed on the tip of my brain—all I had to do was reach out and pluck it from the ether, but I didn't know where to grab. Then again, maybe none of it meant a thing. Maybe the fragments were just that. Fragments. No larger narrative at play. Maybe it was all simpler than I was making it out to be.

I felt my upper body tottering sideways and managed to right myself before I fell clean out of my seat. A group of lumpy women sitting in an adjacent booth snickered. I looked up and saw them gesticulating in my direction. I abandoned the second bottle of Maker's, still two-thirds full, grabbed my hat and jacket, and struggled up from the seat. On my way out, I stopped by the ladies' table. The four of them looked sufficiently mortified by my sudden proximity. One of them shielded her face with her hand and mouthed, "O-M-G," to the two across the way from her.

I motioned to the plate of nachos sitting in the middle of their table. "What are you grazing on there?"

"Excuse me?" the one closest to me, a butchy blonde, said.

I glanced round to the booth I'd just come from. "Something funny?"

"What?"

"In English this time? Am—I—funny? Or amusing? You all look very amused."

Tadpole must have been monitoring the whole thing.

"Quit pestering the customers, Malick," he shouted angrily. "Glide your ass on outta here."

"You see me walking, don't you?"

"Not fast enough."

I turned back to the fat ladies. "No hard feelings. Whatcha drinking? I see umbrellas."

"That's not necessary," one of them said.

"Hey, Malick!" Tadpole hollered.

I pretended to be deaf. I peeled a twenty from my wallet and dropped it on the ladies' table. "'Nother round of nachos, then. On me. You're all on the fast track to diabetes anyway."

I left them there, blinkered and speechless, flipped Tadpole the bird, and stumbled out into the brisk, lonely night. No traps this time. Nobody lying in wait. The only person in sight was the old codger manning the hot dog stand across the way. I put my hat and jacket on and looked down the street to the old high school two blocks away, looming over the sepia-colored landscape with all the charm of a sanatorium. I scanned the windows on the third floor, tried to pick out Karla's bedroom, see if the light was on, but I couldn't tell which one was which and gave up. I wouldn't be welcome there anyway, not tonight, not in this inebriated state. She didn't come to see me, I mused. Probably smart. Probably for the best. But what did it mean? I didn't have the capacity to think too hard about it.

I pulled out my phone to see the time. Just past midnight. Seven missed calls from Karla along with three from Hively. He'd texted me as well.

No money in the ceiling, his message read. *Checking CCTV footage from PO Box place and surrounding buildings. Nothing yet. Talk tomorrow.*

I rocked on my heels, leaned back against the brick wall of the bar and gazed up at the starless sky. Then I was walking, not toward the high school, but in the opposite direction. Under the viaduct and into downtown. Past the courthouse, past the offices of Leach, McKinney & Thurber, past all the bars and clubs, past the banks and churches. I walked and I walked, not knowing where exactly I was headed. Not knowing until I was there. Into the East End, past the Malcolm Terrace housing projects, where I received hard stares from the residents gathered on their stoops, drinking, playing dominoes, listening to music. On down Clifford Avenue. Past the hospital. Past the gas stations and corner stores. To Spring Street.

The road was remarkably visible despite a dearth of artificial light. The street lamps had been busted so many times the city had stopped replacing them. Here and there, a few porch lights beamed out from the blue dark, serving only to illuminate the far greater number of dilapidated houses that sat vacant or condemned. All those trees being chopped down in the superficial effort to deter drug dealers from slinging out in the open made way for the light of the moon to reflect off the pavement and the handful of cars parked along the road.

I shambled along the sidewalk, past all the tree stumps, the yards smothered with weeds, to the shuttered corner house where Nico Blakes's crew had been set up a day ago. I sat on the stoop and watched the neighborhood for a while. It looked empty, felt empty, abandoned, but somewhere close a dog barked. At the edge of a boarded-up house across the street, the tip of a cigarette glowed red. Spring Street, here in the dead of night, may be playing possum, but it was very much alive, and it was scoping me as much as I was scoping it. That was good. I wanted to be seen.

I laid my head back against the top step's hard stone, tugged my cap down over my eyes, and promptly fell asleep.

CHAPTER TWENTY-SIX
SPRING STREET

"The fuck? Y'all know who this nigga is?"

I pushed my cap off my eyes and was greeted by the clean, muted light of dawn. Low puffs of gray clouds were expanding overhead like giant tumors encroaching upon the earth. I sat up to see who'd spouted the expletive that awakened me. Standing side by side on the sidewalk, clad in hoodies and bomber jackets, were the three corner boys Hively had spoken with two days prior.

My head felt like it'd been kicked in by a hoof. I rubbed the fog out of my eyes and worked my chalky mouth loose. "Morning, fellas."

The shortest one, who was flanked by the other two, stepped forward aggressively. "Yo, you like, invading our zone right now. You best move your hobo ass up outta here pronto or we gonna have to move it for you." For emphasis, the kid parted his bomber jacket and lifted the bottom of his hoodie to reveal a .38 tucked into his jeans. The oldest of the three, the one who hadn't taken his cold, murderous eyes off me during our previous visit, said, "Wait a minute. This that white dude who was with Five-O the other day. The one that stayed in the car."

"Bingo," I said, yawning. "I need to talk to your boss."

"You need to talk to who?" Short Stuff snipped.

"Nico. I need you to call him and tell him Nick Malick needs to talk."

"You police?"

"No."

Short Stuff took a brief look up and down the street to make sure nobody was watching. Not that it'd matter if there were. "I look stupid to you?" he said.

"Not yet."

The kid sniffed, making a show of being affronted, and pulled the .38 from his pants, held it loosely at his side.

"How I look to you now?"

"Listen," I said. "You're going through all the options in your head, right? Or if you're not, you should be. Here they are. One, you shoot me. Sure, it's possible, you've got the weapon ready enough. But that's just a lot of hassle for everybody, isn't it? You'd have to dispose of my body, for example."

"It ain't hard to rid a body in this town."

"Don't I know it. Two, you don't call Nico, you run me off. But what if he finds out? That could get you in trouble, see, because Nico knows what I'm about. You don't. Through no fault of your own. You don't know what you don't know. Option three, you call Nico, like I ask, tell him I'm here waiting to speak with him. Simple. No fuss. What's the worst that could happen? He gets a little pissed you woke him up at the crack of dawn?"

"And what happens when he says to get rid of you?"

"I'll walk away, no harm done."

"No, I mean *rid of you* rid of you. Like *ffft*." He dragged his thumb across his neck to illustrate his meaning.

"Yeah, I knew what you meant. Make the call. I'll take my chances."

"It's yo life."

"That it is."

The three of them conferenced for a minute, debated out the actions and consequences. Short Stuff broke the huddle.

"He gonna wanna know what this all about."

"Birdie Bryant and the Stenders."

"The Stenders? Shit, boy, you up in the thick of it, ain't you? All right."

Short Stuff pulled out his cell and stepped away to converse privately. The older one placed his foot on the second step and leaned forward over his knee. The malice was gone from his face.

"What's all this to do with Birdie Bryant?"

"You know her?"

"Yeah. Yeah, we came up together. Used to crush on her big time. Shit, everybody did. We had a dope connection though. I thought we was gonna make it happen. Then, you know how it is, she got grown and all of a sudden she ain't have the time of day for me no more. Started going around with them older niggas. Got knocked up, dropped off, that's that."

"Nick?" Short Stuff called over. He put his palm over the receiver and shuffled a couple steps in my direction. "Nick who you is?"

"Malick."

"Malick," he repeated into the receiver, again moving out of earshot.

I turned back to the older kid. "She was killed yesterday."

"What?" His shock at the news seemed genuine. "For real? Somebody got her?"

"Somebody did."

"Damn," he said wistfully. "Birdie Bryant. I didn't think she'd be one to go out like that. You live long enough though, I guess you see everything."

This statement from an average twenty-year-old would seem ridiculous, but the kids who grew up at the poles of Cain City, in the Malcolm Terrace Housing Projects, on Spring Street, over in The Stend, they aged in dog years.

I said, "Yeah, I guess you do."

"How'd they get her?"

"Trauma to the head. Strangled."

"Damn, ruthless. You know who did it?"

"That's what I'm trying figure out."

"You think Nico's gonna help you out or something?"

"We'll see."

"*Pshh*. I wouldn't hold your breath. I'm Rodney." Rodney stretched a hand toward me. I shook it.

"Nick."

"Yeah, Nick Malick. Nick Ma-Lick," he said, playing with the syllables. "That kinda rhymes."

"If you like your beats funky."

"Ah, I see what you're doing there. 'I'm spunky. I like my oatmeal lumpy.'"

"You know the old-school rap, huh?"

"That was my dad's jam. He used to blast that on his boom box and shit."

"What's his name?"

"My dad? His name was Sam. Sam Slash."

Rodney said the surname as though it were some kind of litmus test. Immediately he looked to see how I'd react.

"Your dad was Sam Slash?"

"You knew him?"

"Everybody knew Sam Slash. He was . . . well, he was one of the meanest son of a bitches that ever came through the East End."

"Yeah, I hear that a lot," Rodney said dourly.

"I saw him play basketball once at the Terrace courts," I told him. "Saw him jump up, no run at it, straight vertical, and put a quarter on the top of the backboard. Soon as he hits the ground he jumps right back up, snatches that quarter off. Craziest thing I ever saw."

Rodney smirked, taking obvious pride in this positive memory of his father, of which I'm sure there were few and far between. Short Stuff stuffed his cell phone into the pocket of his bomber and came over. "This your lucky day. Nico said to wait here. He'll be by in two shakes." He signaled for his colleagues to follow him. "We blowin'."

"Nice to meet you, Nick," Rodney said. "Hope you catch your bad guy."

"Take care of yourself, Rodney," I said, thinking, *Don't turn into too much of one yourself.* The trio moseyed off down the street, cut between a couple of houses, and disappeared.

I sat there and waited, then waited some more. Checked my phone, which was dead. It was good to have the time, clean of distraction, to work the whole thing over with clear, sober thoughts unclouded by liquor, fear, and self-pity. No, my thoughts now were clouded with vengeance, rage, and fury, but it was a clear-sighted vengeance, rage, and fury. Purposeful.

The thick clouds roiled in the sky above. Thunder boomed and the rains came down. I got up and stood beneath a small eave at the side of the vacant house that kept me from getting completely soaked. Twenty more minutes passed before the shiny black 4Runner came coasting down the block and pulled to a stop at the curb in front of me. The back window slid down.

"You gonna stand there getting pissed on or you gonna get in?" Nico Blakes called out. I jogged through the downpour and climbed into the back seat beside him. Junior Brown was in the driver's seat. No Arkell Prince. "Bet right about now you wishing we still had some of them big oaks on this street that you could've taken shelter under."

"That might've helped. Sorry if I woke you up."

"That's okay, we like our days to start out with a little something strange. Believe it or not, things around here can get a little mundane, cain't they, June?"

"Mmm," Junior Brown grumbled, still sounding half-asleep. "Downright monotonous."

"I didn't expect your crew to find me so early."

"Oh, them three boys is crazy. Probably ain't even been to bed yet."

"Rodney seems like a decent kid. I could do without the short one though."

"Pippen? Yeah, Pip always stuntin' on somebody. What'd he do, wave his gun around?"

"Something like that."

"I told June that little nigga gonna get himself in trouble one day."

Nico and Junior locked eyes in the rearview mirror, some non-verbal communication passed between them that I couldn't decipher, and Nico turned his attention back to me. He leaned back into the far corner of the cab. One of his hands was tucked into the front pocket of his hoodie, presumably holding a gun that was pointed in the direction of my abdomen. He laid his other arm across the back of the seat.

"Now that we've gone through the meet and greet, what can we do for you, Mr. Malick?"

"I need to find Momo Morrison."

A twitch of disappointment skipped across Nico's face, but only his face. Not his eyes. He had the calculating eyes of a sociopath or a maniac. They never betrayed a thing.

"Judging by the way your mug look, seems like you already found him. Or he found you, whichever way it went."

"He found me."

"Told you he would. Correct me if I'm wrong, but I believe my part of that business is over and done with. I said I'd pass the word, I passed the word."

"That was official. That was for Willis Hively. I was along for the ride. This would be for me, off the books. I wanna know, if you needed to find Momo Morrison, how would you do it? Not contact him. Find him, if you catch my meaning."

"Oh, I think I'm picking up your vibrations, detective. Here's the thing that intrigues me about this whole scenario we got going on right here. How long you been idling out here? All night?"

"Since two or three, yeah."

"You been out here all night, smelling like you done bathed in whiskey, getting stormed on, all to get up with me and June here, and you think that I'm going to give you a particularly sensitive piece of information because why? 'Cause I said I was grateful to you for getting rid of them Detroit boys?" Nico snorted. "You think that's worth enough for me to tell you something that could start some violence, get them redneck Stenders all in my grill if they connect said violence to me, which they undoubtedly would 'cause I already set y'all up once. That's what you think's gonna happen?"

"Yeah, pretty much."

Nico took my measure, then bared his teeth with that false, ingratiating smile. "You hear that, June?"

"Mmm."

"Everything I heard about you, Malick, says you was smart." Nico tapped a finger against his temple. "But what you doing here ain't that. This plan just faulty from the conception."

"I'm not that smart. Everybody else is just that dumb."

Nico Blakes's smile vanished. "Everybody dumb, huh?"

"Present company excluded, of course."

"Of course. See though, for you to come here, like this—" He gestured to my appearance, which had to be comical, at best. An unshaven, unemployed, waterlogged drunkard. "—got to be more to the story than that."

"There's not."

"Why you want Momo? You think he killed Birdie Bryant?"

"That, or he knows who did."

Nico nodded. "And you want what, to kill him? Little retribution."

"If he did it, yeah. That's exactly what I want."

"Shoooo." Nico pursed his lips and whistled through his teeth. "What you think, June?"

"You know what I think."

"Yeah, I know. Go on and drive then."

Junior Brown put the car into gear and started rolling down Spring Street. He took a right on Clifford Avenue and a left onto Seventh, parallel with the train tracks. Nico took his hand out of his pocket and rested it on the side console.

"I like you, Malick. You my type of lawman. Old school."

"I'm not the law."

"You close enough. But look here, I think you've gone a little nutty in the head if you think I'm gonna burn the Stenders just because you've got some vendetta with Momo Morrison. Now, if I was so inclined, if I saw something in it for me, I could give him to you, 'cause best believe I know a way to get him. 'Course I know a way to get him. Thing is, these Stenders are careful. It's hard to get to them if you need to, so if I burn this one tip, for you, then I'm left empty handed. What's in it for me? You see what I'm saying?"

"Okay," I said.

"What you mean, okay? You giving up that easy?"

"I'm not gonna beg you for it. Do me one favor, please. Don't tell him I'm coming."

Nico laughed. "You hear that, June? Don't worry, Malick. We won't put you behind the eight. I ain't friends with the dude. We don't speak on the reg or nothin'."

Junior Brown drove into the Southside and pulled the 4Runner to a stop outside of the old high school.

"Sorry we weren't able to come together on this one, Malick," Nico Blakes said. "You want an umbrella?"

"No." I went to open the door, but it was locked. "Can you unlock the door please?"

Nico looked at me with a curious expression. "What's Birdie Bryant to you, anyway?"

I started to say, "not a thing," but stopped short and decided to answer truthfully. Maybe truth could work, tug at his humanity. "I cared about her."

Nico cocked an eyebrow. "You was hitting that?"

"Not in that way. I knew her mom. After she was killed, I made sure all her kids were placed in good homes, made sure they'd be looked after properly. Birdie, she was nearly eighteen already, pregnant, all attitude, didn't want anything to do with me at first. Then she made some choices that put her in some bad spots, and bit by bit, she let me in. She wanted to get her life together, get her kid back. I was trying to help her do that. I didn't get her out of it fast enough. I was almost there. I almost had her. And now somebody's robbed her of the chance. So I'm gonna find out who that somebody is and I'm going to snuff out their future. Now if you don't mind, could you open the door please so I can get to it?"

"See, that's where you went wrong 'cause see, there ain't no future out here for us, for the Birdie Bryants of this world. You talking that Barack Obama false hope Americana nonsense. That kind of thinking just invites more trouble. You want to see the future, I'll show you the future." Nico rolled down his window. "There it is. The future is what you see when you look out these windows. Every once in a while, you'd hear about somebody who grew up here, who got out the Terrace, off of Spring Street or whatnot, made something of themselves out there in Magicville, but those stories were like fairy tales. They ain't real. They ain't happening to nobody you know. Nobody I know. And all they do is stoke that false hope, make it harder to live in this here reality."

"Maybe you're right."

"Oh, I know I'm right." Nico narrowed his eyes and studied me. "What you fixing to do now?"

"Don't know," I admitted. "Maybe I'll go door to door down on the West End until Momo opens one of them up. Less you got a better idea."

"Man, you really taking this one to heart, ain't you? What was this girl, like your salvage project or some shit? Your white guilt?"

"No, it's not that. She was my penance."

"Penance? For what?"

"Getting her mother killed by that Detroit crew."

Nico clenched his teeth and folded his lips tightly over

them, then flung his head back, groaned, and looked up at the ceiling. "I can't believe you about to do this," he said to himself. Junior shot a quick look back through the rearview mirror at us, but didn't voice any objection. "All right," Nico said, still addressing the roof, "thing is, this arrangement we've got with the Stenders, it's a precarious ecosystem we got going on. Delicate. You ever watch them nature shows? One little slip-up can throw the whole balance out of whack." Here Nico lowered his gaze back onto me. His tone turned callous. "And all the predators start devouring each other. You catch my meaning? So if I tell you where you can find Momo, and it comes back on me in—"

"It won't—"

Nico lifted a finger to stop me speaking. "If it comes back on me in any shape or form, then I'm gonna go from your friend to your foe in a blink, you understand?"

"Yeah."

"Now, way I figure, a lot in life comes down to who you know. What they can do for you. That's why white people get all the breaks. Because they know all the people who have the good shit. Connections, jobs, property, generation after generation of that shit getting passed down. Black people cain't compete and they cain't get nowhere because the most successful person we see when we growin' up is the dude down there running the corner. But this situation here, I give you what you're looking for—now I know you and you know me, you understand?"

"Yeah."

"You sure?"

"I get it."

Nico took a deep breath and let it out slow. "He's Skittles, man."

"Skittles?"

"He taste the rainbow."

"What does that mean? He's gay?"

Nico grimaced, tick-tocked his head back and forth. "I don't think that's how he would define it, but yeah, Momo don't discriminate when it comes to a piece of ass. How you think he got that nickname?"

"I thought it was short for Maurice."

"Play on words, man. Double entendre. Way I heard tell, he got the taste for it when he was eighteen. Did a little stint up in Moundsville. Assault beef."

"How does this help me?"

"You know that gay joint?"

"Flamboyant?"

"That the one over cross from the junkyard?"

"The Stone's Throw?"

"That's it. Momo's usually there on Saturday nights. They always got some kinda special theme going on. Drag queens, go-go dancers, all that jazz. From what I gather, Momo don't like to miss his Saturday night frolics."

I had to concentrate for a second to compute which day we were currently in. "Today's Saturday, right?"

"Let the man out the car, June."

CHAPTER TWENTY-SEVEN
FREE BIRD

I lumbered up the portico steps to the veranda and entered the old high school. Straight down the main hall, left at the split, another right, and I arrived outside my office. Tacked to the door was another pink eviction notice. I ripped it down, then fished through my pockets, but came up with only my wallet. No keys. I remembered that Hively confiscated them the previous night. Across the hallway was an old locker in which I kept a spare set.

Inside my office, I threw the notice on the counter, kicked off my boots, and went into the back bedroom; the bedroom Birdie would have been occupying, had she not been murdered. I took a long look around the space, picturing her there. The room felt stuffy now, airless.

I stripped and climbed into the shower, turned the knob on the hot water all the way over until it scalded my skin and revived my senses. After, I wiped the condensation from the mirror, examined my reflection. Between the tiny slits on my face, the purple and yellowing swell around my cheek, and the fat lip, I looked as though I'd been ganged up on by a cheese grater and a hammer. I put on some fresh clothes and trudged up to the third floor to Karla's apartment, reached for my keys, thought better of that, and knocked on the door.

When Karla opened it she didn't throw her arms around my neck or stand aside to let me by. At the very least, you'd think she'd be relieved to find me in one piece. None of that. What she did was elongate her neck, set her jaw defiantly, and cross her arms over her chest. She might as well have put on a suit of armor. The warmth faded from her eyes and she gazed upon me as if I were some unwanted solicitor.

Before I could speak, she said, "I'm sorry about Birdie," and in the next breath, "but I think you should stay in your office for a while. I need some space to figure some things out, whether or not this relationship is healthy for me or for my son."

"Fair enough."

Karla bit her lip and nodded incredulously as though I'd confirmed some deep-seated belief that she'd always suspected regarding my lack of commitment.

"That's it? Fair enough?"

"You sound pretty resolute. If a break from me is what you want, then that's what you'll get."

My dispassion seemed to fuel her anger. "Two nights ago you're beaten to a pulp. Then, last night, a totally separate case causes you to go off and get shit-faced and disappear—"

"She's not a case."

"—no texts, no calls, nothing. I've been with guys that disappear, Nick. Guys that do whatever they want with no regard for me or anybody else. I swear, I attract those types like mosquitoes. My dad was like that. Hell, maybe all guys are like that, but I'm not gonna do it anymore."

"You know what happened last night, right?"

"Yes, and I'm sorry. It's horrible. It's a tragedy."

"Yeah, you seem real broken up," I said facetiously. Karla forged ahead, unfazed.

"One thing I've learned in the past two years with you, Nick, is that something is always going to be happening. There's going to be a crisis. Whatever case you're working on, whatever your current obsession is, there's always going to be some drama that takes precedence over us."

"Obsession? What are you talking about, obsession?"

"Yes, Nick. Obsession. You're not happy unless there's some cause to consume you. You can't just be . . . normal."

"Normal? We're talking about the same thing here, right?"

"I hope so."

"You sure? Because I'm talking about the life of a young girl being snuffed out." I was getting fired up now. "I'm talking about people getting murdered. And I'm pretty sure you're talking about me getting drunk and not coming home, which, in the grand scheme of things, who gives a fuck?"

"You can't just disappear, Nick. You can't do that to me, to Davey. I have to be able to count on you."

"Count on me? Have I missed something? When in the last two years have you not been able to count on me? And as for last night, you knew where I was. If you wanted me to come home so bad, why didn't you come down there and get me?"

"Would it have made a difference if I showed up at The Red Head last night?"

"Maybe not, but you could have tried."

"Well, for your information, I did try. I walked down there. You were already gone. I came back here thinking you'd probably stumbled home to your office, but you weren't there either. I called you a hundred freakin' times. I called you all night long."

"My phone died."

"Yeah, no shit. Where were you?"

"I walked around for a little while."

"All night?"

"Pretty much. So I guess we're not getting a house then."

Karla scoffed in disbelief. "You were never gonna buy a house. You were never serious. You did what you had to do, said what you had to say to placate me, string me along and keep things stagnating."

"What are you talking about, stagnating? We were looking at listings two nights ago."

"I was looking at listings. You were nodding along and watching TV."

"That's because you want to buy the most luxurious mansion on the Southside. You wanna be serious? Let's get serious. Hate to break it to you, but those houses are a pipe dream. They're out of our league. So yeah, I let you have your fantasy. I didn't want to spoil it. I've even been trying to save up to make it come true for you, but you wanna buy one of those houses, you wanna leapfrog into the upper crust, it's not gonna be next week or next year or the year after that. I can't go out and plant a tree and watch the money bloom every spring."

"No, you'd need a yard for that."

"You know what I think?" I said, chalked full of scorn. A few of the neighbors had drifted out into the hall to watch the fireworks. I stopped my jawing at Karla and yelled at the lookie-loos to mind their own business, then waited for them to lollygag back into their units before picking up where I left off. "You know what I think?"

"Dying to hear it."

"I think this isn't about me. I think now you've got a new job, some good steady money coming your way, and for the first time in your life you can see a light at the end of the tunnel. A way up the ladder—"

"Don't say anything you're going to regret, Nick."

"We're past regrets, sweetheart. I was good for a time, I checked off all the boxes, a nice bridge from your hardscrabble days, but now you've got prospects, you've got options. Maybe you can even snag yourself a doctor like Joanna did. Hell, maybe you already have."

Karla reared back to slap me, but I'd been slapped by her before and knew how to spot it coming. I caught her arm by the wrist and flung it down to her side.

Karla screamed through clenched teeth. "You want to talk about Joanna?"

"Not particularly."

"Let's talk about her. I'm pretty sure she's still in love with you and I'm more than sure that you're still in love with her, so this is setting up just perfect for you. She's unhappy in her marriage and you're now free as a bird. Free to do whatever the hell you want to do with whoever the hell you want to do it with. You know what? Go for it."

"You sure can twist reality, can't you? It's awfully convenient for you to try and pin this mess on me when this is all you." She tried to say something, but I was on a roll. "You wanna go there, I'll go there. You're right about one thing; I do love Joanna. I love her like you love someone who once upon a time meant something to you, who you went through something as gut-wrenching as losing a child with. That forms a bit of a bond, wouldn't you imagine, that most people don't have the capacity to understand. That you obviously don't have the capacity to understand."

"I'm sorry. That's not what—"

"Don't apologize yet, I'm not finished. I don't love her like that. I could never love her like that again. Not like I love you. God knows why."

Karla, who'd had her eyes locked on mine this whole time, averted them now, sheepish.

"Look." I took a long breath and made a conscious effort to dial down the anger and modulate my tone. "I'll love you for as long as you'll let me, if you let me. I'll love you forever. But if you don't want to be together, then I get it. In fact, I think it's probably a smart decision. I wouldn't want to be with me either. But if this ends, don't put it on me. This here, all this here, is about you."

"No, it's about us," Karla sighed, the fight ebbing out of her. "I want to be with you. Of course I do. But not if you're going to revert back to the Nick I first met. The self-destructive behavior, the drinking, I can't be with that version of you, Nick. At some point I have to move forward in my life. I have to value my self-worth. I can't just keep settling, going through this same toxic cycle over and over again while nothing changes. I need to know who I'm waking up to, who I'm coming home to. I think that's fair to ask."

I didn't know what to say to that. Karla searched my countenance for some answer, some contrition, some sign of a soul. She must have come up wanting because her face cinched tight and her body stiffened. She pressed her fingers against the inner corners of her eyes, sniffed, and shook her head in disgust.

"So that's it? Nothing?"

"What do you want me to say? Good speech. Well executed. Those self-help books have really come in handy."

"You know what, you should go now, Nick."

"I need to grab a couple things."

"I'll bring your shit down to your place. I don't want you in here right now."

"Okay." We stood silent for a handful of seconds. I gazed at her, the soft, gorgeous curve of her cheek. Those sad, hypnotic eyes.

"I need you to leave, Nick."

"Can I get my car keys and phone charger at least?"

"You're unbelievable," she said, subdued. "Wait here."

She shut the door halfway so that I couldn't see inside and withdrew into the apartment. A moment later the door creaked open and Davey appeared.

"Yo."

"Sorry you had to hear that, kid."

"Yeah, my ears feel violated," he wisecracked, trying to alleviate the tension in the atmosphere. "The phrase 'free as a bird' is definitely gonna be a trigger for me in the future. Lynyrd Skynyrd's gonna have to have a disclaimer or some shit."

"Don't worry about this, all right? This is all—it'll work itself out in the end. Always does."

"You gonna be staying downstairs then?"

"For a bit. Till your mom cools off."

"I don't know, Nick. This time seems different. You might've done did it."

"Yeah," I conceded. "I might have."

Karla materialized behind Davey. "What are you doing?" she snapped at him. "Get back in your room please."

Davey cowed, said, "See ya, Nick," and slunk back inside.

"See ya, kid."

Karla thrust the keys and phone charger at me.

"Mind if I say something before you boot me?" I asked, taking the cord.

"It's a free country."

"So they say. Listen, I'm really proud of you. I mean that. Raising Davey on your own, putting yourself through nursing, getting this new job. Not many people can lift themselves up like that. I couldn't have. You're top shelf, Karla. One in a million. And you're right. You should never sell yourself short. You deserve better than me. You deserve better than most."

Her eyes welled again. "Top shelf? Is that the highest compliment you can come up with?"

"Best I've got."

"Fitting," she said, not unkindly. "What am I supposed to do with that, Nick? Huh?"

"Take it with you, I suppose."

"Why are you talking like this is the last time we're gonna see each other? What is going on with you?"

"You don't want to know."

"Right," she said, her hostility toward me easing a little, "that's why I asked. 'Cause I don't want to know."

I raised my hand up and ran the back of my fingers along the soft, beautiful contours of her perfect face. She allowed it. She grabbed the back of my hand and held it there against her cheek.

"Don't do anything stupid," she whispered.

"Why does everyone always say that to me?"

"Because they know you." She kissed the palm of my hand and let go of it. "What happened to Birdie, it's not your fault. It's not your debt to pay."

"Whose is it then?"

"I don't know. Her mother's, her father's, the universe's, it doesn't matter. You don't have to do whatever it is you're going to do. You can bow out of all this. You can step away. It's your choice."

"You're right, it is my choice. And I don't have to. But I want to. You may have had me pegged from the start. It's always something with me, huh? Some compulsion."

"I didn't . . ."

"What?"

"Nothing," she said softly. "Go."

"I'll see you soon," I said, and turned and walked away from her, not knowing if we were finished, not knowing if, in fact, I would see her soon, or ever again.

CHAPTER TWENTY-EIGHT
CHARIOT OF DEATH

Down in my office I plugged my phone in and preceded to eat everything I had on hand, which wasn't much: some southwestern flavored Rice-A-Roni, an orange, a half-bag of stale pretzels, and an expired pudding cup. It took some serious perseverance to see a pudding cup through its 'best by' date.

While I ate I read over the eviction notice. It was more specific than the previous one. The reasons for my eviction were laid out in a crisp Arial font:

1. *There have been multiple complaints about the types of people said tenant's business brings into the building.*

2. *Existing tenants report fear for their safety as long as said tenant remains in residence.*

3. *Tenant's continuing presence lowers the overall desirability of the property for prospective lessees.*

4. *Tenant resides on the first floor, despite the lease agreement stating very clearly that the first floor is arrogated for businesses only, not for residential occupancy.*

Number one was garbage. The class of people who sought my services were no worse than the people who lived here. What were they trying to do, gentrify the place? A gentrified Cain City, that'd be the day. The second, okay, I could see that one. The listed cause in number three was also questionable. Nobody desired to live in these ramshackle apartments in the first place. If they were here it was because there weren't any other options available. However, they had me on number four, though they were late to the game on that front; I'd been living out of my office for years. The listed causes, coupled with the fact that, as of last night, I was no longer employed by a law firm that could assist me in fighting this eviction, meant that my time in the old high school was probably coming to an end. I wish I could say thanks for the memories, but most of them, outside of Karla and Davey, were pretty much shit. *C'est la vie.*

One detail I hadn't paid attention to on the previous eviction slip was the name of the company who'd taken over the property. It was River Path Group. And that I found a little peculiar. Their listed address was 25 Centre Plaza, Suite 300. That was in the Monarch building downtown, across from the library. I pocketed the notice, opened the safe beneath my desk and sifted through its contents: a little bit of cash, my Nikon and its various lenses, a backup snub .32, various recording devices, some file folders, and an extra clip for my subcompact Beretta. I took the clip, shut the safe, and grabbed my phone off the plug. It was forty-eight percent charged. Good enough. There were twenty-three missed calls to go along with three voicemails, all from Karla. Her last call had been placed just after five a.m. She hadn't been exaggerating; she'd waited for me all night. It didn't take a genius to ascertain what was going to be on the voicemails, so I'd listen to those later, maybe. I strapped on my shoulder holster, jacket, flat cap and hit the door.

The storm had passed and the sun parted the clouds, imbuing the cool air with a thick, muggy quality. I set out for The Red Head where my Tacoma was parked. That's where I thought it was parked anyway. When I got there the Tacoma was nowhere in the parking lot, nowhere in sight. Sure that it'd been either stolen or towed, I kicked some gravel, cursed the universe, and stomped around until I was out of breath and had to bend over and cough for a while.

Doing that, I remembered that I hadn't been the one who drove there from the Royal Vista. Hively had. Jesus Christ, I was forgetting everything. The apartment building was only a mile or so away, but my body was sore from the beating I'd taken, stoved up from sleeping on a stoop, and now I was winded from the hissy I'd just thrown. I didn't have another mile in me. I leaned against the wall beneath the awning of The Red Head and rang the cabbie I knew, Dennis Maynard.

"What?" he answered grumpily.

"You working?" I said.

"Huh?" He cleared his gullet for a protracted amount of time and hocked out some bile. "Would it matter if I said no?"

"No."

I told him where I was and to come get me. While I waited I put in a call to the *Cain City Dispatch*. Ciccone was at his desk, doing his best to hammer out a headline story in time for the Sunday edition of the paper. In the background, I could hear his rapid pecking of the keyboard.

"Malick, how you feeling, sweetheart? After the show you put on last night, I wasn't sure if you'd still be gracing us with your presence in the land of the living."

"'Bout like somebody jimmied open my skull, gave my brain a good shake and shoved it back in. We didn't have sex, did we?"

"Ha! A gentleman never tells. Has something else happened?" Ciccone said, putting a halt to the banter. His weaselly voice quivered with anticipation.

"Maybe. Those residential records you researched—"

"Yeah?"

"Were there any other apartments at the Royal Vista that have been vacant long-term?"

A pause on his end. The pecking stopped. "I didn't look for that. Do you think there are more of them? More girls?"

"I know of one other one. I want to know if there's more."

"Aw, shit," Ciccone whined. "It's Saturday. The assessor's office is closed."

"When have you ever let a little thing like operating hours stop you? Do what you do best, Ernie. Grease some palms, lick some ass. I need to know which apartments haven't been leased for long stretches."

Another pause. "Good pep talk, Malick. You gonna pass me whatever intel you find out?"

"Fast as the clap."

"I'll make some calls."

I hung up, sank down onto the asphalt to wait for the cab, thought about the day ahead and made a mental "to-do" list. I needed to figure out how many girls the Stenders were running out of the Royal Vista. See if I could track one of them down to question. I'd talk to Renata, try to shake any details loose from her brain that might be helpful. Then there was the River Path Group, which owned my building, the Royal Vista, and seemingly over half the town. I had to find out if they were culpable for the prostitution racket that flourished in one of their properties. Lastly, this evening I had a date at the Stone's Throw with Momo Morrison. There I could stand to use a little backup, but my intentions weren't exactly pure, so I couldn't involve Willis Hively or Bruce Hale. Maybe I could get Bob Lawson to keep an eye out for me. Pay him out of my own pocket.

That was a good enough plan for now. Best I could come up with anyway. I leaned my head back against the wall, tipped my hat low and closed my eyes. A dozen minutes later Dennis Maynard screeched to a halt at the curb out front of The Red Head. He laid on the horn to roust me from my doze.

"Your chariot has arrived," he hollered, jutting his head out the window. I shoved up off the wall, crossed the sidewalk, and slid into the back seat. Maynard scoped me in the rearview mirror. "My God, man," he chortled. "Who did you like *that*?"

"Fight with a bear."

"Brown or black?" Maynard asked, deadpan. I couldn't tell if he was being serious.

"Polar."

"Now, I'd almost believe that. Them polar bears are mean sumbitches. Tell you what, every time I see ya, you look 'bout ten times worse than the time I seen you before."

"Yeah, well, you smell about as good as I look." This was true. His diseased breath permeated the interior of the cab.

"Two of us make the perfect pair," Maynard snorted. "Halves of a whole. You ain't getting me tangled up in the middle of none of your mischief again, are you?"

"No."

"Shoot me straight now."

"What'd I just say?"

"Okay, okay, had to ask, don't get your tampon stuck. I appreciate the business you send my way, I truly do, but you get in my cab I get jumpy. Seeing your face gives me PTSD, swear to God. I wasn't my natural self for a year after that last ordeal."

"Mm-hmm. Ever thought of investing in some air fresheners? Maybe some Altoids?"

"I got piña colada going in here right now." Maynard sniffed the air. "Smells like Panama City. You don't smell it?"

"No."

"That's vexing. I just got that thing."

I told Maynard where to drive. He immediately pitched a fit.

"You call me down here nine in the morning on a Saturday to give you a two-dollar ride downtown? Nuh-uh, no sir. You can step your hairy little butt right back out onto that curb. I done paid my debt to you and then some."

"Fine. You wanna go further? Drive me out to Becksville. I've got a stop to make out there, then you can bring me back downtown."

"Aw, man, you gotta be kidding me. All the way out Becksville? Again?"

"Pick your poison. What do you mean, again?"

Maynard reminded me that I'd sent him to pick up a pretty little chocolate thing, his words, out in Becksville on Wednesday and that she'd put the ride on my tab. Birdie. The morning I'd had to rush off because Scott Barnhard failed to show up to his appointment with the U.S. Attorney. I'd forgotten that detail. Then Barnhard's body was discovered and all this nasty business kicked off.

Maynard snapped me out of my recollection by asking me how long my sojourn out to the 'burbs was going to be. I told him no time at all and he could keep the meter running. He pulled out, did a three-point turn in the middle of the road and headed back past the old high school, up to the top of Fifth Street Hill where he merged onto the interstate. I'd made this very drive with Birdie, what, three days ago? In that short time the trees that hemmed the road had lost their vibrance. The reds and yellows had started to brown. It happened that fast. Like everything else—in tiny imperceptible increments, and then all at once.

Maynard exited the interstate and steered down the dead-end road to the modest house with the chain-link fence and swing set out front.

"Ten minutes," I said, getting out. I rapped on the front door to the house and stepped back. The chaotic noises of small children sounded from within. Dottie, their foster mother, admonished them to a different room, unbolted the door and swung it open.

"Oh," she said, slightly startled by my bruised and battered self gracing her vestibule. "Hello. Were we scheduled for a visit?"

"Hello, Dottie. No, there was nothing on the books for today."

The way I said it caused her to brace for the news to come. I gave it to her. Dottie invited me into her kitchen and poured me a cup of black coffee from a pot she had brewed. As we sat down, a blur of children flashed by the doorway as they ran wildly around the house, squealing and hollering. I caught sight of Aisha's wild marigold curls bouncing by.

"In the playroom or else," Dottie ordered them. They didn't listen and she didn't have the steam to follow through on the "or else" part. A sip of the coffee seared my tongue.

"What happens now?" I asked.

"I don't know," Dottie said. "As you know, I've steered prospective parents away from Aisha to this point in hopes that Birdie would be able to regain custody. I always hope for that, if there's a chance."

"So you'll—"

"Try to find her a permanent home? I suppose that is the next step, unless you know of a family member who might want to take her in."

"No, there's nobody. Her brothers and sisters won't be eighteen for, I don't know, four more years or so."

"I wouldn't recommend that anyway. Better to place her with someone more suited to fulfill her needs, financially and emotionally."

"Right, of course. You vet them, these families? I mean, she'll get a good one, yeah?"

"I don't vet them personally. CPS does. There is never any certainty, but by and large these are decent families that want to take these kids in." Dottie sighed, sipped at her coffee. "What a shame. I was rooting for Birdie, I truly was."

"Me too."

Dottie reflected silently for a moment, and I listened to the happy, raucous sounds of the children in the next room.

"Aisha is such a delightful child," Dottie said, when she finally spoke. "One of my very favorites to ever come through here. Don't tell the rest of them." She winked.

"You're a special sort, Dottie. It's the hardest job in the world, taking care of littles. You set them on a path they would never have had access to otherwise."

"We all deserve to be loved, Mr. Malick. Especially children."

"I don't know about all of us, but I agree with the children part."

As if on cue, Aisha appeared in the doorframe. In her hand was the unicorn doll her mother had given to her during our last visit. She fixed her bright eyes on me and tilted her head curiously.

Dottie said, "Come say hello to Mr. Malick, Aisha." Aisha smiled shyly and stepped ever so carefully into the kitchen. When she got to within an arm's length, she hopped suddenly against my leg and thrust the unicorn toward my face.

"U-cone," she chirped.

"That's right," I said. "That is a unicorn."

A look of pride swelled on her tiny, beautiful face. I'd forgotten how wondrous an effective communication could be for a child. The unabashed joy for something as simple as a message sent and a message received.

"I forgot to tell you," Dottie said, choking back emotion. "Aisha started speaking this past Thursday. Didn't you, Aisha? You started babbling up a storm. I was so excited to show Birdie."

Aisha glanced back and forth between us with a puzzled expression. "Mama?"

"No mama today," I said mournfully. "Only me. Only Nick."

CHAPTER TWENTY-NINE
THREE TO THE GUT

I paid Dennis Maynard, thanked him for the ride, and got out of the cab in front of the Royal Vista. I walked around to the side where my Tacoma was still parked. Other than the eighty-five-dollar parking ticket affixed to the windshield, the truck didn't look as though it had been messed with overnight. It was still green, the tires still had air in them, and nobody had sawed the catalytic converter off the muffler.

I ascended the three steps to the side entrance, punched in the code, and let myself into the building. I boarded the elevator and rode to the sixth floor. The prostitute that Tom Orvietto frequented in the days before he lucked out with Joanna, the one who went by the name Destiny, used to conduct her business out of apartment 619. Maybe she still did. I rapped on the door and stepped back. Nobody answered so I beat on it some more. The resident who lived in the neighboring unit flung open his door and stepped into the hall.

"You," he hissed. It was the bent old man who'd been wearing the bucket hat and tuxedo jacket the day before. Now he had on a raggedy set of long johns. The white whiskers at the corners of his mouth twitched with recognition. Apparently, he still held some animus toward me for bumping into him during the fracas with the police. "How about knocking off that racket?"

"Sorry, I didn't mean to get you out of bed before noon."

"Don't you sass me, fella," he snapped. "I may be getting on in years, but don't be fooled. Go on and test me. I can still thump you upside the head."

I laughed and told him to go back inside before he broke a hip or gave himself an aneurysm. He mulled that over, decided that he'd blustered enough for one day, and retreated to his apartment.

Before he shut the door the old geezer took one more poke. "At least I'm not deaf, dumb, or blind 'cause that's about what you'd have to be to think there was a living, breathing soul in that apartment that could possibly have failed to hear the cacophony you're making. She ain't there."

"You know who lives here?" I said quickly.

"'Course I do. Nobody." He moved to close the door. I stepped over and stopped it shutting with my foot and forearm.

"Since when? You said she. Where did she go?"

The old man pulled the door back and started banging it repeatedly against my arm. "Out of the way."

"Listen old-timer, I'm investigating the murder of the girl downstairs. I need to talk to the woman who lives in that apartment."

He stopped hitting me with the door. "I told you. She's gone. Been gone six months or more, good riddance if you ask me. Pleasant enough, but she was a good-time girl, if you catch my drift. Had a lot of *nocturnal* visitors. Noisy as hell. These thin walls don't allow for no secrets." He hiked his eyebrows to emphasize his meaning.

"You know where she went?"

"Where she went?" The old man's face puckered as if the question were ridiculous. "No, nobody knows where she got off to. How could we? She just up and *phffft*, skedaddled. Ain't leave no forwarding address or nothing. Mail piled up there for weeks. Halfway up the door. I've still got some of it, case she ever comes back round."

"Was her name Destiny?"

"Destiny?" The old man cocked his head quizzically. "That ain't what the mail says."

"I'm going to need to see that mail."

Marvina E. Justice. That was who the credit card statements, tabloid magazines and Bed Bath & Beyond coupons were addressed to. The geezer had stuffed it all haphazardly into a garbage bag. As I sorted through the parcel, I prodded him for information about Marvina. She wasn't very ingratiating with her neighbors, he told me. Though if spoken to, she was pleasant enough. And she always apologized for the loud noise that came from her apartment all hours of the night: music, yelling, banging. Every so often Gary, that was the old man's name, would hear a scream or a string of curses and wonder whether or not he should phone the police. But he never got around to it and soon enough the screaming would cease. The curses never sounded like the threatening sort. Gary didn't want to get anybody in trouble if he wasn't sure that somebody was being harmed.

"Naturally," I said. "You ever call the leasing office? Make a formal complaint about the noise?"

"'Bout ten times. They'd send some little peckerwood down here, pardon my French. He'd come by and try to smooth things over. Tell me he talked to her, that she'd promised to keep it down, that kind of thing. Couple times he shaved a little off the rent. Enough to string me along till my ears couldn't take it no more again."

"He have a little mustache? Horn-rimmed glasses?"

"You know him?"

"Sounds like the same prick who's trying to kick me out of my apartment."

"I don't know nothing about that," Gary said seriously. I asked him one last question: what did Marvina look like? His description—pretty, pile of curly red hair, lots of freckles, skin so white you'd think it'd never seen the sun—all but confirmed Destiny and Marvina were one and the same.

Justice was a common enough surname, but Marvina, I reckoned there couldn't be too many of those floating around town. Should be simple enough to find some record of her and track her down if she was still in Cain City. I did a quick Marvina Justice search on a couple different social media platforms. Then Destiny Justice. Didn't come up with anything.

I thanked Gary and descended a flight of steps to the fifth floor where I walked to the far end of the hall and banged on number 512. The only clue that this was the scene of a grisly murder less than twenty-four hours prior was a rubber skid mark that streaked the tile floor in the shape of a Nike swoosh. Probably made from the gurney that transported Birdie's body down to the ambulance. I stared at the black swoosh for a moment, then thumped the door again.

"Renata, you in there? It's Nick."

No response. I tried the knob. Didn't turn. When I raised my fist to knock a third time, a shrill, sustained scream pierced the air. It originated from the interior of the apartment.

I drew my Beretta from its holster, kicked the door open and moved in. Renata was on the couch, wide-eyed, chest heaving in and out with panicked breaths. No one else visible in the kitchen or living room. Renata thrust a shaky finger toward the rear of the apartment. Just then a loud crash came from the direction of Birdie's bedroom. I hustled down the hallway, crouched and peered around the doorframe in time to see a large figure in a trench coat hurling itself over the railing of the terrace. The sliding glass door had been shattered. I charged into the room. Broken glass crunched underfoot. I reached the railing just in time to see the fleeing man swing onto the balcony below. I aimed my gun over the side, in case the man's intention was to rappel down the building balcony by balcony.

Someone in the unit below bellowed, "What the—" and had that thought cut short with a dull wallop. I ran back through Birdie's room and the hallway to the front of the apartment. Renata was curled into a ball against the wall.

"Stay put, call the police," I told her, not stopping as I barreled through the door and into the corridor. I sprinted down past the elevators, glanced to see if the numbers were moving—they weren't—and continued into the stairwell. There I stopped, peered over the balustrade, and listened. No sounds, just the groan of pipes, the buzz from the light fixture on the ceiling.

Gun drawn, I edged along the wall, down the steps to the fourth-floor landing. Kneeling beside the heavy metal door that opened to the hallway, I took hold of the handle and cracked it open. First thing, before I could even hazard a glimpse through the slit, a hail of gunshots rang out. Bullets riddled the metal door and the wall I was crouched behind and whizzed through the opening. I let go of the handle, squeezed low against the wall and rode out the gunfire. When it ceased, I chanced a quick look-see and recognized the assailant immediately. It was Lil' Mike Mike, the goon with the dopey face who had accompanied Momo Morrison into The Red Head the other night. I raised my Beretta, but before I could squeeze the trigger Lil' Mike Mike took a running start at one of the apartments, rammed the door and tumbled inside. I waited a few seconds to see if he wasn't setting a trap to lure me into the open. When he didn't peek out I slipped into the hallway and crept toward the apartment. A couple of dimwits ventured out of their units to see what all the hubbub was about. I gestured for them to get back inside. They saw my gun and complied. The door Lil' Mike Mike burst through had been torn from its hinges. I leaned my back against the wall next to it.

"Lil' Mike Mike?" I called out. "You in there?"

For ten seconds, nothing. Then, "Yeah, I'm here." His voice was muffled, as though it were coming from the depths of the dwelling. Or maybe he was smarter than he looked, had covered his mouth with his hand and, at that very moment, had his gun trained on the doorway, waiting for me to show myself.

"Anybody in there with you?"

"Why don't you come on in and see for yourself?"

I removed my cap and slowly raised it into the clearing of the doorway to see if he'd take a potshot. Nothing doing. I put my hat back on and said, "Woke up the neighborhood with those shots, Mike Mike. Cops are sure to be on their way, and you're pretty well cornered. Way I see it, you got two choices. You can surrender and walk out of here, or you can put up a fight and be carted out. Up to you."

"You'd like that, wouldn't you, Malick?" Whatever had suppressed his voice before was gone now. He sounded closer.

"'Fraid you're gonna have to be a little more specific, Mike Mike."

"If you wanna take me down, if the cops wanna take me down, then you're just gonna have to come in here and get me."

"Stretcher then? That's how I figured you'd play it, dumb as you are."

"Fuck you, Malick," Mike Mike hissed. "You little kumquat."

"Kumquat? Either you need a dictionary or you've got me confused with your buddy Momo." The faint wail of police sirens became audible. "Clock's ticking, Mike Mike. You need to borrow some bullets? Can't have too many left in that Sig P."

Mike Mike didn't respond. The sirens amplified with their approach. Brakes screeched outside the building. Car doors slammed. Then, from within the apartment, a signal of movement. The wood floor creaked three times, loud and distinct. I readied my Beretta and braced for the action to come. Suddenly the floor shook with thunderous footfalls. Bullets rained into the hallway. The crazy ogre was rushing me. The concussions from the gunshots were deafening. My brain rattled in my skull. I dropped to a knee and pointed my gun in the general vicinity where I thought Lil' Mike Mike would emerge.

It all happened in less than two seconds. I saw the muzzle flash of his Sig, the massive blur of his body leaping through the doorway, finger on the trigger, firing away. I unloaded my clip. He missed. I didn't.

Lil' Mike Mike's body thudded against the ground, bounced once, and came to rest on the tile. He was so tall he nearly spanned the width of the corridor. I picked his gun up off the floor and used my foot to roll him over onto his back. He was still alive, but just. His breathing was shallow and irregular on account of not being able to suck any air past his throat. Peeling the lapels of his trench coat back revealed five entry wounds perforating his torso. Two to the chest and three in the gut. Another bullet had taken a chunk out of one of his giant ears.

"Was that really necessary?" I said.

Lil' Mike Mike strained to lift his head and assess his condition. What he saw dashed any hope for survival from the equation. Bright blood trickled from the holes in his chest and oozed from the three in his stomach. He dropped his head onto the tile and stared at the florescent tube lights on the low ceiling. His pupils constricted to small dots.

"You shot me," he whispered. "You shot me."

I squatted next to him and spoke urgently. "Who killed the girl, Mike Mike? Who killed Birdie Bryant? Was it you?"

Unexpectedly, his mouth parted into a smile and he began to laugh. A short, weak laugh that curdled into a moan.

"Come clean now," I implored him. "There's nothing left to lose. Give me a name."

Mike Mike struggled to shape his mouth around some words. A jolt of oncoming death twitched through his body.

"C'mon, Mike Mike. One name."

"You wouldn't—" he croaked. "You wouldn't—" A gurgle rose from his throat, his long face went slack, and with those last unfinished utterances, Lil' Mike Mike took leave of this world.

I slumped back against the wall and gazed down at the huge dead husk beside me. *Another one,* I thought. Another snuffed-out life I'd have to account for when whatever entity that held dominion over this existence came to collect my bill. Lil'

Mike Mike was a cretin, sure, and he'd earned the death I dealt him, but he might also have been a husband, a father, a brother. He might have been the light of somebody's life. I highly doubted it, but who knew?

I frisked his pockets, found a set of keys and a money clip, but nothing else.

Movement, out of the corner of my eye. Not the bold approach of police officers, something more furtive. In one swoop, I ejected the clip from my Beretta, retrieved another from my jacket pocket, slammed it into the stock and pointed the gun toward the blurry figure standing halfway down the hall.

Renata froze in her tracks. I lowered the gun and got to my feet.

"It's okay," I said, gesturing toward Lil' Mike Mike. "He's dead."

Renata looked from the body to me, me to the body. Her arms and legs began shaking. The jadedness, the sarcasm, the lassitude that Renata used to protect herself from the world was gone now, stripped away, replaced by fear and panic. There was a child's innocence in her eyes. "I can't be here," she whimpered, hugging herself with her arms. I noticed then that all she had on was a gray tank top and panties.

I stepped toward her, tried to sound comforting. "This isn't your fault, Renata. None of this is. Just tell the police what happened and you'll be fine."

"No." She shook her head desperately, as though she were trying to erase the contents of her brain. "No, you don't understand. They're going to kill me now. The police, they in on it."

"Who's going to kill you? What are you talking about?"

"That one that was talking to me last night, that detective."

"Which one?"

"The one with the red hair."

"What about him?"

"He's one of the men who used to come see Birdie."

"What?" I blurted, even though the implications of what Renata was saying crystalized immediately in my mind. If she were telling the truth, then Red Lewis, the lead detective in the Birdie Bryant murder investigation, had been one of her johns, and if Red Lewis was one of Birdie's johns, it was possible that he'd been videotaped, just as Tom Orvietto had, which exposed him to being blackmailed, probably by the giant dead man at my feet, and, playing that scenario out to its logical conclusion, was likely under the Stenders' thumb. It also made him a suspect in her homicide.

Soon, the police were in the stairwell. We heard one of them yell, "Clear," on the bottom-floor landing. They started thumping their way up the next flight.

"Aw, shit," I said.

"You think?" Renata whispered.

"Is there another way out of here?"

CHAPTER THIRTY
BLOOD SPECTACLE

Renata's eyes darted with her thoughts. "Um. Um" —she flitted her hands beside her head to help jog the words loose— "um—the roof! There's a ladder connects to the next building."

I stripped my jacket off and put it on her. It was long enough to drape over her upper thighs and give the impression that there may be some sort of clothing beneath there, however skimpy. Nothing we could do about the bare feet. I instructed Renata to get to the roof, cross to the other building and go to the library, which was located in the heart of downtown, three blocks northwest of our current location.

"Hide out in one of the study alcoves on the third floor. Wait for me. Don't leave. I'll find you. Got it?" She nodded rapidly. "Good. Run."

Renata took off, hit the stairwell, and bounded up out of sight about twenty seconds before the police stampeded onto the landing.

I stretched my arms above my head. "Over here, fellas."

It wasn't too long before all the principles were convened around the kitchen table in the apartment where Lil' Mike Mike had mounted his last stand. Red Lewis and his partner, Jerome Kipling, had me take them through the events step by step—coming to check on Renata, the knock on the door, the scream, busting in, the jump over the balcony, the chase downstairs, the shootout, and finally the charge, the death deal. Then they asked me to repeat the story to see if I slipped up on any of the details or sequences. Willis Hively leaned against the wall behind them, glowering.

"C'mon," I said. "I know how this recipe is cooked. Story's not going to change. What I told you is what went down."

Red Lewis leaned forward over the table. He had a face like a fat apple and a thick helmet of red hair that clung to his scalp, giving him more than a passing resemblance to Ronald McDonald.

"Something's funky about this," he said.

"I smell it too," I replied evenly. "Why don't you tell everybody what you think is off kilter about this whole scenario, Red?" He leaned back in his chair. "No? Okay, how about this, I'll count to three and we'll both say it at the same time. Ready?"

I thought I saw Red's left eye flutter, but couldn't swear to it. Staring me down, he said, "Why is it, Malick, that whenever there's a blood spectacle in this town, whenever the bodies start piling up, you always seem to be right smack dab in the thick of it?"

"It's a curse really, being so damn prescient in my job. Wish I could get some of it to rub off on the two of you, but unfortunately the magic doesn't work that way."

"How do you think it's gonna play in the public when everybody hears you're in the middle of another fiasco? That you've shot and killed yet another person? Might come off looking a might trigger happy, wouldn't you say? Maybe you won't be everybody's favorite dick anymore."

"Your mother been talking about me again?"

Red puffed out some air and snarled, "You're a gambling man, aren't you, Malick? Like to gamble with your mouth, your life, other people's lives. Doesn't matter as long as it serves your purposes. You know what they say the worst thing that can happen to a gambler is?" I didn't answer. He jutted his neck forward. "You hear the words coming out of my mouth?"

"Was that not rhetorical?"

"Winning, that's what. Winning is the worst thing that can happen to you. You know why?"

"I could venture a guess."

"Tell him what he's won, Jerry."

Jerome Kipling smiled eagerly, like he'd just been tagged into the match. "'Cause when you win, even just once, you get that taste of invincibility, and no matter how many holes you dig yourself into, you believe you can get yourself out of it, again and again and again if you have to."

I understood now that this was a two-hander bit they were performing. Their execution wasn't too bad, as it were. Riffed off each other well, picked up their cues, though they may have played the tough-guy theatrics a tad heavy.

Red Lewis jumped back in. "Sure, you won some, Malick. Hell, you've won your fair share, but how many times you think you're gonna come out the other end of one of these gunfights? Odds are going to catch up with you."

Kipling's turn. He pointed a finger toward the entrance to the kitchen. "You know who that is out there?"

"Who? Lil' Mike Mike?" I feigned a yawn, feigned stifling it. "He a friend of yours?"

"That's a Stender. You talk about gambling with your life. You might as well cash in your chips now because you don't fess up the straight story, let me tell you something, we're gonna let you walk out of this building unprotected, and if we leave you exposed to them, well, compadre, your ass is grass."

"My *ass* is *grass*? Jesus Christ," I exclaimed. "Is this Penn and Teller act how the two of you conduct all your interrogations? Do you guys practice this stuff in the mirror? It's a wonder you make any collars at all."

"Teller never talks, jackass," Kipling said. "It's their whole schtick."

"You'd do well to follow his example," I shot back. "Tell you what. If we're gonna stick to the gambling analogies, here's one for you. I'm all in." I shifted my gaze to Red Lewis. "Got that? *All in.* You can pass that message along to the Stenders next time you happen to talk to them."

Red Lewis's ruddy face flushed to match the color of his moniker or his hair. Whichever metaphor you preferred, I'd struck a nerve. He looked apoplectic. Red made a show of laughter to mask his physically changing colors, but the performance was unconvincing. I was onto him.

He stopped his phony laughing, and growled, "The next time I speak to a member of the Stenders, it'll be because we'll be trying to figure out which one of them killed your dumb ass."

"So you didn't track the deceased here?" Hively said to me, piping up for the first time since the interrogation had commenced. He came off the wall, stood between the two seated detectives and put his palms on the table, leaning forward over them. "Maybe seek retribution against the people you thought were responsible for Birdie Bryant's murder?"

"It's understandable if you were upset after somebody offed your little girlfriend," Red Lewis snarked.

Rage ripped through my body, volted through my veins. My skin burned, my fingertips tingled. I wanted to leap across the table and give Red Lewis a taste of what my vengeance looked like. To wring his neck the way someone had wrung Birdie's. Squeeze the life out of him barehanded. Instead, I locked my fingers behind my head and reclined back in the chair, lifting its two front legs off the ground. A study in nonchalance. I met Hive's eyes, made sure he was looking right into mine before I spoke. "You know better."

"I don't put anything past you, Malick."

I tossed my hands up and put my chair back on all four legs. "Tell me, what would you have me do when I knock on a door and someone inside screams bloody murder? Go down to the corner store for a scone and come back later? Besides—" My gaze shifted to Red Lewis. "I'd have to know who the murderer was before I could get my revenge, wouldn't I?" The tip of Red's tongue poked through his teeth. He looked as though he might bite it off.

Hively said, "Renata gonna back this story up?"

"She's upstairs. Ask her yourself."

"She's not up there," Hively countered. "But why do I get the impression that you already knew that?"

"Beats me. That's where I left her. I have no idea why she'd flee the scene when a couple of fine policemen like yourselves were coming to the rescue. Makes a person pause to wonder."

Jerome Kipling peppered me with a couple more questions about my relationship with Birdie Bryant, to which I gave vague answers, and he asked why I was in the Royal Vista today in the first place.

"I told you. To check on Renata."

"You shtupping her, too?" Red asked bitterly.

Hively dismissed his query. "You have no idea as to Renata's current whereabouts?"

"Not a one. Are you guys gonna book me or what?"

"You better believe we are," Jerome Kipling sneered. "We're gonna throw you in holding with the rest of the scum. You'll be right at home."

"Can I get a word, gentlemen?" Hively said. Reluctantly, Lewis and Kipling acquiesced and the three of them cleared out. I strained to hear whatever they were saying out in the hall, but couldn't make it out. My phone buzzed. Ernie Ciccone. I answered it.

"Yeah."

"Got some intel," Ciccone barked. "Two additional apartments in the Royal Vista have been vacant long-term."

"I'm here now. Which ones?"

"207 and 410."

Hively came back into the kitchen by himself, lowered himself into the seat across the table.

"Okay, thanks. I gotta go."

"Wait a sec," Ciccone groused. "What are—"

I cut the call and tucked the phone into my pants pocket. Hively and I stared at each other for a handful of seconds.

I said, "You planting your flag with them now?"

"I'm police, Malick. My flag's always in the same spot." He took the seat across the table and let out a weary sigh. "You have to get lippy with everyone?"

"What do you want me to do, talk to those two gumps like their combined IQ breaks double digits?"

Either Hively agreed with that assessment of his colleagues or he didn't rate that cap worthy of a response. "Not twelve hours ago you told me you were done. Out for good."

"I *am* done."

"Then you won't be interested to know that Sturges uncovered an interesting little nugget about our friend Judge Blevins."

"Couldn't care in the slightest."

"Don't bullshit me, Nick. I know you. I know you're making a play. What's changed from last night to now?"

"My mood. No, check that. It was when someone tried to shoot a couple dozen holes through me."

"Well, genius," Hively retorted, "now you're gonna have even more psychotic rednecks wanting to do the same thing."

"I'm pissing in my boots," I said.

"You don't tell me what I want to know right now, Malick, that's it. We're through."

"We've broken up before. My heart will recover. If it's all the same to you, let's end this little tête-à-tête, shall we? Whatever you gotta do, Hive, do it and get it over with."

Hively's whole body tensed. He bit his lower lip and extended his neck as though the collar on his dress shirt had become suddenly tight. His Adam's apple bobbed once, hard. "We're gonna cut you loose, Nick. Let you fend for yourself."

"How big of you."

Hively's tone turned officious. "You know the drill. You gotta come to the station, give a formal statement. We'll confiscate the gun. You'll get it back—"

"Soon as I'm cleared of any wrongdoing," I cut in. "Yeah, yeah, that's all well and good. But I'm not coming to the station."

Hively's face tensed. "That wasn't a request."

"Listen, Hive. I've got a lead to run down. If I don't get where I need to be in a timely fashion, that lead might dry up, get lost in the wind for who knows how long. Maybe for good." I was speaking of Renata, though Hive could obviously only intimate that fact. The number of leads or suspects in Birdie's murder could run into the hundreds based off that news interview she gave alone. But Renata, she was afraid for her life. And I wasn't sure how long she'd stick around the library before she spooked or simply got bored and jetted. Getting my statement processed at the station would take hours. I couldn't chance keeping her waiting for that much time.

Hively placed his palms flat on the table and spoke in deliberate syllables as a means to keep his composure. "You were involved in a shooting with a fatality. You know the protocol."

"You need to ask yourself something, Hive. Do you want to catch some killers, or do you want to play by the rules and wait to see what fucked-up thing happens next?"

Hively pounded his fist down on the table, then ran a hand over his face to keep from screaming. "You are the fucked-up thing," he hissed. "What do you want from me, some special treatment?"

"Sure, since you're offering."

"I'm not offering you shit. You gonna tell me what your play is or are we back to you icing me out? Hmm? We back there?" I didn't answer. Hively let out an exasperated sigh. "I don't know what I can do to be any more of a friend to you, Malick."

"Cut me loose, like you said. But let me postpone my statement for a day or two."

"I can't do that." He nodded toward the front of the apartment. "Technically, this is Red's and Kipling's case, and they want to hold you for twenty-four right now, run you through the wringer. They're waiting for me to bring you out so they can process your statement personally. I had to get Hale on the line to tell them I took precedence because you are my asset, but that ain't gonna hold up for long if you don't tell me right this second what you're running. What was the back and forth with Red all about?"

I tilted my head, warningly. "You don't want to know, Hive."

"No, I do want to know. Let me put it to you this way. You tell me what your lead is or I'm turning you over to him and Kipling and washing my hands of the whole thing."

Hively wasn't a hard man to take measure of. He wasn't one for idle threats. I weighed my options, decided there was no harm working in conjunction with him and the police as long as our motivations lined up. I'd freely divulge anything I deemed pertinent to their investigations. But any leads I found to Birdie's killer, those were for me alone. Whoever caused Birdie to breathe her last breath, they wouldn't be getting the benefit of a fallible justice system. No jury of their peers, no burden of proof. I'd be their judge, jury, and executioner. They were mine.

Hively interrupted my ruminating. "Do I need to count to three like I do with my kids?"

"I need you to do things my way, Hive. On my terms."

"You want outta here now? You got no leg to barter with. Spill it."

"It's gonna open a can. And once you hear it there's no going back."

"I'm waiting."

I wet my lips, considered my options one last time and came up with no alternative. So I gave it to him. "Red might be compromised."

Hively didn't flinch. We lived in a town that brought out the basest in a person's instincts, in a world that no longer held shock value. Hively had adapted accordingly.

"How?"

"He was one of Birdie's johns."

There was no need for further explanation; Hively worked the significance out for himself, nearly as quickly as I had.

"How do you know this?"

"Renata." I told him how she'd made a run for it when the police showed up, her escape route out of the building, where she was waiting for me.

"She's still there?" Hively asked.

"Hope so."

"Kipling dirty too?"

"She didn't mention him."

Hively pulled a small, smoothed-out pet rock from his pocket and started working it over while we talked, the way a Catholic works a chain of rosary beads.

"So yesterday, Renata wasn't distraught just because she'd found her roommate murdered. She was scared because she thought the murderer might be the man standing right in front of her, prodding her to reveal everything she might know about it. About him."

"I don't know. I didn't get much of a chance to talk to her before the troops came marching in. That's why I want to get over there before she skips out. I'll put her up at my place or a motel. Nobody'll know she's with us."

"Okay," Hively nodded. "What was your plan before Sasquatch out there started shooting at you?"

"First, tell me what Sturges found out about Judge Blevins."

CHAPTER THIRTY-ONE
THE VACANTS

Rutherford Blevins, as it turned out, had quite the history with the Stenders, though it would take someone parsing through the court records with a fine-toothed comb to suss it out. Plenty of known Stenders came through Blevins's courtroom when he was a criminal judge. That wasn't a surprise. What made it curious was the fact that, time and again, the defendants in those cases either received the lightest sentence the law would permit or got their charges dismissed outright. Not exactly damning evidence, but when measured against Blevins's judgments on the whole, a stark discrepancy emerged. He was typically heavy-handed when doling out punishments, including offenses comparable to the ones the Stenders stood accused of.

"What's that prove, Hive, other than he's racist?"

"Remember that stint Momo Morrison did when he was eighteen?" Hively cocked an eyebrow. "He got sent up for eight months. Should have been two to five years minimum. Got pled down. And Momo appeared two other times in front of him. The first, he received a suspended sentence, and the other one got tossed. Buddy the Face, Lil' Mike Mike, they all went through Blevins's courtroom. Twenty-three cases in total. All of 'em got off light. Hell, Blevins even dismissed a domestic violence charge against the king of the Stenders himself, Fenton Teague, for insufficient evidence."

"To what end though? If you're Blevins, why risk it?"

Hively tocked his head back and forth as he considered the question. "Don't know. This is the same guy who was likely getting mad kickbacks from Scott Barnhard. So, money? Girls? Similar social beliefs? Why does anybody do anything that stupid?"

"Maybe." I told Hive what Ernie Ciccone had discovered about the long-term vacants in the Royal Vista, and the likelihood that more prostitutes were plying their trade in the building. And also Ciccone's suspicion that any kind of illicit activity wouldn't have gone unnoticed by the property's owners, River Path Group. "He's working on an article for the Sunday paper about the possible connection between the two murders. We'll see if that shakes anything loose."

Hive asked me again what my plan had been before Lil' Mike Mike disrupted my schedule with a little gunplay.

"I was going to see what information I could glean from Renata, then try to track down this Destiny woman and do the same. Maybe pay a visit to the River Path offices, ruffle some feathers. They're trying to kick me out of the old high school. Can you believe that?"

"Surprised it's taken them this long. All right—" Hively put his elbows on the table, clenched his hands into a double fist and leaned forward into it. I could see his mind churning. "Before we take another run at the judge, I'm gonna have a chat with the prosecutors who tried those Stender cases. See if they suspected any foul play."

"What about Red and Kipling?" I asked.

"Let me think about it. If Red's on the pad, the Stenders are gonna know real soon you're the one shot Lil' Mike Mike. You gotta be careful. We gotta find a way to smoke him out."

"Yeah, no shit. But I meant right now. How are you gonna get me past them?"

"I'll handle it. Tell them Hale wants me to take your statement. For them to keep working the scene or some shit. We're still gonna have to keep your gun."

"Yeah, yeah."

I neglected to tell Hively that I had a possible bead on Momo Morrison that night. If Momo showed his face at the Stone's Throw, I was planning on breaking a few of the laws Hively was sworn to uphold.

We walked out into the hallway where Red Lewis and Jerome Kipling were hovering over Mike Mike's body. Kipling was speaking with the forensics investigator while Red was telling the police photographer the different pictures he wanted of the scene. Hively instructed me to take a walk. I obeyed and strolled down to the far end of the hall. I surveyed the cluster of pocks in the door and wall where Mike Mike had thrown a bunch of bullets at me. Marveled at how I hadn't been hit by a single one of them.

Hively had pulled Lewis and Kipling aside and was talking animatedly with the detectives. However he was framing the situation, it wasn't going over like gangbusters. Kipling tossed his head back like he couldn't believe his ears, while Red banged the fat underside of his fist on the wall.

Red yelled, "If something ever goes sideways for me, I hope to hell I'll have the same highfaluting friends that he does." He jabbed one of his stubby fingers down the hall toward me. I smiled blithely and waved. Hively listened to a few more of their complaints before cutting them off by walking away. He reached me and didn't slow down. I met him at the elevators. He reached for the down button, but I caught his wrist.

"Let's go up first."

We rode to the sixth floor and walked down to the door I had knocked on no more than an hour ago. 619.

"This one of the vacants?" Hively asked.

"This was Destiny's apartment. Or Marvina's. I think that's her real name."

"Who the fuck names a kid Marvina?"

"Guess they were planning for a boy," I said. "Want to look inside?"

"Is it open?"

I tried the handle. It didn't turn.

"We gotta get a warrant," Hively said.

I stared over his shoulder as though someone had appeared there. "Nothing to see here," I said. Hively whirled around to see whom I was addressing. I reared my leg back and kicked at the soft wood around the knob. The door swung free and banged against the interior wall.

"Look at that," I said. "It is open."

"Fuck's sake," Hively growled.

We entered the front room. The place was fully furnished: sofa, recliner, bar stools at the kitchen counter, dishes in the cabinets, silverware in the drawers. Nice stuff, from Crate & Barrel or one of those places.

"Doesn't look vacant to me," said Hively.

I ran a finger over the countertop and showed him the layer of soot that came off on my finger, then pointed to a bouquet of wilted flowers in a vase by the kitchen window. I opened the fridge. It was dark, airless, and smelled like a morgue.

"Jesus," Hive said. "Shut that."

We moved through the apartment. More of the same. Blankets still on the bed. Curtains still hanging over the windows and the sliding glass door that led to the patio. But there were no clothes in the closets or drawers. No toiletries in the bathroom.

Back out in the living room, Hively remarked, "Somebody left in a hurry."

"Maybe the place she was going was already furnished." I held up the dangling end to a cable cord that was draped over the mantle. "Or she planned on coming back."

Hively called Clyde Sturges and asked him to run the name Marvina Justice, see if he could find a last known address or phone number. It didn't take long. Hively put him on speakerphone.

"Here we go," Sturges said, his reedy voice distorted further by the speaker. "Marvina's last registered address was her parents' house, 319 Third Street West, this was three years and some change ago. She was also registered as a student at Cain

College for two and a half years before dropping out in her . . . fifth semester. Wait a second—" We heard the *click-clack* of a keyboard. "I'm looking up the house address on a real estate site now," he said, narrating his clacking. "Okay, here it is. It looks like the bank repossessed the house from her parents. Let me look them up." Another short wait before Sturges resumed his discourse. "Oh shit, okay. So it looks like the house was repossessed around the same time she dropped out, which was concurrent with her parents having been killed in an automobile accident. From there she drops off the grid."

Hively said, "Sturges, I think we finally found your niche."

"Go suck a—" was all Sturges managed to say before Hively hung up on him.

He turned to me. "So she drops out, lives here doing whatever it is she was doing—"

"Hooking—"

"And then six months ago, poof, thin air. Let's check the other two vacants."

I told Hively the apartment numbers. One was on the fourth floor near our crime scene. The other was on the second.

"You check them," I said. "Let me know what you find. I have to get to Renata."

We hopped back on the elevator and rode down. Before Hively got off on the second floor, we made plans to get back up with each other that evening. I exited on the ground level and was walking toward the side door near to where my truck was still parked when I saw the mob of reporters gathered outside.

"Fuck me," I muttered. I couldn't risk getting held up further, so I turned around, re-boarded the elevator and punched the button to the top floor, then thought better of it and hit five. The elevator doors slid open and I glanced down the hallway to make sure there were no police stationed outside Birdie and Renata's apartment. Yellow crime scene tape stretched across their doorway, but no cops. They were all downstairs. I hurried down the hall and ducked under the tape.

I had never been in Renata's bedroom, nor seen inside. The

door was always shut. I opened it now and flipped the light switch. The room was sparse, its only furnishings a stacked set of plastic drawers and a single sheetless mattress on the floor. Lined against one wall were a dozen or so papier-mâché heads that looked to be homemade. Perched on each of them was a colored wig: pink, red, blue, green, silver, all different lengths and shapes. No other accessories or decorations to speak of. A small round mirror hung from a nail on the wall. Taped beside the mirror were three Polaroids. One was a close-up of Renata laughing. Another was of Birdie sticking her tongue out at the camera. The third was a selfie of both girls. In it, half the frame was blocked by Renata's arm. The other half depicted Birdie planting a big kiss on Renata's cheek, Renata cringing in mock disgust. They looked like the joyous teenagers they may have been in an alternate universe.

I broke away from the photos, quickly sifted through the plastic drawers, and pulled out a pair of jeans to go with an oversized sweater that had two interlocking G's decaled on the front. As I turned to leave, I noticed something else on the floor next to the bed. Birdie's red lava lamp. It was plugged into an outlet by the mattress, but wasn't turned on. I snagged a pair of shoes from the closet and got out of there, walked to the stairwell at the end of the hall and ascended the single flight to the sixth floor. Half a flight up from there was the exit to the roof. A placard screwed to the door read: EMERGEN-CY EXIT ONLY: ALARM WILL SOUND. I ignored it and pushed through. No alarm.

I squinted against the sharp flare of sun that baked the blacktop of the roof. Sweat immediately started trickling down my back and into the crack of my ass. I walked across the roof and peered over the ledge to where the horde of reporters were crammed against the side entrance to the building. I'm sure Ciccone was down there, jockeying for information or a quote. It was plain to see, between the reporters and the police, there was no way to get to my Tacoma without being spotted. Without being hounded.

If I've said it once, I've said it a million times. "Fuck me."

From that vantage I could also see clear to the library, an expansive four-story structure with a shingled red roof that took up the majority of Centre Plaza. The plaza was a series of shops and businesses that bisected the 900 block between Fourth and Fifth Avenues. The Monarch Building, where River Path operated from, was across the street from the library. I mentally mapped the quickest route to get from here to there, then crossed to the other side of the roof to look for the ladder Renata said connected the Royal Vista to the neighboring office building. I thought she meant a ladder that was attached to a wall and maybe I'd have to descend a few rungs to an adjoining roof. That's not what she meant. There was a slim alleyway between the two buildings. Laid across the expanse from one ledge to another was a flimsy extension ladder. The middle of the ladder, where the extension bracketed, was secured with a thin rope.

"You gotta be kidding me."

I peeked down past the ladder to make sure there wasn't a body splattered all over the alley. At least that way I could skip having to traverse the goddamned thing. No such luck. Renata had made it soundly across. I tossed the clothes and shoes over to the other roof. Then I stomped on the first rung of the ladder a couple of times to test the stability. It didn't give too much, so I tried the second rung. Same result. I said what the hell, made up my mind to walk across rather than crawl, and nine rungs later I was safely on the other side.

The rooftop door that led down into the stairwell was propped open by a cinderblock. I descended all the way down to the lobby. There, to avoid any undue attention, I took off my shoulder holster, stuffed it into my pocket and exited onto the street.

The library was three blocks northeast. I cut through a Mexican restaurant and a public parking lot to shave time, but I needn't have worried. I found Renata Jones right where I'd told her to wait for me, in one of the study alcoves on the third floor. She was curled up in a chair with her head resting crooked on the desk, fast asleep. My jacket was draped over her and only the top of her face and her toes were visible. So much for her being frightened and going AWOL. Looking at her like that, you'd think she didn't have a care in the world.

I nudged Renata's shoulder. She came awake with a start, jolting upright, eyes bugging. When she saw it was me she relaxed and blinked her eyes back to their usual circumference. She inhaled deeply through her nose and stretched her arms wide.

"Ugh," she groaned, dropping the stretch, slumping back into a ball. She took in her surroundings impassively.

"Put these on." I tossed her the clothes and shoes. She held the clothes aloft to examine what I'd brought for her, seemed satisfied with the selection, and asked me to turn around so she could get dressed.

When she was decent she said, "M'kay, I'm good," and handed me my jacket. "What now?"

"Now's the part where you tell me what Lil' Mike Mike was doing in your apartment."

"The dude you killed?"

"Yeah."

Renata pulled a series of faces that were meant to convey innocence and virtue. "I don't know what he was doing there. I don't even know how he got in. I thought the door was locked. All of a sudden he just walks up in there, tells me not to say a word, says I'm coming with him."

"Coming where?"

"How I know? Then he walked back into Birdie's room and I don't know what's going on, if I should run or what. I didn't know who the fuck he was."

"You'd never seen him before?"

"Nuh-uh."

"How long was he back there?"

"Not long. You knock on the door. He comes out holding a gun, holds a finger to his lips and tells me not to make a sound. But I wasn't born yesterday. I scream. He takes off. In you come. You know the rest."

"You'd never seen him before?"

Renata shook her head. "Nuh-uh."

"Okay. Listen, stay here. I've gotta check on something real quick."

"Where I'm gonna go?"

From the information Clyde Sturges unearthed, I assumed Marvina Justice had been in high school six or seven years ago. If she had been living in her parents' house on 3rd Street West at that time, she would have been districted to Piedmont High School. The library collected the yearbooks from each school year. They were kept on the second-floor shelf of the Local Publications section. I pulled four of the yearbooks from that time-span and brought them back to the alcove.

Renata held her face in her hands, looking miserable. I sat down at the desk and started thumbing through the class photographs, scanning for the name Justice. It didn't take long. Marvina graduated from Southside seven years ago. The name by her picture read *Justice, Vina*. She'd cut out the "Mar." Vina's senior portrait fit the description both her neighbor, Gary, and Tom Orvietto had given. Thick red curly hair, pearly white skin, gobs of freckles. She was pretty, with scorching green eyes and striking features. Vina wasn't exactly smiling at the camera, but she wasn't not smiling either.

Renata stuck her nose where I was looking. "I know that girl. She live upstairs."

"What do you know about her?"

Renata gave me a cockeyed look like it might be a trick question. "That she live upstairs."

"That's it? You never talked to her?"

"What some fancy white girl got to do with me?"

I took my phone out, snapped a photo of Vina Justice, and stood to leave.

"Where we goin'?"

"My place."

CHAPTER THIRTY-TWO
A FREAK WITHOUT WARNING

The Royal Vista was still overrun with media and police, so I dialed the cabbie again.

"Didn't I just drop you off at your car?" Dennis Maynard said warily into the phone. "What, you got a flat or something?"

"Yeah, it won't start. Come get us."

"Aw, hell's bells. It's always something with you, ain't it? All right, I'll be there in five."

I tucked my phone away and walked across the plaza to The Monarch Building, where River Path's office was located. At three stories high, The Monarch was diminutive compared to the structures on either side of it, but a hundred and some odd years ago it had been the first boarding house to operate in Cain City, thus it had been granted landmark status and turned into an office building. I tugged on the heavy oak doors, but they were locked. I pressed the buzzer on the intercom. Someone with a twerpy voice answered immediately.

I said, "UPS," and the big doors buzzed. A small package had been left on the vestibule. I opened one of the doors and used the package to prop it, then re-crossed the plaza and joined Renata on a bench under the eaves of the library. She was picking at her scalp, watching people go in and out of the library's rotating glass doors.

"Whatchoo doing over there?" she asked, not looking at me.

"Seeing if anybody was home."

"It's Saturday. Ain't nobody work on Saturdays."

"Some people do. Tell me something, Renata. What did you mean when you said the girl in the yearbook was fancy?"

"Whatchoo mean?"

"What made her fancy?"

Renata's demeanor turned salty. "Just the way she carried herself. Way she wore her clothes or wouldn't even look at you. Like she was too good. Petty shit. Let me tell you something, you living in the Royal Vista, you ain't too good for nothing. I don't play those games. That girl is a bitch, straight up."

"Birdie know her?"

"Doubt it."

"Why?"

"Um—" Renata trailed off. A young black mother with two kids exited the library. Renata stopped digging into her scalp and stared intently at the mother. I couldn't tell if the expression on her face was fury, envy, or simply deep curiosity. Renata tracked the family all the way to their minivan, didn't take her eyes off them as the mother buckled her kids into their car seats, climbed behind the wheel, cautiously pulled out of their parking spot and rolled down the lane. When the van turned onto the avenue and drove out of sight, Renata gazed into the space where it had disappeared for a few more beats, then snapped to like she had come out of a trance. She resumed scratching her head.

"Why didn't Birdie know her?" I said.

"Know who?"

"Vina. The girl in the yearbook."

"Oh, right. Birdie didn't pay no attention to nothing like that. She had her own thing going on. She wasn't out here in the world like me. Birdie was basically, like, trapped up in that apartment."

"But you pay attention, don't you, Renata? You see a lot of things."

"Psshh. You can say that again."

"You noticed all the men who came to see her."

Renata frowned as though I were the one who was daft and pitiable. "You got something to ask me, ask me."

"Who came to see her the night she was killed?"

"Now that, I don't know. That was a weird night. Must have been a full moon or something. There was damn near a traffic jam, so many cars in that alley. They just kept coming. Bunch of dogs in heat. Felt like a parade. Everybody was getting play. Least till the cops came round, broke up the party."

"Police raided the alley that night?"

"Yeah, you ain't seen mayhem till you seen a bunch of road-hard hookers scattering like cockroaches, trying to keep from getting locked up."

"What time was this?"

"I dunno. I lose track when I'm working. They'll be times it's like all of a sudden the sun comes up." Renata shrugged as if the whole thing were beyond her control.

"So cops come, what do you do?"

Renata squinted, trying to think back. "I dunno. I might have gone down to The Drop Shop for a drink, I do that sometimes, but let me think. I might have just gone home."

"I thought you were supposed to make yourself scarce when Birdie had a client in the apartment."

"I am. I do. But sometimes you get tired of sitting outside waiting for these motherfuckers to nut, know what I'm saying? So sometimes I might creep back in. If the coast is clear, I book it to my room. What nobody don't know don't hurt 'em."

"That's what you did that night?"

"Yeah."

"You didn't see or hear anything?"

"Nuh-uh."

"But you saw a lot of the guys that visited Birdie, right?"

"I'd say I saw them all one time or another. Coming in the side door. Or going out. They don't never pay attention to me."

"Were there a lot of one-offs, or were most of them repeat customers?"

"One-offs? Like dudes that just came round one time?"

"Yeah."

"Naw, weren't many of them. Birdie got a magic Venus flytrap or something, 'cause once they got a taste of her, they kept coming back. I don't know how she did it, really. Must've been able to fake that shit good like that one movie. What's that movie?"

"Beats me."

"I could never do that, be fake like that."

"Could you identify the men? If I showed you pictures, could you tell me which ones you've seen there?"

"Yeah, that wouldn't be a problem."

"What about names? You ever hear any names? Birdie ever talk about any of them?"

"Naw, not all that much. Billy Bob. 'Cause I'd seen him. That's it really."

"What about the cop, Red Lewis? How often did he come see, Birdie?"

"Standing appointment. Every Thursday ten p.m. See, that's what it was. I thought I saw him with the cops that swooped up on the alley that night. He one of the only ones of Birdie's knew who I was, knew I lived up in there with her. Dude was always giving me the evil eye and shit. Gave me the creeps. That's what he was doing last night, too. I felt like he was staring into my soul, trying to send me like, whatchama-callit, like subliminal messages or whatever, warning me not to say nothing. Or daring me *to* say something. I don't know. That whole night is kind of messed up in my mind."

"I know. I was a wreck too."

"Yeah, I saw them haul you up outta there." Renata turned and appraised my haggard appearance, the cuts and swelling on my face. "So that's what I did when the raid came. I was afraid he was coming after me, like for reals. So I went home, went to my room and locked the door."

"You're sure you didn't hear or see anything? Somebody leaving later that night, nothing like that?"

"Nuh-uh, nothing like that. I crashed out, didn't hear nothing. You think she was already dead?"

"I don't know. I don't know what happened, Renata. That's what I'm gonna try and find out."

Renata nodded, satisfied that someone was on Birdie's side for a change, on her side. Then she got distracted by something she'd picked off her scalp and scrutinized the underside of her fingernails.

Couple minutes later Maynard pulled his cab into the slot the minivan had vacated and tooted his horn. I stood.

"This is us."

"I know that dude," Renata said, under her breath.

"From the alley?"

"Yeah."

Off her alert, cornered expression I said, "He a bad one?"

"No," she said, deflated. "Not *bad* bad. Just—I dunno, gross."

"I tell him how gross he is all the time," I replied. "C'mon."

Renata got to her feet and shuffled over to the cab, climbed in ahead of me and slid to the far side of the backseat. Maynard adjusted his rearview mirror to get a good look at her.

"I know you?" he asked. Renata didn't respond. "You work the window over Taco Bell on Fifth Avenue, cross from the Field House?"

"Don't act like you don't know where you know me from!" Renata blurted. Recognition showed immediately in Maynard's face and his spine seemed to compress into his body like a bashful turtle's.

"I was just trying to be cordial for fuck's sake," he mumbled.

I took a certain amount of pleasure in Maynard's discomfort. "You hungry?" I asked Renata, as though nothing were amiss.

"I was," she answered.

I directed Maynard to hit the Taco Bell drive-thru on our way back to the old high school and bought everybody some MexiMelts and cinnamon twists. Maynard was too rankled by Renata's presence to see the irony in my choice of restaurants, but the free food seemed to pacify the both of them. We ate as he steered down under the viaduct and into the Southside. The processed beef and hot sauce improved the aroma of the cab.

When Maynard dropped us at the curb, I told him I'd be back down in a few minutes and asked him to wait for me.

"Don't think I'm not keeping this here meter running," he warned.

"Wouldn't dream of it."

I led Renata up the steps to the portico, into the high school, and through the maze of corridors to my office. There I gave her the thirty-second tour: front room, kitchenette, back bedroom, bathroom. Renata looked around the space dispassionately. In the bedroom she grunted something that sounded like disapproval, plopped down onto the mattress and tested the squeaky springs.

"So this is where you were going to set Birdie up?"

"This is it. Don't get too comfortable. We can't stay long."

"What you mean?"

"The man that was in your apartment—"

"The dead one?"

"Yeah, the dead one. There are more of him. And they'll be coming for the both of us now."

"You think that man was fittin' to kill me?"

"If he thought you knew something you weren't supposed to, yeah I think he was."

"Why? I told you I don't know nothing though."

"I know. Listen, a lot of shit has happened. I've gotta go do something real quick. Just chill for a bit. Rest a little. I'll be right back and then we're gonna go check into a motel, stay there until I can get this whole thing sorted out. Okay?"

"Choice I got?" she said. Then, mumbling to herself, "Stone-cold killers out here trying to get at me and shit. For what? For nothing. For living." She addressed me again. "What I'm supposed to do somebody comes in here when you're gone?"

"Nothing's gonna happen in the next half hour, but just in case, don't open the door for anyone. Don't even open it if you think it's me."

"Them dudes ain't gonna knock or nothing. What I'm supposed to do if they come bursting up in here?"

"Window's not that high. Jump out of it and run."

Renata stood up and peered down through the window to the ground. She cocked an eyebrow. "But what if they come through the windows?"

"Then you're fucked. Listen, when I get back I'm gonna show you some pictures and have you describe some of the men you saw. Okay?"

"Yeah, yeah, yeah," Renata said, lashing out. "Okay, okay, okay. Can you stop talking at me now? My head is hurting."

I don't know if a foul look swept across my face or what, but Renata's mood shifted at once. Her irritation evaporated. She yawned and her mouth stretched into a chasm wide as a serpent's. So wide you'd think her jaw was double-jointed. Eventually her face reset to its natural position. She flopped onto the bed, situated the pillow under her head, and pointed to the boxy television perched atop the dresser.

"That thing work?"

"It gets the basic channels."

"Basics? It got a remote?"

"Doesn't work, you have to get up and change it."

"Ugh," Renata grumbled. "This situation is lotsa fucked up."

"It's not ideal," I agreed.

"What about my clothes and phone and shit?"

"When the scene at the Royal Vista dies down I'll go grab some clothes for you. Probably best if you don't call anyone now, okay? Anybody knowing what's going on or where you are will be dangerous for you and for them. Got it?"

Renata muttered something that may or may not have been recognized as language.

"Got it?" I repeated.

"Yes, damn, I got it," Renata snapped. "Can you turn that TV on?"

I hit the power button, flipped through the seven channels the bunny ears picked up, found some afternoon talk show she didn't mind watching. With her content to lie there staring dead-eyed at the screen, I went to my safe and grabbed my black-market .32 along with an accompanying box of bullets, slipped both gun and ammo in my jacket pocket and went outside to meet Maynard. A light drizzle spit down from the sky. I jogged down the stone steps, now slick with the moisture, and jumped into the back of the cab.

Maynard must've been working himself into a lather the whole time he'd been waiting for me because soon as I shut the door he unleashed some choice epithets about Renata. Amongst the slew of creative profanities was something about a lack of respect for a man laboring to make an honest living. I'm not sure if there was more to it. The tirade went on for a bit and I stopped listening.

"I don't come to your house and shit on your lawn," he wheezed, gassed from having forgotten to take a breath during his tantrum.

I gave it a second to make sure he was good and spent before instructing him on where to go.

"Downtown."

"Again?" Maynard said, still gulping for air. "You got me running 'round here in circles, chasing my tail."

"I'm paying for it, aren't I? Drive."

CHAPTER THIRTY-THREE
THE MONARCH

It was a quarter to five when Maynard dropped me off in Centre Plaza out front of the Monarch Building. If anyone had come in or out of the building in the last hour, they hadn't bothered to remove the box I'd used to prop the door. I scooted it inside, let the door shut behind me, and hiked up the narrow staircase to the third floor. I didn't have a plan to speak of, didn't know what I was going to do or how I was going to do it. Nor did I have any idea who I might encounter. All I knew was that River Path was linked to everything that had happened somehow, and I wanted to fuck with them a little, see what came of it.

There were two other business suites on the floor, a podiatrist and an accountant. The door to River Path's suite was unlocked. I let myself in. No one was immediately evident in the foyer of the office, which was a modest affair with a lacquered driftwood table; a couple of rose-colored padded chairs on either side of it; and a plush couch to match against the wall. Hanging gallery-style on the wall above the couch were fifty or more framed black-and-white photographs depicting buildings or structures that I recognized from around the city. The Royal Vista was one of them. The old high school another.

"Hello?" a shrill voice called from the neighboring room. A second later the voice was given an owner as Roger Holbrook, bearer of eviction notices, came around the corner with an inquisitive expression on his face that got wiped clean off when he saw me.

"Oh," he remarked with more than a little disdain. Instinctually, he reached a hand toward his horn-rimmed glasses, which still had a crack in one of the lenses from where he'd dropped them. "You."

"Me," I grinned mirthlessly. Reaching into my pocket, I pulled out the latest pink slip that had been tacked to my door and brandished it for him to see. "You want to explain to me what this is all about?"

"That," he said, clasping his hands solemnly and pointing two fingers at the paper, "is your final warning to vacate the premises by the end of the month or face legal action. I'm sorry."

"You will be sorry. We've been over this, Roger. Do we need to do it a second time, or should we skip to the part where you shred this pink slip and vow to never, ever hassle me over this bullshit again?"

"It's Saturday," Roger said suddenly, remembering that this interaction wasn't on his schedule. "How did you even get in here?"

"The door," I said.

"No, I mean—" He made for the exit of the suite. "Doesn't matter. I'm afraid if you want to lodge an appeal or file for an extension to your lease, then you're going to have to make an appointment and come back when—"

"Yeah, I'll do all those things. But I'm not making an appointment and I'm not coming back. I'm here now."

"I understand that." He opened the door for me to leave. "But I'm afraid that's not how this works. I'm not the person who decides these things."

"Who is?" I hooked a hip over the corner of the driftwood table and got comfortable.

"He's not—" Roger sputtered. He pushed his glasses up on his nose. "He's not here. Now please, it's been a very trying day and I don't want to have another situation escalate, but if you don't leave, I'll have no choice but to call the authorities."

"Give 'em a ring, Roger. Mention me by name. It's pretty split over there so you've got fifty-fifty odds between people who despise me or the people who owe me something." Roger Holbrook stood stock still, staring at me. "Go ahead," I goaded him, "I'll wait."

"It's Saturday."

I gestured with my arms to the room. "Yet here we are."

"Please don't make me do this," Roger said, without conviction.

"Do what, Roger? What's so difficult? Whoever I need to talk to, give them a call and get them down here. I've got nowhere to be. I can wait."

"You don't understand. Daniel Solomon, our COO, the person you would need to speak with on this matter, is dealing with a situation right now that cannot be impinged upon for—for this."

"You mentioned that it's been a trying day," I said casually, leaning farther onto the table. "What gives?"

"*Trying* is an understatement. If you must know, if it will help get you to leave the premises in a civilized manner and schedule an appointment, there's been a shooting at one of our properties. Someone's been killed. It's terrible. Not to mention it's a PR nightmare for our company. So if you don't mind, if you follow procedure and make an appointment, I'll see to it personally that Mr. Solomon is here to sort you out. You have my word. Now, please." Roger Holbrook pursed his mouth, extended his hand toward the exit. I didn't move.

"Yeah, I know about that. That's your guys' place, huh, the Royal Vista?"

"Yes."

"That where Solomon is now, is it? Just down the street here?"

He hesitated, then confirmed, "Yes."

"Leaving something out though, aren't you?"

"Excuse me?"

"Someone was murdered there yesterday as well. Two bodies in two days," I clucked. "You're right, that is a nightmare. And, at least to my warped mind—" I twirled a finger next to my head—"a bit ironic."

The thin mustache on his upper lip wriggled as though it wanted to belong to someone else's face. "What's ironic about it?" he said, flat and low, anticipating a dreadful answer.

I leveled my gaze on him. "I'm the one who shot the guy there."

Holbrook emitted a little gust of disbelief. "You're not serious."

"Oh, I'm world serious. Better call up Solomon, Rog. Tell him if he doesn't get over here fast as his fancy shoes will bring him, that little PR nightmare you've got on your hands may get a whole lot worse."

CHAPTER THIRTY-FOUR
ALL IN THE BLINK

Roger Holbrook got on the phone and so did I. I called Bob Lawson, the only other PI in town worth his salt, and explained to him that I needed an extra pair of eyes for a job I was on that night.

"Can't do it, Malick," Lawson chirped. His grating, high-pitched voice over the distorted cell connection forced me to hold the phone a foot from my ear to carry on the conversation.

"You said you needed work, Bob. This is work."

"Yeah, well, if you would have given me more than three hours' notice maybe I could have figured something out. I'm already on the job."

"Can you put the gig off to a different night? Mine's a one-time thing. Solid pay, your standard fee plus ten an hour."

Lawson whistled. "Wish I could, but bird in hand and all that. You understand, right? What's the job?"

"Like I'm telling you. This offer's only gonna come round once, Bob. I'm not coming back to you next time I need somebody."

"Now that's just spiteful, Malick."

"You're right. Tell you what, I'll only hold the grudge until you hit puberty and your balls drop. Should be anytime, you're already a couple decades past due."

"Fuck you, Malick."

"Not on my dime, Bob."

I hung up. That was that, I was on my own with Momo.

Holbrook disconnected his call and informed me that Daniel Solomon would be here in a jiffy. A jiffy turned out to be fifteen minutes. Solomon came storming in, regarded me with a protracted look of derision, and without saying a word pulled Holbrook aside to confer.

Solomon was a slender man with a deep, unnaturally red tan and a salt-and-pepper coif that looked glued on. He was dressed in a gray suit, shiny brown loafers, a crisp white dress shirt, and a silk argyle tie. In aggregate, the attire, his waxed hair and mutated skin tone gave the impression that, if exposed to daylight, he would shimmer head to toe. I recognized him at once as the man I'd seen on the news addressing the crowd at the Cruise Avenue celebration. After some hand wringing, animated whispering, and more than a few glances my way, Solomon was brought up to speed. He turned his back, rolled his shoulders, then spun around and approached me with the hardwired smile of someone who glad-hands for a living. His teeth were so shockingly white they could have been used for solar power.

"You're Nick Malick," Solomon said affably, proffering his hand. I stood from my perch on their fancy table, gave his large paw a shake and confirmed my identity. At six-five, maybe six-six, he was a good half-foot taller than I was. "Mr. Holbrook tells me you're causing a bit of a stink over your eviction notice."

"That's not the half of it," I said, mirroring his phony affect. "I'm looking to pollute the whole joint."

"I'm going to cut to the chase, Mr. Malick."

"I appreciate that."

"Good. Do you know what we're doing here?"

"Cutting to the chase."

Solomon's smile stretched taut. "No, by 'we', I don't mean you and I. I'm referring to the royal 'we' of our organization, River Path. Do you know what *we* are doing here? What our mission is?"

"I don't think you're using that right."

"*We* are trying to make this city shine again. Building

by building. Street by street. Brick by brick. We're going to change the way Cain City is viewed not only by its own citizens, but by the world at large."

"That's a tall order."

"Indeed it is. One that I believe someone like yourself—who, from what I understand, has in many ways provided a great service to this community, having eradicated some of the more seedy elements, if you will—would applaud."

"Oh, I don't know if I've eradicated much. Sometimes it feels more like I've fertilized the soil."

"Well." Solomon's expression turned forlorn, though somehow the smile held steadfast. "You understand the predicament we find ourselves in, as a company. In order for us to make our initiative work, to make this town a place we can all be proud of again, some unpleasant decisions have to be made. It's unfortunate. I wish there were a different solution, but there's no getting around it. I'm afraid you're one of those difficult decisions."

"Wow, did you think of that speech on the way over here, or was that your boilerplate spiel to the people you're kicking out on their asses?"

"What exactly do you hope to accomplish here today?" Solomon retorted impatiently.

"You are aware that someone just tried to shoot me in one of your properties?"

"I have been made aware of that, yes."

"Okay, just making sure. Your underling here"—I motioned toward Roger Holbrook—"called what you've got on your hands a PR problem. But I think it's more than that. I think your company is on the verge of ruin and the way you handle this conversation right here is going to go a long way toward determining whether or not you have a job tomorrow."

"Are you threatening me?"

"Maybe I wasn't clear enough. I was using the royal 'you,' as in this whole goddamned company."

"This is going to be good," Solomon harrumphed. He

crossed his arms and looked over to Holbrook to reinforce his conceit. Holbrook made some sort of grunting noise and mustered an encouraging expression, but he avoided eye contact with his superior. "Care to enlighten us on how exactly the result of this conversation is going to make or break us?" Solomon cocked his head sideways and blinked rapidly a few times.

"Sure. For starters, I'm going to sue you and your investors for all you're worth. You knowingly turning a blind eye to—what did you call it? The seedier elements at play in your properties."

"That's ludicrous. The case would be thrown out before it even made it in front of a judge."

"Maybe, maybe not. But it could gum up the works for you, couldn't it? Stall certain construction projects, things you can't afford to have delayed at such a crux in your business ventures. How much of your capital do you have invested in this Cruise Avenue deal? Most of it? All of it?"

Solomon ignored my questions. "This is the second time you've threatened this company with legal action. I'm told that earlier this week you bullied Mr. Holbrook here into retracting your initial eviction notice. But who in God's name is going to take a no-win case like yours? It's my understanding that you no longer have the backing of the lawyers you used to work for."

I tilted my head sideways and looked at Solomon curiously. "Now how would you know that?"

Immediately Solomon saw his mistake and attempted to cover it by barking, "What do you want, Mr. Malick? Do you want me to rip up your eviction notice, wipe it from our system, is that what you want? Fine, done. Can you leave now, please?"

"That's a start. But I couldn't give two shits about you trying to kick me out of my shitty office. I want to know how you knew I was fired by Leach, McKinney & Thurber. That only happened last night."

The smile adhered to Solomon's face was starting to waver. Little tremors quaked across the muscles of his cheeks. "In my business, Mr. Malick, connections, information—that's currency. And I'm very good at my business."

I rolled my eyes and said, "My turn to cut to the chase. From my vantage, there are three ways this can go for you in the public sector. Cat's already out of the bag. A prostitute and now a gang-affiliated assassin have been killed in your building one day apart. Now, either you knew about the prostitution and the thugs operating the racket and didn't do anything about it or, worse, not only did you know about it, but you encouraged it. Participated in it."

"Ludicrous. We would never, under any circumstances, do such a thing."

"Save your breath 'cause I don't believe a word you say. Now, your only other play, probably the only one where River Path comes out the other end of this thing, is you were simply too neglectful or not diligent enough in your management of that particular property. This way can be spun for public consumption. Act as a kind of evidence to support why your 'mission' to gentrify the community is so important. Crime, malfeasance, is in every nook and cranny of the city and has to be combatted. Even in our own homes, nobody's safe, yadda, yadda, yadda. I'll leave the spin to you. Who knows, maybe this ends up building a stronger rapport between you and the citizens you're looking to subjugate."

I wouldn't have thought it possible, but Daniel Solomon's crimson face turned damned near maroon. "What are you proposing, Malick?"

"I thought you'd never ask. The papers, the news channels, I can make sure they think your company was the unlucky beneficiary of this mayhem. Not the creators of it."

"You can do that?"

"You're the one with the connections and the information, Dan. You tell me if I can do it or not. Or you can just read the newspaper tomorrow and be surprised."

"And what, pray tell, do you want from us?"

"A list of all your investors. I want to know who's really pulling the strings on your marionette. And I want to know how you found out I was fired last night."

"You must be joking. We're a privately-held company. I can't release that information to a civilian."

"Either you tell me and me alone, or by Monday a search warrant's going to be issued on this place and all your dirt will be aired for the world to see."

"I—I can't tell you who our investors are. I'll lose my job."

"I know it's some local rich guys," I said. "Tell you what, you don't even have to say the names. I will. And you can nod your head or blink once or some shit if I'm right. Then you've got plausible deniability."

The last of Daniel Solomon's morbid Joker smile melted away, though the remnants of it lingered in the creases of his weathered face, now plagued by consternation. "Roger, can you leave us for a second?"

"Are you sure? I think I should stay."

"Please, Roger. Give me the room."

Solomon waited for Roger Holbrook to scurry off into the adjoining office, then fixed a spiteful glare on me as though I were the first devil he'd ever struck a deal with. "One name," he said. "I can give you one name. That's it, that's all I can do. I give you that and you'll fix it with your friend in the papers that we knew nothing about what was happening in the Royal Vista. That we were victims in all of this, too."

"That's a little lopsided," I said, "but what the hell. I know where to find you if I need you, right?"

"I think this is a person whom you'll be very interested in."

"We'll see."

Daniel Solomon squeezed his eyes shut, took a deep breath in and out, and physically braced himself for the words he was about to utter. Before he had the chance to utter them, I said, "Rutherford Blevins."

Solomon's eyes popped open. Then, taking care to be exact in his communication, he blinked.

Once.

CHAPTER THIRTY-FIVE
THE RELAX INN

I stood in the alcove of a computer repair shop half a block down from the Royal Vista, a spot that provided clear sightlines to the west-facing side of the building, the alley, and the street where my Tacoma was parked. The ambulances and all but one of the police cruisers were gone from the side entrance. The journalists had dispersed with them. A single uniformed officer I didn't recognize stood sentry outside the door. No doubt there were a few more of them posted around the corner at the main entrance as well as inside by the fourth- and fifth-floor crime scenes. I'd been staking out the area for the better part of a half hour to make sure neither the authorities nor the Stenders were casing my truck, waiting for me to appear so they could detain or follow me, or worse, try to kill me. There was a wide spectrum of possibilities. In that time a few pedestrians had walked by, but none of them had doubled back or come 'round again. A bum had parked his grocery cart under a tree across the street, stretched out across the grass for a nap with a hat over his face and hadn't moved a muscle since. No one was visible in the windows of the Vista or the adjacent buildings, and I hadn't spotted even the slightest flutter of a curtain.

An incoming call vibrated in my pocket. I glanced at the display screen. Ernie Ciccone. I answered it.

"Next time you plan on shooting somebody, you mind giving me a heads up first?" said Ciccone, not completely in jest.

"That's already out there, huh?"

"Yeah, and just as I was putting the finishing touches on a damn good story that I now have to re-write thanks to your itchy trigger finger. On that alone you owe me the exclusive."

"Don't make me laugh, Ciccone. I don't owe you squat."

"Give it to me anyway," he said, attempting to suppress the avarice in his voice. For most, murder, mayhem, and evil were mere curiosities that could be successfully kept at arm's length. They were things that happened to other people, in other towns, on other streets. Things to be riveted by for sixty minutes a pop on television or in a book or online. That is, until they weren't.

For a select group, however—Ciccone amongst them—murder was an aphrodisiac. I'd never understand it.

I described for him what happened, not out of any feelings of goodwill or obligation, but because I wanted him to add a couple details to his story before it hit the printer, including a critical piece of information that might set the whole pot to boil.

I heard something over the line that sounded like Ciccone licking his lips. "You were there to check on Aveena Bryant's roommate and this man, Lil' Mike Mike, started shooting at you?"

"Basically." I told him I didn't know Lil' Mike Mike's real name, though I made sure to give him Renata's.

"Renata . . . Jones," he repeated as he jotted the name down. "Where is she now? Under police protection?"

"No, she's in the wind. Lit out while the shooting was going down."

"Does Renata Jones have a record?"

"I'm sure she does."

"Solicitation?"

"That's probably at the top of the list. Listen, you find anything else out about River Path?"

"No, they've been dodging my calls all afternoon. Won't let me in the building, the smug bastards."

"I did," I said.

"You did, what?"

"Found something out about River Path. You ready for this? Those highfalutin investors you mentioned, guess who one of them is?" I waited for a few beats just to get him worked into a lather.

"Out with it, Malick," Ciccone nearly yelled.

"Rutherford Blevins."

"You're shittin' me."

I got off the phone, kept vigil on the area around the Royal Vista for a few more minutes, and finally decided either there was nothing doing or I was just going to have to risk it. I crossed the street and walked to my truck. No one seemed to take any particular interest in me as I hauled myself up into the driver's seat and got the engine going. The bum didn't rouse, curtains didn't move a fraction. Nary a first glance, much less a second. The cop stationed at the side entrance was too busy with his phone to even look up.

I pulled away from the curb with an eye on my rearview, did some figure eights around a few blocks and didn't pick up any tails, so I stopped my itinerant wandering and steered toward the old high school. I parked on a residential street a block east and cut through some backyards to get to an ingress between the back of the high school and a small building that housed the power generators. An auxiliary door that was supposed to be impenetrable from the outside, used only as an exit in the event of an emergency, was located there. Long ago I'd learned how to pry it open using a decent-sized rock and small switchblade that I kept in the glove compartment of my Tacoma.

I finagled the blade into the doorjamb, held it firmly at an angle, and hit the end of the handle with the rock. The jamb popped open. A passage led to the old gymnasium's locker room, now used for storage. I shoved some boxes out of the way and walked through to the gym, then down the corridor to my office. Once inside, I scanned the street for any signs of surveillance, but again saw none.

Renata was in the same place I'd left her, sprawled out on the bed in the back room watching the fuzzy television.

Her shirt was pulled up halfway over her tits and she was absent-mindedly stroking her belly with her fingertips. When I stepped through the doorway her eyes flicked my way, then back to the television.

"No bad men came to get me. Lucky you."

"Have you moved?"

"Yes," she snapped defensively, "and you out of toilet paper, just so you know."

"C'mon, get up. We gotta go."

I got some loose cash out of my safe, then led Renata out of the high school by the same way I'd come in.

"Where are you taking me?" she asked as we hopped the fence into somebody's backyard.

"Out of the city."

We got in the truck and drove north, under the viaduct and through downtown. The phone reverberated in my pocket. I checked the display, saw that Willis Hively was the caller, and sent it to voicemail. I merged onto the Sixth Street Bridge that crossed the river into Ohio and opened into Route 52. We passed a cluster of fast food restaurants, gas stations, used-car dealerships, motels, and a Wal-Mart. Three miles farther down the line was a lone motel, sitting back from the road. I pulled into it.

"At last," Renata grumbled.

Being isolated from the glut of other businesses on 52 had its advantages—the Relax Inn never had too many junkies loitering about; but also its disadvantages—vacancies were aplenty, as evidenced by the pink neon sign, incandescent against the backdrop of dusk and wilderness beyond. But the proprietors kept the sheets washed—if not the comforters—and for the low sum of fifty U.S. dollars they turned a blind eye to guests unable to produce the requisite forms of identification.

I forked over a crisp fifty. The stolid old woman behind the counter checked the watermarks and the Ulysses S. Grant holograph to make certain the money wasn't counterfeit. Satisfied, she slid the bill smoothly under the register, pulled out a laminated diagram of the property and offered me my choice of rooms. Only three of the units were currently occupied, all of which were situated closed to the ice and vending machines. I selected Room 17, located around the back corner of the motel where my truck couldn't be spotted from the road and Renata wouldn't be seen going in or out. The woman threw in a travel-sized toothbrush and tube of paste on the house.

As soon as we entered the unit, Renata made a beeline for the bathroom, slammed the door behind her and locked it. I looked around the place. Two double beds divided by a bedside table with a lamp. An old chest of drawers at the foot of the beds, TV perched atop of it. Yellowed wallpaper curling up at the corners. Tattered carpet that was pocked with five or six burn marks and sported some dull stains that could have been made by anything from blood to vomit to tobacco juice. The odor of stale cigarettes permeated the drapes, carpet, and blankets.

I sat on one of the beds and listened to the voicemail Willis Hively had left. He said the vacant apartment on the fourth floor was different from the other one we had checked. It was completely empty, no indication that anyone had lived there recently apart from one peculiarity. A phone cord and ethernet cable were connected to their jacks and apparently active. Hively didn't yet realize what that might indicate, but I did. If there was a hidden camera in Birdie's room, the footage from it could have been easily captured via Bluetooth and saved onto a drive or a computer in the apartment directly below.

"Touch base with me. Let me know what you're up to," said Hively, signing off. I put the phone back in my pocket, lay prone on the bed, and closed my eyes for a minute.

The toilet flushed and Renata came back out. She located the remote, flipped on the TV, and collapsed onto the far bed. I sat up.

"There are woods out back here. If, for whatever reason, you have to escape this room, if somebody's trying to get in the door, bar it with a chair, slip out the bathroom window and run into the woods. Find a good place to hide and stay there. I'll find you."

Renata grunted some blasé response. I snatched the remote from her hand and shut the television off.

"I said I got it," she snapped. "Dang."

I peeled a couple fives from my wallet and gave them to her for the vending machines, wrote down my phone number on a pad that I found in the drawer of the side table, and instructed her that she was, under no circumstances, to answer the phone or place any outgoing calls.

"Whatever," said Renata.

"I'll be back late tonight, early tomorrow. I'll bring you some breakfast."

"How long you plannin' on keeping me cooped up in here?"

"Few days, not too long. Before I go I need you to tell me about the men you saw who visited Birdie."

Renata described nearly a dozen different men so specifically I felt as though I could recognize each of them if I passed them on the street. She didn't know any names, outside of Billy Bob, the moniker she and Birdie had made up for Momo Morrison, and Scott T. Barnhard, whom she recognized from the commercials, billboards, and bus-stop ads scattered throughout town. She detailed the two of them well, right down to Momo's toad-like eyes and tiny teeth, and Barnhard's dyed beard that shed an avalanche of dandruff when he scratched it.

"Birdie'd call him Scott T. Bonehard," Renata giggled, "cuz he took Viagra every time they fucked. Gave him one of them relentless boners you can't knock down."

"What about this guy?" I handed her my phone. On its display was the picture of Rutherford Blevins I'd saved from the Cain City government's official site.

Renata sat up, used her finger and thumb to blow up the judge's face and studied the photo.

"Naw, I ain't never seen this mug. Who he?"

CHAPTER THIRTY-SIX
SUNDOWN AT THE STONE'S THROW

The Stone's Throw was situated at the edge of an industrial section just east of downtown, populated with mostly warehouses and factories. The property was hemmed in by a junkyard on its east side, the Eighth Street viaduct on the west, and train tracks that abutted the gravel parking lot in the rear. The bar's doors opened at 9 p.m. Half an hour prior to that I parked the Tacoma a couple blocks away, found a hole in the junkyard's boundary fence, and dipped through. Despite an abundance of *Beware of Dog* signs tacked along the perimeter, there was no proof of any guard dogs patrolling the yard, which was filled with row after row of clunkers. My old Skylark, if it had avoided being crunched into a cube of metal, was somewhere on the premises. I missed that car, shitty as it was, and couldn't help but keep an eye out for it as I made my way to the portion of the fence that bordered The Stone's Throw. It'd been with me during the worst time of my life, that car, and only died after it'd seen me through to the other side.

I found an ancient VW van parked along the fence that provided a clean view of The Stone's Throw entrance, opened its creaky door, climbed into the captain's chair and settled in for what could be a long, futile night of waiting for Momo

Morrison to turn up. I'd been in The Stone's Throw once, two months previously, during a moonlighting job I'd taken apart from Leach, McKinney & Thurber.

The aging wife of a well-to-do pharmaceutical sales rep had suspected her husband was having a romp with the young, breezy woman he'd recently been partnered with. I tracked the pair of them to doctor's offices all across the tri-state, finding nary a hint of impropriety. That is, until one night he knocked off work and came here to The Throw. Turned out the wife's suspicions were well-founded, though the affair was of a very different nature than she'd imagined. Her goal was to catch him red-handed and then bilk him for all he was worth. She achieved that, and now she lived all alone in a big house on Honeysuckle Lane while her husband, though penniless from the divorce settlement, was now engaged to a strapping young lad who worked as a general practitioner in Catlettsburg.

This is all to say I was familiar with The Throw's layout: it had a four-sided bar in the center of an expansive, high-ceilinged room, secluded booths along each wall, six circular platforms adorned with poles for go-go dancers, and at the far end of the place a stage with a runway. Behind the stage was a giant projector screen. On either side of the screen were narrow hallways, one of which led to private suites, the other to the lavatories. One feature I knew could work to my advantage in a pinch—emergency exit doors had been installed in the private suites and bathrooms in case some nutter ever decided he wanted to slaughter some humans for being different from him, or perhaps too similar.

The dying light of the sun flickered out over the western cityscape. Within ten minutes the night had turned cold, black, and moonless. The only source of exterior illumination was a streetlamp attached to the roof of the bar, which poured a pyramid of light down onto the entrance where a doorman squatted on a stool. Everything beyond that pyramid—the gravel parking lot, the train tracks, the wooded area on the far side of the viaduct—was a dark and foreboding abyss. Even with the binoculars I'd brought along for the task, I could only make out shapes and movements in these areas, no details. I hunkered down and waited for something to happen, then waited some more. My cold breath plumed out in front of me, the vapors growing denser with each passing minute.

Around ten-thirty things started to pick up. Car after car came crunching into the gravel lot. In a relatively short span of time the spaces were filled to maximum capacity. The doorway to The Throw was like a portal into another dimension. Each time it opened, flashing lights and thumping EDM screamed into the tranquil night. Every so often a sudden roar, the kind you might hear at a sporting event, would rise up. A good number of cross-dressers had gone in and I figured there was some kind of drag show happening. By midnight at least a hundred people, maybe twice that, had entered the bar, but there was still no sign of Momo Morrison.

I pulled out my phone and dialed the number to Room 17 at the Relax Inn.

"Hello," Renata said in such a way as to make me picture a gob of drool crusted on her chin. The television droned loudly in the background.

"What'd I tell you about answering the phone?"

"Then why you calling me?"

"You doing all right? You get some food?"

"Yeah, I'm straight." Renata groaned as though she were stretching her limbs.

"What'd you get?"

"Some Sun Chips, gummy bears, granola bar, Mountain Dew. When you coming back?"

Just then a set of headlights swung around the bend and a white mini-van rolled into the gravel parking lot, halting beside the doorman.

"I've gotta go, Renata. I'll be back later tonight or in the morning. Get some sleep."

"It stinks in here, you know th—"

I cut the call and peered through the binoculars at the minivan. The driver's side window lowered, but the interior of the car was too dark to make out the identity of the wheelman. Whoever it was traded a few words with the doorman, who hooked a thumb around to the side of the building where earlier he'd blocked off a parking spot with a row of orange safety cones. The minivan pulled around the corner of the building, stopped short of the cones, and to my surprise, Buddy Cleamons, aka Buddy the Face, hopped out from the driver's seat. A black patch with a skull and crossbones covered the eye I'd gouged out. Cleamons seemed to have rather quickly found the equilibrium needed to function with one eye as opposed to two. Enough to operate a vehicle anyway, and he removed the cone barricade nimbly enough.

He clambered back into the car, pulled forward into the slot and killed the engine. The back door slid open and sure enough, Momo Morrison, along with a third man I didn't recognize, climbed out. The unfamiliar guy's body was thin and gangly like a teenager's, his chest concaved. He had on a tattered t-shirt that some wore as a fashion choice and others wore because they had no choice at all. I couldn't discern exactly which category he fell into. Buddy The Face tossed the car keys to Momo, who stuck them into the pocket of his Carhartt jacket. Then Momo signaled for Buddy to grease the doorman with a couple bucks, which he did, and the trio strolled inside.

Momo having his cronies with him complicated matters. Getting him alone wouldn't be so simple as jimmying his car door open and hiding in there until he came out. No, I'd have to force the issue.

I got out of the car and retraced my steps to the gap in the fence. There, I ducked back under and made my way down the dark, eerily quiet block to the front of The Stone's Throw. I hung back at the edge of the building for a minute to wait for a group that I could mix in with. In short order, two packs of young, fashionably-dressed men stumbled past me heading for the entrance. I fell in between the two parties and slunk into the bar on their coattails.

As I stepped over the threshold the music stopped and a huge roar erupted. It took a few seconds for my eyes to adjust to the hazy lighting of the place. When they did, I looked across the room to the stage and saw a long-legged drag queen who, apart from the Adam's apple, bore an uncanny resemblance to Cher. This Cher was straddling a mock cannon that was being rolled onstage by two men costumed as Navy crewmen. She herself was decked out in the same V-cut leather-and-fishnet ensemble that Cher was famous for. The performer stretched her long stockinged leg into the air, swung it over the side of the cannon and slid down. The video for "If I Could Turn Back Time" appeared on the large screen behind the stage and, while the real Cher parted a crowd of seamen on a battleship, Cain City's version raised the mic and began her lip sync routine. This elicited another raucous cheer from the audience.

The place was packed to the gills, but it didn't take long to spot Buddy The Face's scarred head poking out above the fray at the bar. The skinny youth was next to him, sipping on a parasoled cocktail. Momo Morrison was nowhere in sight. I stayed on the fringe of the group I'd walked in with as they weaved through the crush of men. All the while I kept one eye on Buddy The Face to make sure he didn't clock me, the other scanning the floor for Momo.

It wasn't hard to blend into The Throw's clientele. The men in there ran the gamut of ages and styles, from the young hipsters I came in with to an older set who hung back by the bar—from the transgender to a grittier lot more akin to Momo Morrison and Buddy Cleamons.

Two people vacated a booth nearby that was concealed in shadow and afforded decent sightlines down the length of the club. I broke away from my escorts and scooted into the dark corner of the booth. The only visual impediments were the lithe, oiled-up go-go dancers, who were clad only in skimpy thongs and bow ties, and doing things with their hips that I wasn't aware men could do. Guys were queueing up for a chance to stick dollar bills into their thongs and cop a fistful of their junk.

With the majority of the crowd watching the stage, I focused on the crowd, scanning each face. But Momo was a small fry and could easily go unseen in the chaotic discord of The Throw. I ditched that method of detection and instead kept watch on Buddy The Face. With his single eye, there was no masking the direction of his gaze. For him to get a good look at anything his whole head had to turn. And it kept turning to the row of booths on the opposite wall of the bar. I followed an imaginary line from his lonely eye to a darkened booth.

There I found Momo chatting up a bone-thin drag queen dressed in a Western-style corset and a rainbow-colored afro wig. Momo whispered something into his paramour's ear. Whatever he said prompted her to feign a gasp. She clutched Momo's hand and tugged him out of the booth. The two of them sliced through the mass of people by the stage and disappeared down the corridor that led to the bathrooms.

Neither Buddy The Face nor the kid with him moved to follow Momo. I slid out from the booth and forced my way through the commotion next to the stage so Momo's cohorts wouldn't be able to peep me. As I navigated the crush of bodies, a slippery hand reached down from above me, palmed my chest and gave my nipple a tweak. The hand belonged to one of the androgynous go-go dancers, who was gazing down at me as if I were edible. He stretched out the elastic at the front of his thong, invited me to do something about it. I politely removed his greasy paw from my person and kept moving. Once I was safely in the corridor, I reached my hand into the pocket of my pea coat and wrapped my fingers around the handle of my snub .32.

I glanced back to make sure no one was trailing me, then cracked the door and slipped into the bathroom. The reverb from the bass thrummed the walls and the decibel level of the club still rang in my ears, but otherwise the room was quiet. A couple of guys were at the sink washing their hands, preening in the mirror and snickering at the noises emanating from the stall at the end of the row. They saw the sobriety in my face and must have thought one of the carnal participants belonged to me. The two men cleared out quick. I pulled my gun, walked down to the stall. It wasn't locked. Gently, I pushed it open.

Momo, busy getting fellated, didn't register my presence. His head was craned skyward, eyes shut tight, mouth agape with pleasure. His hands clawed into the guy's garish wig. So consumed was Momo with the warm mouth on his crotch, he failed to realize anything was amiss until the cold metal of a gun barrel pressed hard against his eye socket.

Momo's body went rigid. His unobstructed eye popped open.

"Hello, Momo."

The young man on his knees stopped gliding back and forth on Momo's cock.

"Don't move, sweetheart," I said to the guy. "You got him right where I want him. Hands up, Momo."

Momo complied. I couldn't allow the guy on the ground to leave the bathroom only to sound the alarm for Buddy The Face and company, so I ordered him to extend his bony arms out to his sides as well. Momo took in a sharp breath and blew it out with a whistle. "Boy, you leave a wake, don't ya? Where you been? We was looking for you."

I stepped back a hair and took the .32 away from his eye. The man on his knees started to slide off Momo. I reminded him not to move. "I didn't instigate anything that happened today. Your man started shooting at me. I had no choice but to shoot back."

"Listen atcha. Claiming self-defense, you." A sly grin spread across Momo's face. "Okay, say I buy what you're selling. Ain't a stretch. Lil' Mike Mike never could think real straight when shit went sideways, but that don't change this none, do it? Come in here interrupting my boujie. Running around all reckless, bringing a gun into a gay club. That's a bad look, man."

I kept the .32 trained on Momo's chest while I frisked him with my other hand, found a Browning 9mm stashed in the lapel of his jacket. I held the pistol aloft for him to see. "Touch hypocritical, Momo." I slipped the gun into the pocket of my coat.

Momo flipped his raised hands around. "Better safe than sorry, right? What you think you going to do with that little pop gun you got, huh? That thing couldn't hurt a fly. Puny bullets'll probably bounce right off a body."

"Oh, I think it'll do the trick. But say you're right. How about this for an alternative? What do you think will happen if I smack the back of this guy's head with the butt, huh? You think he'll bite your dick off or let you loose?"

Momo's grin washed away. "Everything's that's gone on thus far, Malick, it's all in the course of business. Ain't been personal. But you start fuckin' with my pecker it's gonna get personal real quick."

"Yeah, well, let's see." I tapped the butt of the gun against the crown of the guy's head. Mouth full, he let out a garbled groan that must have had some teeth to it.

"Ahh," Momo winced. "Mother. Fucker." He adjusted his stance to relieve some of the pressure from between his legs. "You got some *cojones* jaunting up in here like this, I'll give you that, Malick. But what's the end game? Don't seem like there was a whole lot of forethought put into things."

I shrugged. "I'm winging it. You want to keep it to business, okay then, let's talk business."

"Hell, man, you the one with the cap gun. I'm gonna talk about whatever you wanna fuckin' talk about."

"Who killed Birdie Bryant?"

"That's what this is about, that little darkie cunt?"

I banged the butt of the .32 against the young guy's noggin again. Momo gritted his teeth and stifled a little yelp.

"All right, all right," he said, blood rushing into his face. "What do you want?"

"Who killed her, Momo?"

"Well it wasn't me, goddammit. Why you wanna know, so you can go and throw them out a window, you fucking loony tune? Yeah, I know about that."

"You don't know shit." I jabbed the barrel of the pistol into his eye. He jerked his head away and cursed.

"You're starting to piss me off," he growled. I poked him again. "I don't know who killed her!" he hollered. "That ain't have nothing to do with me."

"There's a video of Birdie's murder, right? I know you guys taped the girls you had set up in the Royal Vista. I want to see it. That's all I want. I don't give a shit about your buddy the judge, your gang, none of it. I just want the tape. Give me that and we're straight. You'll never hear from me again."

"Never hear from you again? Hell now, the thought alone gives me melancholy. Hate to break it to you, my man, but I don't know what the fuck you're talking about with no tapes. Shit doesn't exist."

I bonked the poor dicksucker on the back of the head for the third time. Momo let fly a string of epithets. "Goddammit. All right, there's a tape, all right? There's a tape."

"Have you seen it?"

"No. What the fuck do you want me to do, go and get it for you right now?"

"That's exactly what I want you to do."

"Ain't no way, that ain't possible."

I reared back to hit the kid again, but Momo pleaded for me to stop.

"All right, all right. I'll get it for you."

"You know where it is?"

Momo huffed, "Yeah, I know where it is. It ain't so simple as all that though. I can't just stroll over there and say 'give me the video.' Shit don't work that way, but I'll get it for you, all right? I'll get it."

"Tonight."

"Jesus Christ. *Fine.* Tonight."

I tapped the kid on his sharp clavicle, told him it was time for him to scat. He slid carefully back off Momo, who popped out of his mouth with a hollow *thwop*, then scrambled to his feet and hightailed it out of the bathroom fast as he could manage in eight-inch stilettos.

"Put your cock away," I told Momo. He bowed his legs, pushed himself back through the slot in his pants and zipped up, looking mighty pleased with himself.

"What happens now, genius?" he said.

"Give me your car keys. We're going for a drive."

CHAPTER THIRTY-SEVEN
COAL TRAIN FLAME

Gun at his back, Momo preceded me through the emergency door that exited out the side of the building bordering the junkyard. The minivan was parked at the southeast corner, maybe thirty feet away. I prodded Momo forward.

"What you think is gonna happen, Malick? They're gonna just let you have the video, give you a playful little pat on your butt and say 'good game?' Send you on your way?"

"Yeah, that's exactly how I think this is going to go." I pushed the button on the key fob to unlock the doors and open the back slider. Momo moved for the back seat. "Nu-uh," I said. "You're driving. Try anything funny and I'll be happy to blow a canyon through your skull."

"Yeah, yeah." We both got in the car. "You gonna give me the keys?"

I inspected the interior of the van—console, glove compartment, beneath the seats—to make sure there were no weapons handy. There weren't, and I handed the keys to Momo. He started the engine, kicked the van into reverse and backed out. As we turned from the gravel lot onto the paved street I heard a commotion behind us and glanced back to see Buddy The Face barreling through a dozen or so people congregated at the entrance. He ran after us for half a block before calling it quits.

"Step on it," I said. Momo pushed on the gas and soon we were driving down Seventh Avenue toward the West End.

"Where's the tape?" I asked.

"They house all that kind of stuff at a place of ours in the Stend."

"What place?"

"You're gonna find out shortly now, ain't ya?" Momo looked at me in the rearview mirror. "Buddy do that to your face?"

"Yeah."

"Well, you got the better of him. I don't know how you managed it, but good on ya. I ain't never seen nobody get the better of Buddy. 'Cept'n that time he set his self on fire. I was there for that. You shoulda seen it. Sparked it too close to the hairdo, whole head blazed up like Ghost Rider or some shit. You and a Zippo," Momo clucked, "the only two losses he's taken."

"I got lucky," I admitted.

"Now, no need to be self-effacing. No such thing as luck. You know something, Malick? I like you. It's a shame we're gonna have to kill you 'cause of all this business. I feel like you and I would be friends under different circumstances, you know it?"

"No."

"Aw, we would now, I'm telling ya. But you was already a pretty big thorn in our side. Now you doing this ill-advised nonsense." Momo tutted regretfully. "Ain't nothing else to be done. That deal you put out there about you getting the tape and walking away, now, you ask me, I say that's a damn good deal. I'd take that deal, get you the hell off my back. But my uncle, mmm, he's more Old Testament when it comes to it. Eye for an eye, you know."

"Reckon something's gotta kill me at some point," I said. "How many of you do you think I'll be able to take with me?"

"Plenty," Momo said merrily. "I'm sure you'd take plenty." He burst into a fit of giggles that started his body convulsing and made him seem like a lunatic.

"All right, calm down."

Momo took a few deep breaths to control the hysterics.

"See, that's why I like you. Nobody messes with us the way you do anymore. Says shit like that. 'How many you think I could take with me?' Everybody knows they shoot off at the mouth like *that*, they're bound to end up in The Trees. So nobody does. It's gotten to be like having a normal job. Boring as hell. Plain tiresome, you know? But this shit with you gets me keyed up. Makes it fun again. I don't know if you dumb or stupid or crazy or what. Well, I guess two of those are the same things, ain't they? I swear, I'm almost gonna be sad to see you go."

"Yeah? I'll tell you where you can spread my ashes then."

"Naw, you don't want to give them to me. I'll dump them on the ground and piss all over them."

"What do I care? If I'm dead you can do whatever you want. Bury me in The Trees with the rest of them. What's it matter?"

Momo chafed. "See now, The Trees is more a figure of speech, really. We might have used to put some people out there back in the day, but it's more of a metaphor now. Easier these days just to concrete over a body. That's probably what we'll do to you. Tell you what, I'll give you the choice. You can replenish the earth—ashes to ashes, dust to dust and all that—or be part of Cain City's foundation. How's that sound?"

"Let me think it over for a few more decades."

"Don't believe you'll have quite that much time to decide, friend."

Momo took a left at the First Street viaduct and drove south until the road dead-ended at the creek that ran along the edge of the southern hills. He hung a right onto Four Pole Road, which, in less than half a mile, tapered into a narrow lane that hugged the base of the hills on one side and was girded by train tracks on the other.

Momo glanced in the rearview just as a pair of headlights swept across the interior of the car.

"You got somebody following us?" he asked.

"No."

"Well, we got company."

I turned around and saw the silhouette of a darkly painted SUV turn our way.

"How do you know?"

"Wasn't sure myself at first. Thought it might've been a different vehicle, but I'm pretty sure that's the one been on our tail since shortly after we left The Stone's Throw."

"It's not one of yours, is it?"

"Nope."

"Keep driving," I instructed Momo. My head swiveled back and forth between him in the driver's seat and the SUV cruising fifty yards behind us. I couldn't tell if Momo was fucking with me or if we were, in fact, being followed. Taken one way, some unknown party with unknown intent was pursuing us. Taken the other, Momo, despite having a pistol trained on his back, felt comfortable enough to play games. Both possibilities were troubling. Momo eyed me in the rearview.

"How many enemies you got?" he chuckled.

"Lost count."

The road narrowed into the tight, winding lane pressed by the hills on one side, a thicket of trees and train tracks on the other. Branches from the trees stretched overhead, creating a natural, claustrophobic tunnel. The van's headlights illuminated the bends and dips of the country road.

"So," Momo said, changing the subject, "Karla Huckabee, huh? You tearing that pussy up or what?"

"What?"

Behind us, the beams from the SUV grew brighter, closer.

"Karla Huckabee. She fine. Didn't know you had it like that. You must got a big ol' dick or something."

"Yeah, well, I wouldn't have pegged you as a Stone's Throw kinda guy, so I guess we both have a couple of surprises up our sleeves."

"Stone's Throw's the perfect bar. Liquor in the front, poker in the back." Momo smirked at me in the rearview, saw that I wasn't amused. "Shit man, ass is ass, ain't it?" I told Momo to keep his eyes on the road. "Aw, hell," he said, "I know this road like the back of my hand. Could drive it in the dark. See?"

He killed the headlights, pitching us instantly into darkness. Rolling blind like that evoked a helpless, floating sensation, the likes of which I'd never experienced. Momo cackled with unbridled delight. I pushed the gun against the back of his head and cocked the hammer. Very calmly I said, "Turn the lights on."

"Okay, okay. Just having a gas." Momo flipped the beams on, illuminating a great green wall of foliage that looked to be hurtling right toward us. I braced for a collision, but Momo spun the wheel as though he were on a leisurely Sunday drive. The van squealed around a sharp curve, shimmied a little on the back end and straightened out.

"Little jumpy, ain't ya?" He laughed, looking over his shoulder. "You should have seen your face, boy. Shit, I been pulling that on people since I was twelve."

"What wires got crossed wrong in your brain?"

"All of 'em. So they tell me, anyway. Hey, you know the dude who knocked Karla up with that pup of hers was a West End boy? You knew that, right?"

"Yeah."

"Ronnie Wellman. Older than me of course, but I heard plenty of stories. My cousin used to hang out with Ronnie. Karla"—Momo puckered his lips and whistled loudly—"she got run through back in the day, boy. Not by me of course, but I've heard the stories. All them dudes used to talk about her. They used to pass her around I think. Take turns. Spit-roast her, you know, that kind of thing. Ronnie felt bad for her, and the kid looked enough like him or something, so I guess he claimed it. Fatherhood didn't take in the end though."

"Shut your fucking hole, Momo."

"What?" he said, feigning innocence. "I don't judge. Good for you is all I'm saying. Taming that sparkplug. She still fine though, ain't she? I wouldn't mind taking a little cut of that filet. Now that I'm thinking about it, I may have to go and pay them a visit soon. Up there in their third-floor apartment."

"You come near them, I'll kill every single one of you. You understand me?"

"You a big talker, Malick. Big talker. But out of you and me, who you think's more likely to make good on their promises, huh?"

"You trying to get shot right now?"

"I don't know, you trying to get in a wreck right now? *Biiiig* talker."

Ahead in the distance, off to the right, a single bright light sliced through the black night, coming toward us.

"Fuck is that?" I said.

Momo leaned forward and squinted. "That there's a train. We gotta cross the tracks up here at this crossing. These night trains are long as hell. Let me see if I can beat it."

Momo punched the gas. The speedometer jumped from thirty miles an hour to fifty.

"What are you doing, Momo?" He didn't answer. "Slow down."

Momo disregarded the directive, instead hammering down on the accelerator. The van leapt forward and careened around a sharp bend. Its left side rose off the ground and thudded back down. The railroad crossing came into view at the bottom of a slope up ahead, its alternating red lights glowing in the dark as the barriers lowered into place. The silhouette of the train loomed larger by the second. Its payload of coal glinting atop the railcars. The train's whistle blew forlornly into the vast, infinite night.

"You know how you said you was going to split my head into a canyon if I tried anything funny?"

I leveled the .32 against his temple. "Don't do it."

"Time to back that big talk," Momo crowed, "'cause I'm about to do something funny."

"Stop the car!" I screamed. "Stop the fucking car!"

"One last thing," Momo said, his tone suddenly placid. "There wudn't never no fucking tape."

Momo slammed the brakes and spun the wheel, sending me banging against the door. The van skidded sideways toward the crossing. Just when it seemed like we were on the brink of sliding clean off the road, the wheels found purchase on the pavement of the lane. Momo stomped on the gas. We shot forward down the slope on a direct collision course with the oncoming train. Momo flung his door open and bailed out of the car. He tucked himself into a ball and I saw him rolling across the pavement. Then I felt the roar of the train bearing down; the metallic screech of brakes, the horn blowing in short, panicked bursts. Its headlamp flooded the van, washing out my vision. Then there was only the shadow of the train. I realized that there was no way the automatic sliding doors could open fast enough for me to ditch. In half a second I would be pulverized.

I dove headfirst between the driver's seat and the steering wheel, reached out and jammed the gas pedal to the floor. The vehicle lurched forward, but not quickly enough to get clear of the train. It smashed into the rear of the van. The sound was deafening, like the earth itself was being torn asunder. Upon impact, the back half of the van was destroyed. The front half was sent spinning ten feet into the air. It crashed down, rolled ass over tit half-a-dozen times until eventually a tree stump halted its progress at the berm of the crossing and the van rocked onto its roof.

I must have lost consciousness momentarily. I came to lying on the roof of the van. The gas pedal, having been ripped from the throttle valve, was still in my hand. My other arm and one of my legs were pinned beneath my back. I twisted free, tossed the pedal aside, and took a quick assessment of my body: arms, legs, neck, torso. Everything moved, everything functioned. I was banged up, my nose was gushing blood, and bolts of pain ripped through my concussed head. But I was alive. I was intact.

I crawled out from the gaping hole where the rear of the van used to be, gingerly got to my feet, and surveyed the wreckage. The back half of the vehicle was strewn about the crossing—tires, glass, chunks of metal. The license plate looked like a crushed soda can in the middle of the road. If I had been anywhere else in the van I would have been a dead man. No question.

The train came to a full stop with a grating metal-to-metal squeal, which intensified the bleating pain in my head and the scream in my ears. As the squeal subsided, an agonized wail that sounded more akin to a mauled animal than a human being arose in its place. The wailing was coming from the opposite side of the tracks. I thought maybe it was Momo, injured when he'd ditched out of the van. I reached for my .32 and realized it was long gone, lost somewhere in the wreckage. So was the gun I'd taken from Momo. I moved toward the train, toward the feral cries. In doing so my vision went topsy-turvy. I started to stumble and would have fallen but for a handrail I grabbed a hold of to keep me upright. Cold sweat broke out over my body as the world around me spun off its axis. I took a few quick breaths to shake the vertigo. The spinning stopped and I clambered through a gap in the train cars.

On the other side, I discovered the source of the wailing. The SUV that had been following us was at the top of the slope, engine running, the driver's side door wide open. Its high beams illuminated the body of a man sprawled across the road, clutching at his windpipe. But the man wasn't Momo. It was Bob Lawson. I hobbled up there and knelt beside him.

"Jesus Christ, Bob. What are you doing here?"

Lawson attempted to speak, but he was still choking for air. "My . . . my . . . my gun."

"What about your gun?"

Lawson flung his arm toward the woods across the lane. "He's . . . he's . . . got it."

I scanned the trees, listened for any movement. Momo could be anywhere in there. I could feel his eyes on me.

"C'mon, Bob. Get up, we gotta go."

I helped Lawson to his feet and shoved him into the passenger side of his own car. From somewhere in the distance, off toward the front of the train, a man called out, "You okay back there?"

I didn't bother to answer. I hurried around to the driver's side, hopped in, did a quick three-point turn and lit out for Cain City proper. As I sped away I peered in the rearview and caught sight of Momo Morrison strolling out from the woods, holding the gun. He stopped in the middle of the road and stood there, bathed in the red glow made from our taillights and the blinking crossing lights, and watched us flee for a few seconds. Then, casually, he raised the gun in our direction and began firing.

I pushed Lawson's head down between the seats and floored it. A handful of bullets plinked against the body of the SUV. Three or four more came through the back window, splintering it into a thousand crackling pieces before it popped and shattered all at once. The shooting ceased. I lifted my head and risked one last look in the rearview. The gun was back by Momo's side now. He stood motionless and watched us until we turned the bend and disappeared out of sight.

CHAPTER THIRTY-EIGHT
THE DEAD OF NIGHT

We sped into the Southside, heading for the old high school, both of us quiet. Lawson's hands shook like he had the palsy. He stared down at them.

"I've never been shot at before," he murmured. His typically shrill voice was chock with gravel now thanks to the chop in the throat Momo had given him. When he'd come upon the carnage of the accident, Lawson noticed what he thought was a boy running at him, flailing his arms and screaming for help. He realized too late that it was Momo Morrison.

"Stick with me," I said. "We'll make it an annual event."

Lawson didn't have a rejoinder for that and we fell back into silence.

A small fleet of police cars blew past us going the opposite direction, blue and reds flashing, sirens blaring. They didn't pay us any mind, but there was a good chance one of the units would peel off to check out the only other car on the road this early in the morning. Up ahead was a utility road that snaked through a wooded area and eventually wound up at a railroad supply factory. I turned onto it, pulled into the black shadows of the woods, flipped the SUV around to face the street and doused the lights. Sure enough, not two minutes later a lone cruiser came rolling by. When it was good and gone, I pulled back out and took a circuitous route through some residential streets the rest of the way.

After a while, when Lawson's shell shock seemed to be subsiding, I said, "So *I* was your fucking job tonight? That's why you couldn't help me out?"

"Yeah."

"How long you been tailing me?"

"Picked you up when you got your car from the Royal Vista."

"Fuck me, that early? You're either getting good or I'm slipping. Who hired you?"

"You know I can't tell you that, Malick."

"Don't make me get nasty. Was it Leach and McKinney?"

Lawson nodded in the affirmative.

"What for, did they say?"

"They just wanted me to keep tabs on you. Way they explained it, you'd gone a little off the deep end with this last thing, the Barnhard thing, and they wanted to make sure you didn't do anything that would further sully their standing in the community."

"Sounds like them. Fuck their standing in the community. Which one sicced you on me, McKinney?"

"No. No, it was Leach."

I explained to Lawson the multitude of reasons why he shouldn't report any of what happened tonight to the firm or the police.

"I have to," he protested.

"Why's that?"

"Morrison stole my gun for one thing. Assaulted me."

"Listen, you want to live to see next week, you don't breathe a word of this to anyone. Not Leach, not McKinney, not your mother, not your boyfriend. You understand me? You don't want to get mixed up in this. The Stenders don't know who you are. Be smart. Keep it that way. For your own good, pretend it never happened."

"What am I supposed to tell the firm?"

"Who gives a fuck? Tell them I went on a bender. They'll believe it."

We reached the high school. I got out of the car. Lawson, faculties restored, slid over behind the wheel.

"I'm sorry, Malick," he said through the open window. "I should've never taken the job when I found out you were the mark. Brotherhood and all. I should've told you."

I reminded him of something he'd said to me once. "Ain't no fucking brotherhood."

"Yeah, well. Regardless. I owe you one."

"Tell you what, you want to get in my good graces, all you have to do is keep your mouth shut. You saw where I went today, who I went with?"

"You mean when you took that girl, the one from the Royal Vista that had on the pink wig, when you took her across the river to the Relax Inn? Yeah, I saw you."

"You told anybody about that?"

"No."

"Good, 'cause you didn't see it, Bob. You didn't see a fucking thing. Understood?"

Lawson nodded. "Yeah, yeah. Understood. Look it, I'm really sorry, Malick. Thanks for getting my ass outta there."

I rapped on the roof of the SUV and Lawson pulled away from the curb. I scaled the portico steps two at a time and ran into the school, up the three flights of stairs to Karla's apartment. I pounded on the door and yelled for her or Davey.

A thin light shone through the crack at the bottom of the door. It swung open revealing Davey, bare-chested and bleary eyed. "What's up, Nick?" he said, squinting against the light from the hall. When the fuzz from his vision cleared and he saw my face, he added, "Aw, shit. Again?"

I hadn't seen what I looked like, but judging from his reaction it couldn't have been pretty. "Where's your mom?"

"She's—"

"It's the dead of night," Karla exclaimed as she emerged from the bedroom. "This better be—" She too stopped short upon catching sight of me. "Oh my God, what happened to you this time?"

346

"Run-in with a locomotive."

"That's not funny. Are you okay?"

"I'm fine." I pushed past Davey and into the apartment. "Get dressed, throw some clothes into a bag. We have to go. Now."

"Why? What's happened?" said Karla, her voice a stunned hush. "What time is it?"

"Three o'clock. I'll tell you later. We have to move."

"You're hurt, Nick. You need help."

"No time."

Less than a handful of minutes later we were banging out the side door of the school and piling into Karla's Nissan Sentra. I got behind the wheel.

"Are you okay to drive?" asked Karla.

"I'm fine."

I peeled out of the lot and pointed the Sentra south, toward the hills. The streets were deserted, no sign of anyone pursuing us. I inhaled a deep breath and let it out easy, realized I'd barely been breathing at all. We drove down around Redding Park, crossed the bridge over the creek and turned left up the lane that wound into the hills.

"Are we going to Joanna's?" Karla said. I must have seemed agitated, because she kept her speech slow and her tone even.

"Oh, snap," Davey yawned. "We gonna be breathing that ritzy air."

In truth, I hadn't known where I was going to take them. My mind was swimming and I couldn't think that far in advance. I just knew I had to get them out, get them safe, and had started driving to Honeysuckle Lane without even thinking about it.

"Yeah," I said, "Joanna's."

I retrieved my phone from the pocket of my coat to call her, warn her we were coming, but the display was shattered and I couldn't get the touch screen to work.

"Give it to me," said Karla. Her touch was lighter than mine and she managed to get into the phone, though she couldn't navigate to the Contacts or Recent Calls screens, just the keypad.

"That works," I told her, and recited Joanna's number.

"You still have it memorized," she remarked.

"Yeah, well, it's been the same for the last fifteen years."

Karla made the call, conveyed our circumstances.

"They'll be waiting," she said, handing the phone back. "You need to tell us what's going on before we get there."

I gave them the straight story, no sugar coating. When I was finished, Davey managed a single syllable, "Whoa," while Karla took a moment to compose her thoughts.

Again speaking deliberately, she said, "How long are we going to have to be here?"

"Until it's settled. You won't have to be here the whole time. We can find somewhere else for you, but this was the best place I could think of in a pinch."

"I'm starting my new job on Monday, Nick. Davey has school. We can't just stop our lives. I can't be a no-show on the first day."

"They'll understand."

"Understand what? That my boyfriend has somehow gotten us involved in a gang vendetta that necessitates us having to go into hiding 'cause it's no longer safe to go out in public? Not safe for them or anyone else to be near us, so, you know, I'll just ask them if they can hold the job for a while?" She ran her fingers through her hair and sighed. "The world won't wait for us, Nick."

I didn't respond.

"Maybe you should like, leave all that out whenever you tell them," Davey suggested from the backseat.

We pulled through the gates and up the long driveway to Jacob's Ladder. Joanna and Tom were on the porch, shivering in the cold, hugging their robes tightly to their chests. Both of them blanched when they saw my face, then tried to mask their expressions.

"I look like the Elephant Man or something?"

"No, it's not that bad," Tom offered, grinning with concern. "Maybe just a close relation."

The Orviettos escorted us inside, got Davey and Karla set up in one of the five spare bedrooms they had in their house, and insisted that I shower while Joanna threw my clothes in the washer. Afterwards she would administer a proper medical examination.

In their bathroom I got naked, tossed the clothes out to Tom in the hall, and took a gander at my reflection in the mirror. Large bruises were purpling up all over my body. The adrenaline from the crash gone, I was starting to feel them plenty. Both my eyes were blackened and my nose had a hook in it that hadn't been there a few hours ago. Dried blood crusted over the lower half of my face, providing a particularly ghoulish touch. Also, there was a gash over one eyebrow I hadn't even noticed. I was beaten to a pulp.

I tapped on my nose a little to see how much it hurt. It was more numb than anything else. Once more I looked in the mirror and took in the whole visage. I laughed at myself. Had to. What else could I do?

I turned all three of the showerheads on in the stall, set the temperature to scalding, and let the water pummel me from all angles for a good long while. I stepped out feeling a little more human, if not exactly refreshed. With the blood washed off, my reflection improved a bit; a little less Elephant Man, a little more like a punched-out LaMotta. Tom provided me with a sweatsuit to wear while my clothes were being washed. They were adorned with the logo of his alma mater, Dartmouth, and so massive they made me look like a little kid trying on his dad's clothes.

Joanna was waiting for me when I got out of the bathroom. She led me into her home office. I'd never been in the room before. There weren't many pictures of Jake around the house, one or two that I'd seen displayed inconspicuously, but her office was a veritable shrine to our dead son. Photographs, framed artwork, some of his favorite toys, the stuffed animal he slept with—it was all there.

"How do you get any work done in here?" I said.

"I can feel him when I'm in here. I don't know, it's somehow comforting. Makes me feel at peace. I can breathe."

The whole space made me uneasy, didn't seem a bit healthy, but who was I to judge how others grieved when my method for the better part of a decade was to destroy everything I came in contact with?

Joanna moved the stuffed fox off the couch and had me lie there. She put me through a battery of physical tests—pressed on my belly, flexed my joints, that kind of thing—to ensure I didn't have any major broken bones or internal bleeding. Her conclusions were as follows: slight concussion, cracked nose, possibly a couple fractured ribs, a dislocated pinky—which she popped into place, no fuss—and something maybe torn in my knee, which I couldn't put too much weight on.

"We need to get x-rays to make certain, an MRI if I can get you to sit still long enough, but I think that's the extent of the damage," Joanna said. "You're very lucky."

"Lucky? I don't think a person in the world would trade my luck for theirs."

"You know what I mean."

I sat up on the couch. "You don't wanna check my prostate?"

"There aren't enough rubber gloves in the world. Are you staying the night?"

"No. I've gotta go."

"You have to slow down, Nick. You can't save everyone all the time."

"I'd settle for saving anyone once. Listen, I'm sorry to bring this to your doorstep, Jo. I needed a haven. You're the only person who popped up in my head. I didn't know where else to go."

"You don't have to apologize. We'll take care of them. We're glad to." She placed her palms behind her on the desk, leaned back onto them. "But, you don't think it's dangerous for us to have them here? I have a baby, Nick."

"I know. If you're not comfortable—"

"It's not about comfort. I've lost one child already . . ."

My eyes were drawn to the eleven-by-fourteen framed photograph on the wall over her shoulder—Jake's kindergarten portrait, the last school picture he'd taken. Two days before he went missing. The proofs came back a week after we buried him.

"I know," I whispered.

"I couldn't bear losing another."

Joanna turned her back to me and bowed her head. I saw her spine and shoulders go rigid.

"It's just a precautionary measure, probably not even necessary, but if it'll make you feel better I'll look for another place to house them. I don't think anybody'd ever think I'd come here in my time of need. My own mother probably wouldn't make the link. Hell, most people don't even remember we were married in a different life."

"In a different life," Joanna repeated wistfully.

"You and Tommy doing okay?"

"I don't know, Nick." She tilted her head slightly my way, enough for me to see a sliver of her profile. "You know what he did. He told you, right?"

"Yeah, he did. Listen, if you would have consulted me before you married the yahoo, I could have told you he was the kind of guy that had to pay for it. You can tell that by looking at him."

"Shut your mouth." Joanna tried her damnedest to never take pleasure when I cracked wise about her husband, but I could tell she appreciated that particular crack. The pleasure was brief. "I'm relieved in a way," she said. "When that lawyer you were working with was killed, I was relieved Tom wouldn't have to give testimony." The admission prompted Joanna to scoff. "I was mortified by the thought of people knowing he'd done that. Knowing the kind of man he is. I realize that's shallow, but there it is."

"You still love him?"

Joanna dabbed at her eye, turned around to face me. "I don't know. I guess. Maybe. I can't tell. It's not the same as it was with you. That was undeniable."

"We were twenty, Jo. It'll never be like that again. There's nothing like the first strike."

"Right."

"Love is a disease in which—how do you docs say it?—the symptoms *present* differently every time."

"I suppose so. What about you and Karla? You're doing well?"

"Ah, I fucked that up finally, I think."

"I'm sorry to hear that," she said, though I thought I detected a twinge of satisfaction lurking behind the sentiment.

"Yeah. Listen, don't be too hard on Tommy. It was before you. You'd be surprised how many men pay for it."

"Ha."

"I'm serious. Tom's a good man, much as I hate to admit. He's a ridiculous human being, don't get me wrong, but he loves you and looks after you. That's all I care about, personally. That's what matters. Now, if he ever stops doing either one of those things, you let me know and I'll rough him up a little."

"You better not, Nick." Joanna thought about something, a memory of us perhaps, that made her smile. Then, fast as it came, the smile faded from her lips. "Sometimes when you see what someone else's life consists of, it gives you a healthy dose of perspective. I see you, all of a sudden my life seems pretty ideal."

"Happy to help."

"How much trouble are you in? As much as last time?"

"Give or take."

"Is there anything else I can do to help?"

"Besides keeping me alive?" I thought about it. "Tommy didn't become a gun owner in the last two years, did he?"

Joanna hitched an eyebrow. "Actually, after those two men threatened him, he went out and bought a small Walther. I'm not sure what caliber. It's a tiny, pocket-sized thing, looks foolish in his hand. I detest having it in the house. You want it?"

Yeah, I did want it.

CHAPTER THIRTY-NINE
NIGHT SWEATS

Karla and Tom were in the kitchen, she sipping coffee at the table, him standing over a couple of sizzling pans at the stove. When we walked in and smelled the food my stomach made a sound like an old boat rocking at sea. I realized that I had no memory of the last time I'd eaten. I took the seat next to Karla, who looked at me with a mixture of contempt and pity.

"Davey asleep?" I asked.

"Mm."

I leaned toward her ear to whisper, "I'm sorry, I swear I'll fix this." She mustered a sporting nod that was dubious at best and I could tell she didn't buy a word of it.

We ate the omelets that Tom prepared, which were, I must say, fucking delicious. Nobody said much, some compliments to the chef, a couple of inquiries about how I got hit by a train in the first place. I kept my answers vague and did my best to pacify Tom and Joanna's fears that he'd be dragged back into the proceedings. Truth was, if I had my druthers, Rutherford Blevins would be made to have a very harsh and very public comeuppance, which meant Tom would be forced to air all of his dirty laundry. But who knew if it'd ever come to that? Who knew if I'd be alive long enough to see it play out? Who knew if I'd survive the day?

When we'd finished eating I went into the bathroom and changed back into my own clothes. Then I came out and told everyone I had to hit the road. Tom stood, shook my hand force-fully, and made a bashful attempt at humor.

"We have to stop meeting this way." He grinned out of the side of his mouth.

"Don't I know it."

I thanked them, gave Joanna a hug, lied and told her every-thing would work out. Karla walked me to the door. Her hands were tucked into the sleeves of her sweater and she held them tightly at her sides. There wasn't much to say. I told her I'd park her car at the high school and stash the key in her apartment. She reached for my face, but stopped short of touching it.

"What are you doing to yourself?" she said.

"Not an improvement then?"

Karla frowned. "Are you going to come back here soon?"

Taking this to be a show of concern or a desire to see me safely on the other side of this conflict, I said, "Yeah, I'll come check on you and Davey. Don't worry, I'll be okay."

"It's just, ah," she stammered, realizing I'd misread her, "in all the chaos I forgot my phone."

"Oh, yeah okay."

"If we're going to be here for a while I'll have to sort everything out," she explained. "With my job, Davey's school."

"Right. No problem. I'll pick it up for you, bring it over."

"Only if it's safe."

"Of course."

"Thanks."

"Yeah."

She saw me off with a half-hearted hug. I limped down the lane to Karla's Sentra, thinking, *So . . .* over then. For the best, I told myself. Karla was still young, gorgeous; she could relegate me to her past, as she had with the many other traumas she'd experienced. Start her life fresh with a new job, find a more suit-able partner if she wanted, a more suitable father figure for Dav-ey. Someone like who Joanna had found, I thought reluctantly. Someone like Tom, minus the proclivity for hookers. No doubt Karla's prospects would queue up around the block. Or maybe she'd choose to live alone. She was plenty strong enough for that, too. With her salary she could afford a house if she wanted. Maybe not on the Southside, but still.

I lowered myself into the Sentra and drove down the hill, through town, and over the bridge into Ohio. It was just before six a.m. The first sliver of sun broke the horizon, sending a shimmer of sparkling lights along the ripples of the river—the river from which I'd pulled my son's bloated corpse, and later watched the man who put him there disappear below its surface. It was a thing to behold, that river, its current cutting a wide swath into the earth as far as the eye could see, and every time I laid eyes on it, I couldn't shake the feeling that my whole life was inextricably bound to that water. To what it gave and took away.

At my request Tom had packed a Tupperware of scrambled eggs with everything he'd put into the omelets: onions, peppers, bacon, cheese. It was for Renata. She was curled into a ball beneath the cheap floral comforter of the motel, gently snoring. Lying there peaceful-like almost made Renata look sweet. I shut off the TV, set the eggs on the bedside table along with my hat, removed my coat, and laid my head on the pillow. In the span of three heartbeats, I was asleep.

I woke some time later, discombobulated, hair ringed with sweat. My first lucid thought was—*pain.* A head-to-toe pain that made it difficult to breathe, misery to move.

I creaked my eyes open, squinted against the sunshine streaming in through the windows and tried to blink the film out of my vision. The TV was back on. Renata was sitting cross-legged on the bed, chomping loudly on some chips, gawking at me. While one of her hands rooted around in the bag, the other gripped the Walther PPK. She held the gun aloft for me to see, then twisted it around to examine it from all angles.

"This real?"

"Very," I said, the words feeling as though they were scraping their way out of my throat. "Mind putting it down?"

Renata aimed the gun at the wall, closed one eye and stared down the barrel, then made a 'meh' face and set it down on the table. Without another thought she turned her attention to the daytime talk show, hosted by some woman who seemed incapable of speaking in complete sentences. I got my limbs moving, sat up and grabbed the Walther, made sure the safety was on and tucked it into my waistband.

"What time is it?" I asked.

"'Bout noon."

"I brought you some breakfast."

"Yeah, that shit cold. And it's got peppers. Nuh-uh." Renata shivered at the thought of eating something that grew naturally from the earth. She crammed some more chips in her mouth.

"What's wrong with peppers?"

"Texture all nasty. Like you're biting into something that's alive or something. Your phone been blowing up."

I pulled my cell from my pocket and studied the shattered display, tried to navigate to the recent calls, but the touch screen was kaput. As I was messing with it, the phone vibrated in my hand. I swiped where the answer feature usually lay. Miraculously, it connected the call.

"Malick," I answered.

"Where you been?" said Willis Hively. "I've been trying to get a hold of you since last night."

"My phone's on the fritz."

Hively hesitated, probably deciding whether or not to believe me about the phone, then said, "You see the paper?"

"No."

"I could kiss that little rat bastard, Ciccone. Man's got a magic pen. Word just came down that his article spurred the U.S. Attorney to open an investigation into Blevins's activities. You should check it out. You're mentioned a couple times."

"I'll do that."

"Blevins gotta be feeling the squeeze," Hively went on. "I was thinking about going over there, rattling his cage a little, see how he responds."

"To his house?"

"Yeah. I'd love to get a shot at him before the Feds come in and steal the show. You want in?"

I mulled the offer for exactly two seconds. "Give me the address. I'll meet you there."

CHAPTER FORTY
A MARVINA
BY ANY OTHER NAME

I ran my head under some cold water, left some cash with Renata so she could eat from the machine, and went down to the motel's office to get some aspirin and a newspaper. Ciccone's front-page headline read:

Recent Murders May Be Linked To Disability Fraud Investigation

The article itself didn't have a lot of bite to it, but it named names, including mine, and apparently it cast enough of a shadow of doubt over Judge Rutherford Blevins to light a fire under the Feds. I imagine quite a few blood pressures spiked when the paper was scooped off the porch that morning. It helped that Ciccone had spoken on the record with the U.S. Attorney, Debra Wilkes, who confirmed that there was indeed an investigation into Scott T. Barnhard's business practices at the time of his death.

There was nothing in there about the train wreck. It'd probably be in Monday's edition.

Rutherford Blevins lived in the next county over from Cain, way out in the boonies. Willis Hively was already there, waiting for me in his idling car, which was parked a ways down the tree-lined lane. When I pulled in behind him, he got out and strolled back toward me. I rolled down the window.

"Detective."

"My God, man, what happened to your face?"

"My parents were ugly."

"What else?"

I didn't answer, saying instead, "What's the play here, chief?"

Hively laid out what he had in mind. It all sounded fine to me, and we walked the remaining hundred yards to the Blevins home: a neo-modern build situated between a bluff overlooking the Ohio River and the par five thirteenth hole on Hickory Nut Golf Course. The entryway to the house was a two-story glass atrium that functioned as the first layer in what looked like a multi-tiered glass wedding cake.

"Let's see if we can get some answers," Hively said as he pressed the buzzer and stood back. A security camera was pointed directly at the spot on which we stood. For the benefit of anybody watching, I waved at it. Nobody came to the door. We tried the buzzer again and knocked on the glass.

You could see clear through the bottom level of the house, from the atrium to the patio and wide lawn out back. We gave the buzzer another go. When there was no activity or sign of life from inside, Hively said, "Wanna wait around for a bit?"

"Bring any snacks?" I said, but before I'd finished the sentence an older, shrivel-faced woman peered around an opaque wall at the left side of the first floor. I alerted Hively to her presence. "Here we go."

Hively pressed his police badge against the glass and pointed to the entrance. "Open the door," he said, taking care to enunciate the words in case the lady was hard of hearing. She shook her head vehemently and slunk back behind the wall.

"I think your fucked-up face scared her off," said Hively.

"Blame yourself. This is Lincoln County. You're probably the first black guy she's ever seen in person."

When the woman didn't come back, Hively cursed under his breath and started around to the side of the house she'd gone off to.

"Wait," I said, "look there."

The old woman reappeared at the back of the main floor. She opened a sliding glass door and hurried out to the back part of the property.

"Where's she going?" Hively wondered.

The woman scuttled over to the edge of the patio where a large swing faced the river. There she stopped and began speaking to someone who must have been lying on the swing. The woman gesticulated wildly and pointed toward the house. A pair of legs lowered down from the swing and the face of a young woman craned around the seatback to get a look at us. We waved amiably, and with some effort, the young lady got to her feet. We saw, even from that distance, that she was heavily pregnant. She placed a hand on the old lady's shoulder to calm her down and they made their way back into the house. The old lady veered into an unseen room while the pregnant girl duck-waddled toward us.

As she drew nearer, I said, "There's one thing answered."

"You know her?"

"Not personally."

Before I could explain further, Marvina E. Justice swung open the thick-paned transparent door and offered us a warm, easy smile that seemed crafted to disarm even the most jaded cranks mankind had to offer. The abundance of red hair and her vivid green eyes were unmistakable. Her face had shed the baby fat that had been evident in her school picture, leaving high, sculpted cheekbones. That, along with the sheet of freckles that overlaid her entire face, even her lips, favored her with an almost alien beauty.

"Hello," she greeted us. Her voice held a country lilt, but the twang typical for this region had been sanded off at the edges. "Are you looking for Rutherford?"

"Is he home?" asked Hively.

"No, sorry," she said earnestly. "Is something the matter?"

"There is, unfortunately. We do need to talk to him, ma'am. You're. . . ?"

"Elena."

"Are you a niece or—?"

"Not hardly," Elena said, amused by Hively's assumption. She placed her hands gently atop her tight, round stomach.

"Do you know where Judge Blevins is, Elena?" I said.

"Where he always is on Sunday. At the club. It's only five minutes away. If it's important I can call him."

"Please."

The woman going by the name Elena showed us into the house and invited us to sit at any of the three couches or six chairs in the living room. We chose our seats, which were cushier than they looked, and we sank down into them.

"Did you get into a fight?" Elena asked me, having taken longer than most to acknowledge the state of my countenance.

"Couple of 'em."

She cocked her head at me curiously, as did Hively, who quickly turned his attention back to our subject.

"May I ask, who is the lady who told you we were here?"

"That's Imogene, our cleaning lady. Would you like water or something to drink?"

We both declined and Elena excused herself to make the phone call to Blevins. As soon as she stepped out of the room, Hively leaned forward and whispered harshly.

"You gonna tell me what the hell it is you figured out?"

"She must go by her middle name now."

"Who? Elena?"

"Yeah, Elena. Though in some circles they call her Marvina, or Vina, or Destiny."

"Our Destiny?"

"Blevins's Destiny by the looks of it."

Elena came back into the room with one hand cupped over the phone receiver. "I'm sorry, I didn't get your names."

We gave them to her and she relayed the information into the phone. After listening for a moment, a startled expression jumped into her face. She lowered herself into one of the soft chairs, listened some more, said, "Oh, okay," and hung up. She stared down at the phone for an extra few seconds to compose herself before lifting her head and reassuming the genial demeanor she'd displayed to this point.

"He'll be here in just a minute."

Elena scooted forward to the edge of the seat and used both hands against the armrests to push herself up, belly-first, from the chair.

I said, "While we're waiting, we actually have a few questions for you, Elena."

"Oh, okay," she said for a second time, sitting right back down.

Hively asked, "What is your relationship to Judge Blevins?"

"We're together."

"Is that his baby?" I asked.

"That's a very forward question." She blushed, or pretended to blush.

"Yeah."

"I don't think—I'm not going to participate in this. You're here for Rutherford, he'll be here any moment. You're welcome to wait here, if you'd like, or you can wait outside."

She edged forward and started the process of standing from the chair again.

"The reason I ask is because there's a significant age gap between you and the judge—"

"Only forty-three years—"

"Is that all? Well, never mind then. That's nothing."

"Rutherford is young in spirit," Elena said, still struggling to rise.

"He's sprightly all right—do you need some help?"

"No," Elena gasped before giving up the effort and sinking back into the seat.

"He told you who we were? Why we were here?" I pressed.

"He said the two of you were the ones who planted that smear job in the paper. The ones who are out to get him. Is that true?"

"More or less."

"Then I'm done answering your questions. I'll have to ask you to wait outside please."

We didn't move.

"When did you start going by Elena?" I asked.

"Excuse me? I've asked you to leave."

"Your given name is Marvina, right? You shortened that to Vina in high school, for obvious reasons. Now you've switched it to Elena. And of course your professional name, as it were, is Destiny."

The veneer of civility she'd been clinging to vanished from her face. I'm pretty certain if she weren't trapped beneath that outsized belly, she'd have leapt across the room at me.

"I don't know what you're talking about."

"Two people have been murdered," said Hively. "You might be familiar with them. One was a lawyer, Scott T. Barnhard, who used to visit a girl who was murdered a couple nights ago in her apartment at the Royal Vista."

"Her name was Birdie Bryant," I said. "Did you know her?"

Elena didn't answer. Her chest heaved with rapid breaths.

"How 'bout Scott Barnhard? Did he visit you at the Royal Vista?"

"No."

"Did you know Birdie was engaged in the same occupation that you were on the floor below?"

Elena pursed her lips in a determined manner that indicated she had no plans on opening them back up.

"What about the Stenders? Momo Morrison?" Hively continued. "Those names ring a bell?" Elena remained mute.

"Here's the thing, Elena, you can answer these questions right now, or we can get a warrant and drag you down the station to answer them. One way or another, they're gonna get answered. Your choice."

"Or," I chimed in, "maybe we'll come to the hospital just after the baby's born, if that's more convenient for you. How'd that be?"

"So be it," Elena said coldly. "This is a malicious attack against a kind and decent man."

"I can see how you'd think so, seeing as he got you out of the life you were living, put you into this." I gestured to the decadent surroundings.

"What are you implying? There is no way he could be involved in any murders," Elena insisted. "Scott Barnhard was like a son to him."

"What are you to him?"

She eyed me viciously. "I'm the one person in this world he loves."

"His children might have something to say about that."

"Rutherford's children treat him like he's only good for one thing."

"Which is?"

"Whatever they can bilk him for."

"Maybe you're right," Hively interjected. "Maybe he has nothing to do with any of it. If that's the case, help us prove it. Clear his name. Tell us what we need to know so we can move on."

"You think I'm stupid?" she huffed. "The police get their sights set on a person, they twist whatever they have to twist to fit the narrative of that person's guilt. It's human nature. Human bloody nature. Doesn't matter who takes the fall as long as someone takes the fall."

"This isn't some petty street crime we're talking about," Hively said sternly. "This is murder, possibly a whole lot more."

Outside, a golf cart came humming around a weeping willow tree halfway down the lane, jumped the curb, and zoomed to a stop on the front lawn. Blevins leapt out of the thing before it even stopped rolling, hiked his golf pants a little higher, and stomped toward the front door.

"Do me a favor and head him off," I said to Hively.

Hive didn't question me. He moved swiftly toward the atrium. I scooted over to the seat closest to Elena.

"Listen to me, Elena," I said evenly. "Birdie Bryant was just like you. She had a child just like you're about to, a two-year-old daughter named Aisha. Birdie didn't want to be a pro. She wanted out of that life, as I'm sure you did when you were in it, but she never got the chance. She was just like you, Elena, and now she's dead."

Elena jerked her head toward me, green eyes blazing. "What am I supposed to do about it?"

"Did you know you were being videotaped?"

Blevins barged into the house, literally shaking with anger. He screamed for Hively to get out of his way.

"Please, Elena," I said urgently, "if there's a tape, then we can find out who killed her. Did you know—?"

"Yes," she hissed.

"Yes, you knew?"

"Yes, we were being videotaped."

Blevins shouted, "Get away from her!" Then, to Hively, who was impeding his path, "By the time I'm done with you, you won't be able to get a job as a goddamned greeter at Wal-Mart."

"Who has the tapes?" I asked.

"I don't know."

"Have you seen them?"

"No." Tears came spilling from her eyes. "And I hope I never do."

Hively could no longer hold Blevins at bay. He got around the box-out and rushed through the room to where we were sitting.

"How?" I said. "How did they tape you?"

"The curtain rods," she whispered. "The cameras were in the curtain rods."

Blevins reached us and knelt at Elena's side. I stood up and took a couple steps as he began cooing in her ear.

"Are you all right, sweetie? What did they do? Did they upset you?"

"I'm fine," Elena gasped.

"Are you sure? Are you sure?"

"Yes." She nodded, sniffing.

"What did they say to you?"

"Nothing."

"It's okay, you can tell me."

"Nothing, I promise. They were just telling me about what's gone on in town. The girl who was killed at the Royal Vista."

"You shouldn't have had to hear that," Blevins murmured. "It's too upsetting." He looked past her to where I stood. "You son of a bitch," he seethed. "Is this how you get your rocks off? Upsetting a woman in her condition?"

"I think mother and child will survive. But speaking of getting your rocks off—"

Hively cut me off. "We came out here to tell you, as of tomorrow you're gonna be under federal investigation. Every move you make is gonna be watched. Every meal you eat, every shit you take. They're gonna squeeze you till there's nothing left to squeeze. You wanna get in front of it, now's your chance. Right here, with us."

"You'd like that, wouldn't you? You have no idea what you've done."

"Enlighten us," said Hively.

Blevins shoved up off his knees. "Get out of my house."

"Tell me something," I said. "Did you set the disability caper in motion to pay for all this"—I waved my arm around to indicate the house—"or so that you could invest in River Path?"

The way all motion in the room froze made it seem as

though time stood still. I didn't know who looked more shocked by the revelation, Hively or Blevins.

"What, you didn't think we'd find out about that?"

"Get out of my house," Blevins repeated with markedly less gusto.

"Last chance," said Hively.

"Out!"

Hively made for the exit. I followed suit. As I stepped past Blevins, he sneered, "I'm going to ruin the both of you."

"Knock yourself out, old man."

He followed us out of the room and through the atrium, cursing and threatening us all the way. When we got out the door, he said, "If you two fucktards know what's good for you, you'll never show your faces near my home again. And if you ever bother Elena—"

"Save your breath, Judge," Hively said, having heard enough. "You'll have my badge, you'll ruin Nick. We heard you the first five times. Here's one last question for you, though. How you gonna explain it to all your redneck Stender friends when that baby comes out a different shade? You still gonna claim it's yours?"

Blevins cast a shrewd eye on Hively. "That will never happen. You want to know why?"

"Sure."

"Because Elena didn't cater to niggers."

With that, Blevins slammed the door in our faces. However, it being glass, each party could still see one another, which undercut the whole scene with absurdity. Blevins made some goofy faces at us before pulling out his phone to make a call. He moved back into the interior of the house, collected Elena from the chair, and disappeared into a room with walls that weren't see-through.

I said, "You gotta admit, he had a pretty good comeback."

"That motherfucker's going down," Hively seethed. "I hope to God that baby comes out black as a fucking eight-ball."

Seeing how Elena was about as colorless as they came, that possibility seemed highly unlikely, but I didn't think it was the right time to mention such things. The key to Blevins's golf cart was still in the ignition. I got it chugging and chauffeured us back down the wispy lane to our vehicles.

"Who do you think he was calling?" asked Hively.

"Feds get a warrant on his cell, we'll know shortly."

"Speaking of the Feds, they're gonna need Renata to give a statement, testify probably."

"They agree to put her in protective custody, they can have her."

Hively gazed out at a couple of golfers lining up their putts on the thirteenth green. "When were you going to tell me Blevins was an investor in River Path?"

"Sorry, I just found out yesterday. You get a chance to talk to the state's attorney that prosecuted those Stender cases?"

"Not yet. It was Lawrence Chabot who tried them. He's on vacation with his family. Back mid-week. Got an interview set up already. What did you ask Elena there at the end?"

"I asked if she knew whether or not she was videotaped with her johns at the Royal Vista."

"What'd she say?"

"Yeah, she said she was."

Hively thought about what that meant. I pulled the cart over where our cars were parked. After a lengthy silence that gave both golfers enough time to four-putt, he said quietly, "So there's a tape?"

"So there's a tape."

CHAPTER FORTY-ONE
ENDLESS BLACK

Hively made me promise to pick up the phone the next time he called, day or night, rain or shine, and also to let him know if I came across anything pertinent.

"Define pertinent," I said. Unamused, Hively got into his car. We went our separate ways, he to his family, and me back to the Royal Vista.

I scoured Birdie's apartment and each of the vacants. Sure enough, in every bedroom there was a curtain rod with the finial on one end missing. Elena hadn't been lying. That's where they'd hidden the cameras. The vacant with the abandoned ethernet cord was probably where they had some kind of drive set up to collect the footage. And Momo Morrison had been carrying something out of the Royal Vista the night Scott Barnhard had been murdered. Something that looked very much like a hard drive or laptop.

I got some more clothes out of Renata's room, threw them in a garbage bag, and drove back over into Ohio, stopping along the way to pick up some burgers, fries, and shakes. Renata devoured the food as though she'd eaten exclusively from a vending machine for two days.

"How much longer I got to be here?" she said between bites.

"Not too much longer. Could be as early as tomorrow."

"Good. 'Cause I'm getting stir crazy something fierce." A chunk of burger escaped her mouth. She caught it and put it back in.

"When this is all finished, you have anywhere you can go? Any people that can put you up for a bit?"

"Got a sister in Florida. Don't know where though. She older, married. Don't have no number. Things didn't part right between us."

"Worth a shot. Give me her full name. I'll see if I can track her down."

"You'd do that?"

"Sure."

Jesslyn Renee Jones. Renata recited her sister's name eagerly, seeming buoyed by the prospect of rekindling their relationship. She didn't know her married name. I assured Renata she could still be found without it, told her I'd be back that night, and set off for the old high school. I needed to retrieve Karla's phone from her apartment, deliver it to her at Joanna's. Then I needed to fetch my truck. Then I needed to find another way to get at Momo Morrison. Unfortunately, I had exactly zero good ideas on how to accomplish that last item on my to-do list. The best way would probably be to sit back and wait for him to come for me, but I had a feeling it wouldn't be him coming. It'd be Buddy Cleamons or another of the Stenders who still possessed both their eyeballs.

Fuck it, I thought. Let them come. Let them all come.

I parked Karla's car in the lot, didn't see any obvious signs of the school being surveilled, no silhouetted figures skulking in the shadows or in the cars across the street at the strip mall. For kicks, I turned the safety off of the pocket Walther and kept hold of it in my coat pocket as I dragged my sorry ass up the steps to the portico and entered the school.

No ambush, no surprises.

I climbed the stairwell to the third floor, let myself into Karla's apartment with my key, and found her phone connected to the charger on her nightstand. The time on the display read 6:23 p.m. I punched in Joanna's cell number, one of the few I still knew by heart.

"Nick," Joanna answered after a single ring. She sounded concerned, which made me feel oddly grateful.

"Hey, tell Karla I've got her phone. I'll bring it up there in a little bit."

"Are you okay? How are you feeling?"

"Like I got hit by a train."

"Normal then?"

"Yeah, normal. See you in a bit."

I slipped the phone and the charger into my pocket, left Karla's car keys on the dining room table, locked the door behind me, and descended the stairs to the first floor. The thought of getting back in the car, driving up to my ex-wife's palace on the hill to face two women I loved but who no longer loved me didn't hold a whole lot of appeal at the moment.

I decided to swing by my office. I wanted a drink, just one drink to blunt the pain in my body and in my spirit. Quiet the debilitating thoughts bouncing around my brain like an incessant echo; all the death surrounding this case. Who killed Birdie? Who killed Barnhard? Who was calling the shots? The Stenders? Judge Blevins? Did they have Red Lewis under their thumb? If so, how many other cops might they have? The one thought that prevailed above all comers was this: there was one common denominator in all the violence, the personal turmoil, the death—me. I'd lost my job. I'd lost my girl. To what end? It was too much to wrap my head around. Fortunately, I had an emergency bottle stashed for just such an occasion.

I went into my office, retrieved the Maker's from back of a filing cabinet and ripped the wax off the top. The first nip travelled smoothly down my throat. The next even smoother. The tension in my body eased. Without bothering to turn on the lights or remove my coat or shoes, I took the bottle to the back bedroom, lay on the bed, and tipped it back a few more times.

I didn't want to sleep. There were things to do, not to mention the last time I'd slept had done more harm than good. Nevertheless, with each successive drink I felt the hypnotic tug toward unconsciousness, toward the sweet bliss of nothingness, an absence of thought, an endless black.

One of the phones in my coat started vibrating. I took both of them out, saw that the one quaking was mine and not Karla's, and tried to make out the ID of the caller through my splintered screen. Couldn't do it, so I just went ahead and accepted the call.

"Malick."

"Now I seen a lot of things in my day," came the cloying voice of Momo Morrison, "but I ain't never seen somebody get hit by a moving train and live to tell the tale. That was something."

"How many people have you seen hit by trains?"

"One or two. You know, I'm glad you made it though. I ain't really want to kill ya. World's more interesting with you in it. But you ain't really leave me much choice in that moment now, did ya?"

"There a reason for this call, Momo, or is it primarily social in nature?"

"Goddamn, you do like to suck the fun out of things. I did want to see how you was doing, make sure there weren't no bad feelings lingering. It was just business, you understand?"

There was a pause where both of us expected the other to speak. Finally, I said, "Sure, Momo, I understand. Are we buds now? You want to send me a friend request?"

"See now, that didn't sound genuine," he said, feigning disappointment. "I guess I'll get down to it."

"Please do."

"Word come down from on high."

"You converse with the Almighty today, did you?"

Momo, starting to get perturbed, took a long, audible breath.

"We all got masters to serve, Malick."

"Uh-huh."

"We need to meet."

I laughed aloud. "I'll take a hard pass."

"I figured you might say that, you're getting predictable. So I sent some of my associates to you. Go ahead and take a gander out your window there. I'll wait."

His words sparked the adrenaline in my body. I bounded off the bed, yanked the pistol from my pocket and skirted along the wall into the main office. I crept to the edge of a shadow near the windows and peered out into the twilight. Down on the avenue, beneath a streetlamp, two men leaned against a Ford Explorer. The first was Buddy Cleamons, the second was none other than Red Lewis. That answered that.

"You haven't left yet, have you? They said you ain't left."

I didn't speak.

"You see 'em?" Momo asked. "I believe the three of you know each other."

"Yeah, we're acquainted. Can't be bothered to come for me yourself, Momo? Gotta send your stooges?"

"Now, don't get worked up. I know what happens when somebody puts baby in a corner. This ain't that. I simply had a suspicion you might still be smarting a little, so I figured it best I stay back from things, sit this one out. You still mad?"

"You could say that."

"See now, I figured. Like I said, word come down. We're gonna make that deal we was talking about. This your lucky day, Malick. Go buy a lottery ticket."

"What deal?"

"'What deal', he says. The deal you proposed last night. That crash turn your brain to mush or something?"

"Must have. Refresh my memory."

Outside, Buddy Cleamons stretched his limbs and used the Explorer's side mirror to adjust his eye patch. Red, for his part, seemed nervous and jittery. He kept peering up and down the sidewalk and at the drivers of the cars zooming past. An old man strolled by walking his dog. Red turned up his collar and tucked his head down. The man got one look at Buddy The Face, his scarred pate gleaming from the glow of the streetlamp, and gave him a wide berth as he moved around them.

Momo groaned. "You recall saying all you wanted was to know who killed Birdie? Once you found that out, you'd leave the other stuff alone? Ring a bell?"

"Vaguely."

"Ain't nothing vague about it. I said I'd make that deal. And here we are. Making that deal."

"You expect me to believe a word you say, Momo?"

"You don't have to believe me. You can mosey on out there and see for yourself."

"They have the tape?"

"They do."

"Call them, tell them to hold it up. And tell them to roll down the windows of their car and open the doors so I can see nobody else is inside."

"Shit, all right. Hold on."

A few seconds later Buddy Cleamons pulled a phone from his jeans, listened for a minute, then went and opened the car doors on the street side of the car, popped the hatch in the back. No one was inside. Cleamons said something to Red Lewis, who lifted a small item above his head.

Momo got back on the phone. "Satisfied?"

"I can't see what Red's holding up."

"It's a thumb drive. Even brought you one of them connectors if you need it. All you gotta do is plug the little doo-hickey in, should play. There is one caveat, Malick. You got to quit barking up trees. You gotta drop all your investigating into that other thing. All of it. You sniff around, talk to that reporter anymore, anything, tell anybody we got cops on the pad, deal's off. Then I will come for you personally. You, Karla, and the boy. Won't stop until the job's complete. Got it?"

"The police are already onto Red."

Momo went silent for a beat. "Well, you don't help them out none."

"All right, but that caveat extends both ways, Momo. I catch sight of one of you in my rearview, see you anywhere near Karla or Davey—hell, if I catch one of you eating in the same restaurant, I'm gonna hunt you and all your friends down one by one."

"I wouldn't expect nothing less. Now, all you gotta do is go out there and get it. Seals the deal."

"That's where we come to an impasse, Momo. No way in hell I'm going out there. Tell them to leave the drive on the bottom step."

"Malick," Momo mocked. "What do you think, they gonna gun you down right there on the street? That's why I sent the cop along, bring you peace of mind."

"Tell them to keep their hands out at their sides. Any sudden moves they get plugged."

"Is that necessary?"

"Do it."

I heard some muffled talk on the other end of the receiver and watched out the window as the message was conveyed, first to Cleamons and then to Red. They both obliged, extending their arms at their sides.

"We got a deal?" said Momo.

"Deal."

"See you around, Malick."

"You better hope not."

The call was disconnected.

I half-expected Momo or somebody else to be waiting for

me on the other side of my office door when I opened it, but no one was there. I walked through the empty halls to the front of the high school, peeked out the square window panel and saw that Cleamons and Red were in the same position.

Gun in hand, I clomped to the bottom of the portico steps where they stood. This was the first time I'd gotten an up-close look at Buddy Cleamons when he wasn't beating the shit outta me. No idea how I'd come out of a fight with him in as good a shape as I had, much less gotten the best of him. His arms were so thick with muscle I wondered how he managed to wipe his own ass.

We all stared at each other for a good duration without speaking.

"I'm sorry, Malick," Red said, breaking the silence. He offered up the thumb drive. I stepped forward, took the drive and stepped back.

"How'd they get you, Red? You on one of these tapes?"

He didn't respond, but I could tell by the contrition on his face I'd gotten it right in one. It was easy enough to see how Red could get from there to here. He had a family—four kids, if I'm not mistaken. A man like him would go to any lengths, make any compromises, to protect that.

Buddy The Face licked his lips and snarled, "You'll slip up. I know you will. And when you do, I'll be there."

"You know something, Cyclops? I believe you."

Only after the two of them got into their vehicle, cruised down the avenue, and dropped out of sight under the viaduct did I look down at the small thumb drive in my hand. I brought out Karla's phone and plugged the converter into the socket. The display went black save for a white triangle in the center. I tapped it. After a few seconds of rendering, a high-angled black-and-white view of Birdie's bedroom appeared on the screen. And as night descended on Cain City, I stood there on the sidewalk and watched a murder.

CHAPTER FORTY-TWO
REVELATION

"This ain't on you," Willis Hively said to me as I clambered out of his car.

"Yes, it is."

I stood there outside the door to Room 17 for a moment, not wanting to go in. The night was crisp, the air clean, quiet enough to hear the electric hum of the Relax Inn vacancy sign, the cars motoring by in the dark up on Route 52. I slipped in the keycard and opened the door.

Renata was sitting cross-legged on the bed, surrounded by crumbs from an assortment of snacks. *South Park* was on the television. As I walked in, Renata was giggling. She brightened when she saw me, and I realized that a bond had formed between us, imperceptibly, in these last few days. She'd begun to endear herself to me, and I to her. Her bright mood went away when she saw the dour look on my face. I sat on the opposite bed.

She flicked through the possibilities. "What's wrong? Something happen? You find my sister? Has something happened to her?"

"No." My voice croaked. "Haven't had the chance. I'll find her." I reached across to her bed and got the remote, switched off the television.

"You starting to freak me out," Renata said, after I didn't speak for a while.

"I found out who killed Birdie."

Renata's eyes went round and wide. She cleared her throat. "Who?" she said, the word coming out soft and brittle.

"You, Renata."

Her eyes flitted to the door, to the bathroom, the two obvious means of flight.

"Don't do that," I said. "There's nowhere to go."

"I don't know what you talking about," Renata said desperately. "I ain't do nothing. I found her like that. I swear to you, I found her like that. It was one of them freaks, one of them men."

"I believed you. I would have gone on believing you. I don't know why. 'Cause I wanted to, I guess. But there's a tape, Renata. I've seen the whole thing. It's over. I just want to know why. Was it for the money?"

Renata opened her mouth as if to continue trying to argue herself innocent, then stopped short as the full impact of what I'd told her sank in.

"A tape?"

I nodded.

Her face scrunched tightly and her eyes filled with water. She tossed her head back and let out a low, guttural sound. "I ain't mean to," she moaned. "I loved Birdie. Oh, God, oh, God."

Renata rolled her head around atop her neck, then shook it hard as though she wanted to rid herself of the thoughts and images stuck inside it. I knew the feeling. When that didn't work she clawed at her scalp as though maybe she could physically pry them from her brain. Renata's breathing grew shallow and rapid. Her hands clenched into fists and she started pummeling the sides of her head. I didn't stop her. When she had exhausted herself, she snorted the mucus from her nose and released a primal growl. Then her body went limp. She closed her eyes, wiped the tears from her cheeks, and when next she looked up there was a glazed, trance-like expression on her face.

Something fundamental had cracked.

"You were arguing," I prompted her.

"Yeah."

"What about?"

"She told me she was leaving."

"Coming to stay with me?"

Renata nodded softly.

"When?"

"After you came through and I saw that suitcase on her bed. I asked her where she was off to."

"What happened then?"

"I was like, 'whatchoo mean you leaving?' She was packing her shit, I thought she meant one of them dudes was taking her somewhere or something. But then she said she couldn't live this life anymore. So I was like, 'what about me?' you know. She started up with all this garbage 'bout, 'this ain't about you, I've gotta do what's best for me and my daughter.' I got it, you know, I understood that, but she act like it wasn't no thing for her to leave me in the lurch like that. I asked her what I was supposed to do? Where I was supposed to go? That's when she was like, I ain't her problem and I got to learn how to fend for myself at some point."

"Is that when you hit her with the lava lamp?"

"Right about then, I guess. I ain't even mean to hurt her. I was just so mad." Renata's eyes refocused to the present and she put them on me. "Birdie was always acting like her life was so miserable. Always annoyed the shit outta me. She ain't know how good she had it. She ain't even have to do anything, you know. Just sit up there in her ivory tower, everything taken care of and shit. Never had to sully herself on the street. And those men that came to see her, they was clean and nice. They smelled good. And you know why they fucked her? You know why?"

"Why?"

"Because they wanted to. Because she was pretty. Them men that cruise the alleys, they ain't so nice." Renata's lip curled into a malicious sneer now. "And they ain't never fuck me 'cause they want to. I ain't pretty like that. Naw, they fuck me 'cause they ain't have no other choice. They fuck me 'cause I'm a means to an end. I'm just a thing to them. Something they can cram they dick in wherever they want. Like your friend, the cab driver."

"Why'd you strangle her?"

"I don't know. I really don't. She came at me after I hit her with the lamp . . . I don't know. I didn't even want to hurt her really. I just wanted her to feel . . ." Renata's sentence trailed off.

"Feel what you felt," I said.

"Yeah, something like that. Birdie had it good, you know. I don't know how she ain't see it. She could get them men to do anything for her. Look at you. You ain't so different. Always coming around, ferrying her all over the place, getting her to move in with you. Girl got people wrapped like it wudn't nothin'. People cared about her. She ain't ever realize how special that was." Renata shook her head in admonishment. "Birdie had it made."

"And all you had was her."

"Yeah," Renata said simply. "I ain't know she was gonna die."

"But she did die. And you staged—" The words caught in my throat. The image of Birdie lying facedown, tied to the bedposts, pants yanked below her knees, flashed like a strobe in my head. I took a moment, blinked the vision away before proceeding. "You staged it to look like it was one of her johns that did it. Then texted me on Birdie's phone to back that up, and erased all her messages and call history."

Renata noticed a trail of chip crumbs on the front her shirt. She dusted them off, rather meticulously, making sure to get each morsel. When she was finished she looked at me with a numbed indifference. "Uh-huh," she said.

"Where's the money?" I asked.

"What money?"

"The money Birdie had hidden in the ceiling above her bed."

Renata stared at me, genuinely puzzled. "What you mean? She had money up there?"

"Yeah."

"How much?"

I shook my head. "Doesn't matter."

Renata looked around the room as though she wanted to memorize it.

"So what now? I'm going to jail or something?"

CHAPTER FORTY-THREE
THE WET DROWN

I sat in the back of Hively's car with Renata for the ride to the station. When we arrived I helped to escort her inside.

I stopped outside the booking room. "This is as far as I go, Renata."

"Oh, okay," she replied. She seemed disconnected from the business at hand, as though she were operating on a different plane of existence. "What happens now?"

"They fingerprint you, take your picture, do a body search, that kind of thing."

"Oh, okay. I've had that done before." Renata looked up at me shyly. "Will you come see me sometime?"

"I don't know, Renata."

Hively instructed one of the officers to lead her into Booking while he hung back. When the metal door clicked shut he turned to me.

"Nick, you being straight with me about the thumb drive?"

"Yeah."

"Doesn't make any sense. Who would leave it on your doorstep like that? You think it could be Blevins?"

"I got no idea, Hive. Weird to me as it is to you."

"Yeah, all right. You good? Need me to arrange a ride for you?"

"Sure, I'll take a ride."

A probationary officer named Mounts was tasked with schlepping me to my truck, which was still parked a few blocks down from the junkyard and The Stone's Throw. I thanked her for the lift, got behind the wheel, and drove straight to The Red Head.

Then I got drunk for a week.

Things happened that week, of course, but I did my best to avoid them. Mostly I trod a beaten path from the high school to the bar, bar to the school. When I got hungry, I'd buy a hot dog at the stand across the street or pick up a soggy piece of pizza from the gas station. If Tadpole had catfish I'd eat that. The sun dragged across the sky, the bad moon rose and the bad moon fell, time marched on. At some point my phone died and I neglected to plug it in.

Despite my best efforts, information from the outside world crept in. At noon, if there wasn't a sporting event to watch, Tadpole flipped the channel on the TV above the bar to the midday news. That's how I saw a segment about River Path breaking ground on the new Cruise Avenue complex. It showed a series of shots depicting the ongoing construction, backhoes digging into the ground, a foreman gesticulating the dimensions of an invisible structure as he talked seriously to a group of workers, that kind of thing. There was one quick shot of a man working a jackhammer. The man was wearing a hard hat, but I could have sworn I saw an eyepatch over his face. The shot cut away so quickly there was no way to be sure.

A couple days later, that same news program is how I learned that Judge Rutherford Blevins committed suicide by jumping from the Sixth Street Bridge into the river.

"C'est la vie," I muttered to myself and raised my tumbler to the television.

No one had witnessed the plunge. In the early-morning hours, Blevins's car had been found abandoned on the middle of the bridge. Later that day they dredged his body out of the water.

It was sometime the following afternoon when Willis Hively slunk onto the stool next to mine.

"You getting your lips wet today, detective, or you on duty?" Tadpole asked.

"Uh, sure, give me a Bud."

"Light or Heavy?"

"Heavy."

As Tadpole twisted off the cap, he launched into his joke of the month.

"So this guy brings his buddy home from dinner after golfing—"

"Not now," Hively said brusquely.

"Well, excuse me for living," Tadpole smarted. He passed Hively the beer and promptly sought out some friendlier patrons to badger at the other end of the bar.

"I think you hurt his feelings," I said.

"I don't have time for that shit. Been looking for you."

"Not very hard, apparently."

"Your phone keeps sending me straight to voicemail."

"It broke." I rattled the ice in my glass and took a swallow. "Forever."

"You hear about Blevins?"

"Saw the crack news coverage right there on the TV." I gestured to the screen above the bar, currently set to ESPN.

"Monday after we saw him, he amended his will. Bequeathed everything he owned—house, equity, his share of River Path, everything—to Marvina Elena Justice. Cut his children out completely."

"Ol' Destiny made out. Good for her."

"Yeah, real good. Another thing that hasn't been released publicly yet, same day he died, Feds raided his house. Found a hard drive in his home office with video files from the Royal Vista. Goes back almost five years, over two thousand videos."

"No shit?"

"Right there sitting on his desk. Might as well have gift-wrapped it. Here's the thing though. Marvina isn't on any of the tapes. It's only Birdie and two other women."

"Blevins covered her tracks, erased the files."

"Yeah, most likely. Unless some other hard drive magically appears, which seems unlikely, Marvina's time as Destiny never happened. It was all a dream. And her lips are locked. She ain't divulging nothing."

"So what now? Case dies with him?"

"There's nothing to implicate anyone else. No indication that River Path had any idea what Blevins was getting up to. Way it looks, the two main people involved in the disability fraud, Scott Barnhard and Judge Blevins, are dead. Birdie's gone. They haven't been able to identify the two other girls. Truth be told, I don't think anyone's in a hurry to find them. Feds are satisfied with the result. If it looks like a win, then it's a win."

"Optics," I said.

"Optics."

Hively had yet to taste his beer.

"You want me to put a nipple on that thing, or you gonna drink it like a big boy?" I asked.

"I don't even want this piss. You want it?"

"Sure. I should hydrate between bourbons."

He slid the beer in front of me. I took a sizeable gulp.

"Anyway, I wanted you to know. You deserve that."

"Yeah, thanks."

"You'd be surprised by the people on those tapes, Malick."

"Oh, I don't think I'd be too shocked. What's gonna be done about it?"

Hively grimaced. "If I had to guess, that shit will get buried. What are we gonna do, go out and arrest half the city?"

"Then that's that."

"Yeah, apparently so. Another funny thing came up."

"Oh?"

"Yeah, you hear about that train derailment last weekend?"

"I heard something about it."

"Turns out the car that caused the wreck was registered to Michael Tackett."

"No shit?" I said.

"Yeah."

"Who's Michael Tackett?"

"Lil' Mike Mike. What do you think about that? Either he rose from the dead or somebody ran his minivan into an oncoming train. Weird that'd happen in the middle of all this other shit. Seems reckless for the Stenders' MO."

I could sense Hively gauging my response to this line of thinking.

"Yeah," I agreed. "Weird."

"Found two unregistered pistols in the wreckage."

"Oh, yeah?"

"Yeah. I was wondering if you wanted yours back."

"My Beretta from the Royal Vista shooting? Sure, I'll take it back."

"Okay," Hively said, seeing that he couldn't trip me up. "Anything else you want to tell me? Maybe how that thumb drive found its way to your doorstep?"

"You know as much about it as I do, Hive."

We sat silently for a few minutes and watched highlights from the World Series game that was played the night before. When the segment concluded, I asked Hive if Red Lewis was on any of the files found on the hard drive.

"No, he's not there. Red's in the clear."

"Or his shit was erased with the others."

"Or that."

I shook my head. "Seems a little convenient. A little too neat."

"I thought so, too. But the Feds, the Chief, everybody wants to put this thing to bed. Shit's closed. Feels like nobody wants to pull the string for fear of what might unravel. Something bigger's at play here, Malick." Hively tocked his head back and forth as though he were debating what to say next. "Anyway, I didn't just come here to tell you the latest. I wanted to bend your ear about something else, too."

"I wondered when you were going to stop playing footsies," I said.

"Blevins didn't read like a guy who'd commit suicide to me. Did he to you?"

"No, but what was he supposed to do, wave a banner? The guy was in a tight spot."

"Yeah," Hively conceded, "he was. Still."

"News said nobody saw him jump. That true?"

"Yeah, no witnesses. A bystander would have made things a lot simpler, that's for sure. Why do you ask?"

"Be nice to know if he went out in style, like with a cannonball or jackknife. Or if he just kind of spread-eagled it."

"You're sick in the head, you know that?"

"Fair enough. What about the security cameras on either end of the bridge?"

"The one on the Ohio side doesn't show anything. West Virginia side went dead two days prior. Wire shorted out. Again, hell of a coincidence, right?"

"Those do keep popping up."

"I finally got to interview the prosecutor who tried those Stender cases. Asked him if he ever felt like there was something extracurricular going on."

"And?"

"He said he never felt that way. He said the reason they always got off or got handed lighter sentences were because they had better lawyers."

A light buzz, like a dull alarm, tickled at the back of my brain. "Who were their lawyers?" I asked, though I was pretty certain I already knew the answer.

Hively confirmed my suspicions. "Your old bosses, Leach, McKinney & Thurber. I had Sturges look it up. Leach was the attorney of record for the majority of their cases."

"Huh. They weren't on the Vista tapes, were they?"

"No. You ever see anything, hear anything while you were working there that struck you as below board?"

"No," I said, honestly. "Then again, I never knew they'd represented the Stenders."

"Most of their Stender cases were before you started working there, I believe. They've stayed off the radar pretty well for the last couple of years. But I need you to think back, see if anything gets jogged loose."

"I will."

"I don't know." Hively blew out a dispirited sigh. "Hit me up if you think of anything. Maybe I'm grasping at air here. But this whole business just feels off. Something just ain't adding right. It's gonna gnaw at me till I know."

I'd put a week's worth of booze in my belly to ward off the very feeling that currently rose in my gut. The feeling that I would never rest easy until I knew the whole story, the whole truth. *All that good Maker's,* I thought. *All for naught.*

"Yeah," I said to Hively. "It's gonna gnaw at me, too."

CHAPTER FORTY-FOUR
THE NEW KINGS

Having been employed by the firm for the past eighteen months, I knew Ed Leach's habit was to arrive at the office before anyone else, putz around a little, read the paper, feed the fish, brew the first pot of coffee the way he liked it, adjust the lighting to his preferred level, and finally, if time permitted, get a jump start on the coming day.

Upon entering his personal office, he didn't notice me sitting in the armchair in the corner for a solid minute—not till after he'd straightened his tie, smoothed out his eyebrows, and sat down to boot up the computer. Leach leapt out of his seat, clutched his chest and screamed, "Oh, Jesus!"

"Don't have a coronary," I said. "Let's talk first."

"You scared the shit out of me, Nick." The adrenaline from the shock subsided and was replaced by an uneasy relief. Leach laughed at his own expense. "How did you get in here?"

"When you fire someone, you oughta change the security code."

"Yes, that is an oversight, isn't it?" Leach said nervously. "We'll have to do that. Is there something I can do for you?"

"You and I are gonna have a chat."

"About your dismissal? I want you to know, Nick, that I was against getting rid of you, all the way. But Kent was furious when you disregarded his instructions to steer clear of the investigation into Barnhard's death. I don't know if he's ready to budge—he was quite miffed about the whole thing—but I can put in a word for you, if you'd like. In time, perhaps, we can mend fences. I'd love to have you back. That other fellow, um . . ."

"Bob Lawson."

"Right, Lawson. He's good, but he's not you."

"I'm not here about the job."

"No?"

"No. I'm here to find out why you had me followed two weekends ago."

"What?" Leach's voice jumped a few octaves. "What are you talking about? Who followed you?" He spotted the gun that I held loosely in my hand now, the pocket Walther on loan from the Orviettos. "Why do you have a gun?"

"In case you need some persuading."

"Persuading for what?"

"I know you traffic in bullshit for a living, Ed, but I don't have the energy today. So go ahead and sit back down, get comfy, and fill in some blanks for me. I think I know most of the story, but for my peace of mind I want to be sure."

Leach pulled out his chair, examined it like there might be a bomb planted beneath the seat.

"Are you going to hurt me?"

"Depends on you, Ed. Of the two of you, I always thought it'd be McKinney that'd be the corrupt one, him being such a dick. You were a surprise."

"Nick, I don't know what you've heard—"

"What'd I just say, Ed?"

"You don't have the energy for bullshit."

"That's right. I'm tired, so let's cut out the pretenses, huh? Sit down." Leach complied, eying me warily as he lowered himself into the chair.

"Lawson been following me this whole last week, too?"

"Yes."

"That's a lot of money to shell out to someone just to watch me get drunk."

"Indeed."

"He hasn't been there for at least the last couple days. When did you knock it off?"

"Thursday. We figured you were pretty much in the bag for good around Tuesday, but kept it going a couple more days just to make sure."

"Few days too soon. He tell you about Momo? About the train?"

Leach nodded in the affirmative.

"So you know about the deal I made with the Stenders?"

Leach took a moment to arrange a response, opened his mouth to speak, then thought better of it and repeated his nod.

"Good. So you know the die's been cast. I agreed to lay off of the whole thing or else they're going to kill me and those I hold dear, so on and so forth, correct?"

"Some may say what you're doing this very instant is a breach of that agreement."

"Some may say that," I granted, "but you're not gonna be one of those people, Ed. And here's why. That deal we made cuts both ways. Except from my end, I included the Stenders and everyone involved in this whole escapade. That means you. In fact, a word of this conversation we're having right now gets breathed to them, you're the first one I'm coming after. And I was gonna leave wives and children out of it, but fuck it." I wagged the gun in the direction of the framed photographs on his desk and on his walls. "Your kids are grown. I'll throw them in for good measure."

"You're not that kind of man, Nick."

"You'd be surprised what kind of man I am when someone threatens the people I care about."

Leach took a big gulp that made his Adam's apple travel the length of his neck. "It wasn't supposed to be this way," he said.

"It never is. You know, it's silly really, but it never occurred to me until yesterday that you, me, and McKinney were the only three people in the world who knew Barnhard was going to squawk to the U.S. Attorney. He'd stonewalled up to that point. But then he spooks, decides to flip." I shrugged. "I didn't tell anyone. Who'd you tell?"

"No one, I swear. I had—"

As he spoke, I casually pointed the pistol in the general vicinity of his chest. His voice faltered.

"Ed, don't lie. I'm only going to ask this once. Did you go straight to the Stenders or did you run it past your buddies at River Path first?"

Leach ratcheted back in his seat. "How did you know that I was involved in River Path?"

"See, I wasn't a hundred percent sure on that, but it makes a lot of things fall into place. Who'd you tell, the other investors? Judge Blevins?"

Leach confirmed it with another nod, then dropped his chin to his chest. "All this death," he whinnied. "They wanted to kill you, too," he said, quickly looking back up to me. "After you nabbed Mr. Morrison from that homosexual club—" Leach snapped his fingers a couple times to recall the name. "Flamboyant."

"It was the other one. Stone's Throw."

"They said you were a menace who threatened the entire operation. I put a stop to it right then and there. I told them in no uncertain terms, if the business goes down, if we lose our investment, then so be it. It was our own fault for biting off more than we could chew, nobody else's, and there would be no more death by our hands. I'd blow the whistle myself if I had to."

"Gee, thanks. My hero. Who is *they*?"

"Pardon?"

"Your partners in River Path. Who are they?"

"I—I—I can't tell you," Leach stammered. But his eyes flicked to a small five-by-seven picture on the shelf behind him, one that wasn't of his family, but of a group of eight men posed on a golf course.

"Is McKinney in on it, too?"

"No, he's not. I promise. But I can't disclose their names. Please understand. I'd be crucified."

"I'm not really worried about you, Ed. But that's alright. We can come back to that one. Who actually did the deed, drowned Barnhard in his pool like that?"

"From what I understand," Leach said hesitantly, "you've already taken care of the person responsible."

"Lil' Mike Mike? That makes sense. Barnhard was a hefty man, took someone strong to hold him under the water. But here's what I want to know. How'd it all start?"

"How did *what* all start?"

"The shady bits. How'd it get to a place where it became necessary to murder a bunch of people? I gotta know. Call it professional curiosity."

Leach sighed heavily. "I fought this eventuality the whole way. You should know that. Even when I realized Barnhard was going to cooperate with the U.S. Attorney, I advocated for patience. I thought we'd skate in the end, but the rest of the collective—we had big things in the works. It was a risk they weren't willing to take."

"By big things, you mean the Cruise Avenue deal?"

He nodded. "Our whole company hinged on that deal. Everything we'd ever done had built to this apex. Individually, we would have lost everything we'd invested if it fell through. Not to mention it'd be a terrible setback for the progression of Cain City. Then this investigation popped up. This would have never happened if not for this perfect confluence of events."

"Which side did Judge Blevins fall on, for or against murdering Barnhard?"

Leach again deliberated the most prudent way in which to respond. "Rutherford didn't want to kill Scott. I believe the thought of it pained him greatly to do so. He resisted for a long time, but in the end, I suppose he saw no other choice. Maybe Rutherford thought that was the only outcome from which he could save his own hide, I don't know."

"He guessed wrong there."

"Yes. In the end, I was the only one who was against that solution, I swear it." Here, Leach gazed into the middle distance as if he were visually remembering the succession of events. "This whole mess would never have happened had we not allowed Rutherford to invest in the collective in the first place."

"Why did you?"

"Oh"—he waved a dismissive hand as if it really didn't matter, though he kept talking—"a few years back the decision was made to expand the core objective of River Path. For a long time we just bought properties, flipped them, spruced them up, rented them out, whatever. It was an investment. That's how it started. Property. A sound, sturdy investment. We never imagined it would prosper the way it did. Pretty soon we had an opportunity to not just put a face-lift on the old, but also to build something new on top of the old. To grow this city. There's been so much upheaval in this town. So many negative forces. It used to be a glorious place to live, to raise kids."

"So the myth goes."

"We had the power to alter the future for the better. To flip Cain City's fortunes. Why wouldn't we do that if we could? But, like most things of that nature, our reach quickly exceeded our grasp. Very quickly, we found ourselves underwater. For lack of a better explanation, we were missing a few key pieces. Rutherford had been pestering us for years to let him invest. First off, this should be said: I never liked him. I was against it. Even when we were kids, when our fathers worked together at this firm, we never got along. Then we inherited the place, were forced to work together. He could schmooze, Rutherford. Yuck it up with the clients better than anyone, but he always cut corners, blamed everyone but himself when things didn't pan out the way he'd envisioned. Never mind that he didn't do the actual work required to achieve his desired outcome. That's how he got kicked out of the firm in the first place. He was trading sexual favors for legal services."

"I thought he left of his own volition."

"No," Leach scoffed. "We were discreet, of course. Kept the real reason hush hush. We didn't want to tarnish his reputation—"

"Course not."

"—so, as long as he didn't badmouth us, we allowed people to believe his side of the story. Which allowed him to go on to the career he had. It was a different time then. I wish now we would have had him disbarred. Anyhow, he wanted to invest, he finally possessed something that we could use and"—Leach tossed his hands up—"the decision was made. We let him in. Worst mistake we ever made."

"His connection with the Stenders, that's what you needed?"

"That, and the influx of cash he pumped into the business initially. We didn't know he was getting that cash from duping the government. As for the Stenders, I always knew Rutherford was, how should we say—?"

"Racist."

"Antiquated . . . in his views. What we needed at the time was someone to grease the wheels with the unions so that we could obtain the building contracts required at a price we could actually afford."

"And the Stenders control the unions," I said.

Leach mulled this over. "'Control' may be a slight exaggeration. 'Heavily influence' is more appropriate. A good many of their members are in one union or another."

"So now you were the one taking the shortcuts."

"Yes. That's exactly what we were doing. And we've suffered the consequences."

"Doesn't seem like you're suffering too much. You own half the city. Seems to me, you're the new kings."

"All the possessions in the world matter little if you live in mental anguish."

"I think you'll be okay."

"Ah, Nick," he moaned. "The whole thing went pear-shaped so fast. I swear, we had no idea that Rutherford was letting the Stenders run prostitutes out of The Royal Vista, or that he was using hidden cameras to blackmail people or whatever it was he was up to. We didn't know he was cheating the government with that damned disability sham either. Turns out, that's how he raised the capital to invest in our company in the first place. We were caught totally unaware. He duped us all. But I tried to warn them. I told them he was rotten to the core."

"Made the decision to kill him easier, I'd imagine."

"Rutherford Blevins," Leach said, annunciating the syllables with more than a little disdain, "committed suicide."

"Sure he did. See, here's how this job works from my end. When a crime takes place, in this case a murder, first thing you ask yourself—who benefits? And with this case, with Judge Blevins, the answer is—*everybody*. Everybody fucking benefited from this. Your company first and foremost."

Leach dragged his hands down over his face and shook his head. "It's all such a terrible mess, isn't it? I keep telling myself it's for the greater good."

Out on the main floor of the office, we heard Betty arrive. She banged around at her desk while humming a show tune to herself. Something that sounded vaguely like *Les Misérables*.

I lowered my voice. "If I dug enough, would I find out the Stenders have done some kind of work on the Sixth Street Bridge?"

Ed Leach nodded. "They were part of the crew who built the new on-ramps ten years ago."

"So they knew how to gain access to the security cameras on the bridge?"

"I don't know."

"Which means Blevins probably didn't jump. He was thrown off."

"I don't know," Leach repeated, desperately. "You have to believe me."

"Ed," Betty called out. "You want me to freshen your coffee?"

Leach shot a look to his door, then back to me.

"What happens now, Nick?"

I stood up and took three quick steps across to his desk.

"Nick, I—" Leach cowered and raised his hands in front of his face as though he were trying to ward off an evil spirit.

"Ed?" Betty called, a hint of worry in her voice.

"No more killings," I said. "You understand me."

"Yes, yes," Leach said between panicked breaths. "I swear it, Nick. I swear it."

I pressed the muzzle of the Walther against his temple. "I'll be watching."

"Yes, yes," he begged, shrinking into himself. "No more. It's done, it's done."

Betty stuck her pert little nose through the door just as I lowered the pistol. "Ed, are you—oh." She saw Leach hunched down, the fright on his face, and me standing there, hands behind my back, and couldn't quite reconcile the image. "Everything okay?" she said, confused.

"Fine, Betty," Leach assured her. "I'll take that coffee, thanks."

"Hi, Nick. You rejoining the team?"

"Not a chance in hell, Betty."

"Oh," Betty exclaimed, taken aback, "alright then."

She went to fetch the drink, leaving the door ajar behind her. I walked around behind Leach's desk and scrutinized the photograph of the eight men on a golf course. I recognized half of them. One was the CEO of the biggest coal company in the state. Another was a man who owned a local medical supply chain. The third person I recognized was Judge Rutherford Blevins. I took the picture from the shelf, tucked it into my coat.

"Enjoy the spoils," I said.

And I left.

I got onto the elevator and waited for the doors to close and the descent to begin. Then I reached into my pocket and turned off the recording device.

CHAPTER FORTY-FIVE
THE SPOTTED LEOPARD

I rapped on the door, stepped back, blew out a short, quick breath, and looked down at my clothes to make sure they hadn't wrinkled on the way up the stairs. The door opened and there stood Karla. She was clad in baggy overalls and a long-sleeved thermal. It had been two weeks since the last time I'd come knocking and the hiatus must have worked to some degree because the door stayed open, she greeted me politely, and there were no outward signs of contempt. In fact, her expression was soft, one might even say compassionate, though she did keep her hand on the edge of the door in case she found cause to slam it.

Karla took me in with one sweep of those sea-green eyes. "Why are you dressed up?"

"Everything else was dirty."

"Your face looks better, the bruises are almost gone."

"Yeah." I ran my fingers absently over my cheeks, which felt like they belonged to someone else since I'd shaved them clean that morning. "I think they rearranged it nicely. Another brawl or two and I'm gonna come out looking like a movie star."

"Let's not get carried away."

"B movies. Schlocky stuff."

Karla's lips curled into a half-hearted smile meant to placate me.

"Are you busy right now?" I asked.

"Nick . . ." She hesitated, peered back into her apartment.

"Look, if you don't mind, I'd like to show you something."

"You want to *show* me something?"

"Won't take too long. Hour, tops."

"I don't know, Nick. Tell me what it is and I'll decide whether or not I'm up for it."

"It's not something I can really explain. You kinda just gotta see it."

Karla tilted her head and pursed her lips.

"Come on," I goaded her. "One hour, that's all I'm asking. If it's the last hour you ever want to spend with me in your entire life, then so be it."

She narrowed her eyes. "Do you always have to be such a drama queen?"

"Only when you force me to pull out all the stops. C'mon, I know you're not doing anything. Davey told me you had the day off and weren't planning on going anywhere."

"Yeah, because I'm cleaning. You two talk too much."

I flipped my palms up, feigning innocence. "We're buddies."

Karla vacillated for another moment before giving in. "Fine. Let me grab my coat."

We walked outside together, down the portico steps and around the building to the parking lot. The day was cold and sunless and the bald trees shivered from the crisp wind that swept down off the southern hills. The dead leaves at our feet rustled in elegy. I opened the passenger door for Karla and gave her a boost into the truck.

"You can't tell me where we're going?"

"What'd be the fun in that? You'll find out soon enough."

I drove us over Fifth Street Hill and hopped on the interstate.

"East, huh?" Karla asked, as if the direction provided some clue to our destination.

"You got me," I said. "I'm taking you hostage. We're not stopping until we hit the ocean."

She didn't laugh and she didn't ask any more about it. We trekked on for a few minutes without conversing. The thick wind breaking against the momentum of the car made a dull, ambient groan. Karla watched out the window as the barren landscape slid beneath the muted sky.

"How's the new job?" I asked.

"It's good. Hard. Harder than I'd imagined it would be. There's so many babies there, Nick, and they're in such pain. Breaks my heart. But it feels good to be doing something to help them. It feels like I'm doing my part to make a difference, you know? However small."

"That sounds really nice."

"Yeah, it is," she said dreamily, as though she were picturing the children. "End of the day comes, I'm tuckered out. Get home and collapse."

"I'll bet."

"What about you? Back to work?"

"No, I'm taking a break for a while. Figure I need to . . . I don't know, work shit out. Figure out what happens next."

Karla didn't say anything to that.

When I pulled off the interstate and down the little dead-end lane to the house with a chain-link fence and a swing set out front, Karla still had no idea where we were going. I realized I had never told her much about Birdie's daughter, about the weekly sojourns we had taken here. I'd always tried to keep business and personal separate, a task I'd failed at so spectacularly it was almost comical.

"Is this where we're going?" Karla asked when I pulled to a stop.

"There's someone I want you to meet."

We got out and Karla followed me through the gate to the porch, where I rapped lightly on the door. Dottie opened up and greeted me warmly. I introduced her to Karla.

"Someone's been waiting for you," Dottie said.

Aisha came galloping out of the living room and leapt into my arms. "Ick!" she chirped.

I heaved her into the air, caught her beneath the arms and twirled her around before setting her back down.

"Aisha, I brought a friend today. This is Karla."

Distracted by me, Aisha hadn't noticed Karla standing there. She became instantly bashful, ducked behind me and clung to my legs, then peek-a-booed around them to see Karla.

"Hello, Aisha." Karla smiled at the little girl. "It's nice to meet you." She turned to me, "Is this—?"

"Birdie's daughter. Yeah."

From the bowels of the house, one of Dottie's other foster children let out a wail. She excused herself to tend to them. I asked Aisha if she wanted to swing. She nodded effusively and bounded toward the swing set in the yard.

"Why did you bring me here, Nick?" Karla said quietly.

"I wanted you to see why everything happened the way it did in these last months. I'm sorry for the way I've behaved, but I wanted you to understand there was a reason for that behavior, and tell you why it will never be like that again."

"I've heard this before, Nick."

I explained to her then, about Aisha's grandmother, her namesake, who'd been murdered because she was my informant. And I told her how, after she'd died, I'd vowed to look after her five children, help them best I could.

"You'd bring Birdie here to see Aisha?"

"Yeah. Once, twice a week. However often she was allowed to come. She had custody of Aisha once, for a short while, but that was it."

"Because she was born with a drug dependency, right?"

I nodded. "She had to be at Maggie's Place for the first month or so of her life, I think."

"And you've been coming here on your own?"

"These last couple weeks, yeah. Wait until you hear her sing. She's a natural."

"Where are the other four children, Birdie's brothers and sisters?"

"They're in good homes. I visit them from time to time. Birdie was the oldest. She was seventeen when her mother died, already pregnant with Aisha."

"How come you never told me any of this, Nick?"

"It was mine to carry. I didn't want to burden you with it. You were burdened enough by me."

We watched Aisha for a moment, who hadn't bothered to wait for me to start playing. She was pushing back and forth with her belly on the swing, Superman-style. Her golden locks dusted the grass with each pass.

"She's beautiful," Karla said.

"I'm going to try and adopt her."

Karla hesitated. Then, speaking delicately, "Is that such a good idea?"

"It's like you said. There's so much pain in this world. So much suffering. If I can do some little part to make it better for one little girl—that little girl"—I gestured toward Aisha—"then I want to do it."

"Nick, have you thought this through? There's so much that goes into raising a child."

"Yeah, I know. I used to have one, once."

"I know," she demurred.

"Believe it or not, I was even pretty good at it. Sure, it'll be hard. I know that. And with my past it's, well, it's gonna be tough to get the board to let me have her. That's why I was hoping you and I could do it together."

Karla covered her mouth with her hand, spoke through her fingers. "Nick, no. This is what—"

"Here me out." Tears bubbled up in my eyes. Seeing that, Karla began to get emotional as well. "I'll be different," I said, the words coming out a little strained. "I promise. I'll give up the job. I'll sell insurance, I'll stock shelves, I'll do whatever I have to do."

"That's not you."

"Sure it is. People do things all the time that aren't them. That's what most people do. You do something long enough, you become that thing."

"It's not that easy, Nick. A leopard can't just decide to change its spots."

"Good thing I'm not a leopard."

Her wet eyes fastened onto mine. Then, as though it were too much to bear, she broke away and gazed out to where Aisha was twisting the swing as tightly as she could, then letting it go so that she could spin with abandon. The little girl squealed with delight.

"I love you," I said.

"I know."

"What do you say?"

Karla nodded her head, then shook it simultaneously. She bit her lip in an effort to quash the fresh tears brimming on her eyelids. "This isn't fair, Nick."

"I stacked the deck a little."

"Yeah, with a toddler." Karla pulled the sleeve of her thermal over her hand and used it to blot the tears away. "You're going to quit being a detective?"

"Yeah, I'm done. I'm sick of the whole business."

"But that's what you do. That's who you are. And you're so good at it. You help so many people."

"I don't know about that."

"I do. It's what you were meant to be."

"I think I should be the one to say what I'm meant to be, don't you? Besides, nobody's *meant* for anything. Anyone who thinks otherwise is naïve or superstitious. Or they believe in hocus pocus."

Karla stuck her hands into the pockets of her overalls, crinkled her nose and shrugged her shoulders inward on her body. "But I *am* one of those people, Nick. Don't you get that? I believe we each have a purpose. Maybe we don't always know what that purpose is, but I have to believe that that's the case. Else, why care about anything? Why try? Does that make me naïve or mean my beliefs are hooey?"

"Okay," I retreated. "Let's say you're right and I'm wrong. What if everything that's ever happened to me happened because it was supposed to lead me right here, right now, to this moment with you?"

"But you don't believe that."

"I don't have to believe it. If it's true, it's true."

"Ick," Aisha peeped. She waggled both her hands, beckoning me to her. "Come."

"I'll be right there, sweetheart," I called. I turned to face Karla. "I want to be with you. I'll do better, I swear. I'll do whatever I have to do, I'll be who you need me to be."

Karla started to speak, but she balked and stayed silent.

"Be with me," I said, voice so low as to be nearly inaudible.

"I just don't know, Nick. I just don't know."

I bowed my head and stepped down from the porch to the lawn. Halfway to the swing set I halted and glanced sidelong back to the porch. "Just . . . think about it, okay? Can you do that?"

Karla took a moment, then nodded slowly. "I can do that."

"Ick!" Aisha demanded, getting impatient now. She marched three steps forward, put her little fists against her hips, and fixed me with an exaggerated glare. Her hair fell onto her face and tickled her nose. She took a quick break to swat the hair out of her eyes and rub the itch from her nose, then reapplied the attitude.

I couldn't help but smile. A spunky little orphaned girl with sun-kissed hair and sass to burn. Just like her mother and grandmother before her. I already loved her as if she were mine. Perhaps one day she would be.

I went to her.

ACKNOWLEDGEMENTS

The day Renée C. Fountain took me on as a client was the single most significant moment in my artistic life, and I will forever be grateful for her belief in my work, her tenacity as my agent, and her friendship. Steve Feldberg at Audible is simply the best editorial partner I could ever hope for. I am tremendously thankful to Otto Penzler and his team at MysteriousPress.com for making the reading of these very words possible. Thank you to Gloria Hanna of the Los Angeles County Sheriff Department Crime Laboratory for helping me design a highly questionable murder. To my first eyes, Cat O'Connor and Kate Martin, thank you so much for your time and efforts and first-rate analytical feedback.

I'd also like to acknowledge two people who have played an instrumental role in my creative development: Darrell Fetty and Steven Anderson. My work, and for that matter my life, is far richer for having had you in it.

ABOUT THE AUTHOR

Jonathan Fredrick is the author of the Cain City Novels, which were inspired in-part by his hometown of Huntington, West Virginia. After working in Los Angeles as a writer, filmmaker, and actor for more than fifteen years, Fredrick now resides in Columbus, Ohio, with his wife and three sons.

THE CAIN CITY NOVELS

MYSTERIOUSPRESS.COM

Otto Penzler, owner of the Mysterious Bookshop in Manhattan, founded the Mysterious Press in 1975. Penzler quickly became known for his outstanding selection of mystery, crime, and suspense books, both from his imprint and in his store. The imprint was devoted to printing the best books in these genres, using fine paper and top dust-jacket artists, as well as offering many limited, signed editions.

Now the Mysterious Press has gone digital, publishing ebooks through **MysteriousPress.com**.

MysteriousPress.com offers readers essential noir and suspense fiction, hard-boiled crime novels, and the latest thrillers from both debut authors and mystery masters. Discover classics and new voices, all from one legendary source.

FIND OUT MORE AT

WWW.MYSTERIOUSPRESS.COM

FOLLOW US:

@emysteries and Facebook.com/MysteriousPressCom

MysteriousPress.com is one of a select group of publishing partners of Open Road Integrated Media, Inc.

THE MYSTERIOUS BOOKSHOP, founded in 1979, is located in Manhattan's Tribeca neighborhood. It is the oldest and largest mystery-specialty bookstore in America.

The shop stocks the finest selection of new mystery hardcovers, paperbacks, and periodicals. It also features a superb collection of signed modern first editions, rare and collectable works, and Sherlock Holmes titles. The bookshop issues a free monthly newsletter highlighting its book clubs, new releases, events, and recently acquired books.

58 Warren Street
info@mysteriousbookshop.com
(212) 587-1011
Monday through Saturday
11:00 a.m. to 7:00 p.m.

FIND OUT MORE AT:

www.mysteriousbookshop.com

FOLLOW US:

@TheMysterious and Facebook.com/MysteriousBookshop

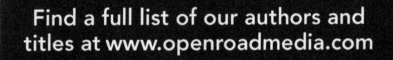